*Praise for J. R. Ward's Black Dagger
Brotherhood series*

'Now here's a band of brothers who know how to
show a girl a good time'
New York Times bestselling author, Lisa Gardner

'It's not easy to find a new twist on the vampire
myth, but Ward succeeds beautifully. This dark and
compelling world is filled with enticing romance as
well as perilous adventure'
Romantic Times

'These vampires are *hot,* and the series only gets
hotter . . . so hot it gave me shivers'
Vampire Genre

'Ward wields a commanding voice perfect for the
genre . . . Intriguing, adrenaline-pumping . . . Fans of
L. A. Banks, Laurell K. Hamilton and Sherrilyn
Kenyon will add Ward to their must-read list'
Booklist

'These erotic paranormals are well worth it, and
frighteningly addictive . . . It all works to great,
page-turning effect . . . [and has] earned Ward an
Anne Rice-style following, deservedly so'
Publishers Weekly

'[A] midnight whirlwind of dangerous characters and
mesmerizing erotic romance. The Black Dagger
Brotherhood owns me now. Dark fantasy lovers, you
just got served'
Lynn Viehl, *USA Today* bestselling author of
Evermore

J.R. Ward lives in the South with her incredibly supportive husband and her beloved golden retriever. After graduating from law school, she began working in health care in Boston and spent many years as chief of staff for one of the premier academic medical centres in the nation.

Visit J. R. Ward online:

www.jrward.com
www.facebook.com/JRWardBooks
www.twitter.com/jrward1

By J. R. Ward

The Black Dagger Brotherhood series:

Dark Lover
Lover Eternal
Lover Revealed
Lover Awakened
Lover Unbound
Lover Enshrined
Lover Avenged
Lover Mine
Lover Unleashed
Lover Reborn
Lover at Last
The King
The Shadows

The Black Dagger Brotherhood: An Insider's Guide

Fallen Angels series:

Covet
Crave
Envy
Rapture
Possession

The Bourbon Kings series:

The Bourbon Kings

J.R. WARD

BLOOD KISS

piatkus

PIATKUS

First published in the United States in 2015 by New American Library,
A Division of Penguin Group (USA) Inc., New York
First published in Great Britain in 2015 by Piatkus

1 3 5 7 9 10 8 6 4 2

Copyright © Love Conquers All, Inc., 2015

The moral right of the author has been asserted.

A CIP catalogue record for this book
is available from the British Library.

Hardback ISBN 978-0-349-40924-5
Trade paperback ISBN 978-0-349-40925-2

Printed and bound in Great Britain by
CPI Group (UK) Ltd, Croydon, CR0 4YY

Papers used by Piatkus are from well-managed forests
and other responsible sources.

MIX
Paper from
responsible sources
FSC® C104740

Piatkus
An imprint of
Little, Brown Book Group
Carmelite House
50 Victoria Embankment
London EC4Y 0DZ

An Hachette UK Company
www.hachette.co.uk

www.piatkus.co.uk

Dedicated with love to the Pup
xxx

ACKNOWLEDGMENTS

Thank you so much to my readers, and to everyone who loves the Brothers as much as I do. And thank you also to Steven Axelrod, Kara Welsh, Leslie Gelbman, and everyone at NAL!

Thanks, too, to Team Waud, and my family, both those of blood relation and those of adoption.

And as always, with love, to my wonderful Writer Assistant, Naamah.

Glossary of
Terms and Proper Nouns

ahstrux nohtrum (n.) Private guard with license to kill who is granted his or her position by the King.

ahvenge (v.) Act of mortal retribution, carried out typically by a male loved one.

Black Dagger Brotherhood (pr. n.) Highly trained vampire warriors who protect their species against the Lessening Society. As a result of selective breeding within the race, Brothers possess immense physical and mental strength, as well as rapid healing capabilities. They are not siblings for the most part, and are inducted into the Brotherhood upon nomination by the Brothers. Aggressive, self-reliant, and secretive by nature, they exist apart from civilians, having little contact with members of the other classes except when they need to feed. They are the subjects of legend and objects of reverence within the vampire world. They may be killed only by the most serious of wounds, e.g., a gunshot or stab to the heart, etc.

blood slave (n.) Male or female vampire who has been subjugated to serve the blood needs of another. The practice of keeping blood slaves has recently been outlawed.

the Chosen (n.) Female vampires who have been bred to serve the Scribe Virgin. They are considered members of the aristocracy, though they are spiritually rather than temporally focused. They have little or no interaction with males, but can be mated to Brothers at the Scribe Virgin's direction to propagate their class. Some have the ability to prognosticate. In the past, they were used to meet the blood needs of unmated members of the Brotherhood, and that practice has been reinstated by the Brothers.

chrih (n.) Symbol of honorable death in the Old Language.

cohntehst (n.) Conflict between two males competing for the right to be a female's mate.

Dhunhd (pr. n.) Hell.

doggen (n.) Member of the servant class within the vampire world. *Doggen* have old, conservative traditions about service to their superiors, following a formal code of dress and behavior. They are able to go out during the day, but they age relatively quickly. Life expectancy is approximately five hundred years.

ehros (n.) A Chosen trained in the matter of sexual arts.

exhile dhoble (n.) The evil or cursed twin, the one born second.

the Fade (pr. n.) Nontemporal realm where the dead reunite with their loved ones and pass eternity.

First Family (pr. n.) The King and Queen of the vampires, and any children they may have.

ghardian (n.) Custodian of an individual. There are

varying degrees of *ghardians*, with the most powerful being that of a *sehcluded* female.

glymera (n.) The social core of the aristocracy, roughly equivalent to Regency England's *ton*.

hellren (n.) Male vampire who has been mated to a female. Males may take more than one female as mate.

hyslop (n. or v.) Term referring to a lapse in judgment, typically resulting in the compromise of the mechanical operations of a vehicle or otherwise motorized conveyance of some kind. For example, leaving one's keys in one's car as it is parked outside the family home overnight.

leahdyre (n.) A person of power and influence.

leelan (adj.) A term of endearment loosely translated as "dearest one."

Lessening Society (pr. n.) Order of slayers convened by the Omega for the purpose of eradicating the vampire species.

lesser (n.) De-souled human who targets vampires for extermination as a member of the Lessening Society. *Lessers* must be stabbed through the chest in order to be killed; otherwise they are ageless. They do not eat or drink and are impotent. Over time, their hair, skin, and irises lose pigmentation until they are blond, blushless, and pale eyed. They smell like baby powder. Inducted into the society by the Omega, they retain a ceramic jar thereafter into which their heart was placed after it was removed.

lewlhen (n.) Gift.

lheage (n.) A term of respect used by a sexual submissive to refer to her dominant.

Lhenihan (pr. n.) A mythic beast renowned for its sexual prowess. In modern slang, refers to a male of preternatural size and sexual stamina.

lys (n.) Torture tool used to remove the eyes.

mahmen (n.) Mother. Used both as an identifier and a term of affection.

mhis (n.) The masking of a given physical environment; the creation of a field of illusion.

nalla (n., f.) or *nallum* (n., m.) Beloved.

needing period (n.) Female vampire's time of fertility, generally lasting for two days and accompanied by intense sexual cravings. Occurs approximately five years after a female's transition and then once a decade thereafter. All males respond to some degree if they are around a female in her need. It can be a dangerous time, with conflicts and fights breaking out between competing males, particularly if the female is not mated.

newling (n.) A virgin.

the Omega (pr. n.) Malevolent, mystical figure who has targeted the vampires for extinction out of resentment directed toward the Scribe Virgin. Exists in a nontemporal realm and has extensive powers, though not the power of creation.

phearsom (adj.) Term referring to the potency of a male's sexual organs. Literal translation something close to "worthy of entering a female."

princeps (n.) Highest level of the vampire aristocracy, second only to members of the First Family or the Scribe Virgin's Chosen. Must be born to the title; it may not be conferred.

pyrocant (n.) Refers to a critical weakness in an individual. The weakness can be internal, such as an addiction, or external, such as a lover.

rahlman (n.) Savior.

rythe (n.) Ritual manner of assuaging honor granted by one who has offended another. If accepted, the offended chooses a weapon and strikes the offender, who presents him- or herself without defenses.

the Scribe Virgin (pr. n.) Mystical force who is counselor to the King as well as the keeper of vampire archives and the dispenser of privileges. Exists in a nontemporal realm and has extensive powers. Capable of a single act of creation, which she expended to bring the vampires into existence.

sehclusion (n.) Status conferred by the King upon a female of the aristocracy as a result of a petition by the female's family. Places the female under the sole direction of her *ghardian*, typically the eldest male in her household. Her *ghardian* then has the legal right to determine all manner of her life, restricting at will any and all interactions she has with the world.

shellan (n.) Female vampire who has been mated to a male. Females generally do not take more than one mate due to the highly territorial nature of bonded males.

symphath (n.) Subspecies within the vampire race characterized by the ability and desire to manipulate emotions in others (for the purposes of an energy exchange), among other traits. Historically, they have been discriminated against and, during certain eras, hunted by vampires. They are near extinction.

the Tomb (pr. n.) Sacred vault of the Black Dagger Brotherhood. Used as a ceremonial site as well as a storage facility for the jars of *lessers*. Ceremonies performed there include inductions, funerals, and disciplinary actions against Brothers. No one may enter except for members of the Brotherhood, the Scribe Virgin, or candidates for induction.

trahyner (n.) Word used between males of mutual respect and affection. Translated loosely as "beloved friend."

transition (n.) Critical moment in a vampire's life when he or she transforms into an adult. Thereafter, he or she must drink the blood of the opposite sex to survive and is unable to withstand sunlight. Occurs generally in the mid-twenties. Some vampires do not survive their transitions, males in particular. Prior to their transitions, vampires are physically weak, sexually unaware and unresponsive, and unable to dematerialize.

vampire (n.) Member of a species separate from that of Homo sapiens. Vampires must drink the blood of the opposite sex to survive. Human blood will keep them alive, though the strength does not last long. Following their transitions, which occur in their mid-twenties, they are unable to go out into sunlight and must feed from the vein regularly. Vampires cannot "convert" humans through a bite or transfer of blood, though they are in rare cases able to breed with the other species. Vampires can dematerialize at will, though they must be able to calm themselves and concentrate to do so and may not carry anything heavy with them. They are able to strip the memories of humans, provided such memories are short-term. Some vampires are able to read minds. Life expectancy is upward of a thousand years, or in some cases even longer.

wahlker (n.) An individual who has died and returned to the living from the Fade. They are accorded great respect and are revered for their travails.

whard (n.) Equivalent of a godfather or godmother to an individual.

BLOOD
KISS

Chapter One

Some graduations happened in private.

Some of these important markers of the next stage of life had no caps and gowns, no orchestras playing the humans' "Pomp and Circumstance." There was no stage to walk across or diploma to hang on your wall. No witnesses, either.

Some graduations were marked by the simple and the everyday, the nothing-special—like a person reaching out to a Dell monitor and hitting the little blue button on the lower right corner of the computer screen. Such a mundane action, done many times in a week, a month, a year—but nonetheless, for one particular instance, a great division between before and after occurred.

As Paradise, blooded daughter of Abalone, First Adviser to Wrath, son of Wrath, sire of Wrath, King of all vampires, sat back in her office chair, she stared at the now-black screen in front of her. Amazing. The night she had been waiting for was almost here.

For most of the last eight weeks, time had been going at a crawl, but in these final couple of evenings it had switched things up and flipped into catapult mode. Suddenly, after having suffered through seven-thousand-hour waits for the moon to rise, she felt like she wanted to slow it all down again.

Her first job was now a thing of the past.

Looking across the desk, she moved the office phone over an inch—then switched the AT&T whatever it was back to where it had been. She straightened the stained-glass dragonfly shade on the Tiffany lamp. Made sure the blue pens were in one holder and the red ones in another. Smoothed her palm over the dust-free blotter and the top of the monitor.

The waiting room was empty, the silk chairs unoccupied, the magazines put in order on the side tables, the drinks that had been served by *doggen* to those who had come all cleaned up.

The last civilian had left about thirty minutes ago. Dawn was about two hours off. All in all, it was the normal end to a night of hard work, the time when she and her father would head back to the family estate to enjoy a meal full of talk and plans and mutual respect.

Paradise leaned forward and looked around the archway of the parlor. Across the foyer, the double doors that led into what had previously been the mansion's formal dining room were closed.

Yup, just a normal night except for the very unnormal meeting that was taking place in there: Right after the final appointment had left, her father had been called into the audience chamber and those doors had shut tight.

He was in there with the King, and two members of the Black Dagger Brotherhood.

"Don't you do this to me," she said. "Don't you take this away from me."

Paradise got up and walked around, re-straightening magazines, re-plumping throw pillows, stopping in front of the oil painting of a French king.

Heading back to the archway, she stared at the closed panels of the dining room and listened to the pounding of her heart.

Lifting her hands, she prodded the calluses on her palms. They hadn't come from working here for her father and the Brotherhood for the last couple of months, organizing the schedule and tracking issues, resolutions and follow-ups. No, for the first time in her life she had been hitting the gym. Pumping iron. Running on treadmills. Working the StairMaster. Pull-ups, push-ups, sit-ups. Erg machine.

Before now, she hadn't even known what an erg machine was.

And it was all in preparation for tomorrow night.

Assuming that group of males in the King's audience room wasn't taking it all away from her.

Tomorrow, at midnight, she was supposed to join the Scribe Virgin only knew how many males and females at a secret location—where she was going to try to make the cut for the Black Dagger Brotherhood's training program for soldiers.

It was a good plan—something she had decided to pursue, a chance to be independent and kick some ass and prove to herself she was more than her pedigree. The problem? Fully blooded daughters from the *glymera*, from one of the Founding Families no less, did not train to become soldiers. They didn't handle guns or knives. They didn't learn to fight or defend themselves. They didn't even know what a *lesser* was.

They didn't even *associate* with soldiers.

Daughters like her were trained in needlepoint, classical music and singing, manners, and running vast households filled with *doggen*. They were expected to know the complicated social calendar and the festival cycles, keep up with the wardrobe requirements of all of that, and know the difference between Van Cleef & Arpels, Boucheron and Cartier. They were cloistered, protected, and cherished as all jewels were.

The only dangerous thing they were permitted to do? Breed. With a *hellren* chosen by their family to ensure the sanctity of their bloodlines.

It was a miracle her father was letting her do this.

He had certainly not been on board when she'd first

shown him the application—but he'd had a change of heart and let her apply to the program: The raids of a couple of years ago, when so many vampires had been killed by the Lessening Society, had proved what a dangerous place Caldwell, New York, could be. And she'd told him that she didn't want to go out and fight in the war. She just wanted to learn to defend herself.

Once she'd framed it in terms of her safety? That was when her father had changed his tune.

The real truth was that she just wanted something that was hers. An identity that came from a place other than what her birthright had forced on her.

Plus Peyton had told her she couldn't do it.

Because she was female.

Screw that.

Paradise checked those closed doors again. "Come on. . . ."

Pacing around, she eventually wandered out into the foyer, but she didn't want to get too close to where the males were meeting—as if that might jinx things.

God, what were they talking about in there?

Usually the King left right after the last audience of the night. If he and the Brotherhood had any private business or stuff about the war to deal with, it was handled back at the First Family's residence, a place so secret that not even her father had been invited to go there.

So yeah, this had to be about her.

Back in the waiting area, she went to the desk and counted the hours she had sat at it. She'd only had the job a couple of months, but she'd liked the work—to a point. In her absence, assuming she stayed in the BDB training program, a cousin of hers was taking over, and she'd spent the last seven nights showing the girl the ropes, clarifying the procedures Paradise had put into place, making sure that the transition was going to go smoothly.

Sitting back down in her chair, she opened the middle drawer and took out her application—as if that could somehow reassure her that this was all going to still happen.

As she held the paperwork in her hands, she wondered who else was going to be at the orientation tomorrow . . . and thought of the male who'd shown up here at the audience house, looking for a printed-out version of the application.

Tall, big shoulders, deep voiced. Wearing a Syracuse baseball cap, and jeans that had been worn out from what looked like actual work.

The community of vampires was a small one, and she'd never seen him before—but maybe he was just a civilian? That was another change in the training program. Before now, only males from the aristocracy were invited to work with the Brotherhood.

He had given her his name, but refused to shake her hand.

Craeg. That was all she knew.

He hadn't been rude, though. In fact, he'd been supportive of her applying.

He'd also been . . . captivating in a way that had shocked her—to the point where she'd waited for weeks to see if he brought the application back. He hadn't. Maybe he'd scanned it and sent the thing in that way.

Or maybe he'd decided not to try for the program after all.

It seemed crazy to be disappointed that she might never see him again.

As her phone went off with a chirp, she jumped and went for the thing. Peyton. Again.

She would see him at the orientation tomorrow night—and that would be soon enough. After that fight they'd had about her joining the program, she'd had to pull away from the friendship.

Then again, if the Brotherhood was putting their foot down in there with her father? That righteous indignation she felt toward the guy was going to be a moot point. But come on, females were allowed to apply.

The problem was, she was not a "normal" female.

FFS, she did not know what she was going to do if her

father took it all back. Surely the Brotherhood wouldn't wait until the last minute to deny her a spot, though.

Right?

Across town, Marissa, mated *shellan* of the Black Dagger Brother *Dhestroyer*, a.k.a. Butch O'Neal, sat back in her desk chair at Safe Place. As the thing let out a creak, she tapped her Bic pen on the OfficeMax calendar blotter and shifted the phone receiver to her other ear.

Cutting into the stream of blabbering, she said, "Well, I certainly appreciate the invitation, but I can't—"

The female on the other end didn't miss a beat. She just kept on talking, her aristocratic intonation sucking up all the bandwidth—until it was a wonder that the entire zip code didn't suffer an electrical brownout. "... and you can understand why we need your help. This is the first Twelfth Month Festival Ball that has been held since the raids. As the *shellan* of a Brother, and a member of a Founding Family, you would be a perfect chair of the event—"

Giving her *no* another shot, Marissa cut in, "I'm not sure you're aware of this, but I work full-time as the director of Safe Place and—"

"... and your brother said that you would be a good choice."

Marissa fell silent.

Her first thought was that she found it highly unlikely that Havers, the race's physician and her very, very, very estranged next of kin, had recommended her for anything other than an early grave. Her second was more along the lines of a calculation ... how long had it been since she had spoken to him? Two years? Three? Not since he'd thrown her out of their house, about five minutes before dawn, when he'd found out she was interested in a mere human.

Who had actually turned out to be Wrath's cousin and the embodiment of the *Dhestroyer* legend.

How ya like me now, she heard in her head.

"So you just *have* to chair the event," the female concluded. As if it were a done deal.

"You must needs forgive me." Marissa cleared her throat. "But my brother is not in a position to proffer my name for anything, as he and I haven't seen each other for quite some time."

When a whole boatload of nothing-but-quiet came over the connection, she decided she should have aired her family's dirty laundry about ten minutes ago: Members of the *glymera* were supposed to observe rigid codes of behavior—and exposing the colossal rift in her bloodline, even though it was well-known, was something that was simply not done.

Far more appropriate for others to whisper about it behind your back.

Unfortunately, the female recovered and changed tactics. "At any rate, it is vitally important for all members of our class to resume the festivals—"

A knock on the door to her office brought Marissa's eyes around. "Yes?"

Over the phone, the female said, "Wonderful! You can come to my estate—"

"No, no. There's someone who needs me." She spoke up louder. "Come on in."

The moment she saw the expression on Mary's face, she cursed. Not good news. Rhage's *shellan* was a consummate professional, so for her to look like that? It was really a problem—

Was that *blood* on her shirt?

Marissa dropped her tone and cut the politeness. "My answer is no. My job requires all my time. Besides, if you're this passionate, you should take the job. Goodbye."

Dropping the phone back in the cradle, she got to her feet. "What's going on?"

"We've got an intake who needs medical assistance STAT. I can't reach Doc Jane or Ehlena anywhere. I don't know what to do."

Marissa rushed around the desk. "Where is she?"

"Downstairs."

The pair of them hit the stairwell at a run, Marissa in the lead. "How did she come to us?"

"I don't know. One of the security cameras picked her up out on the lawn, crawling."

"What?"

"My cell phone went off with an alert, and I ran out there with Rhym. We carried her into the parlor."

Rounding the corner at the bottom, Marissa skidded on one of the throw rugs. . . .

And stopped altogether.

When she saw the condition of the female on the sofa, she put one hand over her mouth. "Oh, dear God . . ." she whispered.

Blood. There was blood everywhere, on the floor in drips, soaking through white towels pressed to wounds, pooling under one of the female's feet on the carpet.

The girl had been beaten so badly there was no way to identify her, her features so swollen that, if she hadn't had long hair and a torn skirt, you wouldn't even have known what sex she was. One arm was clearly dislocated, the limb hanging badly from the shoulder . . . and she had only the left high-heeled shoe on, her stockings shredded.

Her breathing was bad, very bad. Nothing but a rattling in her chest, as if she were drowning in her own blood.

Rhym, the intake supervisor, looked up from where she had crouched by the couch. Through the tears in her eyes, she whispered, "I don't think she's going to live. How can she live . . . ?"

Marissa had to pull herself together. It was the only option. "Doc Jane and Ehlena are both unreachable?" she said in a hoarse voice.

"I've tried the mansion," Mary replied. "The clinic. Their cell phones. Two times in all places."

For a split second, Marissa was terrified about what

that meant for her own life. Were the Brothers in medical trouble? Was Butch okay?

That lasted only a moment. "Give me your phone—and get the residents into the Wellsie annex. I want everyone there in case I have to bring a male in."

Mary tossed over her phone and nodded. "I'm on it."

Safe Place was exactly that—a safe place for female victims of domestic violence to come for shelter and rehabilitation with their young. And after Marissa had spent countless, useless centuries in the *glymera*, being nothing but the unclaimed betrothed of the King, she had found her calling here, in service to those who had been at best verbally abused, at worst, horrifically treated.

Males were not allowed inside.

But to save the life of this female here, she would break that rule.

Answer your phone, Manny, she thought as the first ring sounded. *Answer your damn phone. . . .*

Chapter Two

It wasn't the whole Black Dagger Brotherhood.

In fact, there were only two Brothers with the King.

As Abalone, First Adviser to Wrath, son of Wrath, sire of Wrath, entered the audience room to stand before his ruler, he was acutely aware of the other males. He had never known any of those warriors to be aught than protective and civilized, but considering he was about to turn his only blooded offspring over to them, their more obvious attributes were like screams in the night.

The Brother Vishous was staring at him with diamond eyes that didn't blink, those tattoos at his left temple seeming properly sinister, his muscle-roped body clad in leather and stung with weapons. By his side was Butch, a.k.a. the *Dhestroyer*—a former human with a Boston accent who had been infected by the Omega and left for dead—only to become one of the few to survive a jump-started transition.

The two of them were rarely apart, and it was tempting to assign them bad-cop, good-cop roles. Right now, though, the paradigm had shifted. Butch, the male who tended to smile and talk to people, seemed like the one it would be best to avoid in a dark alley: His hazel stare was narrow and unwavering.

"Yes?" Abalone asked his King. "May I be of service in some manner?"

Wrath stroked the boxy blond head of his guide dog, George. "My boys here need to talk to you."

Ah, Abalone thought. And he suspected what this was about.

Butch smiled for a split second. Like he wanted to preemptively take the sting from whatever was going to come out of his mouth. "We want to make sure you're aware of what's involved in the training program."

Abalone cleared his throat. "I know that this is very important to Paradise. And I'm hoping there are some self-defense courses offered. I should like her to be . . . safer."

That potential benefit had been the only thing that had helped him through the clash between what he had expected for her and her life, and what she seemed to be choosing to do.

When there was no response, Abalone looked back and forth between the Brothers. "What are you not telling me?"

Vishous opened his mouth, but the Brother Butch raised his palm and shut him up. "Your role here with Wrath comes first."

Abalone recoiled. "Are you saying that Paradise is ineligible because of my position here? Dearest Virgin Scribe, why didn't you tell us—"

"We need you to understand that what's going to happen is not all book learning. This is a preparation for war."

"But the candidates don't necessarily have to go fight down in the alleys during the program, correct?"

"What we're worried about is here." The Brother indicated the room. "We can't have anything affect your relationship with Wrath and what you do for the King. Paradise is as welcome as anyone else in the program, but not if the prospect of her dropping out or being cut could create tension between us."

Abalone exhaled in relief. "Do not worry about that.

She succeeds or fails on her own merits. I expect no special treatment for her—and if she cannot keep up? Then she should be dismissed."

In fact, although he would never say it aloud, he both prayed for, and expected, that to be the case. He did not look forward to Paradise being disappointed in herself or her efforts, but ... the last thing he wanted for his daughter was her being exposed to any ugliness—or, God forbid, actually trying to fight in the war.

He couldn't even fathom that last one.

"Worry not," he reiterated, glancing at the Brothers and at the King. "All shall be well."

The Brother Butch stared at Vishous. Then looked back. "You read the application, right?"

"She filled it out."

"So you didn't read it?"

"This is something she's doing independently—as her father and *ghardian*, was I supposed to sign it?"

Vishous lit a hand-rolled. "You might want to be prepared, true?"

Abalone nodded. "I am. I promise you, I am."

Paradise was a female gently raised in the proper traditions of the aristocracy. She'd been working on her physical conditioning for the last two months—quite diligently, actually—and he could feel the excitement rolling off of her as she wound up her duties here and prepared to exit her position. There was, however, a very good chance that after the orientation tomorrow evening, when the real work started, she would find herself either bowing out ... or being asked to leave.

It was going to kill him to see her fail.

But better that than her dying out in the field just to prove the point that she was so much more than what her aristocratic station dictated.

As the pair of Brothers continued to look at him, Abalone lowered his head. "I know this is not going to go well for her. I am more than braced for that. I am not naive."

After a moment, Butch said, "Okay. Fair enough."

"Is there aught else, my lord?" Abalone asked the King.

When Wrath shook his head, Abalone bowed to each of them. "Thank you for your concern. Paradise is my most precious one—all that is left of my beloved *shellan*. I know she shall be in kind and fair hands on the morrow."

As he turned to leave, the Brothers remained grim, but then again, he was not privy to what was going on with the war—and there was always something. The fighting and the strategy were nothing he had ever been involved with, and for that he was grateful.

Just as he would be if Paradise left that program.

Verily, he wished her *mahmen* were still alive. Perhaps this all would be moot if his *shellan* had been present to talk some sense into the girl.

Opening the double doors, he heard a clattering in the waiting area. "Paradise?"

He strode across the foyer, and as he rounded the corner into the parlor, his daughter straightened from picking up red pens that had been knocked off the desk.

"Is all well?" he asked.

Her eyes met his. "Is it? Are you allowing me to go tomorrow night?"

Abalone smiled—and tried to keep the sadness out of his eyes, his voice. "Of course. You're in the program, that was decided months ago."

She ran over and embraced him, holding on tight, as if she had been convinced she was going to be denied what she wanted so badly.

Embracing his daughter, Abalone was vaguely aware of the Brothers and the King leaving out the front door. He paid them no mind.

He was too busy wishing he could save his daughter from any and all disappointment. That was not among the parenting skills he had been granted upon her birth, however.

Oh, how he wished his *shellan* were here with them instead of in the Fade.

She would have handled all of this better.

Standing over the horrifically injured female, Marissa closed her eyes as she got Manny's voice mail for the third time. What the *hell* was going on at the clinic?

Just as she was about to redial, her phone began to ring. "Thank God—Manny? Manny?"

Something about the tone of her voice caused the wounded female to stir, her bloody face moving against the sofa cushions. God, the sound of that wheezing rattle was enough to make the heart skip beats.

"No, it's Ehlena," said the voice in her ear. "Manny and Jane are doing emergency surgery on Tohr. He has a compound fracture of the femur and I have to head back into the OR. Is there something wrong?"

"How long are they going to be?" she asked.

"They just started."

Marissa closed her eyes. "Okay, please have them call me when they can? I've got a . . ." She turned away and dropped her voice. "I have a trauma case that's just come in here. I don't know if we have a lot of time."

Ehlena cursed. "We can't spare anyone here. Can you call Vishous? With his medical training, he may be able to stabilize things."

Marissa tried to imagine that Brother walking through the house. Not her first choice, and not because she didn't trust the male. Her *hellren*'s best friend was a stellar vampire all the way around.

His appearance was just terrifying.

Then again, if everyone was in the Wellsie Annex . . .

"Good idea. Thank you."

"I'll have them call you as soon as we're done."

"Please."

Cutting the connection, she hit up V. And got goddamn, frickin' voice mail. "*Shit.*"

Rhym spoke up from where she was pressing a towel

to that leaking gash in the female's shoulder. "When are they coming?"

It was getting close to the end of the night. V could just be in transit between the alleys of downtown Caldwell and the mansion. Or . . . he could be stuck fighting whoever had injured Tohr like that.

As the female on the sofa began to cough and sputter, the calculation was done in a split second. The last thing she wanted to do was reach out to her brother, but she couldn't live with herself if her personal problems cost someone their life.

Marissa dialed Havers's cell phone number by heart, and hoped he hadn't changed it. One ring, two rings . . .

"Hello?" came his voice.

"It's me." Before there was some kind of awkward silence or hello, she said, "We have a medical emergency here at Safe Place. I need you to come right now—or send someone. The Brotherhood's physicians are in surgery and we don't have a lot of time."

There was a short pause, as if the race's primary healer were switching from a personal track to a professional one. "I shall be there in but a moment. Is it a trauma situation?"

"Yes." Marissa lowered her voice again. "She's been badly beaten and . . . brutalized. There's a lot of blood. I don't know. . . ."

"I'm bringing a nurse. Are you containing the other residents?"

"Already have."

"Unlock the front door."

"I'll meet you at it."

And that was that.

Guess the universe was determined to have her brother on her radar screen this evening. First that idiot call with the socialite, now . . .

Marissa nodded to Rhym. "Help is on the way."

Through the eye that was not swollen shut, the injured female seemed to try to focus.

Marissa leaned in and took a bloody hand. "My brother is going to take very good care of you."

For a split second, she worried whether she should have kept quiet about the fact that a male was going to treat her. But the female didn't seem to be tracking.

Dearest Virgin Scribe, what if she died before he got here?

Marissa crouched down, tucking her blond hair behind her ears. "You're safe, it's going to be all right." That one eye looped over to her face. "Do you have kin we can call? Is there someone who we can get for you?"

The female's head went back and forth.

"No? Are you sure?" The eye shut. "Can you tell me who did this to you?"

That face turned away.

Shit.

Backing off, Marissa went out to the shallow hall in the front of the house. There were long, thin windows on either side of the door, and she looked out to the lawn. The trees that had been so brilliantly colored just weeks before had molted their spectacular red and gold and yellow leaves, the spindly limbs underneath revealed like the bones of a too-thin dog.

It was impossible not to glance at the mirror next to the door and check to see that her hair was in place, and her makeup was holding up even after a ten-hour day.

Back when she had lived with her brother, she had worn silk gowns and heavy jewels, and had her hair styled up high on her head. Now? She had a pair of Ann Taylor slacks on, a blouse with a stand-up collar, and a pair of Cole Haan driving shoes on her feet because they were comfy. No jewelry other than a tiny gold cross that she wore because Butch's God was important to him and her *hellren* had given her the necklace during his last Christmas season. Oh, and she had a pair of pearl studs in her ears.

In spite of Butch's transition having been jump-started, and his status as a Brother and a relation of the King, her male remained fundamentally human, everything from his Catholic belief system to his taste in books and movies to his opinions on what he wanted in a "wife," a product of his upbringing among Homo sapiens.

Touching the gold chain on her neck, she frowned as she had to fight the urge to take the thing off because her brother wouldn't approve of it.

But come on, whether the symbol of her mating was on or off her throat, it wasn't as if that changed anything. In her brother's eyes, she had taken a rat without a tail as a *hellren*, and that fall from grace would never be forgiven.

A split second later, two shadows materialized out of thin air on the sidewalk: one taller and masculine, dressed in a white coat, the other smaller and feminine in a traditional nursing uniform.

As they approached and were illuminated in the security lights, Marissa rubbed her sweaty palms on the seat of her pants. Havers looked exactly the same as he always had, from the bow tie and the horn-rimmed glasses to the dark hair parted on the side and kept in *Mad Men* order.

At the last minute, Marissa switched the cross around to her nape and opened the door. Trying not to sound as if she were nervous, she announced, "She is in the parlor."

No "Hello, how are you?" or "Hey, have you stopped being a prejudicial asshole?"—but then again, this was a medical emergency, not a social call.

"Marissa," her brother said, nodding his head and stepping by her. "This is Cannest, my head nurse."

"My pleasure, I'm sure," the nurse murmured.

Marissa nodded at the female. "This way."

Her legs felt stiff as she led them deeper into the modest house with its common furnishings, and for some absurd reason she pictured herself as a flamingo, her knees facing the wrong way. Meanwhile, all manner of memories boiled under the surface of her conscious mind, only the psychic weight of the tragedy unfolding in the other room keeping a lid on her emotions.

Her brother stopped at the archway into the parlor and gave his doctor's bag to his assistant. "My nurse will do the triage, and advise me as to her condition. It will be better than having a male perform the examination."

Marissa glanced into Havers's eyes for the first time, and noted that his stare had remained the identical shade of blue that hers was. As if that would have changed, though?

"That is very considerate of you," she said before looking to his associate. "Come with me."

In the parlor, the nurse went directly to the sofa, and was kind to Rhym as she took the staffer's place. The victim stirred as if recognizing that there was a new presence before her, and then moaned as her pulse and blood pressure were taken.

Marissa stood off to the side, crossing her arms over her chest and putting her hand up to her mouth. The movements were good, she told herself. It meant that the poor girl was still alive.

"Be careful," she blurted as the nurse felt down that arm and tears mixed with the blood on that beaten face.

Dear God, who had done this? It had to be a member of the species—she couldn't catch the scent of anything human on her.

Marissa had to drop her eyes as the exam became more intimate, and she motioned for Rhym to join her by the archway, as if she were protecting the privacy her brother was already respecting.

After what felt like forever, the nurse spoke quietly with the female and then came back over, nodding for Marissa to follow her out to where Havers was standing with his hands clasped behind his back. He bowed his head as he listened to his nurse speak in a quiet tone.

"She has extensive internal injuries," the female reported. "She will have to be operated on immediately if she is going to survive. The arm is the least of the problems."

Havers nodded and glanced at Marissa. "I took the liberty of arranging for transport. It should arrive in approximately fifteen minutes."

"I'm going in the van with her." Marissa got ready for a fight. "Until her blood comes, I am her *ghardian*."

"But of course."

"And I will assume the cost of treatment."

"That will not be necessary."

"It is very necessary. Allow me to get my things."

Leaving them, she spoke to Rhym, and then she ran up to her office and got her phone, her purse, and her coat.

She thought about calling Butch, as there was some chance she wasn't going to be home for the day, but she wasn't going to know that for a little bit. And unfortunately, if she dialed up her *hellren* every time a crisis hit here at work? She would wear out his ringer.

Halfway down the stairs, she realized there was another reason she wasn't reaching out to him.

Too close to what had happened to his sister.

And there was a possibility things could be completely the same if this female died from her injuries.

No, she thought as she returned to the first floor. He had enough on his plate without having old triggers scatter his grey matter yet again.

"I'm ready," she told her brother, as if daring him to change his mind.

"The ambulance is two minutes out. I shall need to be in it with her as well—she is going to require a feeding if she has any chance of surviving."

Havers gave her a little bow and retraced his steps to the front door. As he turned the corner, Marissa shook her head.

The idea that he would give of his own blood to help some unknown female, who was probably naught but a civilian, was both amazing . . . and a source of frustration.

That the male could be so kind to his patients and so cruel to her personally seemed like an insupportable contradiction.

But that was the *glymera* for you. Double standards abounded.

And typically were used to screw daughters, sisters, and mothers.

Chapter Three

As Butch stood in the BDB mansion's grand, colorful foyer, he frowned and looked at his phone. He'd checked the time on his Audemars Piguet watch about three minutes prior, but figured maybe his Samsung whatever-the-fuck-it-was might give him an answer he could live with better.

Negative.

And his seventh call to Marissa had just gone unanswered. As had the other six.

Off in the distance, the chatter and subtle clanking of Last Meal being consumed bubbled out of the dining room.

For no good reason, he thought about the first night he'd listened to sounds like that. It had been at what was now the audience house. He'd been a homicide detective back then, out of control and looking for a source of total destruction so that he could just be done with life.

And then came the rabbit hole.

Beth had gone down it first, her mixed heritage as half human, half vampire sucking her in. His entrée had been something else entirely.

If you're going to bloody the human, would you be good enough to do it in the backyard?

"You got her yet?"

Butch closed his eyes at the familiar male voice. Even though it was not even partially true, sometimes he felt like Vishous's acerbic mutter had been in his head for his entire life.

"No."

As the Brother approached, the scent of Turkish tobacco preceded him and Butch breathed in deep. Maybe it was a contact high, maybe it was the nasty bastard's presence, but the volume of screaming panic in his ears decreased a little.

"You call her office at the Place?" V asked on the exhale.

"Voice mail. And I dialed Mary, too. Nothing."

"Motherfucker—"

The subtle binging of the security monitor ripped his head around. When he saw the image on the screen, he lunged for the vestibule's door, nearly tearing the heavy weight off its hinges.

"Oh, God, where have you been—"

He was on his Marissa so fast and hard, the rest of whatever gibberish came out of his mouth was lost as he held her against him.

"I'm so sorry," she said in a muffled voice. "I was dealing with a case. I didn't bother calling you because I had almost no time to get home."

Pulling back, he put his palms on either side of her face and looked her over. "Are you okay?"

"Absolutely. And I'm so sorry—"

He kissed her, shuddering as her hands traveled up his back. "No, no. Not sorry. I only care that you're okay."

Fucking hell, that sun was a terrifying thing. A vampire caught out at dawn was nothing but a bonfire in their clothes—and although Marissa was well protected at Safe Place, shit could happen: humans were unpredicable idiots and the slayers were downright deadly.

As she separated them, she smiled. "I'm fine, just fine."

Yeah, right, he thought as her eyes wouldn't meet his.

He tugged her arm. "Come with me."

"But Last Meal is on the table—"

"Who cares."

Drawing her into the billiards room, he would have shut them in together if there had been doors to close.

"What happened," he demanded.

She wandered around a little, her incredible body turning those simple clothes of hers into haute couture. "Nothing you haven't heard before, sadly."

Butch closed his eyes. Sometimes he hated her job; he really did. The harder it got, though, the more she fought—and though it pained him to see her worn-out, worn down, and discouraged sometimes, he respected the hell out of her for what she did for her race. And it wasn't all bad. When people she had helped transitioned back into independent living, his *shellan* glowed like the sun.

Taking her hand, he backed up against one of the pool tables, and pulled her in between his thighs. "Tell me anyway."

Her eyes traveled around the room, but he stayed focused on her. And Jesus, even after a long, hard night, she took his breath away. Her beauty was legendary in the race, something that had been spoken about for generations and was still revered, and it was obvious why. Her face was a compilation of perfect angles, her skin as smooth and luminous as a pearl, her blue eyes the color of a morning glory, those lips so pink and soft. And then there was the blond hair that was down past her shoulders, and yeah, that figure, which was the kind of thing that knocked males on their asses—and kept 'em down.

On a regular basis, he couldn't believe she was with him. Him. A guy from Southie, with a chipped front tooth, a bad background, and a host of addictions he hadn't been able to master until he'd met her.

Plus there was all the Omega shit.

Yet his *shellan* loved him, for some completely unknown reason.

"You're not talking to me," he whispered, sweeping her hair back and stroking her neck, her tight shoulders, her stiff arms. "You know I hate it when I don't know what's doing."

As a chorus of laughter broke out across the way, Marissa nestled in close, her hips coming into contact with all kinds of party time.

And what do you know, his erection was instant, his cock thickening up and getting long behind the fly of his leathers.

Putting her arms around his neck, she leaned in and eased her breasts into his chest. "Aren't you hungry?"

Growling deep in his throat, he reached around and cupped her rear assets. A palmful on either side, nothing more, firm as a gymnast's—oh, God, he was starting to sweat.

Except he shook his head. "This isn't going to work. You're not going to distract me—"

Next thing he knew, Marissa parted her mouth and exposed her fangs. Getting close, she ran one of the canines across his lower lip, the sensation of the sharp point moving over his flesh causing him to moan.

"You sound like you need something," she whispered against his mouth. "Do you want to tell me what it is?" Her tongue extended and licked her way into him. "What is it, Butch. Tell me what you need...."

"You," he groaned. "I need you."

After his transition, when his body had bulked up and become this hulking thing of power, he'd gotten used to feats of physical strength—and also this resonant weakness when it came to his female and sex. He'd needed women from time to time back when he'd been strictly human, but that was nothing compared to the roaring lust Marissa could bring out of him at the drop of a hat. One look, one touch ... a sentence or two ... sometimes it was just the clean ocean scent of her....

Boom! Like someone blew up his brain.

"Marissa ..."

Her pelvis rotated against his arousal and then she was stepping away from him. "Come here."

She could have commanded him to do any number of things—"Stand on your head, shave your eyebrows, pull your own arm off"—and he would have done any of it in a heartbeat. Follow her? With the possibility of giving her an orgasm—or six?

Yes, please, thank you, ma'am, how may I be of service.

Marissa led him behind the bar and pushed him against the shelves of liquor bottles. With fast hands, she went for his fly, and God help him, he gripped the edge of the granite countertop and watched her undo the buttons one by one, the ridge of his erection pushing things open as she went down.

And then she gripped him.

"Fuuuuck . . ." His head wanted to fall back, but he needed to see her—

His whole body swayed as her hand stroked his shaft.

"Do you like to see me do this to you?" She worked him nice and slow, up and down. "Do you, Butch."

"Yes," he whispered, drawing out the word. "I like . . . to see . . . your hands on me. . . ."

"What about my mouth?"

His balls tightened, and an orgasm shot into the head of his cock, ready to explode—and that was before she got on her knees in front of him, disappearing behind the cover of the bar's front section.

He wasn't going to last long, but fuck him, he wanted that sensation, that warm, wet pull, even if for just a second—no watching, though. He had to squeeze his eyes shut. If he saw what she looked like, her mouth stretched wide, her beautiful hair splaying over his leather-clad thighs, that blue stare of hers looking up at him as if she liked the taste of him . . .

Which, of course, couldn't possibly be true. But that was one lie he wasn't going to argue with—

As her name reverberated up his throat, that suction was exactly what he was after, so slick and smooth, so hot that his eyes flared open. With his head on the level, he got a brief hi-how're-ya of the leather couches, the pool tables, the archway into the foyer. If anybody happened to come in — which was unlikely, given Last Meal — they were just going to see him with his porn face on. Marissa was hidden behind the screen of the bar's long, high countertop piece. And more good news? His bonding scent was waaaaaay out there, the dark spices so thick, it would serve as a warning that shit was going down in here, and people needed to give them a little privacy.

Marissa rode his head and shaft with her mouth, working him out like he liked it, and he closed his lids again — thinking of the Patriots playing the Giants . . . what was being served in that dining room . . . whether Lassiter was going to make them watch *The Bachelor* or if it was going to be Rachael frickin' Ray and her EVOO shit.

The image of that bossy little chef was the filter that worked best, blocking some of the sensation — or at least enough so he didn't come all over his *shellan*.

Actually, his fear of that outcome worked even better.

Fucking hell, the horror he'd feel if he ever climaxed in her mouth or, God, on her face . . .

Nope, nope, not gonna happen.

Unhinging his clawed hands from the back countertop, he reached down and gently pushed at her shoulders. "Stop . . ." he choked out. "You need to stop now."

The sensations below his waist were getting loud as a detonation — until even with the distractions and the worry, they were about to take him over, submerging him under great waves of high-octane ecstasy.

Gritting his teeth, he grimaced. "Time to stop — time to —"

At the last possible moment, he forced her head away, jerked his hips to the side, and ejaculated all over the cabinets where the big boxes of Pepperidge Farm Goldfish were kept. As he came, she fought against his hold, like she wanted back at his erection, but he didn't let her go until his hips had stopped kicking and his body was going into a sag.

"You should let me finish," she said quietly. "You never let me finish you."

Refocusing on his mate, he drew her up his body, his still-hard cock bumping against her breasts, her stomach, her thighs—

The sound of the vestibule's door chime brought their heads around—and Butch swallowed a curse. Jesus, how'd he let this happen in such a public damn room? It had seemed like a perfectly acceptable idea when he'd been lust-blind, but this was no place for a lady like her to blow some scrub like him, even if they were mated.

Butch quickly smoothed Marissa's hair and then started doing up his fly. "We need to take this back home."

"It was kind of fun."

"No."

As Fritz let Xhex and Trez in, Butch yanked himself back to reality.

". . . owes me one," Xhex was saying as she strode in.

"I so do!" Butch called out to her. "Call the chit whenever you want."

Xhex shot him a wave, then pegged him with a finger point. "I'm holding you to that."

"You better."

Butch had to smile, but then he refocused on his *shellan*. "Let me feed you. And then get you naked in our bed."

"Good." She kissed him and then turned around to clean up what he had—

"No." Butch stopped her hands on the paper towels. "That's for me to do."

As he eased her out of the way, he could feel her staring at him, but he ignored it. Where he came from, there were two kinds of women, and his mate was in the worship category.

He should know. He'd had more than his quota of skanks.

The last thing he would ever do was disrespect his Marissa. It would be like burning down a church, taking a knife to the Mona Lisa, and driving a 918 off a cliff for no reason at all.

So, no, she wasn't going to clean up the nasty he'd left behind.

Marissa had other fish to fry.

As Butch insisted on paper toweling on his own, she got out of his way and shook her head. She had never understood his quirks about sex, but she accepted them. What else could she do? He wouldn't talk to her about it—whenever she brought up the subject of him pushing her mouth away anytime he was close to climaxing, he shut her down.

Besides, right now that long-running stuff between the two of them was on her back burner.

That horrifically injured female was barely alive after having been operated on—and Marissa had come home only because there was nothing to do but sit outside that ICU room and wait for word that her organs had failed. Or had started to work on their own. God, the surgery had seemed so complicated when the nurse had explained it to her, but fixing her internal injuries and removing her spleen hadn't taken more than an hour.

Unfortunately, she had lost too much blood, and even after Havers giving her his vein, her vitals were jumping all around.

When her brother had emerged from the OR, he had looked Marissa right in the eye and told her that he'd done the best he could.

And their own personal issues aside, she believed him.

The sad part to all of it, and indeed, there was almost too much tragedy to bear with this case, was that they still didn't have a name for the female, and no one had called looking for her—Abalone, the King's First Adviser, had checked the open e-mail box and audience house's voice mail at Marissa's request. There had also been no inquiries at the clinic or Safe Place.

The girl was a figurative ghost . . . on her way to possibly becoming a literal one.

"Shall we?" Butch drawled as he offered her his arm.

Marissa shook herself back into focus and smiled at her mate. "Yes, please."

Taking hold of him, she walked by his side out into the foyer and entered the formal dining room. After the privacy they'd just had, all the chatter, laughter and bustling was a different social time zone, and she found herself feeling a little overwhelmed. Talk about filled to capacity. Even though the muraled ceiling was high as a kite, and the floor space bigger than a bowling alley, with the forty-foot-long table down the center crammed with the Brothers, their *shellans*, and the other fighters and members of the household, there was a joyful congestion ot it all.

Two seats were empty on the far side, and they went around to them, Butch settling her in her chair.

As he sat down next to her, he leaned in and kissed her on the mouth. "Eat fast."

"You'd better believe it," she said—even though she wasn't hungry.

And, she was sad to admit, she wasn't necessarily in a big hurry to get back to the Pit, either. The truth was, she'd seduced him because she'd known it was the only way to get her mate to move on from worrying about her.

When a plate of filet mignon was set in front of her by a *doggen*, Marissa moved things around, cutting up meat that she didn't try, messing the mashed potatoes, scattering bright green peas. And then she took her glass of cabernet sauvignon and sat back, watching the people, listening to the stories.

". . . gonna want me to do?"

Focusing in on her mate as he spoke, she watched as he leaned around John Matthew to put the question to Xhex.

The female fighter laughed. "You should fear me."

"Anyone who doesn't is an asshat."

"You say the sweetest things. And I'm in no hurry to call my chit in. It's a good thing to have a male like you in my debt."

For no particular reason, Marissa took note of how powerful Xhex's body was, her shoulders and torso cut with muscle that was set off by the skintight Under Armour shirt she wore tucked into her black leathers. Between her dark hair that was cut short and her gunmetal gray eyes, she was definitely someone to take seriously.

Meanwhile, Marissa was rocking her office-appropriate slacks and English school marm blouse routine.

As Butch offered his palm for a high five, Xhex laid one on him and the clap was loud in the room even with all the background noise.

"That's what I'm talkin' about," Butch said as he sat back in his chair. "Unbelievable."

"What is?" Marissa asked.

"Xhex was ... well, actually, first, I was in an alley. ... Ah, lemme back up. ..." He swiped his hand through the air. "Actually, it's too much to explain. Bottom line, I was cornered with my pants down with two *lessers*, and Xhex had J.M.'s phone on her when I texted for backup. She came in a flash and—" Butch stopped short and shook his head. "Anyway."

Marissa waited for him to go on. "Anyway ... ? What happened?"

Butch cleared his throat and took a sip from the Lagavulin in his glass. "It's not important. It's just, you know, stuff."

"You were in trouble, weren't you."

He drew again from his rim. "It all worked out."

"Thanks to Xhex."

"You haven't eaten anything."

She glanced down at her plate. "Oh, yeah. No, I had a meal before I left Safe Place."

Both of them fell silent.

As the ribbing surged among the Brothers, Marissa

felt herself receding, stepping behind an invisible screen that dimmed the sounds and the senses.

"You ready to go?" Butch asked a little later as people started to get up from the table.

"Sure. Yes. Thank you."

On the way to the archway, Butch stopped to talk to V, the pair of them putting their heads together and murmuring. Meanwhile, Xhex walked off from the table with her mate, John's hand traveling down onto the tight ass in those pants, squeezing, pulling her toward him. He had eyes only for his mate, his warrior's body clearly needing to blow off steam.

The response?

Xhex let out a growl, the female's eyes locking on John Matthew's as she bared her fangs—like a lioness setting the stage for what was going to be a marathon sex session.

Clearly, she had an edge she intended to file off with her *hellren* as well.

"We're set for tomorrow, then, true?" V said as he offered his palm to Butch.

"It's a go." Butch clapped hands with the Brother, their two heads getting close once more, their voices dropping so she heard only parts of the conversation: "Yeah. That's right. Uh-huh. See you back at the Pit?"

"You got it."

Butch gave Vishous's enormous shoulder a squeeze before turning to Marissa. "You good?"

"Mm-hmm," she said.

When Marissa went to walk along with him, she realized she still had her wineglass in her hand. "Let me put this back, hold on."

Going against the tide, she smiled at Autumn and Tohr, nodded to Payne and Manny—waved across the way at Bella and Nalla. Leaning over her still-full but completely disorganized plate, she put the glass back and wished Fritz and the staff would let anyone help them clear the table.

When she turned back around, she paused.

Butch was standing in the archway, legs braced in his leathers, brows down tight. None of that was unusual. But he'd taken the enormous gold cross he always wore out from under his shirt and was playing with it, winding the heavy weight in and out of his fingertips.

An odd sense of foreboding came over her.

"Marissa?" a female voice said.

Jumping to attention, she smiled at Bella. "Hey. I was watching you two across the table. Are you a cutie?" She gave Nalla's cheek a little stroke. "I think you are, yes, I do."

"She's too much to carry now." Bella bent down and put the young on her now-steady legs. "And I'm investing in running shoes."

"For you or her?"

Nalla took off at a dead run, but across the way, her father was on her, striding tight on those little heels. Even though he looked like a looming monster with his scarred face, skull-trimmed hair and slave tattoos, Nalla giggled in delight, glancing back and smiling up at her daddy as she ran, ran, ran around the table and dodged in and out of the *doggen* who were clearing.

"I need Nikes for the both of us." Bella smiled. "Listen, I wanted to ask you. I heard a rumor you're going to be chairing the Twelfth Month Festival Ball—"

"*What?*"

Bella frowned. "Wait, I thought . . . did I get this wrong?"

"No, it's okay." Great. "What were you going to say?"

"I just wanted to tell you that I'd like to help in any way I can. I was surprised to hear that you took it on, but I get why you would. We need . . . I don't know, I think it's time for the race to reestablish the traditions that worked. There was a lot that didn't, but the festivals are important—"

An unhappy wail lit off in the now-empty room as Nalla lurched and was caught by her father just in time.

"Crap, I gotta go," Bella said. "She's having growing

pains. It's been a long couple of days, I'll tell you. Just remember I'm here for you, okay?"

Bella hightailed off for her family, reaching out for Nalla, who in turn put out one arm for her *mahmen*. The other stayed with Dad . . . so that the three of them were united.

Yes, Marissa, thought. Growing pains were a hard time, at least from what she had heard. For some reason, vampire young struggled with spurts of intense growth, as opposed to the long, slow, steady route to adult height that humans enjoyed.

Just one more fun part to the species.

Like their festivals.

Marissa rubbed her temples as she went back over to Butch. "God, my head is pounding."

"Is it?" he said. "Let's get you into bed."

"Good idea. I think I need some sleep."

"Yeah. Yeah, you look tired."

"I am."

Annnnnnd that was pretty much the end of her night: Ten minutes later she was in bed, eyes closing, images of the last few hours flashing like strobe lights through her head.

While Butch headed back out to sit in the Pit's living room.

Alone.

Chapter Four

The following evening, Paradise took the bus to school.
So to speak.

There were actually two "buses," each holding about
thirty people, and any similarities between the ubiqui-
tous yellow mini-human transporters ended with the
shared name. The vehicles the Brotherhood used to pick
up the training center candidates were like something
out of *White House Down*, all black inside and out, with
thick, darkened windows that had to be bulletproof, tires
like snowplows, and grilles that reminded her of a T. rex.

Like everyone else, she had dematerialized to a tract
of vacant land out to the west of Caldwell's suburbs. Her
father had wanted to go with her, but it had seemed important to start as she meant to go on. This was her independent decision; she needed to do what everyone else
did—and she was pretty certain no one else would bring
a chaperone.

Especially not a chaperone who happened to be the
King's First Adviser.

To see nearly sixty people she didn't recognize had
been a surprise. Then again, the application had made it
clear that anyone was allowed to join the program, so
there were a lot of civilians. Actually, it looked as if it was
all civilians and the male/female ratio was, like, ten to
one.

But at least her sex was allowed.

Refocusing, Paradise shifted in her seat and made sure her elbow didn't disturb the male who was sitting next to her. Other than exchanging names—his was Axe—they hadn't said anything, and his brooding silence fit his image completely: The male had killer written all over him, with his black spiked hair, those black piercings on one side of his face, and that tattoo of something evil running vertically up half of his neck.

If her father knew she was thisclose to a male like that? They'd have to put Abalone on life support.

And this was exactly why she'd wanted to do the program. It was time to break out of the restrictions of her station—and cut the hothouse flower crap. If working around the King had taught her anything, it was that no matter what class you were in, tragedy didn't discriminate, justice could always be served, and nobody got out of this life alive.

"So, you're really going to take it this far."

Paradise looked into the black glass of the window beside her. Reflected in the mirror-like surface, Princeps Peyton, first blooded son of Peythone, was just as she remembered: classically handsome, with those intense blue eyes and his thick blond hair brushed straight back from his forehead. He was wearing his signature rimless, sapphire-tinted sunglasses to hide the fact that he was probably high, and his right-off-the-yacht clothes were tailor-made for his muscled body. With an aristocratic voice that had a rasp, and a brain that was somehow able to counter-act all that THC, he was considered one of the most eligible bachelors in the *glymera*, part Great Gatsby, part Jack Sparrow.

As she breathed in, she could smell his cologne and a hint of smoke.

"How are you, Peyton," she muttered.

"You'd know if you answered your damn phone."

Paradise rolled her eyes. Even though the pair of them had only ever been friends, the bastard was wholly irresistible to females. And one of his problems, among many, was the fact that he knew it.

"Hello?" he demanded.

Paradise turned and faced him. "I don't have a lot to say to you. Which, considering you reduced me to nothing but a pair of ovaries for breeding, shouldn't be a big surprise. I don't have much to offer other than that, right?"

"Will you excuse us?" he said to the male sitting next to her.

"Abso-fucking-lutely." Axe, the tough guy, slipped out as if he were getting away from a stink bomb. Or a squeaky female dressed in pink ribbons and bows.

Peyton sat down. "I've apologized. At least to your phone. What more do you want me to do?"

She shook her head, thinking of that first year after the raids. So many of her kind had been killed by the Lessening Society during that horrible assault on the race, and those who had been lucky enough to survive had left Caldwell, retreating to safe houses outside of town, out of state, out of New England.

Peyton had gone south with his blood. She'd gone west with her father. And the two of them had spent countless, sleepless days talking on the phone just to keep sane and process the fear, the sadness, the horror, the losses. Over time, he had become someone she touched base with not just once a night, but all throughout the endless twenty-four-hour cycles of days, weeks, months.

He had become her family.

Of course, if times had been remotely normal, they wouldn't have gotten so close—especially not if the contact had been in person. As an unmated female from a Founding Family, she wouldn't have been allowed to fraternize so freely with any unmated male without a chaperone.

"You know all those hours we spent on the phone?" she said.

"Yeah."

"I felt like you had my back. You didn't judge me if I was scared or weak or nervous. You were just ... this voice on the other end of the connection that kept me sane. You were sometimes the only reason I made it to nightfall." She shook her head. "And then this comes up, and you body-slam me with the *glymera* bullcrap—"

"Now hold on—"

"You *did*. You laughed at me and told me I couldn't do this." She clamped a hold on his mouth, shutting him up. "Just stop talking, okay? Let me get this all out. Now, you might be right: I might fail out of the program. Fine, I'll fall on my butt—but I'm allowed to be here on this bus, and I have the same shot that everyone else does. And you of all people, who's made fun of every one of the idiot society females your family's tried to set you up with, who's told me you think the festivals are stupid, who's rejected the business expectations your father put on you—you were the *last* person I thought would ever go old-school on me."

He sat back and stared at her through those blue-tinted lenses. "Are you done now? You off your soapbox?"

"FYI, being a smart-ass is *really* going to help you here."

"Just want to know if you're ready to put this feminist shit aside and actually listen to me."

"Are you *kidding* me?"

"You haven't once given me a chance to explain. You're too busy filling in my side of things with all this free-the-nipple crap. Why bother letting the other person in on the conversation when you're having such a great time being judgmental and superior? I never thought you were this way."

Welcome to a parallel universe, Paradise thought.

Before she could stop herself, she snapped, "And here I just thought you were a drug addict. I didn't know you were a misogynist as well."

Peyton shook his head and got to his feet. "You know what, Parry? You and I really do need to take a break."

"I totally agree."

He looked down at her from his height. "Fuck me for thinking you'd need a friend in all this."

"Someone who wants you to fail is not a friend."

"I never said that. Never once."

As he turned away, Paradise almost yelled after him, but she let him go. It wasn't as if the talking was getting them anywhere. What was happening instead? Pretty much everyone on the bus was looking at them.

Man, things were getting off to *such* a great start.

One hour after dark, Marissa dematerialized to a thicket of forest on the far side of the Hudson River. The cold wind whistling through the pine boughs made her shiver, and she pulled her Burberry wool coat closer to her body. Breathing in, her sinuses hummed from the lack of humidity and the fantastically clean air of the Canadian high-pressure system that was blowing in from the north.

Looking around, she thought there was something fundamentally dead about November. The colorful leaves of Fall were down and rusted on the ground, the grass and underbrush were wilted and gray, and the cheerful, false-cozy of winter's snowfalls had yet to blanket everything in white.

This was the vacant transition between one version of fabulous and the next.

This was nothing but cold and empty.

Pivoting around, her keen vision zeroed in on an utterly unremarkable concrete structure about fifty yards ahead. Single-storied, with no windows, and only one dark blue door, it looked like something that the city of Caldwell had built for water-treatment purposes and then abandoned.

As she took a step forward, a stick broke beneath her loafer—and she froze at the sound, wrenching around to make sure there was no one behind her. Damn it, she should have told Butch where she was going. He'd been so busy getting ready for the new recruits' orientation, though, she hadn't wanted to bother him.

It was okay, she told herself. There was always Last Meal. She would talk to him then.

Crossing the distance to the door, her palms broke out into a sweat in her gloves, and her chest got so tight, she felt as if she were wearing a corset.

God, she hadn't had one of them on in how long?

As she tried to do that math, she thought back to her life before she'd met Butch. She'd had all of the status and none of the position that anyone from the *glymera* could have asked for. As the unclaimed betrothed of Wrath, son of Wrath, she had been a cautionary tale, a beautiful curse who had been pitied and avoided at the aristocracy's events and festivals.

Her brother had always watched over her, however, a largely silent and yet loyal source of comfort. He had hated that Wrath had always ignored her except when he'd needed to feed—and in the end, that hatred had driven her brother to try to kill the King.

One of many attempts on Wrath's life, as it had turned out.

She had been suffering and limping along in her un-happy lot, expecting nothing more, but wanting a proper life for herself . . . when she had met Butch one night at Darius's former house. Her destiny had changed forever as she had seen the then-human standing in that parlor, fate giving her the love she had always sought but never had. There had been repercussions, though. Perhaps as part of the Scribe Virgin's dictate of balance, all of that goodness had come at a huge cost: Her brother had ended up kicking her out of his house and his life just moments before dawn one morning.

Which was what happened when you were a Found-ing Family's daughter and you were dating what was then assumed to be a mere human.

It had turned out that there was a lot more to Butch, of course, but her brother hadn't stuck around long enough to learn about all of that—and Marissa hadn't cared. She would have taken her male any way he came to her.

Save for running into Havers at a Council meeting, she hadn't really seen her brother since.

Until last night, that was.

Funny, she hadn't spent any time looking back at what she'd once had, where she had been, how she had lived. She had cut herself loose from everything that had come before her mate, living only in the present and the future.

Now, though, as she walked up to the threshold of her brother's new state-of-the-art clinic, she realized that the whole clean-break thing had been an illusion. Just because you moved on didn't mean you shed your personal history like a suit of clothes.

Your past was the same as your skin: with you for life, both the proverbial beauty marks . . . and the scars.

Mostly the scars, in her case.

Okay, where was the bell? The check-in? Last night, they'd come in the ambulance to a different entrance — but Havers had told her to go here if she were dematerializing in.

"Are you here to meet with the doctor?" a disembodied female voice said over a speaker.

Jumping to attention, she pushed her hair back and tried to find the security camera. "Ah . . . actually, I don't have an appointment. I'm here to see — "

"That's all right, dear. Come inside."

There was a *thunk* and a push bar was revealed on the door's face. Giving it a shove, she emerged into an open space that was about twenty by twenty. With inset lights in the ceiling, and concrete walls that had been whitewashed, it was like a prison cell.

Glancing around, she wondered . . .

The red laser beam was wide as a palm, but no thicker than a strand of hair, and she noticed it only because of its warmth, not because it immediately registered to her eyes. Traveling in a slow, steady sweep from her feet to her head, it emanated from the corner up on the right, from a dark pod that was mounted with bolts to the ceiling.

"Please proceed," the female voice said through another hidden speaker.

Before Marissa could bring up the fact that there was nowhere to go, the wall in front of her split down the middle and peeled back, disappearing to reveal an elevator that opened soundlessly.

"Fancy," she said under her breath as she got in.

The trip down lasted longer than a one-story drop, so she had to imagine the facility was not just nominally subterranean.

When the elevator finally bumped to a stop, the door opened again, and . . .

Busy, busy, busy, she thought as she stepped out.

There seemed to be people everywhere, sitting in chairs around a flat-screen TV over on the left, checking in at a reception desk to the right, hustling and bustling through the center of the large room if they were in scrubs or white nursing outfits.

"Hi! Do you have an appointment?"

It took her a moment to realize she was being addressed by the uniformed female sitting behind the front desk. "Oh, I'm sorry, no." She went over and lowered her voice. "I'm the nominal *ghardian* of the female who was transferred from Safe Place last evening? I've come to check and see how she's doing."

Instantly, the receptionist froze. And then her eyes went up and down Marissa, rather like the laser beam had done at ground level.

Marissa knew exactly the narrative that was going through the female's mind: Wrath's unclaimed betrothed, now mated to the *Dhestroyer*, and most of all, Havers's estranged sister.

"Will you please let my brother know that I'm here?"

"I'm aware of your presence already," Havers said from behind her. "I saw you on the security camera."

Marissa closed her eyes for a brief second. And then she turned around to face him. "How is the patient doing?"

He bowed briefly. Which was a surprise. "Not well — please come this way."

As she followed his white coat toward a pair of heavy closed doors, she was very aware of many eyes on them.

Family reunions were good fun. Especially in public.

After Havers swiped his card through a reader, the metal panels opened to reveal a medical space as sophisticated and intense as anything Shonda Rhimes ever thought up: patient rooms full of fancy medical equipment were clustered around a central administrative space staffed with nurses, computers and various other kinds of support, while three hallways led off in different directions to what she assumed were specialty treatment pods.

And her brother manned it all by himself.

If she hadn't known what he could be like, she would have been in awe of him.

"This is quite a facility," she remarked as they walked along.

"It took a year to plan, longer to build." He cleared his throat. "The King has been quite generous."

Marissa shot a look at him. "Wrath?" As if there were another ruler? Duh. "I mean—"

"I provide essential services to the race."

She was spared having to make any further conversation as he stopped next to a glassed-in unit that had drapes pulled into place all along its interior.

"You should prepare yourself."

Marissa glared at her brother. "As if I haven't seen the result of violence before?"

The idea that he would want to protect her from anything at this point was offensive.

Havers inclined his head awkwardly. "But of course."

With a sweep of his arm he opened the glass door, and then he moved the pale green curtains out of the way.

Marissa's heart dumped into her gut, and she had to steel herself against wobbling. So many tubes and machines ran in and out of the female that it was like something from a science-fiction movie, the vital mortality on the bed overtaken by mechanized functions.

"She's breathing on her own," Havers intoned as he went over and looked at the reading on something. "We took the tracheotomy tube out about five hours ago."

Marissa shook herself and forced her feet to move toward the bed. Havers had been right to warn her— although what did she expect? She had seen the injuries firsthand.

"Has she . . ." Marissa fixated on the female's battered face. The bruising had discolored the skin even more, great patches of purple and red marking swollen cheeks, eyes, jaw. "Has—ah, has any family stepped forward to claim her here?"

"No. And she hasn't been conscious enough to tell us her name."

Marissa went to the head of the bed. The quiet beeping and whirring of the equipment seemed very loud, and her vision was way too clear as she looked at the IV bag with its constant dripping, and the way the female's brown hair was tangled on the white pillow, and the texture of the knitted blue blanket on top of the covers.

Bandages everywhere, she thought. And that was just on the exposed arms and shoulders.

The female's slender, pale hand lay flat beside her hip, and Marissa reached out and clasped the palm. Too cold, she thought. The skin was too cold, and not the right color—it was a grayish white, instead of a healthy golden brown.

"Are you coming around?"

Marissa frowned at her brother's comment—and then realized the female's eyes were flickering, the thickened lids batting up and down.

Leaning over, Marissa said, "You're okay. You're at my br—you're at the race's clinic. You're safe."

A ragged moan made her wince. And then there was a series of mumbles.

"What?" Marissa asked. "What are you trying to tell me?"

The syllables were repeated with pauses in the same

places, and Marissa tried to find the pattern, unlock the series of words, grasp the meaning.

"Say it again—"

All at once that beeping in the background accelerated into an alarm. And then Havers ripped open the drapes and the door and shouted out into the hall.

"What?" Marissa said, getting down closer. "What are you saying?"

Nurses came running, and a cart was rushed in. When someone tried to get between her and the patient, Marissa wanted to tell them to stop—but then the shift in the room sank in.

"I don't have a heartbeat," Havers said as he pressed his stethoscope to the female's now-bare chest.

The connection between Marissa and the patient was broken, their palms unlocking—and yet the female's eyes stayed on Marissa's even as people and more machinery got in the way.

"Start chest compressions," Havers said as a nurse hopped up on the bed. "Charge the cart."

Marissa stepped back a little farther, and yet kept the eye contact. "I'm going to find him," she found herself saying over the din. "I promise you. . . ."

"Everyone clear," Havers commanded. When the staff backed away, he hit a button and the female's rib cage jerked up.

Marissa's heart thundered, as if it were trying to make up for the deficit on that bed.

"I'm going to find who did this to you!" she shouted. "Stay with us! Help us!"

"No pulse," Havers announced. "Let's do it again. Clear!"

"No!" Marissa yelled as the female's eyes rolled back. "*No* . . . !"

Chapter Five

It was . . . a cocktail party?

As Paradise stepped into a gymnasium that seemed as big as a professional football arena, she was surprised to find uniformed *doggen* holding silver trays of *hors d'oeuvres* in their white-gloved hands, a bar set up on a table draped with damask, and classical music playing in the background.

Mozart's violin sonatas.

The ones her father listened to in front of the fire after Last Meal.

Over on the left, there was a sign-in station, and after some coalescing, all sixty of them formed a line in front of a female *doggen* with a happy smile and a laptop computer. Not wanting to look like she expected to be treated any differently, Paradise fell in somewhere in the middle and patiently waited to give her name, confirm her address, get her picture taken, and file off to the side to check her satchel and coat.

"Would you care for a *canapé*?" a *doggen* asked her.

"Oh, thank you, no, but I appreciate the kindness."

The *doggen* bowed at the waist and approached the male who had been behind her in line. Glancing over her shoulder, she nodded to her fellow candidate—and recognized him from the festivals that the *glymera* had put on before the raids. Like all members of the aristocracy, they were distant cousins, although she was not close to him or his people.

His name was Anslam, if she remembered correctly.

After he nodded back, he popped a *canapé* into his mouth.

Pivoting around, Paradise checked out all the athletic equipment that had been set up throughout the open space. Parallel bars, chin-up bars, mats for tumbling, a pummel horse, leg press . . . oh, good, they had an erg machine.

At least there was one thing she wasn't going to fail at.

Glancing over her shoulder, she found that many of the recruits were awkwardly fending off the *doggen* with the trays, looking as if they had never seen servants before. Peyton was hitting the munchies hard—not a surprise. And Axe, the latent serial killer, was standing at the edge of things, arms crossed over his chest, eyes surveying the landscape like maybe he was picking out victims.

Why half of him with the tats? she wondered. And the piercings?

Whatever.

And yeah, wow, looked like there was only one other female at the moment. And given the hard-as-nails expression on that lean face, and her broad shoulders, she was probably more suited to the program than a lot of the males in here.

Rubbing her damp palms on her thighs, Paradise shook off a feeling of disappointment: That male, Craeg, who'd come to the audience house for the application wasn't in the group.

But come on, that was probably a good thing. He'd been a total distraction the second he'd walked up to her desk—and she was going to need all her focus to get through this.

Assuming tonight was anything other than a *canapé* hour.

Where were the Brothers? she wondered.

A flash of movement at the corner of her eye turned her head. One of the males had hopped up on the pummel horse and was slowly spinning his lower body in circles as his massive arms held his weight aloft. The smacking of his palms hitting the padded leather formed a beat that gradually got faster and faster as his speed increased.

"Not bad . . ." she murmured as his incredibly strong torso threw his legs out and around in a blur.

He never missed a beat. Not once. And the more he whirlwinded, the more she became convinced she should have spent eight years in the gym instead of weeks. If the rest of the applicants were like this guy? She was screwed.

Then again, she didn't seem like the only one who was intimidated. The entire class had stopped milling about and was staring at him, transfixed by the sheer excellence of the performance in the otherwise empty expanse of the gym.

Clank.

The sound of a door closing made her glance over her shoulder—and she gasped before she could help herself.

There he was, the one she had waited for, the one she had hoped to see again.

Paradise patted at her ponytail, some estrogen-linked receptor going bat-shit, sixteen-year-old as the male walked over to the sign-in station.

Taller. He was so much taller than she remembered. Broader, too—his shoulders stretching a huge Syracuse sweatshirt to its seams. He was in blue jeans again, different ones that nonetheless had the same kinds of rips and tears the other pair he'd worn had. His shoes were scuffed and dirtied Nikes. No baseball cap this time.

Really nice dark hair.

He'd recently gotten the stuff cut, the sides so tight she could see his scalp underneath the fine dark shading around his ears and at his nape, the top short enough so that it stood up on its own. His face was . . . well, it probably wasn't a showstopper for anyone else, his nose a little too big, his jaw a little too sharp, his eyes too deeply set to be even remotely welcoming. But to her he was Clark Gable; he was Marlon Brando; he was the Rock; he was Channing Tatum.

It was like having beer goggles without the beer, she supposed, some chemistry in her transforming him into so much more than he appeared.

Breathing in deep, she tried to catch his scent—and then felt like a stalker.

Well, because she *was* a stalker.

After his picture was taken, he turned to the crowd, his eyes sweeping over the assembled, no reaction showing on his face. Dimly, she was aware of the *doggen* who'd checked them all in packing up her things and departing—along with the tray-wielding servers who were probably going back for reloads.

But like she cared about any of that?

Look at me, she thought toward the male. Look at me....

And then he did.

His eyes moved past her—but then doubled back, locking on. As a blast of electricity went through Paradise's whole body, she—

All at once, the gymnasium went pitch-black.

Pitch.

Frickin'.

Black.

Back at the Havers's underground clinic, if it hadn't been for the glass wall Marissa was leaning against, she would have fallen down.

Especially as she watched her brother pull the white sheet up and over the frozen features of the female.

Dearest Virgin Scribe, she had been unprepared for the silence of death ... how, when Havers had called time, everyone and everything just stopped, the alarms silenced, the effort extinguished, the life over. She had also been unready for the withdrawing of the equipment that had tried to keep the female with them all: One by one, the tubes in her chest, her arms, and her stomach had been pulled free, and then the cardiac monitoring hookups and pads had been removed. The last thing stripped down had been the compression sleeves on her thin calves.

Marissa had had to blink fast at the gentle hands of the nurses. They were as careful with her in death as they had been in life.

As the staff filed out, she wanted to thank the females in their white dresses and discreetly squeaky shoes. Clasp their hands. Hug them.

Instead, she stayed where she was, paralyzed by a sense that the death that had occurred was not hers to witness. Family should be here, she thought with dread. God, where was she going to find the family?

"I'm so sorry," Havers said.

Marissa was about to ask him why he was apologizing to her—when she realized he was addressing his patient: her brother was bent over the bed, one of his hands resting on the motionless shoulder beneath the sheet, his brows drawn tightly beneath his tortoiseshell glasses.

When he straightened and stepped back, he popped up those glasses and seemed to wipe his eyes—although when he finally turned to her, he was fully composed.

"I shall ensure that her remains are attended to appropriately."

"Which means what."

"She will be cremated with a proper ritual."

Marissa nodded once. "I want her ashes."

As Havers nodded in turn, and arrangements were made for pickup the following evening, Marissa was very aware that she was running out of time. If she didn't get away from her brother, this room, that body, the clinic . . . she was going to break down in front of him.

And that was simply not an option.

"If you will excuse me," she cut in. "I have some business to take care of back at Safe Place."

"But of course."

Marissa glanced at the female, noting absently that the sheet was staining red in a couple of places, no doubt from the removal of the tubes.

"Marissa, I . . ."

"What?" she said in a tired voice.

In the tense quiet that followed, she thought about all the time she'd spent being mad at him, hating him—but at the moment, she couldn't muster up any of those emotions. She just stood in front of her kin, waiting in a position of neither strength nor weakness.

The door opened and the curtain was pulled back. A nurse, one who had not been involved in the death, put her head in. "Doctor, we are prepped in four."

Havers nodded. "Thank you." When the nurse ducked back out, he said, "Will you excuse me? I have to—"

"Take care of your patients. By all means. It's what you do best, and you are very good at it."

Marissa left the room, and after a split second of which-way, remembered to go left. It was easier to regain her composure out in the open and keep her mask in place as she walked back down to the reception area—and all eyes were on her as she departed, as if word had spread among the staff. Strange that she recognized no faces—it made her realize anew just how many had been killed in the raids, how long it had been since she had been around her brother's work.

How the two of them, in spite of blood ties, were essentially strangers.

Taking the elevator back up to the surface, she emerged in the cell-like pre-building and punched her way out into the forest.

Unlike the evening before, tonight the moon shone brightly, illuminating the forest . . . and the absolutely no road in. It dawned on her then that there truly were a multiple of entrances to the subterranean complex, some for deliveries, others for patients who were able to dematerialize, and then that one for ambulances.

All of it so logically set up, undoubtedly due to her brother's input and influence.

Why hadn't Wrath told her that he was helping Havers with all this?

Then again, it wasn't really her business, was it.

Had Butch known? she wondered.

I am so sorry.

As Marissa heard her brother's voice in her head, her anger came back tenfold, to the point that she had to rub a heartburn sensation away from her sternum.

"Water under the bridge," she told herself. "Time to go back to work."

And yet she couldn't seem to leave. In fact, the idea of heading to Safe Place made her want to bolt in the opposite direction: She couldn't tell the staff there about what had happened just now. The female's death was like a negation of everything they tried to do under that roof: intercept, protect, educate, empower.

Nope. She couldn't face going there right away.

The problem was . . . she had no idea where to go.

Chapter Six

In the darkness that was as dense as that of a grave, Paradise could hear only her heart thundering behind her ribs. Squinting, she tried to get her eyes to adjust, but there was no light source anywhere—no glow from around the doors, no red Exit signs, no emergency lights. The void was utterly terrifying and seemed to defy the laws of gravity, the sense that she had maybe floated off the floor even as her weight remained on her feet confusing her, nauseating her.

No more classical music, either.

But things were far from silent. As she forced her ears to reprioritize away from the castanets in her chest, she could hear the muttering, the breathing, the cursing. A few must have been moving a little, the rustling of clothes, the shuffling of feet, like background chatter to the more prominent vocal noises.

They can't hurt us, she told herself. There was no way the Brotherhood was actually going to hurt any of them: Yes, she had signed a consent and waiver form on the back of the application—not that she had read the fine print with much interest—but in any event, murder was murder.

You couldn't sign away your right to remain breathing.

This was just the Brotherhood making their grand entrance. Any moment now. Yup, they were going to emerge spotlit from some door, silhouetted like superheroes against a rolling white fog, their awesome weaponry hanging from their larger-than-life bodies.

Uh-huh.

Any minute now . . .

As the darkness continued, her fear spiked again, and it was hard not to give in to it and run. But where would she go? She had some vague sense of where the doors were, where the bar was, where the sign-in table had stood. She also thought she remembered where that male, Craeg, was—no, wait, he had moved. He was moving.

For some reason, she could sense him among all the others, as if he were a kind of beacon—

A breeze brushed against her body, making her jump. But it was just cool air. Cool, fresh air.

Well, that ruled out an electrical short if the HVAC systems were still working.

Okay, this was ridiculous.

And clearly, she wasn't the only one getting frustrated. Other people were cursing more, moving more, stomping their feet.

"Brace yourself."

Paradise shouted into the darkness, but then settled as she recognized Craeg's voice, scent, presence. "What?" she whispered.

"Get ready. This is going to be the first test—they've opened the way out, the question is how they're going to drive us toward it."

She wanted to seem as smart as he was, as calm as he was. "Why don't we just go back over to the doors we came through?"

"Not a good idea."

Right on cue, there was a coordinated shuffling in the direction of the way they'd all entered, as if a group had coalesced, agreed on a strategy, and was putting a plan in action.

And that was when she heard the first screams of the night.

High-pitched, and obviously of pain and not alarm, the horrible sounds were accompanied by a buzzing she didn't understand.

Blindly—literally—she threw out a hand and grabbed onto Craeg's . . . except no, the flat, hard expanse was his stomach, not his arm. "Oh, God, I'm sorry. I—"

"They electrified the doors," he said without acknowledging her gaffe or apology. "We can't assume anything is safe in here. Did you drink what they served? Did you eat any of that stuff on the plates?"

"Ah . . . no, no, I—"

From over on the left, the unmistakable sound of someone dry-heaving cut into the chaos. And two seconds after that, like a bird answering the call of its species, someone else started to vomit.

"They can't make people sick," she blurted. "Wait, this is . . . this is school! They can't—"

"This is survival," the male said grimly. "Don't fool yourself. Trust no one, especially not if they're a so-called teacher. And do not expect to make it through this—not because you're a woman, but because the Brothers are going to set the bar so high, only one in ten of us has a shot at still being on our feet at the end of this night. If that."

"You can't be serious."

"Listen," he said. "Do you hear that?"

"The throwing up?" Her stomach rolled in sympathy. "It's hard to miss."

Hard to smell, too.

"No, the ticking."

"What are you . . ." And then she heard it, too . . . in the background, like the auditory equivalent of someone moving behind a curtain, there was a steady clicking sound. "What is that?"

"We don't have a lot of time left. The intervals between the beeping are getting shorter and shorter. Good luck."

"Where are you going?" Don't leave me, she wanted to say. "Where are—"

"I'm going to track the fresh air. That's where everyone is going to be headed. Don't touch any of the exercise equipment, either. Like I said, good luck to you."

"Wait!" But he was already gone, a ghost that disappeared into the blackness.

Abruptly, Paradise became downright terrified, her body shaking uncontrollably, her hands and feet going numb, a cold sweat breaking out over every square inch of her skin.

Father was right, she thought. I can't do this. What was I thinking—

And that was when all hell broke loose.

From up above and all around, explosions erupted as if the gymnasium had been wired to detonate, the sounds so loud her ears registered them as pain, not noise, the flashes of light so bright she went from one version of blind to another.

Screaming into the maelstrom, she put her hands up to the sides of her head and crouched to the ground, ducking for cover.

Ahead of her, she saw people on the floor, some who were in a defensive curl like she was, others who were vomiting, still more by those doors who writhed and curled their arms in tight as if the pain were too great for them to stand.

There was only one person who was up and moving.

Craeg.

In the intermittent flashes, she tracked his movement to the far, far corner. Sure enough, there appeared to be an opening, a door that offered nothing save more blackness— but that had to be better than getting blown up.

She took a couple of steps forward, and then realized that was bullshit. Run. She needed to run—there was nothing holding her back, and she didn't want to get hit with falling debris.

Don't touch the exercise equipment.

Considering what had happened when those people had tried to get out those metal doors? No shit.

It was a great relief to bolt forward, but she toggled back on her speed because her vision couldn't keep up; she had to wait for the flashes. It was the only way to be safe.

Talk about an ugly stride. Tripping, scrambling, slipping, she began to fight her way through stinging noise and light, the threat to her life, the terror that gripped her.

She had just entered the maze of athletic equipment when she came to the first person on the ground. It was a male and he was moaning and clutching his stomach. Her instinct was to try and help him, but she stopped herself.

This is about survival.

Something whizzed by her ear—a bullet? They were *shooting* at them?

Throwing herself down, she skidded across the slick floor on her stomach and then crab-walked through the overwhelming chaos.

She was fine until she came up to the next male who was down and writhing, his arms locked around his abdomen.

It was Peyton.

Keep going, she told herself. Get yourself to safety.

As another explosion went off, right by her head, she belly-flatted to the floor and yelled into the maelstrom, "Shit!"

As Craeg, son of Brahl the Younger, started across the gym, he was surprised that the idea of leaving that female behind bothered him as much as it did. He didn't know her; he didn't owe her—she was Paradise, the receptionist from the King's audience house, the one who had given him a printed application weeks ago.

Which he'd needed because he was too poor to have Internet access, much less a computer or a printer.

Back in that parlor, she had been . . . too stunning to

look at. And then when he'd heard about her wanting to try out for this program? The only thing that had gone through his mind had been what humans could do to her if they caught her. Or *lessers*. Or the wrong kind of vampire male.

Someone as beautiful as her was not safe in this world.

Yet she seemed naive about the crucible they were all facing as trainees. The Brothers had engineered every part of this environment. Nothing had been left to chance, and nothing was going to work in favor of the candidates. Telling her what she should have already known had seemed like the only way he could help her at all—but he couldn't waste even a moment wondering what happened to her.

What he needed to focus on was the flashes.

Although on the surface they seemed random, in fact there was a subtle pattern to them, and as with the beeping before the light and noise show had started, the intervals were getting shorter and shorter—so they were running out of time again.

He had no idea what the second phase was going to be, but he knew he'd better be ready for it.

At least none of the were going to die.

In spite of the atmosphere of danger, he had the sense that the Brotherhood wasn't actually going to hurt any of them: The "explosions" were just a lot of sound and light; there was no debris, no structures falling, no smell of smoke. Likewise, whatever was making those people throw up couldn't be anything fatal. The folks down on the gym floor were not in their happy place, for sure—but among the flashes of illumination, he saw that some of the first who'd fallen were already getting to their feet.

This was a test, an elaborate, God-only-knew-how-long test—and at the rate things were going, the program's passage rate might be even lower than what he'd quoted Paradise.

Craeg paused and looked back for a split second. He couldn't seem to help it.

But there was no telling where she was in the fray. Not enough sustained light, and too many bodies.

Just keep going, he told himself.

You've done it before, you're going to do it tonight.

Pressing on, he worked his way around the periphery of the exercise equipment. Really not a good idea to take cover behind or under any of it. From time to time, he'd see out of the corner of his eye some poor soul give that a shot—only to appear to be electrocuted, their bodies going all bad angles in the strobing light as they jerked back and twisted and fell.

He really hoped she'd listened to what he'd said.

Ducking his head and moving fast, he eventually came around to the open doorway in the far corner. The scent of fresh air was intoxicating, a respite that charged his body with additional power. But he couldn't see what was on the other side—and cursed himself that he hadn't followed through on the passing impulse to keep a flashlight on him.

Okay, fine, so even he hadn't expected things to get this frickin' intense.

"This is where we have to go."

At the sound of a low voice, he glanced behind himself—and was shocked to find a female standing next to him. It wasn't the lovely blonde, not even close. In fact, this one seemed to suggest that the term *fairer sex* was a serious misnomer: She was nearly as tall as he was, muscled under her athletic clothes, and the way she looked him in the eye, he knew immediately she was even smarter than she was strong.

"I'm Craeg," he said, putting out his palm.

"Novo."

Unsurprisingly, the shake was tight and short.

"This is next." She nodded at the void. "Why the hell didn't I bring a flashlight?"

"I was thinking the same—"

"This way!" someone hollered. "This is the way!"

In the strobe lighting, Craeg saw a group of three

males gunning for the open doorway, led by a big muckling guy who wore an expression of anticipatory triumph that Craeg was pretty damn sure wasn't going to stay in place for long.

Craeg shook his head and stepped back. However he went in there, it wasn't going to be headlong and at a dead run. For all they knew—

One . . . two . . . three . . . the trio passed by him and the female, who also stepped aside.

Right away the door slammed shut with a loud clang. And then there were screams from the other side.

Craeg looked around. Maybe something else was going to open? Or was he not casting a wide enough net? It was possible that there was another answer—

At that moment, he saw a pair of ropes hanging from the ceiling about thirty feet away. He could have sworn they hadn't been there before—who knew.

"That's the next option," he said.

"Let's do it."

The pair of them took off, running around the exercise equipment, heading for the ropes before anyone else went over there. There was no telling where the lengths led to—he couldn't see that far up—but the lights were strobing with greater intensity, and there were no other options.

"Rock, paper, scissors for who picks first," she said, putting out her fist.

He did the same. "One, two, three." Craeg threw rock, she threw paper. "Your pick."

"Right."

Craeg grabbed the left one and pulled so hard his palms burned. Certainly seemed strong enough. But if he was wrong? Long way to fall, and there was no padding underneath.

He and the female went hand over hand, gripping, pulling up, using their feet to clasp the loosey-goosey they left behind as they ascended. And she was nearly as fast as he was, not that he spent a lot of time measuring her progress. Up, up, up—until the speakers from which the explosion noises ripped were directly above his head and the light boxes generating the jagged illumination overwhelmed his vision from straight ahead.

"Now what," he barked when he was about six feet from the ceiling.

"Scaffolding," she yelled back, shifting her grip and pointing.

Sure enough, there was some kind of catwalk suspended from metal wires. Glancing down, he said another prayer that the platform was strong enough to hold his weight.

"I'll go first."

"Rock, paper, scissors," she hollered. "One, two, three."

He threw scissors; she threw paper.

"Me first," he announced.

Except the catwalk was a distance away even as he came up to its height. Holding on to the thick rope, he used his lower body to create a swaying motion ... that increased to a full-on swing. It was going to require perfect timing to get this right—he was going to have to go hands-free for a good five feet of nothing-but-net. And shit only knew what he was going to find when he landed.

More metal with an electrical current piped through it?

Craeg pumped his pelvis one last time, brought his knees up, and sent his weight away from the scaffolding; then as momentum brought him forward again, he arched his back and kicked his feet out ahead of him.

At just the right time, he released the rope, giving up his tether.

At least ... he hoped it was the right time.

Chapter Seven

"Get up! Peyton, get up—now!"

As Paradise lost the fight with her survival instinct and rolled her friend—or nemesis or whatever the hell he was—over onto his back, she cursed him, herself, the Brothers, pretty much anything that was a noun.

That whole faceup thing didn't last long. As he began to heave again, she shoved him back over so he didn't aspirate.

Glancing around, she saw . . . so many on the ground. As if it were a battlefield.

"I'm gonna die," Peyton moaned.

In the back of her mind, Paradise noticed that although the noise was just as calamitous, there was more illumination, the flashes coming faster and staying lit longer.

"Come on." She pulled at his arm. "We can't stay here."

"Leave me here . . . just leave me. . . ."

As Peyton vomited again and not much came up, she looked to the far corner of the gym. There were a number of people standing around the dark opening that Craeg had told her to head toward.

"Peyton—"

"We're all gonna die. . . ."

"No, we're not."

And it was a shock to realize she actually believed that—it wasn't just a line to offer false hope to Mr. Smooth with the stomach issues. The thing was, all this noise and light wasn't actually producing any debris, smoke or dust, any structure rattling, any sort of real impact on the space or the people in it. It was a light and sound show, like a thunderstorm or a theatrical production—and that was as far as it went.

She also had the sense that the lights were changing, and that had to mean something.

Probably nothing good.

"Peyton." She grabbed his arm and pulled him over onto his back again. "Get your ass up off this floor. We've got to make it over to the corner."

"I can't—it's too—"

Yup, she slapped him. And she wasn't proud of it or satisfied by sharp contact, either. *"Get up."*

His eyes popped wide. "Parry?"

"Who the hell did you think you were talking to? Taylor Swift?" She pulled his upper body off the gym floor. "Get on your feet."

"I might throw up on you."

"Like we don't have bigger problems? Have you seen this place?"

Peyton started babbling, and that was when she decided enough was enough. Straddling his legs, she took hold under his pits and used her newfound strength to walk back and drag him upright onto his pair of Adidases.

"Paradise, I'm going to be—"

Oh, fantastic.

All down the front of her.

And he was weaving so badly that walking in a straight line was going to be a challenge. Running? NFW.

"Fuck this," she muttered, grabbing him around the waist and jerking him into a dead lift off the floor.

Heavy. Really heavy on her shoulder.

Now she was the one with the whoa-nellies: It was like trying to balance a piano up there—made worse by the fact that the weight was arguing with her—and barfing down the back of her right leg.

Paradise set off, ignoring everything but the goal of getting to that godforsaken door across the way. Her head was wrenched to one side, her neck straining so badly it burned; her shoulder was going numb from lack of circulation; and her thighs were already quivering from the stress on them.

The temptation to get lost in all those physical sensations was strong, especially as they grew ever louder and more insistent. But she wanted to . . . well, she wanted to get to that door, to the fresh air, to the end of all this shock-and-awe business. Then she could take a deep breath, put Peyton's whining deadweight down, and sit in a nice, clean classroom.

Maybe share a laugh with the Brotherhood that she had made it through the worst part and now the self-defense and schoolbook training could start.

To keep herself going, she tried to remember the classrooms she'd seen as the trainees had walked from the parking area to the gym. They'd had fluorescent lighting, and banks of tables with chairs in orderly positions facing the blackboard —

"Stop," Peyton said. "I'm going to die. . . ."

"Will you shut up and stay still?" she said with a grunt.

"I'm going to —"

Oh, for fuck's sake, she thought as he lost it again.

As she trudged along and panted from the exertion, the maze of athletic equipment was a total pain in the ass, the various stations seeming to have been spaced and angled in a way that made it incredibly awkward to get through, past, around.

Especially with Peyton draped over her.

And then there were people who were scattered along the ground.

Every time she stepped by somebody or had to lift a foot over one of their hands, their feet, their leg or arm, she wanted to stop, ask if they were okay, call for help . . . do something. The fact that she couldn't save anyone but herself and Peyton made her scream on the inside, her lungs burning in her chest, a strange anger motivating her.

She kept looking for blood. Obsessively.

But there was no sign of it: no red stains on clothes, no red streaks on skin, no red sweeps across the honey-yellow floorboards. There was also no scent of it that she could detect—although there were plenty of other smells, none of them pleasant.

No blood, though. And that had to be good . . . right?

"Ahhh!" she screamed, as a white-hot blast of pain shocked her.

Applecart. Over.

The pain in her left elbow destabilized everything, her body becoming like a folding table that had had a leg kicked out—and just like a bowl of fruit on a previously level surface, Peyton crashed to the ground, his limp limbs bouncing like McIntoshes.

"Oh, my God," she gritted as she grabbed her arm and massaged where the electrical current had licked into her.

She'd gotten too close to a chest-press machine. And as she measured the amount of equipment she still had to work through, she thought . . . *I can't do this. I can't. . . .*

"Can you stand up?" she said.

Peyton answered in a non-verbal fashion that didn't just suggest *no*, but emphatically announced that that was still a negative.

God, how could there still be anything left in his stomach?

"I can't do this," she moaned as she looked around and massaged her elbow.

As her eyes bounced back and forth, she realized that she was searching for help, some kind of lifeline, a rescuer. There had to be somebody she could turn to. . . .

For only the second time in her life, she prayed to the Scribe Virgin, squeezing her lids closed, trying to find the proper words against the jarring backdrops of the sounds, smells, sights, and the razor-sharp adrenaline spasms racking her internal wiring. Somehow, she managed to ask the race's deity to send someone to make this stop, to take care of Peyton, to rescue all the other people who were down, to get everyone out of this hellhole—

Stop wasting time, an inner voice commanded.

It was such a shock, she wrenched around, expecting to find somebody behind her. No one was there.

Maybe it had been piped in from overhead?

Stop wasting time. Go!

"I can't pick him up again!"

You'd better fucking figure out how!

"I can't do this!"

You'd better fucking do this!

"Okay, all right, okay, all right."

She mumbled those words over and over again as she restraddled Peyton and humped him back up into position. The second dead lift was even more uncoordinated than the first, her body loose in places that really, totally didn't help—but Peyton seemed to be recovering strength, his hands gripping her hips and holding on.

By the time she cleared the obstacle course, she was running out of energy, and she performed a quick calculation on the distance to the door—and then added ancillary factors like how much her shoulder was deforming under the weight, and the fact that, inconveniently, she needed to pee so badly she felt like someone was daggering her lower abdomen.

Breaking into a shuffling gallop, her feet skimmed over the blessedly unobstructed floor, and the less shimmying, the better for her passenger and her whole body.

Wait a minute.

The door was shut.

As she closed in on her destination, she frowned and commanded her eyes to focus through the flaring lights. Shit, the door was *shut*. But there had been people standing around the opening only moments before?

Coming up to the panel, she let Peyton slide off her

back and barely spared him a glance as he sprawled out flat on the floor.

What had happened to the frickin' door?

No handle or doorknob. No hinges. No glass to break.

Pivoting around, she surveyed—Jesus, there were gym ropes hanging about thirty feet away. The thick lengths had appeared from the ceiling, and there were two people climbing them with the kind of speed that made her want to sit down and give up right where she was.

"Peyton?" she said as she angled her head to watch the pair ascend. "I'm not going to be to carry you up those."

Hell, she didn't think she could drag her own weight on the twirling lengths.

Where were the two of them going? she wondered as they disappeared out of sight.

"Peyton, we're going to need to—"

One after the other both ropes fell to the floor, the slaps of the thick, woven lengths sounding out even over all the other noise.

Where had the two people gone?

Rubbing her eyes, she wanted to scream. Instead, she gritted out, "What the hell are we going to do—"

A fresh blast of cool, clean air had her twisting back around. The door had opened again, revealing a dense black void.

As though it had consumed the other trainees who had entered and was ready for another meal.

Peyton struggled to his feet, his shaking hands wiping down his face. "I can walk."

"Thank God."

He glanced over at her. "I owe you."

"Let's see if heading through here actually gets us anywhere first."

"We go together." His eyes burned as he offered her the crook of his elbow—as if they were going into a ballroom full of silk gowns and white-tie tuxedoes. "I'm not going to leave you."

Paradise stared at him for a moment. "Together."

Linking her arm through his, she wasn't surprised that he used her to steady himself. Still, this was a huge improvement over his comatose-but-for-the-barfing.

They stepped forward at the same time, the doorjamb wide enough to accommodate them both—

The door slammed shut behind them and cut off all light—and she opened her mouth to scream, but then sucked back the sound, holding it in. That feeling of the floor slipping out from under her feet happened again, a lesson on the significance of vision to things like balance and the spatial orientation of limbs and torso.

Beside her, Peyton was panting.

From out of nowhere, rough hands grabbed at her hair, latching on, yanking hard. And she screamed bloody murder as fear made her contort and spasm and fight against the hold.

"Paradise!"

They were ripped apart and something was put over her head and tied around her neck. Forced to the ground, her legs were bound and then used to pull her along on her back. Twisting and turning, trying to kick, to breathe, to stay even partially calm enough to think, she felt like she was suffocating.

She felt like she . . . might be dying.

Up on the scaffolding, Craeg learned the hard way that you'd better frickin' balance yourself—the electrical shock he got each time his arms flailed into something metal sent his heart racing and shorted out his mind for a split second that he couldn't afford to spare.

And naturally, the goddamn platform was as rickety as an old man, shifting this way and that, swinging like a baseball bat.

"Get in a rhythm!" he shouted to Novo. "Follow my steps!"

Strong hands grabbed onto his waist. "Got you."

They fell into a walking stride that was quick but cautious, lurching from side to side, the heat from the lights and the mass of bodies down below making him sweat. Extending his arms, he counter-balanced himself and her, and began to make even better time, heading for God only knew—

All at once the scaffolding went rock-steady, and that was bad news. What had worked on an unstable surface didn't fly at all on a stable one, and both of them careened into a series of electrical shocks that sent them reeling, their bodies slamming into each other and then hitting the metal supports, only to get reshocked. Muscles began to cramp up and refuse to loosen, his limbs unable to follow his mental commands.

"Fuck!" Craeg barked as he tried to stop his body from reacting to the stimuli.

"What the fuck!" Novo yelled.

Or some version of that.

Thin air.

Next thing he knew, he had fallen off an edge he hadn't seen coming and gone into a free fall that left even him screaming at the top of his lungs. All around him, air rushed up, traveling through his clothes and making them flap, streaking his hair and the skin of his face and back, riddling his ears with a buffering sound. He was going to snap both of his legs if he landed feet-first, but there was no time, and no distance—and no reason to even try to broker a landing that wasn't going to be devastating—

Sploosh!

He hit an unanticipated pool of water on his side, his body getting caught in the safe hold of cold, fresh liquid. The relief as he didn't end up with both his femurs coming out of the tops of his shoulders was short-lived. His Tasered, tortured, overheated muscles immediately cramped on a oner, everything freezing up, his lack of body fat turning him into an anchor, not a buoy.

The shock of the unexpected bottoming-out had caused him to pull in a tremendous lungful of air, but that oxygen supply wasn't going to last. He needed to get to the surface.

With clawed hands, and only one leg that had any mobility, he scratched and kicked in what he hoped was the way up. He had no visual orientation at all, nothing but a black abyss that was going to consume him if he didn't save himself.

The surface of the pool, pond, lake, whatever it was rearrived with the same unexpected, unannounced surprise that he'd plunged into it with. Coughing and trying to suck in air were two mutually exclusive activities, and he had to force his primordial sense of survival to regulate his diaphragm's spastic responses.

Chlorine. They were in a pool.

He didn't spend a lot of time thinking about that. The pain in his cramping muscles was unbelievable, like having daggers driven into his thighs and his ass and his gut, and he started to sink back down before he'd caught his breath—and that was a no-go. He was going to die that way.

Fighting against his body's impulses, he used his mind to override his sympathetic nervous system: Taking an enormous breath in, he stroked his arms out and down, creating an artificial current that swept his torso flat across the top of the water. Then he stopped ... fucking ... *moving*.

And let the air in his chest cavity become the life jacket he wasn't wearing.

It wasn't a perfect float. His legs continued to sink, and he had to kick every so often to stay on top, but it was a hell of a lot better than hitting the bottom and drowning.

From time to time, he expelled his breath and reinhaled.

He wasn't sure how long he could last like this. But he was going to find out.

God ... his cording muscles were a torture to endure, and to distract himself, he relived being up high on that catwalk. The Brothers were brilliant, he decided. Going from that heat to this cold? After the electrical shocks?

It was an engineered environment guaranteed to put someone exactly where he was: fighting against his body's natural responses to certain stimuli and environments.

What was happening to everyone else? he wondered.

Where was the female?

Not the one he'd been on the elevation with ... but the other one? Paradise?

As water clapped in his ears, it was like the light show from the gym, obscuring and then letting in sensory input. He heard splashing, both close to him and farther away ... a lot of shouting and gasping from others in the pool ... echoes—they must be somewhere large with a relatively low ceiling and a lot of tile.

Releasing the air in his lungs, he immediately reinflated them ...

... and waited for whatever was next.

Chapter Eight

"...pair in the mouth. ETA four minutes. Clear entrance and far right side of pool ..."

Pressing the release button on the wire that ran from his earpiece down the side of his neck, Butch said quietly, "Roger that."

As he strode around the edge of the pool, he tracked the movements of the candidates in the water with his thermal-imaging goggles. Two more had just fallen in from up above; both had surfaced and assumed a dead man's float so they were tight and relatively quiet. Not always the case. He and Tohr had had to pull four candidates out already, which meant there were only three other males in with the new couple.

Everyone was far away from entry point B over on the right. Good.

Butch checked his watch. Whoever was left behind in the gym was going to be timed out in another six minutes. And all this stuff was just the preamble to what he and his Brothers were referring to as the Final Destination—and that last stop was going to be shut down by the sun at dawn, so it was mission-critical that the group who made it through these early tests had enough time out there.

Doc Jane and Manny's clinic was filling up. The mild herbal emetic had more than done its duty, and there had been a variety of minor cuts, scrapes, muscle pulls and burns. Two loads of dropouts were already on their way off the property, and there were going to be more.

This was the thing with a meritocracy: Shit had to get real fast, because he and V weren't going to waste time on anybody who couldn't make the cut.

"Is it my turn yet?" Lassiter asked over the earpiece. "I was born ready for this."

"Of all the people who could be immortal," V muttered, "why are you one of them?"

"Because I'm awwwwwesome," the fallen angel sang. "And I'm part of your team—"

"No, you're not—"

"—living your dream!"

Butch's head started thumping even worse. "Shut up, Lass. I can't do singing right now."

"It's from *Despicable Me*," the angel commented. Like he was being helpful.

"Shut up," V cut in.

"Shut up." Butch fought to keep his voice low. "We've got another four minutes in the gym. I'll let you know when you can—"

"I'm losing air over here, you know," Lassiter bitched. "My inflatable is deflating."

V cursed. "That's because it doesn't want to be around you any more than we do."

"You keep this up and I'm going to start thinking my enmity is mutual."

"About fucking time."

Right, Butch didn't get off on dragging soaking-wet, panicked idiots out of a pool—but, man, he was really frickin' glad he wasn't on the back side of the house with those two fighting. "Sit tight, Lass," he said. "I'll be in touch—and, V, for the love of God, will you turn off his fucking mic—"

"Ow! Hey! What the fuck, V—"

Annnnnnd everything went blissfully silent.

As his headache tried to kick down the door to his skull, Butch wanted to pop his goggles off and rub his eyes, but he wasn't about to lose sight of the candidates for even a moment. The last thing the program needed was someone getting seriously hurt, or worse, waking up dead.

Besides, he was distracted enough on his own, even with the 20/20 headset.

Something was wrong with Marissa.

Shit knew he'd spent enough time being a walking zombie back during his human days to recognize the numb preoccupation she'd been rocking.

The trouble was, she was giving him nothing to go on. Every time he asked her what she was thinking about or whether she was okay, she smiled at him and made some BS excuse about things being busy at Safe Place.

Undoubtedly that was true, but that was always the case. And she didn't always look like she had for the last night and day.

Maybe they just needed an evening off—and not only in terms of not working. The mansion was a great place to live—the chow was good, and the company even better. The problem was, you didn't get much privacy. Short of retiring to your bedroom, which in their case was a shoe-box-sized enclave with a thin door and thin walls at the Pit, you weren't ever truly alone. Intrusions happened without warning by everyone from the staff, to other Brothers, to mates.

The Irish Catholic from a big family in him loved that.

The worried *hellren* part of him was not quite as enthused.

I need to go on a date, he thought.

"Where are we going?" V asked in his ear.

Shit, he'd said that out loud. "Not you."

"Hurt. Seriously hurt over here," came the tinny reply.

"Marissa and I need. . . ."

"If it's sex ed, I could have sworn you two figured that out. Unless all those sounds are just the pair of you thumb-wrestling."

"Really."

"You're saying that shit is origami? Jesus Christ, the paper cuts ... can't fucking imagine, true?"

"Stop it."

"Says Marissa never."

"Not been the case recently," Butch retorted.

"You got problems?"

"I don't know."

There was a long period of silence. "I have an idea."

"I'm open to anything—"

"That's what she said!" Lassiter cut in.

"V, I thought you took that away from—" The sounds of the two males wrestling on the up-close had him popping his earpiece out and grimacing.

Lassiter was clearly getting the beat-down he'd been begging for, and under any other circumstance, Butch would have found the pair, and not to play referee. But he had more important things to worry about.

Especially as he had two new visitors to welcome to this liquid-ish round of the party.

And when V came back on, maybe Butch would get some good advice. Provided his best friend could think outside of the spiked-collar/black-candlewax/nipple-clamp world.

Shit.

Paradise thrashed against the hold on her ankles, fishtailing her torso back and forth on the floor she was being dragged over, clawing with her hands. Inside the sack around her head, her hot breath suffocated her—or maybe she had just sucked all the oxygen out.

In response, panic gasolined her entire body, spasming up her muscles and turning her brain into a superhighway of thoughts that did absolutely nothing to calm her down or help her out. Part of her wanted to call out to Peyton, but he wasn't going to save her. They'd gotten him, too. The other half was extrapolating all kinds of bad outcomes.

What next! What next! What next what nextwhatnext—

"Next" arrived with the same lack of warning that everything else had: the forward momentum stopped, a second person stepped up and grabbed her shoulders, and she was flipped off the ground.

Paradise screamed again in the bag, and tried to break herself out of the holds. Not possible. The grips were so strong, she might as well have had vises biting into her skin and bones—

Swinging.

She was being swung left and right, momentum growing, as if she were about to be thrown.

"No!"

Just as she was released at the top of the left arc, the bag was ripped free of her head. She had two incredible gulps of air—and then she was falling, falling, falling, through a darkness marked with strange sounds—

Splaaaaaaash!

Water everywhere—getting into her nose, her mouth, encapsulating her body. Instinct took over, her senses immediately calibrating that "up" was the opposite way she was sinking. Spidering her arms and legs out, she found that the binding on her ankles had been freed.

She broke the surface with such force her torso popped free like a cork, and she coughed so violently she nearly lost consciousness. In between the racking, though, she was able to get air down . . . and then she was sucking in great hauls of oxygen, the simple luxury of being able to breathe preoccupying her with a gratitude that brought tears to her eyes. That didn't last long. All around, she could hear people struggling in the water, sounds of them coughing, breathing, paddling to stay afloat.

How many?

Was this the second part?

Treading water, she wanted to call for Peyton, but wasn't sure that drawing attention to herself was a good idea. For all she knew—

"Paradise!"

The sound of Peyton's voice was close by and to the right. "Yes," she choked out. "I'm here—are you okay—"

"Are you all right!"

"I'm right here." She spoke a little more loudly. "I'm right—"

Next thing she knew, a strong hand had taken her arm and was pulling her through the water.

"I can stand here," Peyton said. "Let me hold you up."

"I don't need—"

"You have to conserve your strength. This is just beginning."

He sounded so reasonable, like maybe the shock of the water had sobered him up. And then his hands were smooth on her waist as he turned her around so she was facing away from him.

"I've got you," he whispered.

His arm locked around her, and the feel of his strong body behind her made her tense up. When all he did was breathe like he was in recovery, too, she began to relax a little, even though she couldn't see anything and her legs kept brushing up against his.

She'd never actually been this close to a male before.

Although, given the situation they were in, now was hardly the time to waste a second on that nonsense; Peyton had nothing on his mind other than survival.

With tenuous relief, she sagged in his hold, letting herself go. Her instincts remained on high alert, but at least her body had a brief respite, her heart rate slowing, that horrid burn in her lungs extinguishing—

Splash! Splash!

Two more candidates—or victims—hit the water far, far away, giving her a sense of exactly how big the pool or pond or lake they were in had to be. Except . . . no, it wasn't a lake. The water was chlorinated.

A pool. They were in a pool underground—probably not far from the gym, given that she hadn't been dragged miles.

"What comes next?" she said.

"I don't know. But you and I are going to stay together."

"Yes." She was shocked at how much his presence calmed her—in spite of the fact that there was still nothing to see, and she had no clue as to what they were going to be hit with next—

Splash! Splash! Splash!

"How many are in here?" she said.

"Five just came in. So there are at least seven of us."

"Out of sixty . . . ? There have to be more." How could she be one of such a small number to make it this far? "Surely, there are—"

Four more came in—one dropping really close to them, three others entering far off on the other side.

"Am I too heavy for you?" she asked.

"Oh, please."

As he switched his grip, her body moved in the water, her backside pressing against the front of his pelvis. She didn't feel anything there . . . but she wouldn't have known what to be worried about even if he had been aroused.

Another person hit the pool.

And then . . .

. . . for a long period of time there were no more additions. In reality, it was probably just a couple of minutes, but it felt like hours . . . days.

Her fear kept humming along, but with nothing to immediately feed off of, the anxiety began to cannibalize her rational side, all kinds of craziness running through her mind. What if this wasn't a training program? What if this was some kind of . . . social experiment? A body-snatcher routine . . . or an attempt to . . . jeez, she didn't know.

A wave of terror shot through her. She couldn't see anything, and the roar inside her head was drowning out the sounds in the pool, and her body was too tired to process the shaking that racked her.

"What comes next?" she moaned.

"I—"

Before Peyton could answer, she became aware that something had changed around them. The others noticed, too, the bodies in the water stilling as if they were trying to assess what was different.

The water level was dropping.

The choppy surface had been at her shoulders—but was only now to her upper arms, then her elbows.

Her heart rate ramped up once more, a buzzy, trippy dizziness making her head spin.

"What are they going to do to us now?" she gasped.

Lower ... and lower still ... until her feet hit the bottom like Peyton's could. She stayed in the circle of his arm, though—at least with his big body behind her, she knew that her back was covered.

I just want to see, she thought into the black void. God ... please, let me see something—

Over in the corner, a brilliant, blinding light appeared.

It was so overwhelming that she lifted an arm up against the glare, and in its lee, she saw that yes, they were in a pool, one that was very clean and had a nice tile border that was pale blue and green. And then there was Peyton, looking wrung out behind her. And other candidates in the water.

Pushing her dripping hair out of the way, she winced and tried to focus—

What the ...

"—fuck is that?" Peyton finished for her.

On the far side of the still-emptying pool, a huge male with blond-and-black hair had entered the space—and at first, she thought he had brought the light with him. In fact, his body *was* the light. He was glowing as if he were a living, breathing incandescent lightbulb.

But the crazy thing was ... that wasn't actually the biggest shock.

He was wearing a scuba mask and snorkel set pushed off his handsome face ... a set of flippers that slapped

over the slick floor as he approached the pool's edge . . .
a slingshot bathing suit that was hot pink . . . and a children's yellow-and-blue floaty around his waist.

Every single one of the soaking-wet half-deads in the
pool stared at him like he was the second coming in a
SpongeBob–meets–Magic Mike parallel universe.

Slapping, flapping his way down to the diving board,
he stepped up, took great pains to arrange a flesh-
covered nose plug on his snoz, and cleared his throat.

After a couple of "me-me-me-mes"—like he was
warming up to do a solo—he took a great breath and—

"Cowwww-a-bunga!" he hollered, and ran down to
the end.

Springing high off the tip, he held the kiddie floater in
place as he executed a perfect tuck-and-roll and nailed
the dwindling water with a cannonball that kicked up
spray to the ceiling.

As Paradise ducked so she didn't get hit in the face
with the tsunami, she thought . . . points to the Brothers.

Whatever she might have expected?

That was *so* not it.

Chapter Nine

Craeg's running shoes found the bottom of the pool just as the . . . well, it was a male, that was for sure . . . hit the water with an impact like a sedan had been tossed in there. After the deluge settled, the environment became evenly illuminated, the light emanating from that big, ridiculously outfitted body creating a glow that turned the Olympic-sized bathtub into its own lamp.

The guy was like part pro wrestler, part Toys "R" Us.

But Craeg wasn't going to waste any time figuring that combo out.

Wiping his face, he identified the possible escape routes first—there were four or five doors, including the one that thing with the floaty corset had come through, but he was willing to bet they were all locked. Nothing on the ceiling. On the walls. On the bottom of the pool.

Second check-in was to see if there were any other third parties in the mix. Yup. Over on the periphery, there were two huge males dressed in black with hoods over their heads and night-vision goggles on their eyes. They were armed heavily, but their weapons were holstered—and they appeared to be monitoring everyone in the pool as if searching for signs of weakness or danger.

Third assessment was of who else had made it to this stage. Ten—no, twelve . . . wait, thirteen people were in the pool with him, including the female he'd fallen from that great height with.

And the blond receptionist, Paradise.

Although she was not alone.

Nope, she was up against one of the males, her hand resting on the protective arm that was around her waist.

Hardly a surprise. Females like her were never without someone of the opposite sex around them. Moths to a flame and all that bullcrap.

Craeg forced his eyes away from the pair of them—and that worked for maaaaybe a minute. Next thing he knew, he was leveling a combat assessment at the guy, taking note of the male's size, the strength in his shoulders, the set of that jaw.

As if the two of them were going to come into conflict.

Which was insane, of course.

He had no right to that female—and more to the point, the only thing he needed to care about was making it to whatever finish line was waiting for him at the end of this—

Conventional lights came on all around the room, cutting the shadows down to nil, showing nooks and crannies that hid no further threats.

But he didn't think it was over yet. He certainly wouldn't have stopped now if he were the Brothers. Too many people still standing.

The door in the far right corner blew open as if it had been kicked in.

And that was when the next wave appeared.

One by one, a group of almost a dozen warriors marched in—the Brotherhood, he thought. This had to be the Brotherhood: Their bodies were enormous, dwarfing even him, and like the other two guards, they had masks over their faces and black leather covering them from boots to heads.

Unlike the other two, they had guns in their hands.

In a flash, the one who'd made the big appearance with the kiddie props up and disappeared. And then the last of the water glugged out the drains in the deep end of the pool.

All around him, candidates milled in their soaked clothes and relative exhaustion. He stayed still—as did Novo, who seemed to sense, as he did, that things were only going to get harder.

So it was best to conserve their energy until they had something valid to confront.

Those guns, he thought, were bad news.

With classic group-think, the other candidates congregated together, people in the shallow end backing up as the fighters came down the long side of the pool and made the turn to the set of steps that were slick and led to nothing but concrete and puddles now.

And then those menacing males with the guns were descending into the basin, their shitkickers landing like thunder, the shifting of their holsters making creaking sounds. When they came to a halt, it was impossible to know precisely who they were focusing on, as their heads were all facing the group, but their eyes were covered.

Triangulating his position, Craeg decided that, for the moment, sticking with the pack was for the best, so he—

One by one, the Brothers raised their autoloaders, aiming directly at the trainees. And then the tallest of them stepped forward, swinging his muzzle in a slow, lazy circle as if looking for the best target.

Talk about herd panic. Candidates freaked out, running this way and that, fighting to get behind others, slipping, falling. A couple of them went down on their knees, blubbering and begging before there had even been any shooting.

Craeg was having none of that. If the trainees were going to get hit with some lead, it wasn't going to be anywhere lethal. There were too many precautions in place so far. And he was ready to take a bullet—if that was what he had to do to get to the next round?

Hit him. He wasn't afraid of pain.

Squaring his shoulders, he faced off—and was aware that there was probably another reason why he halted. But he refused to acknowledge it in any way.

Come on, he thought. Over here.

Over here . . .

But they didn't go toward him.

No . . . they went toward someone else.

Not her, he thought. Shit, not Paradise.

"Hey," he called out. "Hey, asshole!"

As soon as those males in black stepped into the pool area, Paradise recognized the Brothers. After having spent so much time working around them, their scents, their auras were well-known to her—and she had grown to consider them like protective pseudo-fathers of hers.

That was not the case tonight.

Especially as they came down into the now-dry pool, lifted their guns . . . and one of them settled on her as a target.

Rhage. It was Rhage who trained his weapon on her and then began to walk forward. She knew because his body was so much larger than the others'.

No, no, she thought. You can't do this. My father—

But he didn't hesitate. He came right up to her and Peyton, leading with that firearm, finger on the trigger.

"Hey! Asshole!"

From out of the corner of her eye, she saw one of the recruits step forward and wave his arms.

It was her male—the male, that was. Craeg—

"Shoot me! Hey! Motherfucker! Shoot me instead."

And so the Brother did.

Without turning his head away from her, Rhage's arm swung to the side and he pulled the trigger, a bullet exploding out from the muzzle.

Paradise screamed and jerked against Peyton's hold as chaos went hog-wild, shrill voices echoing around like the panicked clatter of a thousand flushed birds. "No! Oh, my God—no!"

"Shut up," Peyton hissed as he kept her in place. "*Just shut it.*"

NFW. As Craeg fell over, she broke free and lunged in

attack at the Brother. It was like a bug hitting the wind-shield of a car, but none of that mattered. She just couldn't have anyone get hurt—especially not that male. Slapping, hitting, she clamped her hands on the muzzle and held on for dear life, trying to control the weapon. She failed. Before she knew what was happening, she was facedown on the damp concrete, and pinned at the back of the neck and small of the back. Turning her head, she looked frantically across the pool bottom to see if Craeg was still alive.

The male was down on her level, writhing while hold-ing what looked to be his thigh. The only other female in the group crouched beside him, forced his hands away, inspected the wound. Then on a quick jerk, she pulled her shirt out of her waistband and ripped it off, exposing a muscled torso and a black sports bra. With a tear, she took the hem off all around the base, freeing a strip of cloth.

She tied a tourniquet on his upper thigh as if she had been trained.

"Let her go," Peyton demanded from behind her. "Let her fucking go!"

"Or what," came a distorted voice from speakers overhead—as if someone had spoken into a microphone with a synthesizer attachment.

That was when Peyton lost his mind. Craning to twist her head around, she caught the unbelievable sight of him in full aggression, fists flying at Rhage, feet kicking, his fangs bared in a snarl as he tried to get the Brother off of her. And then suddenly he wasn't alone—the male who had displayed such athletic ability on the pommel horse joined in.

Pop! Pop!

Both of them were picked off with bullets by another Brother. And so were another two males who likewise tried to get involved. Meanwhile, people were climbing the walls, using the stainless-steel ladders to try to leave the pool—only to be electrocuted and fall back down.

A door opened.

From overhead that voice announced: "Anyone who wishes to leave may do so. No harm will come to you. This can all be over—right now. All you have to do is run for that door."

At that moment, she was released, Rhage hopping off, stepping back.

She scrambled across to Peyton, rolling him over once again. "How bad? Where?"

"My arm—my fucking arm."

Paradise yanked her shirt up and followed the example of the other female, tearing a section with one of her fangs, ripping a strip free, and trying to tie it just above the bleeding wound on his triceps.

She glared up at the Brothers. "Are you out of your fucking minds! This is school, not war! What the fuck!"

"You may leave now," the voice from overhead droned on. "Just proceed to the stairs at the shallow end of the pool and let yourself out of this."

A sudden sharp rage had her seeing white, and before she knew it she was up and at the line of Brothers. "Shoot me! Come on! Do it, you bunch of fucking cowards!"

She had no idea what the hell she was saying. What the hell she was doing. She had never seen so many guns before, much less deliberately put herself within point-blank range of such weapons—but she had snapped and discovered a surprising surge of power came with the unhinge.

Not that the Brothers seemed to care. They just stood there, unmoving and unreactive, as if they were content to wait until she ran out of gas.

So she turned on the trainees who were leaving. "Where are you going! You need to fight! This is wrong—"

Just like that, the door was closed and the unmistakable sound of a bar being clamped into place ricocheted around the space.

"You will now be required to complete First Night,"

the overhead voice stated. "The final session begins in three ... two ...

"... one."

And that was when the illumination went from incandescent to the purpley-blue of blacklight.

Also when the Brotherhood opened fire on all of them.

Chapter Ten

Rubber bullets hurt like a motherfucker.

As the first of a countless number of rounds hit Craeg in the pecs, he rolled away and offered his back instead of his more vulnerable front. Down below the waist, the one real bullet wound was like a firebrand in his skin—just as he'd predicted, though, the expert shot had done nothing but graze his flesh so that tourniquet was unnecessary. No time to take it off—he grabbed Novo's hand and yanked her into a belly-flat on the pool's bottom. Keeping their heads down, they crawled away from the barrage, heading up and over the hump that took them to the ten-foot end.

Glancing behind him, he found that the Brothers, who had realigned themselves to block the steps at the shallow part of the pool, had begun to walk forward like they were driving cattle into the chute of a slaughterhouse. Fucking hell—the metal ladders mounted up high on the pool walls by the diving board were juiced with electricity—and those warriors seemed to have an endless supply of the fucking dummy bullets. Even though the impacts were more like exaggerated bee stings through his clothes, with enough of them, his pain threshold was going to get triggered to a point that incapacitated him.

Wrenching around again, he measured how fast the Brothers were coming at them.

Fast enough so that he had maybe sixty seconds to figure this out.

"Dematerialize," he said as much to himself as anyone else who would listen. "Only chance."

Freezing his forward motion, he closed his eyes and started to breathe. The first vision he had was of that slender blond female attacking that impossibly large Brother with a gun.

To defend him after he'd been shot.

"Stop it," he hissed.

Control. He needed to get control of his mind and his emotions, focus himself, and dematerialize up and out. Focus . . . *focus* . . .

Pain in his body: in his thigh, in the other impacts along his shoulders, his spine, his hip. His head was thumping. His ribs were tight. His elbow still throbbed from when he'd been nailed by the electricity on the scaffolding.

All around, people panicking, crying, cursing. Tripping. Falling.

And still those bullets, driving into him. Into all of them.

The harder he tried to ignore the fear and panic, the louder the chorus of discomfort and distraction became.

He needed a target image, a place to train his brain to.

From out of nowhere, he pictured that receptionist when he'd first seen her. She'd been sitting behind a neat little desk in a majestic sitting room. Everything had intimidated him—the silk wallpaper, the fancy rug, the clean smell . . . her.

But she hadn't treated him like the scrub he was. She had looked up at him with eyes that had stopped his heart in his chest—and then she'd said her name.

Paradise.

Her voice had been so beautiful, he hadn't even heard her properly. And then he'd blown things completely by not shaking the hand she'd offered. The trouble was, his brain had frozen because she was so . . .

His body dematerialized without him being aware of it. One moment, he was suffering and stuck in his corporeal form . . . the next he was flying out from the pool.

With no destination in mind, he tumbled through the air as he had the first few times he'd tried the trick after his transition—and then he got hold of himself and projected his form into the far corner, against the wall.

As he re-formed, Novo was already there, braced and ready, but massaging one of her shoulders as if she were either rubbing pain away or assessing if the damn thing had dislocated.

One by one, four more dripping and damp trainees made it out of the pool: The athletic male from the pommel horse. The one who looked like a murderer, who had piercings and tats on only one side of his face and neck. The guy who'd had his arm around Paradise. Another male who was tall and strong.

He had no idea what happened to—

The receptionist was the last to re-form, and Craeg had to turn away or exhibit an emotion that was unacceptable. To distract himself, he tried to see what was happening in the pool to the five who'd been left behind—

A door opened right beside them all, and as a stiff, cold breeze came at them, he smelled the outdoors.

Whatever was on the other side was dark.

"Who goes first," Paradise asked.

"I will," the pierced, Goth-looking male answered. "Nothin' to lose."

Craeg frowned as the sudden silence around them began seeming like a bad omen: The shooting had stopped. Which could mean that that part of the test was over . . . or the Brothers were taking aim again.

No, they were gone—all that was left in the pool were a couple of trainees who had broken in half, the soaking wet, sobbing figures sitting on the damp concrete with their heads in their hands or their bodies in the fetal position.

Shit. Where were the Brothers now?

"I'll go with you," he said to the Goth.

The pair of them were the biggest of the group, the tip of the spear, so to speak—and though he'd gone into this

thinking about solo survival, he was beginning to reconsider that strident position. At least for the short term.

If an attack came at them, two were better than one.

Novo spoke up. "I'll take the rear."

The athlete fell in beside her. "I can help cover that,
too."

"You three," Craeg ordered the blond female and
her . . . mate? BF? And a guy who was good looking in a
pretty-boy kind of way. "In the middle."

At least that way, he wouldn't worry about her.

Not that he was.

"Move out," Craeg said.

He and the hard-core male went over the threshold
together, their combined shoulders nearly filling what
turned out to be a tunnel—and once they were in there,
a distant flickering light became a guide they slowly progressed toward.

"What's your name?" the Goth whispered.

"Craeg."

"I'm Axe. Nice to fucking meet ya."

Paradise expected anything to happen as they made
their way as a group through the tunnel. Tight quartered,
anxiety ridden, slow moving and wrung out, she waited
for another shoe to drop, something to jump at them, fall
on top of them, knock them down.

When they simply emerged outside by a bonfire, her
jangling nerves didn't know how to process the lack of
attack.

And then her brain really couldn't grapple with the
fact that there was a table set up with bottles of water on
it and energy bars and pieces of fruit.

Was this the end? she thought as she looked around
at the pine trees, the underbrush, the stars above.

"I'm thirsty as hell," Peyton said, beelining for the Poland Springs.

The male she couldn't help but keep track of stopped
him. "It could be a trap," Craeg said, going over.

"You're paranoid."

"Did you try the food before? You like throwing up?"

Peyton opened his mouth. Closed it. Cursed.

Craeg measured the setup. Tapped the earth with the toe of his wet boot. Moved forward from the side in a crouched position. When he got close, he bent down and put his eyes on a level with the orderly array of bottles. He lifted the skirting on the table and looked underneath.

Then he picked one of the Poland Springs up slowly.

Paradise's heart thundered. She was dehydrated, too—even after feeling like she had swallowed half that pool. But she was scared to get poisoned.

God, she had never been in this situation before—consumed by thirst, confronted by drink, and yet frozen from getting what she wanted.

"This is not sealed," Craeg announced.

He picked up another one. And another. On the third, there was a *crack!* as he freed the cap. Taking a sniff of the open neck, he tested a sip.

"This is good." He passed it back without looking—and as soon as Peyton grabbed the thing, Craeg kept going, inspecting more tops, weeding out the unsealed ones. Peyton was the one who divvied them among the group until everybody had water.

Craeg kept a bottle for himself, but didn't drink much, tucking the thing into his belt. Then without any comment, he moved on to the energy bars, tossing out the ones that had rips in the wrappers, sharing those that were okay.

Paradise ate even though she wasn't hungry, because she didn't know when they would stop again or how much effort was going to be required for the next stage—and talk about food as fuel and that was it. The energy bar was a nasty mix of cardboard, fake sweet, and goo, but she didn't care. She was going to need the calories.

If only to stay warm, she thought as a shiver went through her. November night and wet clothes. Not good for your core temperature if you were standing around.

Or stuck out in the elements for very long.

"What do we do now?" she asked everyone and nobody at the same time.

Behind them, the door to the facility slammed shut and locked.

The serial-killer guy, Axe, drawled, "That's okay, I wasn't looking for a reboot of that pool action anyway."

"There's a fence over there," the other female said, pointing to the left.

"And over here," the athlete chimed in.

"Bet it's electrified," Peyton muttered. "Everything else that's metal has been."

The question was solved when someone picked up a stick, threw it at the chain link — and the thing got toasted in a shower of sparks.

With some further exploration, they discovered they were in a chute of some kind, one that offered them a single outlet: straight ahead, into the dark woods.

"We go together," she said, staring past the flickering orange light of the bonfire. "Again."

"I hate teamwork," Axe muttered.

"And I'm *so* excited to be doing this with you," Peyton drawled back.

Without talking about it, the group fell into the lineup order from the tunnel. And then they were off, moving forward as a unit, mindful not to get too close to the chain link as the fence narrowed in on both sides.

Twigs cracked under their wet trainers. Someone sneezed. A breeze blew in from one side that turned Paradise's arm to ice.

But all that barely registered. As she walked along, her body was a live wire, energy coursing through her veins, her instincts prickling and ready for input from somewhere, anywhere: She was on the razor-sharp lookout for anything that was wrong, a snap on the ground that was too loud, an awkward shift of Peyton's body beside her, a creak from a tree branch over on the left ... and that which she couldn't immediately sort into the non-threatening category made her twitchy muscles and her bouncing brain want to freeze and assess. Or break out into a run to escape.

And yet they kept going. And going. And . . . going.

Time was passing, she thought, glancing up at the position of the stars.

And still they kept on, their ragtag group schlepping along, shuffling over the ground, limping, lurching, everyone injured in their own way and yet remaining on their feet.

Several miles later—or was it more like a hundred?—nothing had come at them.

But she wasn't fooled.

The Brothers would be back. They had a plan for all of this.

She just needed to stay tight, keep with the group, and—

Up ahead, Craeg and Axe stopped.

"What is it?" she said as she grabbed for Peyton's arm. Why did she smell . . . fire?

"We're back where we started," Craeg replied quietly. "This is where we began."

When he pointed to the ground, she saw footprints, their footprints, in the loose dirt. Except the table with the water and the food was gone . . . and the bonfire had been put out—which explained the scent . . . and the fence had been moved into a different position.

It had been closed off to form a loop or a track.

"They have us going in circles?" Peyton demanded. "What the fuck?"

"Why?" Paradise asked, looking over at Craeg as their de facto leader. "Why would they do that?"

Thanks to her eyes having adjusted to the darkness, she could make out his strong features as he frowned and glanced around. When he shook his head, her stomach became a pit.

"What?" she said.

That only other female spoke up. "They're going to wear us out. That's why—"

The popping sounds of gunfire came from the left, another round of chaos lighting up along with those flashing muzzles as the group banged into itself, bodies colliding and causing bolts of pain to flare in Paradise's shoulder and lower leg.

"Walk!" Craeg yelled. "Just walk and it'll stop!"

And he was right. The instant they began moving in the direction they'd been going, everything went still and silent again.

It didn't take a genius to figure out that if they halted, they were going to be hit with more of those rubber bullets.

Paradise drew in a steadying breath. This was not so bad, she told herself. Their pace was slow and even, and she liked walking.

Better than being shot at, for sure.

This was going to be just fine.

Better than the pool. Better than being dragged over the floor while bound and head-bagged. Better than the explosions in the gym.

All she had to do was put one foot in front of the other.

To pass the time, she focused on what she could see of Craeg up in front, tracing the movements of his big body, from his broad shoulders to the way his hips shifted with each step he made. When the wind changed direction from time to time, she caught his scent and thought it was better than any cologne she'd ever smelled.

Who were his people? she wondered. Where was he from?

Did he have a mate?

Funny how that last one made her feel a pang in her chest. Then again, after everything she had been through tonight, no wonder her mind and her emotions were all over the place ...

Around and around they went, until she began to pick out familiar trees and specific branches, until their footfalls carved a track in the earth, until the dull monotony began to get to her: No one aggressed upon them, fired anything at them, jumped over the fence to terrorize them.

It didn't mean that couldn't happen ... but the longer none of that went down, the more her brain started to cannibalize itself, flipping from random thoughts about Craeg, to baseless panic, to images of her father, to ... worry over whatever was coming next.

Glancing up at the sky, she wished she knew what the positions of the stars meant. She had no idea how much time had passed since they'd arrived in the gymnasium or even come out here for that matter. It felt like a lifetime since she had checked in and gotten her photograph taken. Even longer since she and Peyton had argued on the bus. But that was most certainly not true.

Three hours? No, too short. Five or six, she estimated.

The good news was that this had to stop at dawn. Sun was a non-negotiable even for the Brothers—and clearly no one was going to be killed. Yes, that gun stuff had been terrifying, but the people who had had real bullets shot at them were up on their feet, their wounds clearly superficial—and it was the same for anyone who had eaten or had anything to drink that had been tampered with.

So many weeded out. They had started with sixty. They were down to seven.

And she was astonished to find she was still hanging in. In fact, if she'd known that a stroll through the woods was the end to it all? Everything would have been so much easier.

Considering how bad it could have been, this was a piece of cake.

Chapter Eleven

One by one, they all went down.

The first to drop out was that male she knew from the *glymera's* festival parties, her very distant cousin, Anslam: After a while, he began slowing, his gait falling off with a limp that gradually grew so pronounced, his entire body became affected by it. And then he just stopped.

There was some encouragement offered by the group, but he just shook his head and sat down to loosen the laces on his left Nike.

"I'm done. Let 'em shoot me. I'm fucking done."

Even in the darkness, she could see the blood on his white sock.

"Come on, Paradise," Peyton said, nudging her. "We gotta keep going."

Looking into the dense forest, she wondered where the Brothers were. What was going to happen to him.

When the group started off again, she followed because she didn't want to quit, and also—even though she was ashamed to admit it—because she'd never really liked the guy. He had a bad reputation with females.

It wasn't long before the next fell by the wayside. And then, one after the other, they all crumpled. The feet were the thing. Or a thigh. Or shoulder. One by one . . . everybody took to the ground, to the well-worn dirt track they had created with their countless footfalls. And Paradise had the urge to help everybody, especially when

Peyton began to sway next to her ... and then weave as if he wasn't sure what was in front of him anymore.

For him, it was the aftereffects of the vomiting. The water he'd taken in had refused to stay put, and dehydration had made him delirious.

She couldn't not try with him, and she pulled at his arm, attempting to get him up from his knees when he finally collapsed.

"... home now," he babbled. "I'm going to go home now. Bed, I need ... food. ... I'm right by my house, look."

It was terrifying to watch as he pointed ahead to the forest, his eyes rapt, as if he were actually seeing the mansion he lived in.

And it was then that she knew she shouldn't push him.

"Come on," the other female said to her. "If you're still on your feet, you need to keep going."

Paradise looked into a set of teal-blue eyes. "I hate this."

"Nothing will happen to him. No gunshots, remember—for any of the others who gave up."

"Go," Peyton said with sudden focus. "I'll be fine."

In the end, she couldn't really say why she put another foot in front of herself again. Maybe the lack of introspection was a symptom of her own exhaustion. Maybe she was delirious in her own way and she followed what was left of the group because her brain mistook them as a "home" of sorts.

Maybe her body was simply on autopilot.

And then there were two.

That other female, the one with the bright blue eyes, soon followed what Paradise now recognized as a pattern. First, she slowed and began to trip; then she outright stopped. When she didn't fall to the ground, Paradise doubled back, thinking there was a chance.

"No," the female said, cutting off conversation. "I'm staying here. You keep going."

Paradise glanced at the single male who was still

trudging forward: Craeg was still in the lead. Had been the whole time.

He hadn't stopped for anyone.

He hadn't offered any encouragement.

He just kept his pace without deviation or distraction.

"Don't waste time or energy on me," the female said. "I've made my decision. I can't feel my legs anymore, and I think my shoulder is broken. If you can keep moving, you need to do it. You're too tired to carry me, but even if you could, I will be no one else's burden."

Paradise's eyes stung with tears. "Well . . . shit."

The female smiled a little. "You're going to win this."

"What?"

"Just go. You got this, girl."

Okaaaaaay, and someone else had gone delirious, clearly.

The female gave her a shove and a nod. "Prove to the boys we're not just equal, we're better than them. Don't let me down."

Paradise shook her head. If anyone was going to win a war of the sexes, the better bet was on the female in front of her.

"Go. You can do this."

Paradise was cursing to herself as she turned away and resumed walking. Craziness. Just insanity.

As her feet skimmed over the now-packed dirt, she checked the sky again. The stars shone as bright as ever, which told her that dawn remained a ways off.

How long had they been walking? she wondered. And how much longer . . . ?

By now, Craeg was well off in the distance. From time to time, she caught his scent on the breeze, but it was just a faint hint. Talk about winners? He was the one who was going to "first place" this: He was stronger and tougher—and she had to believe, even if it went against every core principle she personally had, that his single-minded, unwavering commitment to himself was going to see him through this better than her compassionate interest in others.

Weight carried, whether it was physically, mentally, or emotionally, slowed you down.

And as she kept going, through the cold wind that no longer registered, she felt the loss of each member of their little group—and all the others who had suffered before, whether it was in the gym, the pool. . . .

No, that male up ahead of her was going to be the last candidate standing.

As she rounded a bend in the track, a barrier in her path registered. It was some ways away, but it was definitely an obstacle on the ground in the center of the trail.

Not just an obstacle.

It was . . . Craeg.

Her brain flipped into a faster gear, ordering her to rush to him—her body, however, could not respond to the flush of adrenaline. Even as her brain hit all kinds of alarm buttons, her pace didn't change, that shuffling of her feet and lurching of her upper torso unaltered by the panic.

Coming up to him, she discovered that he had collapsed facedown in the path, his arms flopped at his sides as if he had lacked the strength or consciousness to brace himself for the impact. His legs were lax, his Nikes turned inward.

"Craeg?"

When she went to crouch down, she fell herself, because her knees refused to bend—and then, as she tried to roll him over, her hands kept slipping free of the grip of his clothes, his shoulder, his arm.

Although maybe that was because he weighed twice as much as Peyton did.

She could get him only half on his side, and God, he was so pale that his face glowed like a ghost's. At least he was breathing, though, and after a moment, his eyes opened in a series of messy blinks.

It was bizarre, but her first thought was to offer him her vein—which was something that hadn't occurred to her up until now, even when Peyton had hit the ground.

The impulse was so strong, she brought her wrist up to her mouth—

He stopped her, slapping her arm down. "No . . ." he rasped.

"You're bleeding." She nodded down at the big red stain on his jeans. "You need strength."

As his eyes locked on hers, a strange kind of tunnel vision reduced the entire world to just the two of them: The forest around them, the construct under which they had been laboring, the toil they were both enduring . . . it all disappeared along with the aches and pains in her body and her head.

His gaze wiped her clean. Refreshed her. Energized her.

"Leave me here," he mumbled, his head shaking back and forth on the ground. "Go ahead. You're the last one. . . ."

"You can get up. You can keep going—"

"Stop wasting time. Go . . ."

"You have to get up."

He closed his eyes and turned his head away from her, as if he were done with the conversation. But then he said, "This is about your survival. Survival means you continue no matter the cost, no matter the sacrifice. So stop wasting breath, get back on your feet, and move."

"I don't want to leave you here." Also didn't want to look too closely into why she had walked away from Peyton, but couldn't seem to bear leaving this total stranger behind. "I'm not going to leave you."

His eyes swung around and they were pissed. "How about this. I don't want help from the likes of you—I don't want to be rescued by some dumb female . . . some dumb, weak, fumbling female who should never have been allowed into this program in the first place."

Paradise fell back onto the forest floor, a blazing pain ripping through her chest. Except then she shook her head. "That's not what you really believe. That's not what you told me the first night we met. You told me to come here even when my father didn't."

"I lied."

"You're lying now."

He closed his eyes again. "You don't know me."

When he stayed silent, she felt a tidal wave of exhaustion hit her. "No, I don't."

Looking past him to the trail ahead, she tried to imagine herself getting to her feet and walking again . . . and couldn't get there. Sometime between when she'd last been on the vertical and this current, on-her-ass moment, she had gained seven thousand pounds of body weight—and that wasn't all. Somebody had come along and beaten both her feet with hammers. Her head, too. And one of her shoulders.

Paradise glanced back at where they had come from. Had she really thought a little walk wasn't that bad?

"You don't belong here," she heard him say.

Paradise rolled her eyes. "I'm bored with that line of reasoning. If you really believed it yourself, you wouldn't have given me that advice at the beginning of tonight."

"I felt sorry for you. I pitied you."

"So you do have a heart."

"No."

"Then how can you feel sorry for me or anybody else?" When he just grunted, she was very aware they were two pushed-to-extremes individuals, neither of whom was making much sense. "Fine, take me out of this. You have no heart, why did you bother testing the bottled water out for everyone. The energy bars. That wasn't just for me."

"Yes, it was."

Paradise stilled. His head was angled away from her, but she had the oddest sense that he had spoken the truth there.

"And yet I'm just a stranger to you," she said.

"Told you. Felt sorry. The others could take care of themselves and there is safety in numbers."

"So wait, which one is it—misogynist with a conscience or teammate-even-though-I'm-a-girl? You're flipping back and forth like a politician."

He groaned and brought up an arm. "You make my head pound."

"I think that's the endurance test at work. Not me."

"Will you just leave? Much more of this conversation and I'm going to get as sick as your boyfriend was."

"My b— Peyton? You're talking about Peyton?"

Okay, were they really sitting here talking like nothing much was going on?

Well . . . *arguing* like there was nothing going on?

"Do me a favor," the male said. "You see that rock over there?"

She glanced to the left. "That one? That's the size of an ice cooler?"

"Yeah. Could you pick it up and drop it on my head? That'd be great. Thanks."

Paradise rubbed her eyes, and then put both hands down when keeping her arms up on her knees became too much like work. "What's your full name? If I'm going to kill you at your own request, I need to know what to inscribe on your grave marker."

Those eyes came back to hers. Sky blue. They were a shockingly bright blue.

"How about we compromise," he muttered. "You just leave me here to die on my own and then you won't have to worry about getting blood on your shoes—or what my name is."

Paradise looked away. "Three times is not a charm."

"What?"

She waited for him to tell her his lineage. When he didn't, she chalked it up to exhaustion . . . and his commoner's background.

"Will you please go now?" he whispered. "As much as I've 'enjoyed' this little talk, I'm about to pass out—and I'd just as soon get on with that. I need the sleep."

"You can do this—you can keep going."

He made no comment to that or acknowledgment of it—and stupidly, she felt as though he'd rejected a gift she'd tried to give him. And how arrogant was that?

"So this is it, huh," she said—mostly to herself.

Again he said nothing, but she didn't think he'd actually passed out.

And then, just as he had before, he spoke up when she didn't expect it. "It's time for you to decide who you are. It happens in moments like this. Are you someone who quits—or who keeps going?"

But I'd always stop to help you, she thought to herself. And helping another person isn't quitting.

"Don't you want to find out who else you are—other than a receptionist?"

She frowned. "There is honor in all work."

"And maybe there is greatness waiting for you—if you only get back up on your feet and keep going."

God, she didn't know . . . pretty much anything at this point.

With the heat of her anger dissipating, she was left with a weariness that threatened to collapse her bones in her skin.

Who am I, she wondered.

Good question.

And she had no idea what the answer was. What she *was* clear on? Paradise, blooded daughter of Abalone, First Adviser to Wrath, the Blind King, was not the kind of person who was going to sit next to some stranger who didn't want her around and wasn't asking to be saved while there was even a possibility she could go one more foot, one more yard, one more mile in this challenge.

She glanced down at Craeg. Like her, his clothes were ruined by blood, sweat, and dirt, his hair stiff from having dried without being brushed, his body a limp rag of bad angles.

"Take care," she said as she struggled to get up.

He didn't reply. Maybe he had finally passed out? Or perhaps he was simply relieved she was going. Either way ... not her concern.

When she went to move her right leg forward, she found that everything about her corporeal form—from her neck to her spine to her calves and all the joints and straightaways in between—was one hot mess of pain. But she got her foot in front of herself. And she did it again. And again. And ...

She had no idea what made her keep going. She didn't care about winning. She wasn't doing it to prove anyone was wrong or that females mattered. She wasn't even aware of having any conscious thoughts.

Paradise just kept on walking ... because that was what she did.

Burning.

Sometime later, all she could feel was burning: in her legs and her feet ... in her gut and her lungs ... down her throat—God, her throat was on fire ... in her skull ... on her face.

Fire all around her, in her, through her, as if her veins had lit gasoline in them and her muscles were charring from the inside out.

Brilliant light in her eyes, too.

Light so bright.

Too bright.

Except it wasn't dawn. The sky was still dark—at least ... she thought it was ...

Dimly, a thought sprouted above all the agony. Was this the Fade? she wondered. This illumination, this pain? The heat?

Had she died somehow?

She didn't recall dying—wouldn't you know that you had? But what else could explain this incendiary agony?

Walking ... she was still walking. Or maybe the world was moving under her feet and she was standing motionless? It was hard to tell. She was seeing double, the trees thickening up on either side of the electrified fence, the trail she was following bifurcating off into the distance so she kept feeling like she had to choose a left or a right—except when she looked down there was only one path again.

Fire . . . the Fade.

No! she thought in a scramble. God, her father! Oh, this was terrible—Abalone was going to be all alone now, no one in that huge Tudor mansion, both of his females gone. . . .

Paradise stopped.

The path ahead was no longer clear.

As she focused on the tall, solid barrier before her, her double vision coalesced into what was a more accurate representation of reality . . . and she saw that it was a lineup of males.

There were . . . a dozen, maybe more.

And they were all dressed in black with hoods over their faces and guns on their bodies.

The Brotherhood was welcoming her unto the Fade?

This made no sense.

As she weaved on her feet, she realized they were coming to her now, walking in a thick group of impossibly huge bodies.

Run! an inner voice commanded. *Run! This is another test!*

Except there was no energy to do that. No energy even to sustain that panic longer than one single burst of action-oriented thought.

Weaving in thin air, on fire inside and out, she thought, Fuck it. She'd violated the time limit, failed the module, flaked out of whatever part of the training this was—and it was gameover for her. There was no reboot, no motivation available to her, either internally or externally. If they shot her, carved her up into bite-sized pieces, pushed her down to mow her over? She had no fight left to offer them.

So this was her end, huh. Man, her father was going to be so pissed when they killed her.

On a coordinated halt, as if they were functioning out of one brain, the Brotherhood halted in front of her and lifted their hands. Bracing herself for something else that hurt, she—

They started to clap.

One by one, they brought their broad palms together, clapping while they stared at her. And as the round of applause continued, they took their masks off, revealing themselves to her.

"What?" she mumbled. "I don't understand."

Or rather, that was what she'd meant to say. She had no voice left, nothing to carry forth the words her mind wanted her to utter.

Butch, the one with the Boston accent, came forward. "Congratulations," he said grimly. "You are the *Primus*."

Paradise had no idea what that meant. And there was no chance to ask him for a repeat.

Like someone unplugging a computer ... everything went dark on her between one heartbeat and the next.

Chapter Twelve

As Butch waited outside of Doc Jane's exam room, he put his ass against the concrete wall of the training center's hallway and let his head drop forward on his spine. From time to time, he rubbed his eyes.

Which didn't help much.

It didn't help at all, actually: With every blink of his lids, he saw Paradise weaving down the middle of that track they'd made through the forest for the trainees, looking as if she had been through a war, her hair all matted, dirt on her face, clothes a mess, blood on her hands. And when she finally focused on the Brothers, her stare had been hollow as an empty skull, her body a jangly mess of floppy, loose limbs, her spirit broken.

Goddamn it, he couldn't help picturing her from the night before, when she'd been wrapping things up for her father at Wrath's audience house. Neat as a pin, then. Awake, alert, happy, although nervous that her application was going to be revoked by her father, the Brotherhood, the King.

Fucking hell, maybe they should have locked her out.

But that wouldn't have been fair.

The good news, he supposed, was that the program that he and Vishous had devised had worked. Their goal had been to crush the class from sixty applicants to under ten students.

They had seven to work with.

Everyone who had made it out to that track was in.

He couldn't say he felt tight about it, though. Maybe if the last one standing had been one of those strapping males. Like that kid Craeg who was a natural-born leader, the kind of guy who was perfect for the life of a soldier—if he'd lasted them all out, Butch was pretty sure he wouldn't be having an attack of conscience right now.

It wasn't that he didn't believe females could handle shit. He just—

The door to the clinic opened and V emerged. As the brother immediately lit up a hand-rolled, Butch wondered if he wasn't also struggling with what they'd done. Not that the hard-ass would ever admit it.

"Well, that was fun," the brother said grimly. "Can we do it again tomorrow night?"

"Is she all right?"

"Fine." V exhaled as he put his lighter away. "Dehydrated. Feet are torn up. Chafed in places. She's being rolled into the bunk room by Ehlena right now."

"She's still out cold?" Fuck, this was bad. This was very bad.

"More like in and out. We don't want a slip-and-fall situation, true?"

"Yeah."

There was a pause. "What's wrong with you? Look, I told you, she's gonna be fine."

Butch just shook his head. No doubt, given V's S-and-M background, he was used to females—and males—looking wrung-out, and yet walking away from seshes just fine. As a former homicide detective, however, Butch took things in a different direction: He saw victims.

He relived crime scenes where females' bodies were mangled like cars that had been crashed—and no, they did not walk away, they were not "fine."

For fuck's sake, he remembered what his own sister

had looked like as she'd stared out the back window of her murderers' car, never to be seen alive again.

So, yeah, the associations were not the same.

"You want a drink?" V asked him.

Read: You look like roadkill, true?

Butch took out his phone. He'd texted Marissa as soon as they'd carried Paradise back inside, but no, no response. Busy night for his mate, apparently.

"You mind if I duck out?" he asked his roommate.

"You going to church again?"

Man, the son of a bitch knew him too well.

"I still have two hours before dawn." He clapped his best friend on the shoulder. "See you at Last Meal."

He was halfway to the office, where the entrance to the tunnel was, when V called out, "You didn't do anything wrong tonight."

Butch nodded. Then looked over his shoulder. "Doesn't mean I'm happy about introducing a bunch of children into the war."

"We either make the intros, or the war will find them on its own terms."

"Yeah, this shit might be necessary—might even be for their own good. Doesn't sit well with me, though."

As he kept going, he could feel those diamond eyes watching him, and he was glad he was walking away from the guy instead of toward him. Vishous was too good at reading him, and he wanted to keep all the unstable he had going on to himself.

And yes, that was why he was going to church. It was what good, God-fearing Catholic boys did when they were suffering from mind fucks like this.

Paradise came awake on a jerk, not so much surfacing back to consciousness as catapulting into awareness, her hands slapping out at whatever she was lying on, her torso jacking up, her eyes popping wide.

She was ready for anything. . . .

Except for the clean, well-lit room that was full of bunk beds and completely empty of anyone but her.

"What . . . the . . . ?"

As she went to look around, her neck cracked, and that opened the floodgates to all kinds of unpleasantness: Her feet were throbbing, her hips were killing her, her thighs were on fire, one calf was seized up, and her stomach was aching like she'd been punched in the gut.

Shifting her legs to the floor, she discovered she was in a hospital johnny and a soft robe.

"Don't worry, both the doctor and the nurse are females."

She snapped around to the doorway. "Peyton?"

Her friend was half in and half out of the jamb, his wrecked clothes gone, a loose, belted robe in their place. He'd clearly had a shower and some food and drink—he was close to normal, his good looks, his sardonic smile, his lidded eyes revived.

"Or call me Santa Claus." Her friend came forward and held out a mug. "I brought you a present, after all."

"Wait, wait . . . where are we? What are—"

"Here, drink this." Peyton sat down on the bunk next to her. "And before you ask, nothing's in it except for two sugars and two creams. I remember how you like it."

"What time is it?" She took the coffee, just to be pleasant. "Oh, my God—my father—"

"I called him myself. We're all here at the Brotherhood's training center. The seven of us made it into the program—especially you. Congratulations, Parry. You did it."

She frowned and took a sip—then moaned. "Oh, my f— this is the best thing I've ever tasted in my life."

He got back up and went over to a side table. "Last Meal, m'lady."

As he brought her over a tray of covered dishes, she had to force herself not to pound the coffee. "Where are the others?"

"In a cafeteria, break room thingy right outside this

place. Most of them are sleeping. I had the nurse put you in here for obvious reasons."

"Obvious . . ." Oh, right. "Thank you."

"Yeah, no chaperones. But I've been checking on you every fifteen minutes."

After everything she had been through during the nighttime hours, her virtue seemed like the last thing she needed to worry about. But you didn't shake your entire upbringing justlikethat.

"Eat," he said. "Everything gets better after you eat."

He put the tray next to her on the bunk and began popping the lids off. One look at the slices of roast beef and the baked potato and she was ravenous.

But before she tucked in, she had to ask, "All seven of us? From the . . . you know, we walked together? All of us?"

"Axe, Boone, Novo, Anslam, and Craeg."

She ducked her eyes at the last name. "So that's our class?"

"Yeah."

Picking up the fork and knife, she groaned as she twisted toward her plate and her ribs let out a WHAT ARE YOU DOING. "Crap, I can't move without—"

"Advil. I'll have them bring you some more." Peyton headed to the door and stopped. "I owe you an apology."

"For what?"

"Thinking that you couldn't do this." He glanced back at her. "You were right to call my shit out on the bus. You proved me wrong. I'm sorry."

Paradise exhaled. "Thank you. That means a lot."

He nodded. "Come out when you're ready. We're just shooting the shit."

"Hey, Peyton?" she said before he reached for the handle.

"Hmm?"

"Do me a favor?"

"Name it."

"Don't tell them about . . . you know, about who I am.

I don't want to be treated any differently. I just want to
be like everyone else."

"Anslam knows. But I can talk to him and give him a
gag order."

"Thank you."

Peyton looked at the floor for a moment. "Anything
for you."

After he left, Paradise ate as much as she could—
which turned out to be everything on the tray, including
the fresh roll and the peas. She finished the coffee and
drank both of the bottled waters that came with everything. Then she limped over to the bathroom in the corner.

The shower she took was so hot, she was surprised she
didn't melt the paint off the walls, but oh, how her body
loosened under the penetrating spray. The blisters on her
feet stung, and so did various random places, like her
right elbow and her left knee that were scraped and the
tops of both her shoulders for some reason. She didn't
care. It was heaven.

Hanging her head, she let the rush of water run down
the back of her neck.

She was glad that Peyton had called her father. It was
almost dawn, and she didn't want the male worrying, but
she wasn't ready to talk about what had happened. She
needed time—to think, to reassess, to process.

There was shampoo. She used it without checking the
label. Same with the conditioner. And the soap.

By the time she got out, she felt closer to herself—but
that changed when she looked at her reflection in the
mirror over the sink.

Leaning in close, she regarded her features as if they
were someone else's—and they did look unfamiliar. Her
face seemed so much leaner, and even with no makeup
on, her big eyes seemed to take over everything as a
child's would.

"Who am I?" she whispered to the reflection.

Chapter Thirteen

St. Patrick's Cathedral in Caldwell was a grand old lady, rising up from the pavement as a testament to both God's mercy and man's ability to glue blocks of stones together. As Butch pulled up in his new Lexus and parallel-parked, he thought it was pretty damn funny that of all the human traits to have survived his transition into a vampire, the one that had stuck the most was his faith.

He was a better Catholic now than he had been when he'd been a Homo sapiens.

Tugging his Boston Red Sox cap down low, he went in through the front portal that was bigger than the house he'd grown up in, in Southie.

The cathedral was always open, a Starbucks of spirituality, ready to serve up what was needed when souls were lost and fumbling.

Monsignor, I'd like a venti of forgiveness tonight, thanks so much. And a scone that will magically tell me what the fuck is wrong with my wife.

The security guard sitting in an armchair in the vestibule looked up from his *Sports Illustrated* and nodded at him. The guy was used to him coming in before dawn.

"Evenin'," the guard said.

"You good?"

"Yup. You?"

"Yup."

Always the same conversation, and the six-word exchange was now part of the ritual.

Crossing over the thick red carpet, Butch breathed in deep and caught a contact calm from the familiar smell of incense, beeswax candles, lemon floor polish, and real flowers. And as he pushed through the carved double doors to the majestic sanctuary, he didn't like keeping his hat on, but he had to stay on the DL.

His mother would have had a fit, though—assuming her dementia lifted long enough for her to track anything.

The fact that she had lost her mind had made leaving the human world so much easier—and from time to time, he and Marissa went to see her, materializing into her room at the nursing home up in Massachusetts and visiting with her because they knew that no memories of them would stay—

Butch stopped and inhaled deep, his blood surging, his skin tingling. Pivoting in a jerk, he frowned as he saw a lone figure seated in the rear pews.

"Marissa?"

Even though his voice didn't carry far, his mate looked up, his presence registering to her.

Rushing over the stone pavers, he went sideways and shuffled down the row she was in, trying not to trip over the needlepoint prayer stools.

"What are you doing here?" he said as he caught the scent of her tears.

Her eyes were watering as he came up to her, and she tried to smile, but didn't get far with that. "I'm fine, really, I'm ..."

He sat down next to her—collapsed, was more like it—and took her cool hands. She still had her Burberry wool coat on, and her hair was tangled at the ends, as if she had been out in the wind.

Butch shook his head, his heart going trip-time on him. "Marissa, you gotta talk to me. You're scaring the ever-loving shit out of your man."

"I'm sorry."

She didn't say anything else, but she leaned into him, allowing his body to support her weight—and that was an explanation in and of itself: Whatever it was, he wasn't at fault.

Butch closed his eyes and held her, rubbing her back. "What's going on."

The story came out in fits and starts: a young female ... lawn of Safe Place ... brutalized ... Havers operated ... died anyway ... no name, no information, no family.

God, he hated that his precious *shellan* had to be exposed to all that ugliness. Oh, and P.S., fuck her brother for real.

"And now I don't know what to do for her." Marissa let out a shuddering breath. "I just ... I feel like I didn't do enough when she was alive to save her and now she's gone ... and I know she was a stranger, but that doesn't matter."

Butch stayed quiet because he wanted to give his mate every chance to keep going—and as he waited, he thought, Shit, he knew that feeling of untethered accountability. Back when he'd been working homicide for the CPD, he'd felt the same way about every victim in his case load. Amazing how strangers could become a sort of kin.

"It's just so unfair to her. The whole thing." Marissa turned away to her purse, took out a Kleenex, and blew her nose. "And I didn't want to say anything to you because I know you're really busy—"

"Wrong," he cut in. "There is nothing more important than you."

"Still ..."

He tilted her face toward him. "Nothing."

As she teared up again, he brushed her cheeks clear. "How can you doubt that?"

"I don't know. I'm not thinking right." She pressed the tissue wad to her nose. "And I came here because this is where you always go."

Okay, that warmed the crap out of his heart. "Has it helped?"

She smiled a little. "Well, it brought us together, didn't it."

Arranging her into his side, he put his arm around her and stared up the rows of glowing wood to the magnificent altar with its golden cross and its twenty-foot-tall statue of Jesus on the crucifix. Thanks to external security lights, stained glass glowed in the great arched windows that stretched up to the Gothic flying buttresses high above. And the chapels that honored saints flickered with votive candles lit by midnight visitors, the marble statues representing the Virgin Mary, and John the Baptist, and the archangels Gabriel and Michael offering grace to whomever needed it.

He didn't want his mate to suffer, but he was so damned relieved she was turning to him. As a bonded male, his first instinct was always to protect his *shellan*, and that withdrawal thing of hers, even though it had lasted for only a day, had been a kind of amputation.

"AndIdidn'twanttotellyoubecauseofyoursister."

"What?" he murmured, kissing the top of her head.

"Your sister . . ."

Butch stiffened, he couldn't help it. But then, any mention of that slice of his past was enough to make him feel like someone had juiced him with a car battery.

"It's okay," he said.

Marissa straightened. "I didn't want to upset you. I mean, you never speak of . . . well, what happened to her."

He looked down at his female's hands. They were twisting and turning in her lap, trading off the tissue that was now a ball.

"You don't have to worry about me." He moved her hair back over her shoulder, stroking the fine, smooth strands. "That's the last thing you need to do."

"May I ask you something?"

"Anything."

When she didn't immediately come back at him with something, he moved his face into her line of vision. "What?"

"Why don't you ever talk about your life before you met me? I mean, I know some details ... but you never speak about any of it."

"You're my life now."

"Hmm."

"What are you getting at?"

She glanced over at him and shrugged. "I don't know what I'm saying. I think I'm babbling."

Her purse let out a *bing!* and she pulled the thing over into her lap. As she took out her phone, he studied her from a distance even though she was right next to him.

"It's a text from Havers," she said. "The remains are ready to be picked up."

Butch got to his feet. "I'm going with you."

Marissa stared up at him. "Are you sure you have time?"

All he could do was shake his head at that one. "Come on. I'll drive you across the river. We still have a good hour of darkness left."

As Craeg sat in a relatively comfortable chair with a padded back and padded arms, everything hurt so badly he might as well have taken a load off on a set of fireplace pokers. Part of it was his own fault. After he'd been brought in from the field on a stretcher, he'd refused the OTC pain meds he'd been offered following his physical exam. He had, however, taken advantage of the food, the bathroom, and the drinks.

That was about it, though. Ever since the six of them had been shown into this cafeteria/hangout room, with its college dorm, concrete-and-throw-rug-style decor, TV, and galley kitchen, he'd been staying away from the others. Short of learning their names, he'd kept on the outside of the group, listening to their stories without offering any details of his own.

Wasn't like he had much to share. He was the only one of his family left, and he was not about to air his personal memories of the raids.

What he did pay attention to was the back-and-forthing of that Peyton guy. The SOB was up and off his couch, checking the bunk room every ten seconds.

Why the guy didn't just stay in—

This time, when Peyton poked his head through the door, there was some conversation. Then he went in and shut the door solidly. When the male came back out after a little while, he went over to the Anslam guy and whispered something. Whatever it was, Anslam agreed with a shrug and a nod.

And then Peyton went back to sitting in the middle of the room.

Not long thereafter, Paradise came out— and the instant she was through the doorway, everyone looked over at her, the conversating about *Tosh.0* stopping.

Craeg turned away from her, mostly because he resented like hell the fact that his blood pressure rose and his heart rate increased just at the sight of the female.

Damn it, none of these people were his business. Especially not her.

"Lady and gentlemales," Peyton said. "We have our *Primus*."

"Don't call me that," she gritted before any kind of applause could happen. "Ever."

"Why?" Novo challenged. "You beat all of us. You lasted the longest. You should be fucking proud of it."

Okay, now *there* was the female he should have been going for—not that he was interested in anything sexual from anybody at the moment. Still, Novo was his kind of "lady"—one who knew her way around an obstacle course and was clearly the type to clock an offender first and ask questions only after the jaw she'd broken had been reset.

Novo also looked damned good in that loose Hanes

T-shirt and those surgical scrubs she'd traded her trashed clothes in for.

He wasn't the only one who'd noticed, either. Anslam, Axe, and even that Peyton fucker had been checking her out surreptitiously—not that she'd seemed to care, or even notice.

The receptionist, on the other hand, was no doubt very used to everyone looking at her. Blondes like her never failed to get attention.

It could make them targets, too.

And yeah, that was what he'd been thinking when he'd stood over her desk and suggested she enter the program. Sure, a female such as herself was protected by the males in her family, but that didn't always work, did it?

His own sister would have been alive today if that had been true.

"... with us?"

Craeg looked up at Novo. "What?"

"We're going to go find someone to get us more to eat. We've finished everything in the fridge and the cupboards here. You want to come?"

"No."

"Then I'll get more of those double-stuffed Oreos for you. You ate them all."

"You don't have to."

"I know," she said as she turned away.

Crossing his arms over his chest, he winced as he shoved his ass further down in the chair and kicked out his legs. Shut-eye. That was what he needed—and as he heard the door close, he exhaled.

"You aren't hungry?"

His lids popped open and he shifted his head. Paradise was still by the door of the bunk room, and she looked about as relaxed as he no longer felt, standing there with her arms around her middle and her robe lapels tight to her throat.

"No," he snapped.

Shit, there was no reason to bite her head off.

"I mean . . . no." Great, he sounded like a total idiot.

"How are your feet?"

"Fine." There was a pause, as if she were waiting for him to ask the same of her. "Look, why don't you go with the others—"

"You can't kick me out of here, you know."

He lowered his lids. "You've got to get over this thing about trying to talk to me."

"Why? What did I ever do to—"

Craeg sprang up out of his chair and crossed the distance between them. Getting all into her space, he made sure she had plenty of time to measure exactly how big he was.

"You were saying?" he said in a low voice. "Or are you leaving."

Her blue eyes stretched wide. "Are you threatening me?"

"Just suggesting a relocation that will be better for both of us."

"Why don't *you* leave?"

"I got here first."

"Because you failed . . . riiiiight. You lost to a girl . . . riiiiiiiiiiiight."

Craeg ground his molars. "Don't push me, okay. I've had as long a night as you have."

"You were the one who came over here like a charging bull. And I would leave—because I really don't like you as much as I thought I would. The truth is, though, my feet hurt so badly I can't really walk, and I have too much pride to ask for a wheelchair."

Total.

Fucking.

Asshole.

Yeah, that was pretty much how he felt as he dropped his stare further and saw her shoeless, sockless feet in all their gory non-glory: Angry red welts had sprung up on the sides and across the tops, and the right one was so swollen, it looked like it didn't belong at the end of her slender ankle.

He closed his lids for a moment. Walk away. Just go back to your little chair, buddy, sit down again, and let her limp on over to the sofa and stretch out or . . . head back into the bunk room . . . or sprout wings and fly away from your sorry, nasty ass.

Instead, he found himself sinking to the floor. Both of his knees cracked so loudly, it was like snapping a pair of branches in the quiet room, and his thighs and calves screamed at the change in position.

"They look really bad," he said softly.

He didn't mean to reach out and touch her skin. He really didn't. But somehow his hand went forward and he brushed the top of the left one—on what was the only stretch of non-red skin.

Above him, he heard her inhale sharply, and for some reason, he didn't trust himself to look up at her. "Did I hurt you?"

It was a while before she answered in a breathless voice, "No."

He ran his fore- and middle fingers so lightly across the top of her foot that he could only sense the warmth in her skin.

Craeg's own body shuddered. And his voice wasn't steady as he said, "I hate to see these marks."

She probably had them elsewhere, too. Contusions, bruises, scrapes, places that were rubbed raw. He wanted to touch all of them.

Touch other parts of her, too.

This was bad, he thought. Dear God, this was very bad. . . .

His sex drive had been asleep for a long time and the last thing he needed right now was for it to wake up, especially under these conditions. Especially with a female like her.

You didn't have to be an aristocrat to be a lady. Even commoners who were working girls could have standards and appropriately save themselves for a proper mating.

Which would not be to an orphaned floor layer's son.

Oh, and she was very, very clearly a virgin.

The way she held herself told him that. The way Peyton, who was clearly a player, respected her space told him that.

But mostly he knew it because of that inhale, that whispered *no*.

This was realllllly bad.

Chapter Fourteen

Paradise's heart was like something out of a drum section, and the surges of heat crashing through her body were as bold and bright as a set of cymbals.

Craeg was down on the floor in front of her, his huge body folded into some kind of awkward sitting position, the muscles of his shoulders straining the thin white T-shirt he was wearing, his dark head bent as he carefully ran his fingertips over the top of her foot.

Even though she was exhausted, she felt every nuance of his touch—and also became achingly aware that she was naked under the robe and the johnny.

Man . . . forget about the aches and pains. What agony?

The only thing that registered from her body was some great, undefined potential she didn't fully understand, but wasn't completely ignorant of, either.

This was . . . sexual attraction. Lust. Desire.

Right here, right now.

Unrepentant, unforgiving, uncompromising chemical attraction.

"I shouldn't be touching you like this," he said softly.

No, she thought. He shouldn't. "Don't stop."

His head angled up, and his eyes met hers. "This is not a good idea."

Definitely was not. Really, totally, definitely was not. "I feel drunk."

Craeg closed his eyes and winced. "I gotta stop."

But he didn't. He just ran that finger up onto her ankle and then higher to her shin.

"I don't have any clothes on," she blurted.

Now he bowed his head and rubbed his face with the hand that wasn't touching her. "Please don't tell me things like that."

"I'm sorry. I don't know what I'm saying."

"I realize that."

As his body seemed to tremble, she whispered, "Is this why you don't like me? This connection?"

"Yes."

"So you feel it, too."

"I'd have to be dead not to," he muttered.

"This is what they talk about, isn't it. This need."

He groaned and swayed even though he was already on the ground. "Don't . . ."

"Don't what?"

Craeg just shook his head, and pushed himself away from her. Putting his knees up, he rested his forearms on them and seemed to try to gather himself. After a moment, he awkwardly shifted his pelvis a couple of times, as if something were stuck or cramping there.

"I'm not going to do this with you," he said in a low voice. "The training program is all I've got. It's the only future I have—so staying in it and doing well is not some vanity thing to me. I'm not trying to prove anything to my parents, either, and I don't just have some jones to get out and fight the world. I literally have nothing waiting for me. So I won't let anything or anyone get in my way."

"You can't do both?" she said, even though she wasn't sure what she was suggesting.

Oh, bullshit on that. She knew *exactly* what she was suggesting: Having had his hands on her ankle, she wanted to know what they felt like all over her body.

"No," he repeated. "I can't do both."

With a curse, he struggled his way to his feet, his palms going in front of his hips and covering something up as he walked back over to where he'd been sitting before. He didn't lower himself into the chair, though. He stayed standing, staring down at the cushions, big body tense.

"You don't have to protect me," she said.

After a moment, he looked over his shoulder at her — and his face was grim. "Fuck that. I'm protecting myself."

As Butch drove them over the river in the Lexus, Marissa stared out the window next to her. The supports of the bridge made a pattern that cut through the view of the water down below, making her think of windshield wipers on a slow repeat. They were up so high, she couldn't tell if there were waves on the surface. Probably not. It was a quiet night weather-wise.

For some reason, she kept going back to when the two of them had fallen in love — probably because her brain couldn't handle where they were headed and so it was escaping to a part of her past that had been filled with wonder and joy and excitement.

Nothing like that first touch. That first kiss. That moment when you had sex for the first time, and you looked at the face above yours and thought, *I can't believe we're really doing this!*

"What are you thinking about?" Butch asked, squeezing her hand.

"Do you remember where we first kissed?"

Her mate laughed softly. "God, yeah. It was out on the second-story porch at Darius's. I broke the arm off that wicker chair."

She smiled and looked across at him. "You did, didn't you."

"I hadn't expected you to be so . . . strong."

In the dim light of the dashboard, his features were just as sexy as they had always been to her, and she thought about what he looked like when he was aroused, his hazel eyes going all hooded, his face becoming so serious, his body stilling before he pounced.

"I want to have sex with you when we get back home," she said.

His head whipped around so fast, the sedan swerved in its lane. "Well, what do you know. That can *so* be arranged."

"I feel guilty about it."

"Don't." His eyes met hers. "It's very natural. You want to feel alive in the face of death—it doesn't mean that you aren't sad for the girl, or won't do right by her. The two are not mutually exclusive."

"You're very smart."

"Just had a lot of experience in nights like tonight."

Easing back in the luxurious seat, she let the familiar, erotic sensations pump through her body . . . and imagined herself ducking underneath his arms, and getting into his fly, and sucking on him as he drove along.

But he would never let her do that.

And besides, as they hit the far side of the Hudson, her brain switched gears. "Please don't hurt him."

"Who? Your brother?"

"Yes."

"I'll be a gentleman through and through."

She glanced over at him. "I mean it."

"So do I." He gave her hand a squeeze. "You got nothing to worry about. I wouldn't do that to you—and that makes him a very lucky guy."

Butch followed the directions that had been texted to her when she'd asked for the way in by car, and about fifteen minutes later, they were bumping down a dirt lane that meandered through the forest. This time, the entry building was a modest two-story farmhouse, and there were a couple of sedans parked on its cobblestone driveway. When they got out, they proceeded around back to what appeared to be an outbuilding for tractor equipment, but which was actually the same kind of kiosk she had been to earlier in the evening.

The procedure was the same: checking in, stepping in, getting scanned by a laser. And then a wall of tools was displaced and they were in an elevator, heading down into the earth.

"This must have cost a lot of money to build," she murmured as they both stared up at the dinging lineup of numbers over the doors. "Four stories underground? Wow."

"It needed to be done."

She looked across at him. "Wait, so you know about this new clinic? Why didn't you tell me?"

Butch shrugged. "I didn't want to upset you by bringing up your brother." He glanced over at her pointedly. "Tell me Havers behaved himself when you were here earlier."

"He did."

Her mate nodded and jacked up his fine black slacks. As always, when he was off duty, her Southie cop *hellren* was dressed like something out of the Neiman Marcus catalog, his crisp white shirt and his paper-thin suede jacket every bit as expensive as they looked. He smelled good, too, although that was courtesy of his bonding scent and not any kind of cologne—and his Piaget watch and that large gold cross he always wore were sexy without being overdone.

And yet he was right. If he'd wanted to, he could have killed her brother with his bare hands—and he probably did want to. She believed him, however, when he said he would never do that in front of her.

"He's amazing to his patients," she heard herself murmur.

"That has never been his problem."

No, it hadn't.

The elevator bumped to a halt and they emerged into another waiting area that was smaller and more self-contained than the other one she'd been in.

The receptionist at the desk looked at Butch first— and then took her time in giving him the once-over. Not that he noticed. "Welcome," she said. "The doctor knows that you're here. May I get you coffee while you wait?"

Or perhaps something more personal? her tone seemed to suggest.

"We're good, thanks." Butch took Marissa's elbow and led her over to the line-up of chairs against the far wall.

As they settled in together, she was glad when he held her hand.

"So how was the program's first night?" she asked, both to make conversation and because she cared.

His brows locked together in a frown. "It was good— no one got seriously hurt. We have seven who made it through. They're going to spend the day with us—mostly because we don't want their parents to see them that beat-up. Also, it's a good chance for the group to start getting tight. I teach the first class at nightfall, and then they'll be allowed to go home after a workout."

"I'm really glad it went well."

"We'll see. Hey, you know Abalone's daughter, Paradise? Who helps out at the audience house?"

"Oh, she's lovely."

"She lasted the longest. That girl has a core of steel."

"Abalone must be so proud."

"He will be."

They fell silent. Until she spoke up again. "I think I'm going to be sick."

Butch immediately started to jump up, but she patted his arm. "I mean that more as an expression than an actual intention."

"Do you want to go back to the car? I can bring the remains out to you."

Marissa shook her head. "No, she's mine. Until we find her proper family, she's mine."

Butch put an arm around her shoulders and drew her in close. "Be ready for that not to change even when you give her back to her bloodline."

"Is that how you . . . when you were working, is that how you felt?"

"With every one of my victims." He exhaled long and slow. "For me, they never went away. Even now, when I can't sleep, I see their faces on the ceiling above our bed.

I remember what they looked like in life, and can't forget how they lay in death. It's a stain on my brain."

Staring at his profile, his hard, beautiful, imperfect profile, she plugged into all the love she had for him. "Why don't you wake me up and talk to me when you're like that?"

His tight smile was all about the downplay. "You have a job, too."

"Yes, but I—"

"It doesn't matter. It's in the past now."

Not if it's still keeping you up, it isn't, she thought.

"You and I are so alike," she murmured. "We've both shelved our old lives."

"You make that sound like it's a bad thing."

Before she could say anything else, the door across the way opened and a nurse in a white uniform walked in with a black box that absurdly—and inappropriately—made Marissa think of the pair of Stuart Weitzman stilettos that had been delivered to her the other night. Same size.

She'd expected the container to be bigger. Smaller. Different.

God, she didn't know.

"We're so sorry for your loss," the nurse said as she went to hand it off to Butch.

Marissa stepped in and took the thing. It weighed less than she'd thought it would. Then again, it was only full of ashes, wasn't it. "Thank you."

The female flushed at the lack of protocol: As Marissa was a female from a Founding Family, it was assumed that she would never touch anything pertaining to the dead: In the Old Country, such contact was seen as bad luck, particularly if one was pregnant or of young-bearing age.

Screw that, though.

"Was there anything else with her things?" Marissa asked.

The nurse cleared her throat like she was trying to swallow her disapproval and choking on the stuff. "Actually, there was something." She glanced at Butch as if she were looking for him to step forward and get his mate to be reasonable. "Ah . . ."

To his credit, Butch just cocked a brow like he didn't know what the hell the female was going on about.

The nurse cleared her throat again. "Well, there was one thing. It was the only personal effect we found—it was tucked into her . . ."

"Into her what?" Marissa demanded.

"Into her brassiere." The nurse put her hand into the pocket of her uniform and took out a length of black something or another with a ribbon of red fabric on it. "Are you sure you want to . . ."

Marissa snatched the thing out of the nurse's hold. "Thank you. We'll be going now."

Before anything else could be said, she headed over and punched the "up" arrow on the wall. As if the elevator had been waiting to help her GTFO, the doors opened and she stepped inside. Butch was, as always, right behind her.

It was only when they were ascending back to ground level that she looked at what she'd taken from the other female.

"What is this?" she said, turning over the four-inch-long piece of black metal in her hand. There was a red silk tassel hanging off a cut out on one end, and on the other, a pointed, notched portion seemed like something that would fit in a lock. "Is this a key?"

Butch took it from her and examined the thing. "You know, it might be."

Chapter Fifteen

By sundown the following evening, Peyton had decided he didn't like any of them.

Look, it wasn't that he thought he was better than the other five trainees. There was just something off with each one.

Axe, that outlier with the punk/Goth, yeah-we-get-it-you're-a-hard-ass style? Obvious. The bastard was one kitchen knife away from being a serial killer. Boone, the Adonis with those muscles? Uh-huh, we know you can walk on your hands and throw your ass around like it's attached to your throat with a rope—but who cares. You're here to fight, not slap on a tutu and try to get into the Cirque du Soleil. Anslam? Nothing but an also-ran in the *glymera*, not even from a Founding Family. Irrelevant, and a shock that he'd made it as far as he had.

The one he really didn't like, though, was that Craeg guy—although that was actually more because of the way everybody, even Paradise, treated him like he was the anointed leader of the group.

Not that Peyton was looking for that job, but come on. Nobody had a lock on any of this yet. There was no reason to be getting out the pedestal so soon.

And that wasn't the only thing that bugged him about the guy. There was something else about the male, something he couldn't quite put his finger on. An instinct, maybe? A sense of some kind of threat?

He didn't know—but he was damn sure going to figure that one out.

And then there was that Novo female.

Stretching in his chair in the break room, Peyton surreptitiously glanced in her vague-ish direction. She was
laying out on the sofa to the left, her long, long, long legs
crossed at the ankles, her hands clasped over her flat
stomach like she was dead. Her hair was iris-black, stick
straight, and plaited tight as a rope. Her skin was honey-
brown, and he had never, ever in his fucking life seen a
female built with that kind of muscle.

He'd spent most of the day trying to avoid measuring
her breasts—mostly because he wasn't sure whether
she'd cut his balls off if she noticed.

Rubbing his eyes, he wanted a blunt so badly he was
shaking from it.

Maybe Paradise had a point about the drug use.

Then again, it had been one long frickin' night and one
weird frickin' day. After he'd made sure Paradise was
awake and eating, the rest of them—except for Craeg the
Great Fanged One who was better than everybody else—
had gone for a wander around the facilities, found a *doggen* and asked for more food. Then they'd come back here
to find Paradise once again in the bunk room asleep, and
Craeg sitting up in a chair with his eyes closed.

Probably contemplating how superior his belly lint
was to everyone else's.

At that point, without a lot of conversation, they'd each
picked a spot in the unadorned room and proceeded to
not sleep very much or very well. Much as he hated to
admit the weakness, he was still jumping at any sound
that was out of place, his adrenal gland on hyper-alert
even though the nurse who'd examined him had told him
that the trial was over and nothing else of an electrical-
shock/throat-punch nature was going to come at them—

Without warning, Paradise stuck her head out the
bunk room door, like maybe she was expecting to find
herself left behind.

As Peyton opened his mouth to say her name, he caught Craeg's eyes shifting over to her . . . and pulling the classic head-to-toe males did when they were frickin' man-whore sonsabitches.

It was his own signature move, for fuck's sake.

Before he could bark at the guy to back off, the door to the outer hall opened wide, and two enormous males walked in like they owned the place.

Brothers.

Talk about coming to attention. All six of the loafer trainees were up and out of their whatevers like someone had goosed them in the ass. By the bunk room door, Paradise straightened and pulled her robe lapels even closer.

The Brother on the left was dressed in jeans and a black shirt—and he was quite possibly the largest living thing Peyton had ever seen outside of an elephant. He was also so good-looking, you had to wonder why the Scribe Virgin had dumped all that hotness on one guy—as opposed to spreading it more evenly over a cast of thousands.

And next to him was a slightly shorter male who was built like a bulldog, drinking a coffee, and wearing a Boston Red Sox sweatshirt.

"The beauty queen next to me is Rhage," the guy in the sweatshirt said. "I'm Butch. And we already know who the fuck you are. The time is currently six o'clock in the evening. You will have one hour to shower in the locker rooms, dress in the uniforms that will be brought to you, and come back here to eat. After that, we want you lined up outside in the corridor. Anyone who is late is out of the program."

Butch? Peyton wondered. The Brother's name was *Butch*?

As in from the human world . . . ?

Wait a minute.

"You're the *Dhestroyer*," Peyton heard himself say. "Holy shit, I know who you are. You're mated to Marissa, blooded daughter of—"

"Any questions?" Butch talked over him. "Good. I didn't think so. One hour. That's all you got."

With that shutdown, the male turned and left.

The Brother Rhage gave them a smile. "Try the tenderloin. It's fucking awesome. And the lamb, too. Oh, and the mashed potatoes. Skip the salad. Waste of chewing. Later."

At least he didn't seem to want to kill them, Peyton thought as the door closed once again.

"Wonder what the uniforms look like," Paradise said.

"This isn't a fashion show," Craeg bit out.

Peyton bared his fangs at the guy. "Do you want a problem, asshole? 'Cause I can arrange that."

Craeg's head swiveled toward him. "I wasn't talking to you."

Peyton had no clue what got his feet moving, but before he knew it, he was nose-to-nose with the SOB. "Let's get this straight. You don't look at her. You don't talk to her. And you really, totally *fucking* do not disrespect her. Are we clear."

The male's eyes shifted to Paradise. "Think your boy over here is a little territorial. You mind calling him off before he gets hurt?"

Annnnnnnnd it was on.

Peyton had no conscious thought of going for the motherfucker, but next thing he knew, he was on the male like a coat of paint, fists punching, arms grappling, legs kicking.

He'd actually never been in a fight before, but for some reason his body seemed to know what to do—not that he didn't get his ass kicked. Craeg was taller and heavier, and his reach was like Stretch Armstrong, those punches coming from every direction, reaching his face, his gut, his chest.

People were shouting around them. Furniture got knocked over. He was slammed against the wall—and then paid that back by spinning Craeg around and pushing him into the door to the corridor so hard, he busted the panels clean apart, wood splintering as the pair of them ended up brawling out in the hall.

And still they fought.

For being half-dead only twelve hours before, Peyton found himself with plenty of goddamn energy.

It was like watching something from *Maury*.

As Paradise followed the fight into the corridor, she was having an out-of-body experience. Half of her was in the drama, trying to grab onto a flying arm, or yell in the hopes of getting through to one of them. The other half was in the land of OMG!—because she could not believe this was happening in front of her, on account of her.

Peyton was a lot of things, but never violent.

And Craeg—well, she didn't know much about him, but he'd seemed so much more self-controlled than this.

"Come on!" she barked. "Just stop it!"

The male bodies careened into the concrete wall, some horrible crack suggesting something had gotten broken on one of them—no, actually, it was a cinder block. Meanwhile, blood went flying from Peyton's nose, splashing brilliant red on the white paint, and Craeg's shirt got ripped in half, falling free from his—

Okay, WOW. The guy was lean, but built, great fans of muscle flaring out from either side of his spine, his shoulders bunching up and releasing with every fist he threw, his incredibly tight waist—

Right, this was inappropriate.

But *damn.*

Shaking herself, she lunged forward in another attempt to catch hold and slow things down, and she aimed for Peyton's right arm, because all that nakey was way too much to handle—

Novo grabbed her and dragged her back just when she would have gotten hit in the face.

"Let 'em go," the female said.

"Someone's going to get hurt!"

"Better them than you." Novo rolled her eyes. "Males are idiots. They're just fighting for dominance. Personally, I'd rather save my energy for the real work, as opposed to this social-posturing bullshit."

Paradise panted and cursed. "They're going to get themselves kicked out!"

"If they do, that's on them."

Next to the combatants, Anslam laughed and clapped his palms. "Smack him like a bitch, Peyton!"

Paradise glared at the male. "This is not cockfighting, you know."

"The hell it isn't."

Adding his name to her growing Jackass List, Paradise looked up and down the corridor. No one had come out of anywhere, but given the number of closed doors, that was not going to last—

Suddenly, Craeg changed places, grabbing Peyton by the shoulders, spinning him around, and shoving him up against the wall like he intended to break through the concrete with the guy.

"This is nuts," a male voice drawled.

Glancing behind her, she saw Axe leaning against the doorjamb of the break room, his arms crossed over his chest, his expression that of someone watching paint dry.

Paradise narrowed her eyes at him. "You've got to stop this!"

One of his jet-black brows lifted. "Do I."

"Yes! They're going to get kicked out!"

"And that affects me how?"

She deliberately stopped herself from smacking that sardonic expression off his half-pierced face. "You'd want someone to help you."

"I wouldn't have picked a fight over you. No offense, but fucking you would be like having sex with a department-store mannequin. You're beautiful, but going to be totally useless in the sack."

Paradise's jaw dropped open. "That is the rudest thing anyone has ever said to me."

"Then you've led as sheltered a life as I thought. And whether you're offended or not, the truth is what it is."

Turning to Boone, she opened her mouth—but he shook his head, all nope-not-me. "What is wrong with you people?" she demanded.

At least the fight was slowing down—oh, yeah, no, it was still going strong: Craeg grabbed Peyton around the waist and took him to the floor, the males grappling now, bare feet squeaking on the polished stone, palms slapping.

And that was when Butch and Rhage came storming down at the group.

Putting her head in her hands, she waited for the yelling to start. If this was anything like the human army she had read about or seen in movies, they were probably all going to get punished for this. Maybe she would get thrown out for being a troublemaker, even though she had done nothing except make a nervous comment.

Maybe just Peyton and Craeg would get disciplined.

After either one or both of them were out of their body cast(s).

When the combat only continued, she glanced through her fingers at the Brothers. The pair of them were standing off to the side, watching the action, talking to each other. And then Rhage nodded . . . and they shook hands.

Paradise looked around at the other trainees—and found that everybody else had disappeared back into the sitting room.

It was sometime later that Peyton finally lost.

One misplanned head butt sent his forehead directly into the concrete floor. At which point there was a horrible sound, like a bowling ball had been dropped onto a slab of stone—and the guy's body went lax as if his bones had been liquefied.

Craeg shoved him away and collapsed flat on his back, breathing hard, coughing, wiping blood out of his eyes.

"How much was it?" Rhage asked Butch.

"Fiver."

"Damn, I thought my boy was going to do better than that." Rhage shoved his hand into his pocket and took out a black wallet. Withdrawing a bill, he slapped it into Butch's palm. "We're going double or nothing the next time one starts."

Paradise recoiled as they turned away and walked off like absolutely nothing had happened.

"Are you kidding me," she said under her breath.

She wanted to call after them that Peyton was still passed out cold—no, wait. He was groaning and rolling over onto his back.

At least he was alive, she thought as she walked over to him.

"What the hell is wrong with you?" she demanded. "You want to get kicked out?"

Granted, that threat would have had more teeth if their two professors had been doing something more stern than betting on the damn fight.

The two males looked up at her with lolling stares. God, they looked as bad as they had the night before— maybe even worse. Hell, they were both going to have black eyes, and Craeg's lip was split so deep, he probably needed stitches.

"I'm . . . fine," Peyton mumbled before spitting blood.

"Yeah," Craeg lisped. "Just fine."

Which came out something like *Jusssth phine.*

"Tell me," she barked, "how many fingers am I holding up."

Putting out her middle one, she gave the pair of jackholes a chance to focus on the fact that she was flipping them both off. And then she marched away to find somebody in a nurse's uniform . . . doctor's scrubs . . .

Goddamn janitor's uniform.

God knew the corridor was going to need to be cleaned up—and anyone with a broom could start with the two wastes of space that had made the mess.

Chapter Sixteen

Twenty-five minutes, two stitches in his lower lip, and a snatch-and-grab First Meal later, and Craeg was front and center in the gym with the other six members of his class. Well, not front and not in the center of the lineup — he was more off to the side and back a little.

He was also weaving on his feet.

The last thing his body had needed was another full-on, high-contact, knuckle-cracker of a fistfight, but he wasn't going to back down from class. And as for Peyton, Paradise's so called "not boyfriend?" Uh-huh. Riiiiii-ight.

Fucker.

Him, not her.

The good news was that as bad off as he himself was, Peyton wasn't even able to stand. He'd been wheeled in on a stretcher like a piece of meat.

Wheeled in.

Who won that one, bitch?

Oh, and neither of them had been kicked out. Apparently, short of betting on the outcome, the Brothers weren't going to get involved —

One of the doors to the gym was punched open, and this time, as the Brothers Butch and Rhage came in, they were dressed in the same loose-fitting cotton pants and shirt that everyone else was.

The Brother Butch didn't waste any time as they

came to a halt in front of the group. "So, in light of all the Mayweather/Pacquiao going down, we're gonna start with hand-to-hand combat instead of book learning."

"Please note," Rhage said with a smile, "that your unis are white."

"It's because OxiClean is wicked good on bloodstains, but we're prepared to use Clorox if we have to."

Craeg swallowed a curse. Just what he needed.

"We're going to pair you up," Butch continued, "and get an assessment of how much you know. Since one of you is already on the horizontal, no one has to worry about fighting Hollywood over here."

"Personally, I'm about to cry over that," Rhage said. "So let's put Novo with Boone—Axe, you take Anslam. That leaves Craeg and Paradise."

"Hold up," Craeg said. "I can't . . . I won't do that."

"Hit her? Why? 'Cause you can't lift your arms up? Not my problem."

Craeg leaned in and dropped his voice. "I won't hit her."

Rhage shrugged. "Fine, you can get your ass kicked again."

Butch cut in. "Actually, he won that fight, remember. And I got your five bucks to prove it."

"Only because golden boy over here knocked his own self out."

"A loss is a loss." Butch refocused on Craeg. "But my brother is right. You either defend yourself or go back for more of Doc Jane's thread. Your choice."

With that, they were told to spread out into different quadrants of the enormous gym, and Peyton was wheeled off to the side.

Craeg watched the others go, trying to think of a way out of this. Funny, when he'd told her way back when that she should enter the program to learn self-defense, he hadn't considered that he was the one she'd have to be defending herself against.

Even in a "classroom" situation.

"Well," Paradise said as she came up to him. "Are we going to do this?"

"I'll wait until one of the males is finished."

"You're serious."

He looked down at her from his much greater height. "I don't want to hurt you."

"You didn't beat Peyton with ease," she muttered. "That took, like, half an hour."

"You're actually comparing yourself to a full-grown adult male. Who I put on a stretcher."

"Oh, you're right. That wouldn't be fair. Because compared to the two of you, I'm a goddamn genius."

As she put her hands on her hips and glared at him, he wondered what in the hell else was he going to say to her? He didn't want to spout the real truth—which had everything to do with the fact that he could still remember what her soft skin felt like . . . could still picture how small her ankle had been compared to his palm . . . could imagine so many things he wanted to do to her, absolutely none of which involved violence of any kind.

Absolutely all of which included contact with his fingertips, his lips . . . his tongue.

Craeg crossed his arms over his chest. "I'm not going to fight you."

"So if I swing at you, you're going to do nothing."

He cocked a brow. "I'm not worried about getting knocked out."

"Oh, really."

"No. Your lesser endurance aside, you're not going—"

The next thing that came out of his mouth was a high-pitched scream that left everyone in the gym ripping around to see what the hell had happened.

And he might have told them—but he was too busy covering his nuts with both hands and bending at the waist.

She had kneed him in the groin.

In the groin. With her knee.

"What the fuck!" he sputtered. "Why did you do that?"

She seemed as surprised as everyone else. But she recovered fast—by clamping a hold on either side of his head, bringing up that knee again, and nailing him so hard in the face, he saw more stars than a human Christmas tree had lights.

As he let out another howl and lurched off balance, she locked both of her hands together, extended her arms, and swung around in a tight circle like she was throwing a discus—catching him in the temple with enough force to knock his legs right out from under him.

Boom! Down he went to the blue mats.

Everyone came running as she stood over him, braced for whatever came at her—while he made out with the floor.

Shoving his palms into the mats, he hefted his upper body to the vertical and looked at her. "You really want me to do this."

"You haven't done anything yet," somebody cracked.

"Tell me," another one chimed in. "Do you take a piss sitting down?"

"He does now," came a reply.

Paradise just tracked every move he made, each twitch and breath and shift of his eyes. But she had no idea what she was doing. He could tell by the way her hands were trembling, and the fact that her ribs were pumping way too hard for the physical activity she'd just done.

She was also ever so slightly aroused.

Okay, that was straight-up trouble. The scent of her sex triggered the very male part of him—and made him want her to run just so he could chase her and catch her and get her underneath him to take her hard. He wanted her nails scratching his back as she came . . . and her fangs bared right before she took a vein at his throat.

The lust was so strong, he could have fucked her even if there were people watching—and as if she recognized the change in him, she took a step back.

And then suddenly no one was laughing or joking at him anymore.

Butch stepped in between them. "Easy, there, big guy. How about you come at me?"

The Brother sank down into a fighting stance, his fists up in front of his chest, his eyes narrowed.

But Craeg wasn't interested in the male. He looked around those mammoth shoulders to Paradise, who was staring at him with an inscrutable expression on her face.

This time, when a punch came at him, Craeg went into full fight mode, something that had not happened with Peyton. With the other trainee, he had given about sixty percent of what he had, holding some of his strength back because he had been afraid of killing the piece of shit, or doing permanent damage—and thereby getting booted from the program. Now? The knife-edge of his arousal cut through all restraint as he went into the hand-to-hand battle, ducking, throwing a fist of his own, ducking again, jabbing. The Brother was viciously quick, mercilessly powerful, eminently trained.

Not like Peyton at all.

And as the fight wore on, as they traded kicks and dodges, grabs and grapples, more people came over and stood around, until there was a crowd of ten, fifteen . . . twenty in the gym.

It was about fifteen minutes in when the daggers got tossed at them.

The two razor-sharp, black-handled, silver-bladed knives flew through the air from out of nowhere. Butch caught one on the fly. Craeg caught the other. And then they were circling, searching for a way past defenses, weaving the weapons back and forth—lunging, retreating, the stakes so much higher.

Butch wasn't breathing heavily at all. Craeg, on the other hand, was panting like a motherfucker—sweating like one, too.

First blood was drawn when Craeg misjudged one arc by a millimeter and got his cheek cut open. When he miscalled another, he started leaking at the shoulder. Mistaking a third, he got his thigh sliced.

It was then that he realized the Brother was giving him just sixty percent of what the male was capable of: The precision of the cuts told Craeg that his opponent knew more than he did, was stronger than he was, and was prepared to nick his way to a victory based on incremental blood loss.

But Craeg wasn't going to give up. Not yet, at any rate. Not until he couldn't stand, couldn't see, couldn't move.

His will would accept nothing less.

Paradise recognized immediately that this fight was a totally different thing than that mad, sloppy scramble that had rolled out into the corridor earlier. In fact, back with Peyton, Craeg had been reining himself in for some reason; he was no longer. His coordination as he faced off against Butch with his fists, and then—oh, God, those daggers—told her, and everybody else in the gym, that he was an incredible fighter, capable of great strength, balance, flexibility, and power.

It was enough to make her entire body light up like a switchboard.

And no, she thought, as much as she respected Novo's females-can-do-everything-males-can, it was very clear to her that she could not have handled the likes of what Craeg was putting out now. He would have knocked her cold with just one of those knuckle punches. Or snapped her head clean off her spine. Or broken one of her legs with an easy twist.

Not that she couldn't learn appropriate defenses and counter-measures, she just didn't know them now—and he had, in fact, been prepared to attack her: When he'd crouched down and bared his tremendous fangs, she had stumbled back—and yet, for some insane reason, she hadn't been afraid of him. Which was just plain nuts. He had more than a hundred pounds on her, and he'd been out for blood.

So yeah, what was totally insane? She had suddenly wanted to run from him—but not too fast. She'd wanted him to come after her, and catch her on the fly . . . and . . .

Well, it was back to that moment they'd shared when they'd been alone in the break room.

But Jesus, I can't handle him, she thought as she watched him move. And not just in a fight: Any female who set chase to a male like that wasn't getting a sweet kiss at the end of the running—she wasn't getting a hand held and a sacred promise of a bonded mating and a conversation with her father where said suitor bashfully asked for permission.

This was not the kind of refined male one was expected to give one's virginity to on the night of her mating before the Scribe Virgin and her family.

No, he was an animal with only a modicum of higher reasoning.

And the way he'd looked at her in that moment had suggested that his brain had checked out entirely.

She should have been afraid, she told herself again.

Instead, she wanted him to catch her—

All around, the crowd let out a hiss as Craeg took another cut, this time right across the chest. He was bleeding in several places now, his sparring uniform stained red, blood dripping from his chin from the slice on his cheek, dripping from his thigh, dripping from his pecs.

Another flash of the Brother's blade caught him on the opposite shoulder. Then it was the side of the throat. The other thigh, the abdomen, across the back.

"Stop," Paradise said under her breath. "Stop coming at him."

But every time that vicious blade of the Brother's struck, Craeg went back for more, reengaging over and over again, until he was slipping in the puddles he was making on the blue mats, and his uniform was stained red and plastered to his body.

He wouldn't relent.

And Butch gave him no quarter except to spare him death.

"Craeg! Stop!" she called out because she couldn't help herself.

Putting her hand to her mouth, she felt her heart go back into panic mode as she wondered whether he really would keep going until he'd lost so much from his veins there was no coming back.

"Craeg! This is crazy!"

But still he continued, until he started to sag into his knees, and lurch instead of lunge, and wobble when he retreated. Now, the sloppiness came to him.

God, he was too pale.

"Stop!"

From over on his gurney, Peyton sat up and yelled, "Craeg! Come on, man—he's gonna kill you."

Ripples of unease passed through the other trainees, but not through all the Brothers who had come to watch the show. The medical people, in contrast, also didn't look thrilled—however, when the female doctor with the blond hair went to step forward, the Brother Vishous shook his head and made her stay beside him.

Craeg went down for the last time forty-two minutes and many, many liters of lost plasma later.

He just dropped to his knees, swayed for a moment . . . and then fell facedown in his own blood. Exactly as he had done out on the track.

Paradise rushed to go forward, but Rhage caught her and yanked her back. "No. You allow him his honor."

"What are you talking about?" she hissed.

Rhage just nodded toward the two combatants. "Watch."

Butch stood over the fallen male for a moment, giving Craeg a chance to get back to his feet. When he did not, the Brother waited for Craeg to look up at him.

Unfocused eyes struggled in an ashen face to lock onto the Brother. But when they finally did, Butch switched the weapon to his other hand . . . and scored his dagger palm deeply with the blade.

As Paradise gasped, the Brother extended his palm to Craeg—who, from out of nowhere, suddenly found the strength to reach up and accept what was offered.

The Brother pulled Craeg to his feet . . . and embraced him. "Good job, son. I'm proud of you."

Craeg blinked his eyes fast, as if he were tearing up. Then he seemed to give up the fight against his emotions by closing his lids, tucking his head and sagging into the Brother's arms.

"And that," Rhage said in a loud, approving voice, "is how you do it."

Chapter Seventeen

Sitting at her desk at Safe Place, Marissa had all kinds of work to do: patient files to read, intake papers to approve, bills to process. Instead of tackling any of that, she just sat in her chair and stared at that black strip of metal with its red tassel.

After she and Butch had gotten home, she'd shown the odd, key-like object to a number of the Brothers, and none of them had recognized it or been able to put a solid name to the thing. Then Vishous had done an Internet search on an image of it—and come up with nothing.

By the time she and Butch had gone to bed, she'd been so exhausted, she'd fallen asleep as soon as her head had hit the pillow.

But she hadn't stayed that way.

Her eyes had opened at around three in the afternoon, and she had lain on her back, staring up in the darkness while Butch had snored quietly next to her.

It was just as her *hellren* had said. Images of that female had played across the blank ceiling, a photo montage that had made her tear up. And the sad thing was, the urge to cry had gotten even worse as she'd thought of her and Butch.

Which was crazy.

There was nothing wrong between them. He couldn't have been more supportive, taking her out to Havers's, sticking with her through her efforts with the key, being understanding of everything she was feeling.

"I'm losing my mind," she said—

"That's what I'm here for."

Marissa jerked her head up. "Mary, hi—sorry, I was talking to myself. I'm a little scrambled right now."

Rhage's *shellan* came in and closed the office's door. "Yeah, I got that impression—I've been saying your name three or four times and not getting through."

Marissa eased back, pushed her hair over her shoulders, and forced a smile. "What can I do for you?"

"You can talk to me." The female sat down in the chair across the desk. "I'm worried about you."

"Oh, God, don't waste a second on that. We've got people here who are seriously in need of your help—"

"Good Samaritans like you and I have trouble doing our jobs if we don't talk about the hard cases. It's a fact. I'd also like to point out that I'm a friend of yours."

In the silence that followed, Marissa kept quiet about all the paperwork she hadn't been able to concentrate on because her head was messed up. And then she remained silent about the day she'd spent not sleeping. And finally, she said nothing about the strange distance between her and Butch—

"I can't get her out of my mind," she blurted.

Immediately, tears came, and she cursed as she reached for a Kleenex. "I don't want to talk about this."

"I know," Mary said gently. "Trust me, I've had a lot of personal experience with not talking. It wasn't a good strategy."

"Oh, come on, you're the most self-actualized person I've ever met. You're like a ten out of ten on the relating scale."

"You've only seen a snapshot of my life, Marissa. You didn't know me before. And I still struggle, just like everyone else."

Marissa blotted under her eyes and had to fight a

wave of straight-up bawling. "How do you deal with that."

"The struggling? I talk to people. I talk to Rhage. I write things down."

"No . . . the clean cut."

"I'm sorry?"

Marissa waved her tissue around. "I'm not making any sense. Just forget—"

"You mean the fact that one life ended for me and another began when I got with Rhage?"

God, her heart was pounding for no good reason. "Yes. That's exactly it."

Mary crossed her legs and chewed on her lower lip, and as she took time to compose her thoughts, Marissa studied her even-featured face, and her newly bobbed brown hair, and her aura of calm confidence.

Yes, Marissa thought, Rhage was right. The female was gorgeous—not in the flashy, beauty-queen kind of way, or the all-angles, no meat, anorexic model stuff, and not even the girl-next-door standard. Mary was like the glow of a banked fire in the deep vicious winter, warm and sustaining, captivating and illuminating.

No wonder the Brother adored her.

With an exhale, Mary said, "I think it was different for me because I was dying—so I knew I was leaving? Even though I wasn't aware of the cancer being back for a while, I'd been preparing for the day when they'd tell me it had returned. So I'd checked out. Packed my mental and emotional bags, got my ticket, was ready to go. I mean, my mother was gone, I hadn't really connected with anyone else on the planet . . . there was nothing for me so there wasn't anything to walk away from, if that makes sense?"

Marissa thought about the night her brother had kicked her out for being with Butch.

"If I understand things correctly," Mary said, "that was not the case for you. Was it."

Marissa had to look away. "No, it was not. I came back to the house Havers and I shared one evening just before dawn and he . . ." Now, her tears welled and fell in a rush, one after another, landing on her blouse, her slacks. She mopped up before she could go on. "All of my things had been packed. He told me he didn't care where I went, he just wanted me out of his house. He put money . . ." She had to clear her throat. "He put money on one of the bureaus. It was as if he didn't want to touch me."

Sniffling, she popped free another tissue and blew her nose. "I kept the cash. I still have those hundred-dollar bills. Sometimes, when I run into them in my drawer, I think, why do I keep them? Why am I—oh, for heaven's sake." She had to take a third tissue. "What is wrong with me? That girl is dead, and I can't find her family or who killed her—and I'm sitting here whining about my stupid-ass brother who's old news. This is ridiculous."

"This is past trauma," Mary pointed out evenly.

"I am annoying myself."

"Well, have you thought about what really happened last night?"

"Are you kidding me? There's nothing else on my damned mind."

"No, I mean have you *thought* about it."

"If your point is that I had to watch a young female die in front of me and that her loss is a tragic waste of life that I am apparently powerless to make right, yes, of course I have."

Mary shook her head. "With all due respect, you're missing my point. Last night, for the first time since Havers ended your relationship with the only blood you have, you were forced to rely on him for help. You couldn't save the girl, so you had to turn to your brother and hope and pray he did the right thing for her."

"He did, though." Marissa released a hard curse. "I mean, he was amazing with her."

"And how did that make you feel, considering how badly he treated you."

Annnnnd cue more tears. "I did think of that. When I went to see her just before she died."

"Here's what I know to be true. We can bury the past all we like. We can use a hundred thousand distractions, some of which are healthy, some of which are not, to keep it under the ground—but when something isn't processed, it will absolutely, positively come back and bite us on the ass. You had a hard life before you and Butch fell in love, and it was no doubt a huge relief to leave all of it behind and start fresh. But you can't outrun what came before. Remember, Marissa, we are every age we have ever been at each moment in our lives. We carry it all with us like luggage. Sooner or later, the stuff with your brother was going to come up again. That's just life."

Marissa performed another re-blot under her eyes. "I'm having trouble connecting with Butch right now."

"Of course you are. He's the one who caused the break."

Marissa recoiled. "Now, wait a minute, hold on—he has been nothing but good to me—"

"It's not an issue of fault, Marissa. You were on one path, he came into your life, now you're on another. I'm not judging him or even saying he did anything wrong—I'm just stating a fact."

For some reason, she remembered staying wide awake while she let Butch sleep. That never would have happened even a year ago. "What do I do?"

"You're not going to like what I have to say."

"It feels like it can't get worse."

"You're going to have to make peace with your brother."

Marissa closed her eyes. "I will never be able to forgive him."

"Making peace doesn't mean you absolve him of his wrongdoing. And honestly, he isn't the only one you need to come to terms with. The *glymera* treated you horribly, your position within the aristocracy was untenable, and Wrath was a royal shit—and I do mean that with love. You've got a tremendous amount of pain and rejection that you at first held in because it was the only way to survive, and then you put aside because you finally got a break and a chance to feel good in your own life." Mary nodded at all the paperwork on the desk. "If you want to get back to being productive, you're going to have to look under all those rocks, feel your feelings, and come out on the other side of that journey."

Tissue number four came out of the box with a snap, but she didn't end up using it. She just twisted the thing in her hands. "I don't want to forget the girl. I don't want this to be all about me."

"No one says you have to stop trying to find out who she is or do right by her. Just don't use that as an excuse to pack up all this dirty laundry and shove it back underground. That's a short-term coping strategy that will not hold—and the next time this all comes up again—and it will—it's going to be even harder, because you'll relive all this with the girl, too. See, this is how people get paralyzed. They stuff and stuff and stuff, and the triggers keep coming and the layers continue to build until the load becomes too heavy, and they fold."

Marissa kept twisting and untwisting the tissue. "You're right."

"I know."

After a deep breath, Marissa looked across the desk. "Can I give you a hug?"

"Please! Are you kidding me?"

They both stood up and Marissa came around to embrace the smaller female. The hug she got in return was so strong and steady, she teared up all over again.

"You're always there when I need you," Marissa choked out. "I love you too much for words."

"That's what friends are for." Mary pulled back. "And you're going to do the same for me sometime."

Marissa snorted and rolled her eyes. "Doubt that."

"Trust me."

"I'm too much of a mess."

"No, you're human." Mary shook herself. "Sorry, term of art. You're alive and you're struggling and you're beautiful inside and out—and I love you, too."

"I'm still not sure what exactly to do next."

"Think on it. It'll come to you. Remember, forgiving doesn't mean forgetting, hiding isn't a long-term strategy, and distraction isn't your friend. Hit this head-on—and know that I've got your back, 'kay?"

After the female left, Marissa went around to her office chair and sat down again. For some reason, her eyes fixated on the phone—the desk one, not her cell.

The past. Her brother. Butch. The girl. The *glymera*.

Mary was right. There was a lot she wasn't dealing with.

And to start things off, she might as well tackle the one that seemed the least scary. Or . . . well, maybe the most doable, how about that.

Picking up the receiver, she riffled through the papers and found the pink While You Were Out slip that had been given to her two nights before. Dialing the local number, she took off her pearl earring and leaned back in her chair.

A maid answered the line, put her on hold . . . and then a haughty female voice said, "Oh, hello! So very glad you've called."

Marissa gritted her teeth. "I'll do it. I'll chair the festival."

"Oh! This is marvelous! What wonderful . . ."

As the platitudes droned on, Marissa closed her eyes and heard Mary's voice in her head: *You're going to have to make peace with your brother.*

Oh, God, she thought. She had no idea how that was going to happen—but she did know about parties, damn it.

Start small. Then get to the big stuff.

Chapter Eighteen

Paradise dislocated her finger when she blocked a heel-of-the-palm punch thrown at her by Rhage. She'd meant to duck and defend using her forearm as he'd taught her to, but her arms and legs didn't always follow directions correctly—the result being that she caught her hand spread wide on the punch.

"Fuck!" she barked as she spun away and tucked in around the injury.

"Lemme see," the Brother said.

"Owowowow." Okay, fine, she sounded like a girl, but how did this hurt so much? "God!"

"Parry, lemme see."

She put her arm out and his big hands, which were now gentle, examined what was an extraordinarily cock-eyed version of her middle finger.

"What is wrong with it?" she said, even though she knew.

"Off to the clinic, come on."

As he led her out of the gym, she glanced over her shoulder. Anslam was giving Boone a helluva fight, and that surprised her. Peyton was sitting up and icing his shoulder, staring across at her like he wanted to know what the hell was going on. Novo and Axe were circling each other, the Brother Tohr offering instruction.

"You're going to be fine," Rhage said as he opened the heavy door for her. "Back at 'em in no time."

She made some kind of *mmm-hmm* as they hit the corridor—and she knew he was right. As long as she didn't look at the digit, the pain was actually okay.

"You guys have only got an hour left tonight, then we're going to let you go," the Brother said as they came up to one of the swinging doors of the medical clinic. "And tomorrow you're going to be in the classroom most of the time."

Cue another *mmm-hmmm*. "Has Craeg left already?"

"He's still being treated."

The exam room was tiled from floor to ceiling and filled with glass-fronted stainless-steel cabinets, medical equipment that was worth a fortune, and all kinds of computer screens. In the center was a massive table under a chandelier with enough globe lights to turn midnight into noontime over a surface area of several acres.

A tall, dark-haired human male turned from what looked like the image of a knee X-ray. Dressed in blue surgical scrubs and a white coat, he seemed very big, very broad . . . and very not-vampire. "Hey, what have we got here?"

Paradise took a step back. She couldn't help it.

"Yes, I'm one of those guys," the man said as he flashed teeth that lacked prominent canines. "But I'm all right, promise."

Rhage went over and gave the guy's shoulder a squeeze. "Great surgeon. Fantastic dude. Tragically proficient poker player, but at least he sucks at pool. Meet Manny Manello, MD."

"So what have we got going on?"

"Dislocated finger," the Brother said.

Both of the males—well, the male and the man—looked over at her.

Paradise cleared her throat—and intended to go with a "Yeah, my finger is . . ." Instead she blurted, "I've never seen a human up close before."

Dr. Manello smiled, put his arms out, and did a slow pivot. "Not that different from you. And I've been to the

audience house a couple of times while you were working."

She hadn't noticed then, probably because she'd been
so focused on her job—and surrounded by other vampires.

"I don't mean to be disrespectful," she whispered.

"I'm not offended. I had a worse reaction when I
learned about you people, trust me." When she looked at
him in surprise, he shrugged. "Bear in mind, in my cul-
ture, your kind are the bad guys. You know, fangs, blood-
sucking, the whole Halloween thing."

She traced his features, and was surprised to find that
he was handsome—and he seemed smart, too. Not like a
rat without a tail at all.

"He's operated on me twelve times," Rhage cut in.

"Thirteen. We did your shoulder again last week."

"Forgot." When Paradise glanced up at the Brother,
he shrugged. "I lose count. Shit happens."

Taking a deep breath, Paradise put her busted hand
forward. "Is this going to hurt? What you need to do
with it, that is."

Dr. Manello smiled again and took what she put out
so lightly she could barely feel his touch. "Pleased to
meet you, Paradise. Don't worry, I'm going to take really
good care of you."

And what do you know, he did.

After Rhage left to go back to teach, Dr. Manello
took an X-ray, showed her that nothing was broken,
numbed the area up, and popped the middle knuckle
back into place.

"You won't have to wear this splint for long," he said
as he encased her finger in a padded metal sheath that
he taped up with strips of sticky white cloth. "You guys
heal so well—it still amazes me."

When he stepped back, she looked his work over.
"Thank you so much."

"You're out of commission for the rest of tonight. You
and Peyton can hang out in the gurney section."

There was a knock on a door over to the left.

"Come on in," he said as he went over to a red bin and snapped off his bright blue surgical gloves. "I know you've met Ehlena, our nurse." The man frowned at the female's tight expression. "Is he still refusing?"

The nurse shut the panel behind her before answering. "He sent the Chosen away."

Dr. Manello muttered a curse. "I'm not releasing him if he doesn't feed."

"Is this Craeg?" Paradise asked. "Is it—"

The man smiled and talked over her. "So we're done here. Why don't you head back to the gym? You guys must almost be done for the night."

"I'll feed him," she said roughly. "If he needs it, I'll feed him."

What. The hell. Was. She. Doing.

As the daughter of a Founding Family, she wasn't supposed to give *anyone* her vein. Ever. That was solely for her intended mate. And if she herself ever needed to feed, it had to be in the company of a male relative of hers and several witnesses.

If she did this for him, it was akin to her losing her virginity before her mating night.

"That's okay," Dr. Manello said. "We'll take care of it."

Paradise was escorted out into the corridor, and as the door shut behind her, she could hear the two of them talking in hushed voices.

Go back to the gym, she told herself. Go on, now. Just head back to class and . . .

Looking around, she found that she was alone in the corridor, nobody coming or going, no sounds of footfalls or voices.

She really should rejoin the others.

Except as soon as she had the thought, her feet turned her to the left and took her away from where the hand-to-hand was being taught. Going down to the next door, she pressed her ear to the closed panels and listened.

Breathing in deep, she caught the shadow of Craeg's scent.

He was in there.

Right, she *really* needed to go back to the—

Her hand pushed the door open a crack and she peered in—and there he was, lying on white sheets on an enormous hospital bed that he nevertheless managed to dwarf. His eyes were closed and his breathing shallow. His skin was . . . not much different from those bleached sheets—except for the incredible bruises on his face, his throat, his . . . everywhere. And then there was the patchwork of bandages that covered the worst of the blade strikes.

Stepping inside the room, she forced the door to close faster than it wanted, and waited for him to look over.

"What?" he said without opening his eyes.

She went across to the bed—and wondered idly if she was ever going to be around the male without her heart pounding.

"Why aren't you feeding?" she demanded.

"Why are you bothering me?"

"You turned down a Chosen?"

"Why aren't you in class?"

"I got hurt. I'm not allowed."

That brought his head around and his lids up. "Are you okay?"

"I'd show you, but it would mean I'm flipping you off."

"You kicked me in the balls, remember? You think I'm worried about your finger?"

"And it wouldn't be the first time, either. I think I flipped you and Peyton off in the corridor."

"After the nut shot, my memory is fuzzy."

She wanted to sit on the edge of the bed, but she was scared of what she was proposing. "You can take my vein, you really can."

Craeg stared at her for a moment. "Can I ask you a question?"

"Please."

"Were you born to a family of saviors? Is it in your blood or something? Because I have never met a pain in the ass like you before, and this Mother Teresa stuff can't be learned behavior. The world is too nasty a place for it."

"They aren't going to let you go home."

"They can't keep me here."

She laughed. "It's the Brotherhood. I'm very certain that nobody is getting out of this place without their permission."

He grunted and fell silent.

"Come on, it'll make you feel better." She put up her left wrist. "And it'll help me feel less guilty about the . . . um, yeah."

"I turned down a Chosen, you know."

Paradise rolled her eyes. "You have the strangest way of being a prick when you feel threatened. Did you come from a family of pricks or did the nasty world just teach you to protect yourself like that?"

"The nasty world killed all of my family. Two of them in front of me. So yeah, you could say it's learned behavior."

Paradise dropped her arm and looked down. "I'm sorry. I didn't—"

"And besides, aren't you afraid that I'll do something I shouldn't?"

"I'm sorry?"

"You saw what happened when you pushed me in the gym. You know exactly what I'm talking about."

Paradise felt her body start to warm—and it was then that she owned up, at least to herself, that she had come in here to offer her vein because she wanted more of that . . . whatever it was . . . with him. That connection. That . . . electrical charge.

That sexual burn.

And if there was one sure way of getting it? It was offering a starving male her vein: She might be a virgin, but she wasn't that naive.

"Do you like playing with fire, girl?" he growled. "Because if you keep looking at me like that, I'm going to burn you to the ground."

She knew without opening her lips that her voice was lost. So in reply, she simply, and mutely, offered her wrist.

When he didn't take it, she upped the ante by bringing it to her mouth and scoring her flesh with her own fangs.

. That did the trick.

As the scent of her blood hit the air, his eyes rolled back in his head and his body surged under the thin blankets that covered him, his hips rolling, his legs sawing.

"Take my wrist," she said in a low voice. "It will help you."

His hand shot out and grabbed a rough hold of her forearm, jerking her vein to him. But before he struck, he looked up at her with wild eyes. "You're going to need to yell for help."

"Why?" she breathed.

"Right now. Do it."

Except he didn't wait for her to respond. He yanked her toward him—then with a ferocious growl, he struck at her skin even though she had already opened up access for him. As he began sucking with great pulls, she felt an erotic charge all over her body. Opening her mouth so she could breathe, she braced her hand on the bed and held herself up, balancing on the precipice of falling over on top of him. Her mind gone, she was nothing but instinct, and her body knew exactly what it wanted—naked skin on naked skin, the malest part of him in her core, pumping ... coming.

Screw her virginity.

Literally.

And he was thinking the same thing. As he fed, his eyes roamed over her face, her throat, her breasts—and something was going on under the sheets, his hips moving, his torso arching, his expression one of pain as if he hurt from the wanting.

No, she was not calling for help.

It was, of course, totally insane, but that didn't seem to matter—and dimly, in the very back of her mind, she had a thought that this was why feeding was so closely monitored for females of her class: There was going to be absolutely no crying for help. She didn't want any because she had no interest in stopping anything that was going to happen next—this hot, wild moment was not about her being from a Founding Family. It wasn't about the mansion she lived in with her father or the money in all those bank accounts. It had nothing to do with social position or posturing.

It was raw and it was honest, just between the two of them.

And that made it . . . beautiful.

Because it was real.

Chapter Nineteen

No wonder her name was Paradise.

As Craeg took long draws off of the single most incredible blood source he'd ever had in his entire life, all he could think of was how apt her name was.

Well . . . that wasn't *all* he was thinking of.

His body reawakened with lightning speed thanks to the strength she provided him, that heady wine of hers flowing down the back of his throat and pooling in his gut before being sent out in all directions like a restorative fire: Beneath his battered skin, deep in his aching bones, he began to fill up with power.

And with that power came a gnawing, grinding need.

Under the thin covers, he popped an erection as hard as steel and as long as his leg—proof positive that her solid groin hit hadn't castrated him. And between his ears, his brain latched onto the idea of getting inside her with the same tenacity as his fangs were locked on her vein.

He was slightly more decent than he would have guessed, however.

Instead of ripping her pants in half and muscling her up and over his hips, he forced himself to stay right where he was—because that kept her where she was.

His pelvis was not about to get the memo, however.

With great, rolling thrusts, he worked himself against the sheet and blanket, each push up offering a tantalizing stroke that was too soft to do much more than drive him fucking insane, each retreat making him more desperate than the last.

And then his hand started to itch to get involved.

No-go. Even if Paradise wouldn't have admitted it unless she had a gun in her face, he knew she was already in way over her head. If he whipped himself out and started stroking one off? She was going to get one hell of a show to tell whoever her father was about—even if that hand job option was better than drilling her sex so hard she saw stars.

Which was what he really wanted to do.

Damn it, why did he have to be attracted to a nice girl?

"You can . . ." she started. There was a pause and her eyes flicked over her shoulder like she was checking to make sure the door was still shut. "You can do what you want."

He frowned through the bloodlust, trying to make sense of what she was saying.

"I see where your hand is. I'm not stupid."

Craeg tried to shake his head, but he didn't get anywhere with that, because his mouth was not interested in breaking the seal.

Paradise nodded. "It's okay . . . do it. Take care of yourself."

And that was when light dawned on Marblehead—shit, she wanted him to . . .

For a split second, his conscience threw out a hell-no, but with her eyes so steady on his, and the scent of arousal coming off her, that didn't last longer than the formation of the words.

Talk about your yes-ma'ams.

Drunk on her taste, stretched on a rack of lust, body whacked out and mind blown up, he had enough left in him to will the locks into place on every door there was—including the closet. It wouldn't keep people out forever—but certainly long enough so that her virtue wouldn't be completely—

Peyton.

As the other male's name popped into his head, she frowned as if she had read his mind. "What did you say?"

Guess he'd spoken it out loud—sort of.

Craeg loosened his latch enough to say clearly, "Peyton."

"I told you, there's nothing . . . God, no. Not ever. He's like my brother."

Staring up at her, he decided she was either utterly guileless and talking the truth as she knew it—and in fact had no idea the guy wanted her—or she was the best actress outside of Hollywood and playing him.

Breathing in, he caught no scent of subterfuge—and then he thought of Peyton's haughty act and his perfect accent and his expensive watch. He might actually be a true aristocrat—in which case, there was no way the male was going to hook up long term with a receptionist.

And apparently the motherfucker was honorable enough not to lead her on. And successful enough that she'd bought the act, even if he had reacted as a possessive male back in the break room.

Guess maybe Craeg didn't have to hate him quite so much.

"There's nothing with Peyton and me," she repeated. "And there never will be."

Good enough for his palm.

Next thing he knew, he'd disappeared his free hand under the—

Craeg groaned and arched up as he gripped himself. Slowing down on the feeding, he found himself wanting to prolong this moment between the two of them. He wanted the sex *and* the blood from her.

And it looked like, for this brief moment, he was going to have some of both.

It would be, however, the one and only time any of this happened.

There was something inevitable about it all.

That was the thought that went through Paradise's

mind again and again as she looked down and watched Craeg's hand move under the covers. He was stroking himself, his tremendous body torquing at strange angles as he rode waves of pleasure.

And yet, as inevitable as this felt, there was so much that was unexpected, too.

She hadn't anticipated feeling so . . . powerful: She got the very clear sense that as big as he was, as strong as he was, she was in charge—anything she wanted from him, needed from him, he would give her, do for her, find for her.

After he was finished with the sex.

Craeg's eyes were heavy lidded and violently hot as they stared up at her from his battered face. And the straining muscles in his neck and his chest seemed ready to break through his skin. And his scent had bloomed into a roar of something spicy and delicious.

And then he started moaning.

God, she wanted to be the one with her hand on him—she'd never done anything like this before, but come on, it wasn't like she couldn't go up and down like that . . . the trouble was, her good hand was by his face, and her bad one with its finger splint wasn't gripping anything at the moment—

Without warning, Craeg released her wrist and let out a sound that was all animal, not even a little civilized. Then his free hand grabbed onto the sheets next to her hip and twisted them into a wad. His chest pumped once, twice . . . he arched again, this time with a groan . . . and then his hips jerked hard over and over, raw grunts coming out of his mouth as his eyes focused on her face.

The stillness that eventually came was just as surprising as the rest of it: After what seemed like an eternity, his body went lax and he collapsed back onto the bed, eyes closing, breath sawing, sweat gleaming on his chest.

"Lick . . ." he mumbled.

"What?" God, her voice was hoarse. "What did you say?"

"You're ... bleeding. ..."

Paradise looked at her wrist. He was right. The multiple puncture wounds were only partially closed. Bringing her arm up, she sucked on the—

The soft growl that rose up from him made her freeze.

That hot stare of his was focused on her lips.

Except then he turned away. "You need to go."

"What?"

"You heard me. Go."

Paradise exhaled as a surge of pissed-off ushered out all the lust she'd been enjoying with the efficiency of a bulldozer. "Why are you always dismissing me?"

"Because I don't think you're going to like someone coming into this room as it is now."

She glanced around. Okay, fine, there was a small amount of blood on the sheets by his mouth, but other than that, nothing was out of place. "There's nothing—"

"It smells like sex in here," he muttered. "I just came all over the place—and if anybody walks through either of those doors, they're going to know you're the reason. Leave with a little virtue left in you, will you?"

Paradise lowered her brows as her mouth fell open. "I *beg* your pardon."

"We're done here." He shrugged. "You asked me to give myself a hand job. I did—and you got to watch what it looks like when a male orgasms. So we both got something out of this sesh. What did you expect, a mating proposal?"

Pain lanced through her chest as she fell momentarily speechless. And then the only thing that went through her mind was something involving "Fuck" and "You."

Pushing herself back, she squared her shoulders and walked away from him. When she came up to the door to the corridor, she was surprised to find the thing locked. She hadn't done that.

Perhaps he had.

Who the hell cared.

As Paradise unlatched things, she glanced over her

shoulder. "I can't pretend to be sophisticated, or worldly about sex, but I know damn well that the need to diminish others when one is threatened is the mark of a coward, not a hero. Have a good rest of the night. I'll see you tomorrow—if you decide to show up."

Stepping out, she let the door close behind her and walked off a couple of feet, a couple of yards ... halfway back to the gym.

She intended to keep going.

Her feet refused to cover the rest of the distance back to class.

With a curse, she leaned against the concrete wall, crossed her arms over her chest, and stared at the polished pavers that formed the corridor floor ... then the inset fluorescent ceiling lights above her ... then the doors, the many, many doors. Off in the distance, she heard shouts coming from where the sparring continued. There was also an ambient hum from the HVAC system. And after a moment, her stomach let out a growl, reminding her that the calories she'd taken in at the quick-stop First Meal she'd had were long gone.

That had been her first sexual experience.

And when it had been happening, it had been wondrous, exciting, beyond tantalizing.

Craeg had just ruined all that, though. With only a couple of sentences, he had blown the whole thing up and made her feel ashamed of herself—

"I'm sorry."

Jerking her head around, she recoiled. "What are you doing out of bed?"

Craeg shuffled out of his room, seeming to rely more on the IV pole than his own legs for ambulation. He was determined to come over to her, however—and God knew he'd already proven he would go until he dropped.

Walking toward him, she put both palms out to stop him. "You need to get back in—"

"Look, I ..." He cleared his throat. Scratched under his nose even though there was nothing there. Rubbed his thumb across one eyebrow and then fiddled with his hospital johnny. "I can't be anyone other than who I am right now. Maybe in a different time, maybe if certain things hadn't happened . . . maybe I'd have the energy to try to file down these edges of mine. The problem is, I just don't have that extra effort in me at the moment—and there's not a lot of anything warm and fuzzy in here." He pointed to the center of his chest, his IV line draping across the front of him. "I'm not saying I'm right or that I'm proud of myself. I'm just telling you like it is. And that's all I can give you—tonight, tomorrow . . . next week. That's all I have to offer anybody."

As he stared down at her, his eyes were steady and grave.

And there was no doubting his somber voice or his carefully chosen words.

In the silence that followed, she thought of the great human writer and orator Maya Angelou's statement about people: When someone shows you who they are, believe them the first time.

Or something to that effect.

"If you want a male, go hang out with your boy, Peyton," he continued. "You're so spectacular, there's a chance he'll end up overriding that dumb *glymera* stuff. And hey, you wouldn't have to be a receptionist for the rest of your life. I couldn't offer you anything close to what he can—even if my personality did a one-eighty."

As he continued to speak, his words didn't sink in much. All she was thinking about was how unfair it was that she finally met a male she was attracted to at the precisely wrong time in the precisely wrong context for anything meaningful. And then there was his I-am-an-island stuff. Which she wanted to call bullshit on, but which might, actually, sadly, be the truth.

"Okay," she said finally. "Thank you for being honest."

There was an awkward pause—as if he'd expected some kind of protest from her, some indignant marching around, maybe some harsh words.

Then his lids lowered as if he didn't want her to see what was behind his eyes.

The hand that wasn't on his IV pole lifted toward her face. But then he dropped it back down and shook his head. "I have a lot of regrets in my life. Next time you wonder whether anyone cares about you . . . know that you're on that list."

Craeg turned away and limped back down to his hospital room.

She watched him until just before he opened the door and disappeared.

Pride made it important for her to go her own way first.

Bracing herself, Paradise headed for the gym, for class, for learning and self-discovery. After all, like him, her future was with the training center. Not some pipe dream with a male stranger that was never going to happen for so many reasons.

Chapter Twenty

Two hours later, Paradise rode a bus back out of the training center. There was only one leaving, as there were just the six of them, Craeg having not been medically cleared to go home.

Looking across the aisle, she met Peyton's eyes. He had stretched out across a row of seats, his back on the bank of blackened windows, his legs fully extended and crossed at the ankles.

It seemed like a lifetime since they had argued on the way in the night before.

You okay, he mouthed.

She nodded and mouthed back, *You?*

He shrugged, grimaced as he rearranged himself and closed his lids.

Nobody else was talking much, either.

Several rows in front of them, Boone sat with his head bowed, a set of Beats helmeting his ears, shutting out the world. He didn't seem to be able to find a song he liked, his thumb hitting the screen of his iPhone every second or two, the covers of albums flashing briefly before they were rejected. Anslam was asleep sitting up across from him. Novo was closest to the driver, staring out the windows through which you could see nothing.

Axe was all the way in the back, keeping to himself.

From time to time, Paradise shifted her body, and found herself pulling a Peyton with the wincing. She was exhausted; she was aching all over; she was worried about what the next night would bring in terms of tests.

She also kept thinking about what had gone down in Craeg's hospital room. And then what had been said between them out in the corridor.

"Stop it," she murmured to herself.

It wasn't like reliving the stuff was going to change the outcome, and if she was honest with herself, she did want that. It would have been amazing to be free to explore that kind of connection.

Not in the cards, though.

Hoping to distract herself, she looked down at the Bally leather satchel she'd checked with a *doggen* when she'd signed into the program. She remembered exactly what was in it: the protein bars, the extra socks, the change of clothes and underwear, her wallet, phone, a picture of her parents in an old gilt frame. She recalled quite vividly packing all of those things, too—the drawers she had opened in her walk-in closet, the choices she had agonized over, the stuff that she had wanted to bring but decided to leave home.

The disturbing thing . . . was that none of what was in there felt like hers anymore.

It was more like it was all owned by some kind of little sister or something, some younger relation who looked like her from a distance, but who, up close, was totally different.

Peyton shifted his feet to the floor and shoved his body across the aisle. This time, when he sat next to her, she was grateful.

"You don't look okay," he said softly.

The concern threatened the dam that was holding back her emotions, but she kept that wall in place for fear of losing it in front of her fellow classmates.

Primus, my ass, she thought.

"I don't know." She shook her head when the words came out. Not what she had meant to reply. "Actually, I'm all right."

"Last night was a lot to go through."

"We made it," she murmured. "Go, us."

"Yeah."

As her friend went quiet again and stared at the back of the headrest in front of him, she could only imagine what he was thinking of: throwing up, getting bagged over the head, the pool ... the longest walk of their lives.

That fight with Craeg.

"How are you feeling?" she asked. "You seem better."

"I'm going to need to feed."

As he rubbed his face like he was trying to stop more memories of school, she felt a stab of guilt—because unlike Craeg, who she'd been in a big fat hurry to offer a vein to, helping her friend wasn't foremost in her mind.

Plus also, she wasn't sure she could go through that with Peyton ... if he had the same response Craeg had.

Not that she was some sexpot to males, but because maybe that kind of lust was just a natural by-product of feeding and she didn't want to cross that line in her friendship.

"I texted my dad." Peyton patted the front pocket of his coat. "He has someone waiting for me. Gonna be the first time I don't have sex when I take a vein." He frowned and glanced over at her. "Sorry. TMI."

What was he talking about? Oh, right. "It's okay. I'm not offended."

You want to cover the TMI bases? she thought. What was *really* TMI was what she and Craeg had done in that clinic. Or rather ... what he had done to himself.

She looked away just to be sure the blush that hit her face didn't get noticed.

"You're different," he remarked.

That brought her head back around quick. "How so?"

"I don't know. Maybe it's because I remember how great you did."

As he stared over at her, she knew he was saying sorry again, and without thinking, she leaned in and gave him a hug. "Thank you for that—"

A series of bumps and then a noticeable decrease in speed made her break away. "Are we there already?"

Peyton took out his phone and checked the time. "Forty-five minutes since we left. So yeah, probably."

The *doggen* who was driving announced over the loudspeaker that their destination had, in fact, been reached, and one by one, they all stood up, filed out, got off.

The night was cold, very cold—and for some reason, she thought that if the color light blue had a scent, it would be what was in her nose as she breathed in the bracing, dry air.

Turning to the others as the bus left, she found that everybody was just standing around in the open farm field as if no one quite knew what to do.

Anslam was the first to say good-bye, although only to Peyton, and then he took off. Axe didn't speak to anyone before dematerializing.

"Until tomorrow then," Peyton murmured as he looked at Novo and Boone.

Before he ghosted out, he came over. "You're going to be hearing from me in about two hours. I really hope you answer that phone."

"I will."

"Good."

With a brief smile, just like that, he was gone.

Paradise said something to the others; she didn't know what—and they said something to her; which she didn't quite track.

And then she shouldered her satchel and was gone, gone, gone, spiriting away in a jumble of molecules that somehow fit her mental and emotional state far better than being in her corporeal form.

As she came back into her body on the lawn of her father's mansion, she stayed where she was and stared up at the magnificent facade of the Tudor's great sprawl. Lights glowed from indoors, the buttery illumination passing through the diamond-paned windows, creating the illusion of a fireplace's warmth. From time to time, through parted silk drapes, she saw a *doggen* walk past, carrying a silver tray, a feather duster, a bouquet of flowers.

The wind was fierce here, and the longer she stood on the browned, frosty grass, the more it got through her jacket, her clothes, her skin.

She and her father had lived on the estate for a very long time, and there wasn't a room that she didn't have a memory in—even the hidden ones.

Yet tonight the manse seemed as the objects in her satchel were: someone else's.

Amazing . . . how a journey that started and ended in your hometown, and didn't actually require you to leave your own zip code, could distance you so completely from your life.

When she began to shiver, she forced herself to walk forward. It was about two a.m.—and though it made her feel guilty, she was so glad her father would still be working down at the audience house. She just didn't have the energy to tell him all about her "studies."

More to the point, she hadn't really processed anything for herself yet—so it was just too early to explain the experience to anyone else.

Coming up to the front entrance, she reached out for the doorbell—and had to stop herself.

Really, she thought. You're going to ring the bell on your own house?

And yet she felt like a stranger as she put her forefinger on the print reader and sprang the lock.

Stepping into the warmth, she closed the heavy door behind her and took a couple of deep breaths. There was no sense of calm as she looked around at the familiar oil paintings and the Orientals. Instead, she felt a creeping unease—

"Mistress! You return!" As the butler, Fedricah, rushed over to her, he was all smiles—and he bowed so deeply his forehead nearly Swiffered the floor. "What may I get you? Would you care for a meal—no, a bath. I shall have Vuchie run you a—"

"Please, no." She put both hands out as his face fell so fast, so far, he was liable to start talking out of his bow tie. "The Brotherhood fed us very well—and honestly, I need to retire to bed." Words, she needed the right combination of words here. "Will you please tell my father it was a wonderful learning experience . . . tell him I'm okay—I'm very well, in fact, and I made it into the program. We're doing classwork. It's all very safe."

And the last two things technically weren't a lie. Rhage had said they would be in the classroom tomorrow evening, and no one had gotten seriously hurt.

"Oh, of course, mistress! He will be so pleased! I do not believe he slept during the day—but please ring if you require aught. We are always at your service."

"I will, I promise. Thank you."

She escaped up the stairs quickly, some irrational fear of her father getting home early driving her to her room. When she closed herself in, she looked at the canopied bed and the needlepoint rugs and the antiques . . .

. . . and really wished she were crashing in an anonymous, clean hotel room.

Walking over to her bed, she sat down on the supersoft mattress and put her satchel down by her feet. Then she laid her palms on her knees and stared at the wall.

Craeg wasn't the only thing she thought about. But there was a whole lot of him in her brain.

Shoot. Now that she was up here hiding, she felt trapped—

As her phone went off in her bag, she cringed. Undoubtedly Fedricah had called her father the moment she'd come up here, and the question was whether it would be worse for him to go to voice mail . . . or for her to try to force an everything-is-normal across the connection.

Later was not much better, she decided: If she didn't talk to him now, he was liable to come knocking on her door as soon as he got home. And then she'd have to do it face-to-face.

Fishing her iPhone out, she frowned as she saw the picture of a five-pointed weed leaf on her screen. "Peyton?"

"Hey. I couldn't wait two hours. I've got a serious case of the heebs."

Even though he couldn't see her, she nodded. "I know. Me, too."

When there was a pause, she waited for the customary sound of a bong being drawn on. Instead, there was only silence.

After a moment, he said, "I feel like I've been gone for a decade."

"Same for me."

"I don't want to even smoke up. How fucked in the head is that?"

She pushed herself back until she was leaning on her pillows. "Maybe that's a good thing."

"Just one more part of the weirdness, you know?" There was some rustling, as if he were doing the same thing. "Okay, so what the fuck is up with that Axe guy. I mean did you see him when he was fighting with . . ."

As her friend launched into all kinds of commentary, Paradise closed her eyes and took a slow, deep breath.

Funny, this was just like after the raids. The two of them talking in the night, tethered by two phones, an invisible connection open between them that was nonetheless tangible.

He was her only friend, she realized.

And she was very grateful they'd come out the other side of their argument—and also that first night of training.

Suddenly things didn't seem so foreign anymore.

"Damn, I'm good," Marissa said as she sat back and looked at the stack of five-by-seven card stock in front of her.

It had taken her hours, but she had managed to computer-generate one hundred color invitations to the

Twelfth Month Festival Ball. Yes, it would have been so much better if the damn things were engraved, but they were out of time: There were only about fourteen days before the event on its mandatory first full moon of December, so nobody was in a position to get fussy over cutting corners.

Next stop was addressing the envelopes, and Mary and Bella had offered to help with that at the mansion. After that, Marissa was going to talk to Fritz about whipping up the food, and ask around for some of the traditional Old Country musicians to cover that hole.

Oh, and may the Scribe Virgin bless Abalone forevermore: The male had agreed to let them use the ballroom at his estate. It was a much better option than that other venue at the rich-old-male/gold-digger-female combination's place: That pair had hosted the secret Council meeting to plot against Wrath, so there was no way any of the Brothers were going back there unless it was with a bunch of flamethrowers—and by extension, she didn't think Butch would have been all about her spending time under that particular roof.

So, invitations. Venue. Food. Entertainment.

She was on it, but she wasn't fooling herself. She knew why she'd been asked to chair the event, and it wasn't her competence: The people pushing for this were having trouble drawing the *glymera* out after all the drama around Wrath's democratic election. As there was nothing that the aristocrats loved more than a scandal, what could be more fun than watching her in action at the party?

Her presence was going to up the acceptance rate through the roof.

And it was funny. In a sick way, she found herself looking forward to holding her head up high in that bunch of sharks—and at least Butch wouldn't have to deal with the bullcrap. He was going to be out working and teaching. Besides, he'd have no patience for that party kind of thing.

She would travel this stretch backward into her history alone.

Checking her watch, she noted that it was three o'clock. Usually she waited until four a.m. to go home, but if she and the females could get these invitations addressed before everyone retired, then Fritz could take them to the human mail system and they would be received the day after.

With quick efficiency, she packed the invites and envelopes into the LV Neverfull that Butch had gotten her a while ago, and shut down her computer.

Her sense of satisfaction was short lived.

After checking in with her staff and excusing herself for the evening, she left the Wellsie wing and spirited back to the mansion. As she waited for the vestibule's inner door to be opened for her, she went right back to worrying about the female.

Still nothing on that "key." And no e-mails to the general accounts at Safe Place or the audience house about a missing female. Nothing on the closed social media groups. No phone calls or texts, either.

But her family had to be missing her, right?

Fritz, the beloved butler, opened the door with a wide smile. "Mistress, how fare thee?"

Fucked-up, thank you. "I am very well, how are you?" She shook her head as he went to take her bag. "I've got this, thanks. Have you seen—"

"We're ready! And Mary's on her way!"

Marissa looked over at the archway into the billiards room. Bella, Beth, and Autumn were standing together, glasses of white wine and plumed pens in their hands.

"We're prepared to scribe up," Bella said. "And then we've asked for Last Meal on special service, because we're doing movie day upstairs in the theater."

"*Magic Mike XXL* just came out on DVD," Beth chimed in. "We have a moral obligation to support the arts, even if they're just the human ones."

"I haven't seen the first one," Autumn murmured. "They tell me his pelvis is double-jointed. Is that true?"

Beth came forward and took the Neverfull. "Come on, you look like you need a girls' night. Payne and Xhex are joining us. So are Cormia, Layla, Doc Jane, and Ehlena. We're getting all of us together—it's about time."

For a split second, Marissa felt guilty about easing into the friendship that was being offered. It seemed ... too frivolous when she thought about all she wasn't able to do for that unknown female.

Bella leaned in. "We've told the males that they can't come in. Mostly because if they see that Channing guy up on the big screen—"

Beth finished, "—we're going to need to do a remodel after they're done with things."

"Back to the double-jointed business," Autumn kicked in. "I mean, how does he walk?"

"Very well, my friend." As Bella answered Tohr's mate, she put an arm around Marissa's shoulders. "Very, very well."

As Marissa let herself get drawn into the billiards room—where ink pots had been set up on one of the coffee tables and there was already a glass set out for her—she began to blink fast. Part of the emotion was the fact that that female who had died wasn't ever going to have anything like this again—if she'd been lucky enough to find good people surrounding her while she'd been alive.

The other half was a gratitude so great, her chest could barely contain the emotion.

"Ladies," she said, putting her arm around Bella's waist. "Let's do the addressing quickly—so we can get to the undressing."

Chapter Twenty-one

"I'm sorry . . . they're doing *what*?"

As Butch spoke, he looked at the males-only group sitting around the mansion's dining room table. Not one of his brothers or any of the soldiers was laughing or talking loudly. The bunch of sad sack losers was just sitting in front of half-eaten plates and untouched rocks glasses of vodka, bourbon and whiskey like a roll call of bassett hounds who'd lost their anti-depressants.

Not what he'd expected to find as he came late to Last Meal.

When Marissa had texted him and told him she was working with the females on something, it had seemed like a good idea to take care of some trainee stuff.

He hadn't banked on this funeral thing just cuz the ladies were doing a project.

"Hello?" he demanded. "You guys lost your hearing along with your sac or something?"

Wrath inhaled like he was about to break the news of a death in the family. "They're having a movie night."

Butch rolled his eyes and went over to his chair. Yeah, it was a little weird to sit down without his Marissa by his side, but for crissakes, it was nothing to go Prozac over. Besides, he was glad his woman had friends in the house —

"They're watching *Magic Mike*," someone said.

"Is that a children's show?" He sat back as Fritz put a heaping plate of lamb in front of him. "Thanks, man — oh, thanks, yeah, I'd love a drink. I'll take a Lagavulin on the rocks—"

Butch stopped talking as he realized the entire table of males was looking at him. "What?"

"You haven't heard about *Magic Mike*?" Rhage demanded.

"No." He leaned back again as his drink was delivered. "Thanks. Is it like Barney?"

"It's about strippers," Hollywood countered.

Butch frowned and lowered the glass from his lips. "I'm sorry?"

V came in from the pantry with a thick pouch of tobacco, a pack of rolling papers, and a scowl like somebody had stripped his favorite sex toy of its batteries.

"Naked," Vishous muttered as he sat where Marissa should have been. "Buck-ass naked. And they're humans. Christ, it's like being shown up by a pack of dogs."

"In thongs," someone else bitched. "Dogs in thongs."

Butch followed through on taking a drink this time, swallowing the burn, welcoming the heat in his gut. Okay, fine, it was a bit of a surprise to find that he kept going until the glass was empty, but hey, he had a lot to think about. On one level, the fact that his *shellan* was watching a movie with her buddies, even if it did involve some nakey, really wasn't a big deal.

On another level, he wanted to find the electrical box and cut the power to that part of the mansion.

Then torch the DVD. And the screen.

And take his mate to bed just to show her all the tricks he had over some actor in a—oh, God, a *thong?*

"It's fine," he heard himself say as he motioned to a *doggen* for a refill. "I mean, first of all, they love us—and second, it's not like it's an X rated—"

"They show a cock pump," Lassiter said with a wide smile, like he was helping. "And in action. You know, it's on a cock and it's pumping—"

Vishous unsheathed a dagger from somewhere and pointed the thing at the fallen angel's head. "You keep talking like that and I'ma trim your hair. With my eyes closed."

Lassiter laughed. "Yeah, whatever, big boy. I thought you had more mojo than to get worked up over something like this. You really that insecure?"

"You want insecure," V said. "I'll make you—"

"Okay, okay," Butch cut in. "Leave it, V. It's fine, it's great—they're just enjoying themselves. What's wrong with that? It's not like they're sleeping with the guy."

"You sure about that?" Lassiter smiled. "You don't think they're fantasizing about—"

The collective growl that rose up from the Brotherhood was so loud, it managed to agitate the crystals in the enormous chandelier hanging over the table. And the fallen angel was an idiot, but he wasn't stupid.

Moving slowly, like there were multiple guns pointed at him, he put his hands up in submission. "Sorry. Whatever. I'll stop before all this lame-ass uncomfortability you bunch of morons are sporting kills me."

"Wise choice," Butch said dryly. "Not that I wouldn't mind hitting you right now. Although that's not specific to this sitch."

Lassiter went back to eating, shoving food into his face.

The Brothers weren't so quick to do a reset on things, those narrowed eyes and bared fangs still trained on the angel with the big mouth.

"Come on, boys, it's *fine*." He cut a piece of lamb off and put it in his mouth. "Mmm. Delish."

In reality, the stuff tasted like cardboard, but he made a show of the yummies. He couldn't keep it up, though.

Two minutes later, he was shoving a full plate away and nursing his second whiskey. "Really. They should have a little independence. They don't need to be locked at our hips, and listen, life here revolves around us. It's about time they do something just for them. Really. This is great."

Next to him, V lit up a fat hand-rolled. "Is it. You like the idea of Marissa looking at some other male's junk?"

"It's not an X-rated—" As his voice squeaked, he cleared his throat. "I mean, it couldn't be. . . . no, it's not—"

"I already checked," Rhage muttered. "They have the DVDs—they're probably watching the extended, uncut versions."

"So the strippers aren't circumcised?" Lassiter put his palms up again before the growling got even worse. "Jesus, you guys are *so* damn touchy."

Butch shook his head and decided the angel was on his own. "So, yeah, I mean, a little gyrating—a pec pump or two. It's nothing to get worked up over. Fritz, can I have a refill over here again?"

The butler hustled over to pick up the empty glass. "Would any of you care for dessert? We have homemade ice cream and *Petit Gâteau.*"

Butch glanced at Hollywood. "What do you say there, my man?"

When Rhage just swished his ginger ale around in his glass, Butch cursed and said to Fritz, "This one here will have some even if no one else does."

"Bring me the dessert," Rhage spoke up.

Fritz bowed with Butch's glass in his hand. "But of course, sire. I shall fix you a plate directly—"

"No. I want the whole dessert. All of the cake and all of the ice cream."

Annnnnnnnnnnnnnnnnd that was how Hollywood ended up with a morose audience of however many playing witness to his consuming fifteen small chocolate cakes and two gallons of vanilla ice cream.

It was like watching paint dry, except there was no chemical smell and the room was the same color before and after.

The good news was that the booze was doing its job, fuzzing out Butch's mind, making his body both numb and horny. "May I have another?" he asked a passing *doggen* who was removing the final chocolate-smudged plate. "Thank you so much."

When his glass came back, he pushed his chair away from the table. "I'm out. I've got some work to do."

And no offense to any of them, but hanging around in their vibe was just making him more depressed. Any more of this and he was going to start braiding the noose.

Walking out, he paused in the grand foyer. Looked up the stairs. Tried to imagine his Marissa ogling some actor in his underwear.

"Really. It's fine. Good for her."

He took his phone out and called up their text string. Hesitating, he thought he'd just send her something, you know, to remind her that . . .

Wow.

In his human iteration, he would never have given a shit about something like this. Marissa wasn't only the love of his life; she was a female of worth who would never cheat on him. And *hello*, it wasn't like she'd checked into a seedy motel with the guy, for fuck's sake. She was hanging with her friends just like he hung out with his.

This was ridiculous.

He was *not* the jealous type—

The sound of shitkickers approaching had him glancing over his shoulder. It was Rhage, and the brother had a frothing glass of Alka-Seltzer in his hand.

Hollywood looked up the stairs. And dollars for dipshits, he was thinking exactly what Butch was.

"I'm going up," the guy announced.

"Now, wait, wait, wait." Butch grabbed that huge forearm and squeezed. "It's not like you can just burst in there."

"Why not?"

"It's girls' night."

"So I'll put on a dress."

"Fucking hell, Rhage. *Really*?"

Next out were V., John Matthew and Tohr. And everyone else, including Wrath—and even Manny, who, in spite of being a full-blown human, was right there along with the hound-faced rest of them.

"We are *not* going up there," Butch announced. "We're going to go play some pool, and get drunk, and talk about all the kills we had in the attack on Brownswick. We're going to have a great fucking night—day, whatever the hell it is. Now pick your balls up off the floor and let's start behaving like men."

"He has skills. I'm just saying."

As Doc Jane spoke up, the captivated audience that was focused on the big screen was in total, very unmuted agreement.

Payne let out another of her now-trademark wolf whistles.

Xhex cursed and threw more Milk Duds at the image, yelling, "Damn, son, you get that shit! You get it!"

Marissa just laughed again. She couldn't decide what was more amusing, the movies or the company—probably the company. Although the humans were not hard on the eyes, she had to admit.

And then it was time for another round of hooting and hollaring.

God, she couldn't remember the last time she had laughed this hard. There was something about being with the girls that made the jokes both worse and better at the same time, and the giggling louder, and the silliness more stupid.

All of which was a very beautiful thing, as it turned out.

It also reminded her of how great it was to be accepted for exactly who she was, no external expectations laid on her, no shortfalls she hadn't volunteered for cutting her down. No judgment, just love.

Plus a number of naked guys who were almost as hot as her male? Not a hardship.

When the final scene was over and the credits started to roll, they clapped like the actors could hear them all the way out in California.

"Can you teach me how to whistle like that?" someone asked Payne.

"You just put two lips around your fingers and blow," the female replied.

"Isn't that a line from a movie?" somebody chimed in.

"Are they going to do a third one—"

"Magic Mike Ginormous—"

"We need to watch one and two again first as prep—we've got a tradition to uphold—"

"Anybody see *Nine and a Half Weeks* lately—"

"What's that—"

One by one, they stood up from the padded leather recliners and stretched in the dim, windowless room, backs cracking, shoulders unknotting. And it was funny—Marissa felt the urge to cut through the conversation and say something profound and meaningful, just to acknowledge the space they'd been in. But the right words didn't come.

Instead, she said, "Hey, can we do this again?"

Then again, maybe that was exactly what she meant.

Well, what do you know, the peanut gallery was so on board: The rousing cheer was as loud as the hoots at the dance scenes, and the idea that this special time wasn't a one-off made her feel a piercing kind of relief.

"I think we need a Chris Pratt marathon next. *Guardians of the Galaxy*," Beth said.

"Is he the guy with the brother?" Bella asked.

"That's Hemsworth," someone answered.

Starting the line for the departure up the middle aisle, Marissa wadded her empty Milk Duds box and made a rim shot with it into the trash. Abruptly, she realized that she couldn't wait to see Butch—and not because of all the scenes of half-naked bodies. She missed him—which was ridiculous, considering neither one of them had gone anywhere.

Heading for the door by the glass display of candy bars, she was smiling as she pushed open the—

"Dear . . . God," she blurted as she recoiled.

The hallway beyond was filled with the males of the house, the Brothers and other fighters and Manny sitting on the floor with their backs to the bare walls, their legs stretched out, propped up, crossed at the knees or crossed at the ankles.

Apparently there had been quite a bit of drinking going on, empty bottles of vodka and whiskey littered around them, glasses in hands or on thighs.

"This is *not* as pathetic as it looks," her Butch pointed out.

"Liar," V muttered. "It so fucking is. I think I'm going to start knitting for reals."

As the females emerged with her, each one of them registered shock, disbelief, and then a wry amusement.

"Is it me," one of the males groused, "or did we just perform our own mass castration out here?"

"I think that just about sums this shit up," somebody agreed. "I'm wearing panties under my leathers from now on. Anyone joining me?"

"Lassiter already does," V said as he got to his feet and went to Jane. "Hey."

And then it was group-reunion time.

While the other pairs found one another, Butch smiled as Marissa came over to him and put out her hand to help him off the floor. As they embraced, he kissed her on the side of the neck.

"Are you out of love with me now?" he murmured. "'Cuz I'm pussy-whipped?"

She leaned back in his arms. "Why? Because you pined after me while I was watching a dirty movie with my girls that wasn't all that dirty? I think it's actually— and brace yourself—really pretty cute."

"I'm still all man."

As she rolled her body against him, she let out a *mmmm* as she felt his erection. "Yes, I can tell."

With Butch's bonding scent roaring, he took his female's elbow and drew Marissa deeper into the staff wing. Except for V and Jane, all the others had a shorter distance to go than they did: The Pit was just across the courtyard, but it was daylight now, and that meant a trip all the way downstairs, into the tunnel, and through the underground passage to get back to their bedroom.

He wasn't going to last that long.

Not even close.

The first available vacancy with any privacy came in the form of an unoccupied staff bedroom that had pulled drapes, a twin bed with no sheets on it, and a very handy brass lock.

Butch didn't bother turning the lights on; he just pulled his female against his body and kissed the everloving crap out of her as he kicked the door closed and worked that dead bolt like a pro.

"I need you so bad," he growled.

"You've got me," she said against his mouth.

Fucking perfect, his cock roared in his pants. And talk about following orders: with a quick shift, he backed her up to the bed, sat her down and knelt in front of her. As he inhaled deeply, he started to laugh.

"What?" she murmured, all half-lidded and wholly edible.

"You're aroused."

"Of course I am."

"You weren't when you came out of the movie."

"Why would I have been? That was just good fun with the girls. Like going to a museum, you know? You appreciate the art, but you wouldn't take it home with you."

"So I'm still your favorite flavor?"

"You're my *only* flavor."

Well, didn't that make him go all robin-breasted, dick swing with the ego. Flashing his fangs, he said, "Now, that's what I'm talkin' 'bout."

"Were you really jealous?" she said. "Of a movie?"

"Yes."

The laugh that came out of her was so easy and relaxed, such a happy sound, that it made him hope she and her girls got together again and, yes, to watch sexy humans gyrate on the screen, if that was what made his mate uncoil like this. Granted, he wasn't about to write that Tanning Chatum guy a fan letter, but he was more than grateful for those females and that friendship.

Anyone, anything that took care of his *shellan* was all right in his book.

Refocusing, he split Marissa's thighs and eased her upper body down on the little bed. He had a lot of plans that involved him going down on her for two hours—but his cock wasn't going to be able to wait for all that.

He needed in her. Now.

Zeroing in on the fastening of her slacks, he had her naked from the waist down with some quick hand work and one pull down her long, lovely legs. And then his palms were traveling up her calves, her thighs. With a moan, she spread further for him as if she wanted this as badly as he did, revealing her bare, glistening sex—and that was when he lost his damn mind.

Outing his erection, he went right for the heart of her, no preamble, no foreplay—they were both beyond ready.

"Marissa," he groaned as he penetrated her, sliding in deep, the sensation at once familiar and bracingly electric.

Cursing on the exhale, he reared up and his hips took over, grinding, thrusting, pumping—and he loved how she held on to his neck and shoulders.

"Take my vein," she ordered.

His fangs had already punched out of the roof of his mouth, and he bared them with a hiss. Striking in his favorite spot, on the left side, he drew deep, drank hard, got high on her taste as well as the sex.

He couldn't last long with that, though. Shit was getting too hard, too fast down below. Licking the puncture wounds closed, he repositioned her so he could go even deeper—then he grabbed onto her hip bones and dug in, pistoning her body, rocking things so hard the thin metal frame banged into the wall and the tinny mattress springs became a symphony of wild creaking.

He heard her come, which was what he'd been after, heard that common, nothing-fancy name of his erupt into the sex-scented air—and he wanted to stop so he could feel that rhythmic gripping of her core. He was too far gone, though. His balls were tucking up and going hot, his pelvis was doing that autonomic jerking shit that he was no more capable of reining in than he could stop his own heart, and his cock was that bizarre combination of numb and hypersensitive—

Butch came so hard he got a load of fireworks across his vision, and even as he started to ejaculate, he knew he wasn't finished.

He kept riding her, shifting positions again, arching farther over her body until his weight was braced on the balls of his feet and his arms were supporting him so he didn't crush her.

Even deeper. Which was amazing.

Not so hot for the bed, which started to migrate across the floor.

But again, there was no stopping. He just walked along with it—until the frame fit itself obligingly into a corner.

Talk about some leverage.

Fucking. Perfect.

Butch kept going at it, pounding her, his body doing an uncoiling of its own, the weeks—and maybe, if he was honest, months—of feeling somewhat separate from her disappearing like he was fucking that subtle distance out of existence.

Lot of orgasms. The fantastic ugly kind where your face screwed up hard, and you were going to be sore when you woke up, and shit got really, really messy down below.

When it was finally over, he collapsed on top of her. He meant to roll over, though, so she could breathe easier. He really did. Yup.

Rolling over would be good right now.

Uh-huh.

In three . . . two . . .

... one.

Except he couldn't quite manage the effort: He felt like someone had parked a Hummer on his spinal cord.

Marissa ran her hands up and down his arms. "You are *incredible*."

He tried to lift his head. Discovered that the same rat bastard with the Hummer had left a four-wheeler on the back of his skull.

"No, that's you." Or at least, that was what he'd meant to say. What came out of his mouth was a stroke victim's speech.

"No ... that's you," he repeated.

"What?"

All he could do was laugh, and suddenly she was laughing, too—and that was when he forced himself to get with the program and ease off the poor female. She followed with him, and then they were scooting around so they were lying on the bed properly. With their bodies still throwing off tremendous waves of heat, they were warm, warm, warm even without a blanket.

"I love you, Butch," she said.

In the dense darkness, he knew she was looking at him, and he fucking loved it. He wanted her undivided attention, craved it, needed it to ground him on some pathetic, talk-about-castrated level. But he would never demand that kind of thing from her—and for an impatient SOB, he was very, very willing to wait for it. God, when given freely? Her love, her focus, was a gift that, like her, never grew old to him.

Closing his eyes, he felt how much she loved him—and it was funny, sometimes, when you were with a person for so long, married to them, living with them, moments like this were just as wondrous and magical as that incredible instant when *I love you* had been said for the first time.

"God, I love you, too."

The kiss he gave her now was soft and gentle, and not because he was spent—because, actually, if she'd been up for another round, he was more than capable of going the distance. No, he kissed her with care because the emotional tie between them was at once strong as a steel cable and delicate as a blade of grass.

With a light touch, she ran her fingertips over his chest. "Do you ever wish I were different?"

"Not possible. You can't improve on perfection. And no, I don't."

"You're sweet."

"That is one thing that has never been said about me."

"Well, you're sweet to me." There was a pause. "May I ask you for some help?"

"I'd be pissed if you didn't."

Cue another long pause. To the point that he eased onto his side and propped his head on his hand. Now, he wished there was more illumination in the room other than that thin strip around the doorjamb. "What's up?"

"Well, I know you're busy with work and the training center—"

"Stop. Really?" He frowned at her even though she probably couldn't see it. "You're going to suggest anything is more important than you?"

The curse she let out was a kind of defeat. "Can you help me find out who killed that female? Who she was, what happened to her, who did it to her?"

He didn't hesitate. "Yes, I will. It would be my honor."

Her exhale of relief was another compliment the likes of which he would never stop relishing.

"Thank you," she murmured.

"I was going to offer, but I wanted to respect where you're at."

"I can't leave her in an unmarked grave."

"Not going to happen. I'll take care of it." He frowned again in the darkness. "You should know something, though."

"What?'

"I'm not the type who's going to let it go."

"Oh, I know. You and I will dig until we find out everything."

Butch shook his head. "Not what I mean. The vampire race doesn't have a police force. There are no jails—"

"There's a penal colony out west somewhere. At least, there used to be. I'm not sure what happened to it?"

"Which is my point. There's no real procedure or consequences for crimes within the race. No way to punish the guilty or handle false accusations. Wrath doing the audiences again has helped with certain kinds of conflict, but he's judge and jury all at once—which is fine until we get some capital murders and felonies into the system. And they will come. That's a fact of society whether you have fangs or not."

"So what are you saying?"

His voice lowered to a growl. "If I find out who did that to some innocent girl? I'm not going to be able to let that go without reprisals. Do you get my drift?"

Chapter Twenty-two

Raging. Hard-on.

The following nightfall, as Craeg resurfaced from the kind of sleep that was so dense it was practically a solid, he had a big-ass chubby straining at his hips: Laying on his side, having rolled over into his preferred position at some point, his hand was about three inches away from his cock—and on the backs of his closed lids, images of Paradise played like a slide show calculated to get him sprung and keep him that way until he got off.

Yeah, sure, his conscience put up a fight, but it was a battle doomed to be lost.

He wasn't going to work himself out in the bed, though. The nurse was coming in to check on him every fifteen seconds, and knowing his luck, she'd pick just the right time to crack the door and make sure he was still breathing.

Bracing himself to sit up, he—

Had absolutely no problem moving. Shifting his legs off the bed. Getting to his feet. In fact, he felt as though he'd slept for a month.

Huh.

It was Paradise's blood, of course. And that made him a little afraid of her for some reason.

One by one, he unhooked himself from the various machines and bags of fluid, and when an alarm sounded, he punched at the buttons of the monitor until the thing fell silent. Then he headed for the bathroom, cranked on the shower, and shut himself in, figuring the nurse who was no doubt going to run in like a fire truck to a house blaze would see for herself that he was up and at 'em.

Sure enough, there was a knock on the loo's door just as he ditched the johnny and stepped under the spray.

"Craeg?" she said. "Everything all right?"

"Yup. Showering and ready to eat."

"That's good. Be careful, though—do you need help?"

He glanced down at the enormous erection sticking straight out in front of his hips. "No. I think I can handle things all on my own."

"Okay, but you know where the call button is, don't you? Just let us know if you feel woozy."

"Yup. Thanks."

He waited a moment longer to see if there was anything further coming at him. When there was only blissful, no-more-questions, he picked up the bar of soap—but he didn't go for his cock and balls. Running the thing over his chest and shoulders, his neck and face, his legs and feet, he gave his body a chance to get over the bright idea.

Nope. If anything, the smooth feel of the suds over his flesh made him think about sitting on the floor in front of Paradise and stroking her fine skin.

The shampooing didn't help, either. And as the air in the bathroom became dense with humidity, and he ran out of places to wash, he conceded defeat, ended the negotiation, resigned himself to the inevitable.

"Oh, fuck," he groaned as he gripped himself.

Putting one arm up on the tile wall, he leaned in until his forehead was on his forearm. The stroking was too damn good—he couldn't remember, actually, the whole jerking-off thing feeling this incredible before. It was . . . paradise.

Or, Paradise, as the case was.

Harder, faster, until he dropped his other arm and squeezed his balls with a twist—

In a series of lightning bolts, his cock kicked against his hold and he ejaculated onto the wall of the shower over and over again.

And when he finally sagged, he cursed over and over again.

After everything he'd been through, why now. Why did he have female-on-the-brain *now*?

It was just stress, he told himself. This attraction thing was just a reaction to the stress he was under, a wormhole for him to focus on so that he didn't implode.

Out. Towel off. There was a razor so he shaved, and deodorant for his pits, and a comb for his hair, short though it was.

Shit, he needed clothes.

Stepping out . . .

He found another loose shirt and pants uni on the bed as well as a pair of running shoes that, yup, were in his size. Absently, he wondered how many sets they had on hand for the candidates. The whole height/weight/shoe-size thing had been part of the check-in process, but still.

A couple of minutes later, he was out the door, down the corridor, and walking into the cafeteria room.

Talk about a spread. The first thing he saw as he entered was a table with enough food on it to feed an army. Plates were lined up, ready to be filled, damask napkin rolls held sterling silver forks and knives, and the "bar" had about every kind of non-alcoholic anything you'd like—including a milkshake machine.

Clearly, the Brothers were refining things as they went along.

"None of it is tampered with," a male voice said behind him.

Craeg wheeled around and put his fists up like he was going to be attacked. The Brother Butch was sitting at the corner round table, legs propped up on an empty chair, a plate of food by his side. With careful, precise movements, he shifted scrambled eggs to his mouth without dropping anything off his fork.

"G'on," he said around chewing. "Get food. Sit with me. I'm not gonna fuck with you."

Craeg nodded once and hit the lineup. He wasn't shy about portions—he had no idea what was in store for all of them, but he could guess an energy reserve was the best way to prepare for the evening.

Picking a seat two over from the Brother, he had a good view of the door, something he regularly found himself requiring: Always know your escape. That was how he had lived through the slayers coming to his home.

"Look, I'm not going to beat around the bush," the Brother said before Craeg had gotten a fork load even close to his lips.

Great. So the guy had planned this, knowing that Craeg was in house and likely going to eat early.

Lowering the hash browns, Craeg forgot about the food and focused on the door. "What."

"I think you need to stay here in the training center."

"Excuse me?" He shifted his eyes back to the Brother. "I got a place."

The guy put his boots down on the floor and moved around so they were face-to-face. "I know where you live."

There was something about that direct stare that freaked him out, so he made a show of eating. "Yeah. I didn't lie about my address."

"It's not safe."

"Been there since the raids."

"That tenement barely has plumbing. And there's no shelter from the sun."

"I'm in the basement."

"A fire would cure that quick, putting you in the position of having to choose incineration by flame or noonday light."

Craeg cut a breakfast sausage in two and put half of it in his mouth. "I'm not moving."

"You got food and water here—and a good bed to crash on. No rent, either."

"I don't need charity." Okay, now he was beginning to get pissed off. "I came here to learn how to fight, not make you guys feel good about yourselves."

Butch leaned in. "You think we want to wipe your ass every time you take a shit? Really, you think that's where we're coming from?"

"Look, I don't need this—"

"Asshole," Butch snapped. "We are about to invest over the next year a couple hundred thousand dollars into you free of charge—you think we want that up in smoke 'cause your pride has a hard-on? This is not charity and it is not negotiable. I will take you home tonight after class, watch you pack up your shit, and then I will drive your miserable carcass back here or you can fuck off. What's it going to be, tough guy."

Craeg cursed long and hard, but it was under his breath.

Talk about by the short hairs.

"Fine," he muttered.

Butch clapped him on the shoulder. "And to show there's no hard feelings from you being a douche just now, I'll set you up with a good TV, Internet and a twelve-month calendar of Rhage so you have something pretty to look at."

With that, the Brother got up from the table, taking his still-full plate with him.

So that "meal" of his had just been to prove that it was safe to eat.

"See you in class," Butch said by the door after he'd bused his dishes at the sink. "Classroom tonight. Bombs, detonation systems, defusing. Fun stuff."

Left by his little lonesome, Craeg put his head in his hands.

Plans, he'd had plans for all this, people.

WTF.

"And then what transpired?"

As her father asked the question and spread more marmalade on his crust-less toast, Paradise tried to formulate another lie. Which, considering she had gotten about two hours of sleep and was still in physical recovery from everything, was like trying to button up a shirt in the dark.

"Ah ..." She broke off a piece of her croissant and put some strawberry jam on it. "Well, after we checked in, there was a cocktail hour of sorts." Vomitorium. "We milled around the gym getting to know one another." Nearly were electrocuted in the dark. "Went for a swim." Had a drowning party. "At the end, we took a walk." Dickensian death march. "And then everybody had a physical exam." Cardiac resuscitation. "It was a long evening, so that was why they wanted us to stay." Half-dead and barely breathing. "And that's it."

Great. She was channeling Mr. Subliminal.

Her father nodded. "The Brotherhood was most kind in calling me — Peyton as well. They said you did a wonderful job — that you were at the top of your class."

"I surprised myself."

And was still lost in her own home. Sitting with her father in the same seats they always did, under the same crystal chandelier, with the same porcelain plates and cups and saucers, watched over by the same oil paintings of ancestors, she felt like she was in a nice hotel that was furnished like a castle, and had a staff so well trained they were able to anticipate everything she wanted ... and was in a foreign land.

Then there was her father ... God, her dad.

As Abalone sat at the head of the long, glossy table, his handsome face was aglow with relief and pride — mostly relief — and didn't that make her feel even worse. The fact that her fabrications were having their desired, de-escalating effect distanced her even further from him . . . plus there was the added layer of her guilt.

Which was not just about the training.

It was impossible not to remember and obsess about what she'd done with Craeg, and what he'd done to himself. Part of her was constantly re-running every nuance of the experience, all the eye contact, all the sounds, the scents . . . the expression on his face as he —

Okay. She was not going *there* at the damned dining room table.

Where she would go, though? God, much as she hated to admit it, she worried that that interlude, even if it proved to be a one-time only, made her unmateable in the eyes of the *glymera*. Sure she was still sexually pure, but her vein had been good and tapped and that had led to . . . that certain exhibition, as one might call it, on Craeg's part.

Indeed, she hated the fact that she was wasting even a thought on that load of judgmental BS — but sitting here with her father, it was an unavoidable burden.

You didn't ditch an entire upbringing's worth of context that quickly.

Especially when you thought about what your next of kin wanted for you in life.

"Paradise?"

She shook herself and smiled. "I'm sorry, what?"

"I think you have enough jam on there, darling."

Paradise looked down and saw that she had put about half the jar on a piece of croissant the size of her thumb. The red sweetness was dripping down onto her plate, all over her knife, onto her hand.

"Silly me." She started trying to clean things up. "So how was your night last evening?"

Fortunately, he went into his work and a grand festival ball that was coming up and some other things, and she was able to listen well enough to nod in all the right places.

What were the Brothers going to do to us tonight?

she wondered. And how the hell was she going to act all normal around Craeg?

Thirty minutes later, she was in her uniform, had her satchel sorted, and was out the front door, dematerializing to the meeting place. The bus was already parked in the wooded lot, and the folding door opened as soon as the driver saw her.

Going up the three steps, she loosened her coat and met the eyes of the group. Novo was lounging back, earbuds plugged in, her iPhone front and center. Boone was the same. Axe was asleep in the back again, no doubt dreaming about things that hopefully would stay in his brain. Anslam was typing into his phone, probably updating his Facebook status to being in a relationship with the Porsche his father had just bought him as a reward for being in the training program. And Peyton was rubbing his face as if maybe that would wake him up.

"Hey," he said as she came down to where he was.

As she took a seat across the aisle from him, he shifted around, leaned against the blackened windows, and stretched his legs out.

"You ready for this?" he asked.

"I could answer that better if I knew what we were in for."

He grunted. "Okay, I'll change the subject. So, guess what I heard?"

Peyton was the source of all gossip—always had been. He'd been the one to tell her about the new toy parked in Anslam's family's garage, and the latest scandal involving his second cousin and the fact that she'd lied to her parents about where she was staying in town, and the one about some female who was married to an old goat and fucking rounds of males in her guest cottage on her estate.

But that last one had to be hyperbole.

"What?" At least the chatter would take her mind off

of seeing Craeg. "And embellish if you can. This trip is going to take a half hour at least."

"I got more stories. Don't you worry."

"Thank God." And this was in spite of their having spent all those hours on the phone during the day. "Have I mentioned lately that I love you?"

"Yes, but if you really wanted to prove it, you'd get that tattoo we were talking about."

"I'm not having your picture put on my ass."

"When you pass me by, though, it'll give me something pretty to look at."

"Not if I'm wearing pants. And hey, shouldn't I be offended by that comment?"

"Yeah, I'm sorry to break this to you, Parry, but blondes with perfect bodies and smart blue eyes don't go anywhere in this world. You might as well get used to this sad truth right now."

She threw her head back and laughed. "Okay, what's your story."

"My third cousin told me the Twelfth Month Festival Ball is being held in your daddy's ballroom. Why the fuck didn't you tell me?"

"I heard that, too," Anslam said without looking up from his phone.

Paradise glanced around. Boone and Novo couldn't have heard a thing, and Axe was out of it. Lowering her voice, she said, "Peyton. You need to chill about stuff like that, remember?"

Her buddy cracked his knuckles. "Sorry. But we're basically alone—and that's some big shit. You want to go with me? Or can I come with you." He gave her a winning smile. "That sounds dirty, doesn't it."

Paradise shot him a glare, but wasn't offended in the slightest. "You're a pig. And yes, please be my escort. I'm going to need you to help me get through the night."

"I shall be a gentlemale and a scholar—well, at least for most of the evening. Maybe till two a.m. I'm going to get hammered, though. Just want to warn you up front. That's the only way I'm going to make it to dawn."

Paradise leaned across the aisle and put her palm out. "High five."

As their hands smacked together, she thought, Thank you, baby Jesus, at least I'm going with a friend.

Chapter Twenty-three

Britney fucking Spears.

As Craeg sat in the rear of the classroom, all he could think of was that dumb-ass "Baby One More Time" video from a million years ago. He'd seen the damn thing only once, when an older, post-trans cousin of his had been watching it with a fascination he hadn't understood. At the time, Craeg had wondered why the hell some idiot human school girl with a pair of braids, a pleated skirt, and half her belly hanging out would be on anyone's radar.

Now? He so got it.

"... this detonator's primer is lead azide, lead styphnate, and aluminum, and you want to place the compound here, about the base charge, which in this case is tetryl." When Boone put his hand up, the Brother Tohrment nodded. "Yeah?"

"Are there other primary charges?"

"Good question. There's dizodinitrophenol and also you can use mercury fulminate mixed with potassium chlorate. But we're ASA in the Brotherhood."

The lesson continued, with Tohr, as he'd told them to call him, walking them through Bomb Making 101—and Boone, the class hand popper, interrupting from time to time with yet another "good question."

If the guy hadn't been so tight at the hand-to-hand, and otherwise quiet and not a problem, you'd have pointed to him as the classhole.

Meanwhile, Craeg was doing the right brain/left brain polka and he guessed the creative/analytic bucket labels held up: The analytical side of him was plugged into the front of the room, with its long countertop of chemicals in various forms and containers, and its blackboard on which there were scribbles and diagrams.

The "creative" side, or "nasty man-whore repository of all things heeeeeeeeey-now," kept pulling his eyes over to Paradise. She was sitting in front of him, at the table over on the right, and unlike him, she certainly didn't appear anything other than strictly focused: she was leaning in, intent to the point of obsession on the information being given, taking notes on a pad.

Half of her hair was pulled back into a loose knot she'd tied with some kind of thick black elastic, and she was wearing the same loose white *ji*-like uniform they all were. But fucking A, she might as well have been in a string bikini with all those blond waves down around her shoulders and her breasts—

Stop it.

To fuck with that, his libido shot back.

Fantastic. Now he was distracted *and* arguing with himself. Any more data processing under his helmet and he was liable to have a skull meltdown of Three Mile proportions.

And what do you know, he went right back to staring at her.

The root of his problem, apart from the orgasms he'd had in the shower, was the nape of her neck.

That skin right there had to be as soft as the stuff on her foot.

Had to be.

Shifting in his seat, he surreptitiously dropped his hand under the table and rearranged himself. Damn it. He really had to reel this shit in.

And yet even as his stare went back to Tohr and the bomb talk, he had a fantasy of getting out of his chair, going up behind her, and running his lips across the pale stretch between her hairline and the collar of that loose white shirt—

"Craeg?"

"What?" he squeaked to Tohr. Clearing his voice, he tried again in a more manly tone. "I mean, what."

"Come up here and walk us through all this."

Craeg glanced down. And wondered exactly what kind of a tent show he was going to give everybody if he got to his feet. Big top. Three ring. Barnum & Bailey. Yup.

And then he felt Paradise look at him—and his cock kicked hard enough to make his hips jump.

Right. He was pretty sure that was not the kind of detonation the professor had in mind.

"Craeg?"

As an awkward pause ground things to a halt in the classroom, Paradise braced herself and glanced over her shoulder.

She had been achingly aware of where Craeg had chosen to sit the entire class, to the point that it was almost like she had a compact open and had angled the mirror just so she could watch him watch the teacher. Which was nuts. She was pretty sure, given his Not You, Not Now speech from the night before, that he wasn't giving her a second thought—so it seemed particularly ridiculous to waste even a nanosecond on the guy that wasn't related to training.

Besides, it wasn't like he'd done anything to bring notice to himself.

Not so with the other trainees. Boone had asked a lot of questions—starting with, "Why can't I use my laptop to take notes?" To which the Brother Tohrment had replied, "Because the tap-tapping of a keyboard makes me want to get my shotgun. Do you feel like having a cranial leak tonight?" And culminating about two seconds ago with another inquiry that, frankly, helped the class.

Boone was the smart one.

Axe just sat by himself, hands steepled, brows down, not writing a thing—but the guy's dark aura meant that even if he didn't say much, you couldn't help knowing he was in the room. Novo didn't talk much either, but when she did, everyone listened. And Peyton, yes, Peyton cracked the occasional joke.

Yet it was Craeg, silent, brooding Craeg, who was the one she was tuned in to.

And P.S., she couldn't figure out why in the hell he wasn't getting up.

It was more than a lack of verticality, actually. He was sitting there like a deer in the headlights, staring at the blackboard like he'd forgotten how to rise out of a chair.

"Craeg?" Tohr prompted. "Have you separated from reality? Having a little vacay on me?"

Peyton got to his feet. "Lemme give it a shot," he said, scooting out and heading around behind the counter of chemicals to the blackboard. As he picked up a piece of chalk like it was a dead spider, he glanced at the Brother. "I thought this stuff was outlawed after the turn of the century?"

"You want me to write using your face instead?" Tohr drawled.

"Are you allowed to say that to students?"

"You a good enough fighter to get me to stop?"

Peyton shook his head. "Nope. Not even close."

"Smart answer, son. You're going to do well." Tohr clapped him on the back. "Why don't you save your shy little buddy back there and show us what you know."

Paradise looked down again at what she'd written in her notebook. Back at the beginning of the night, it had been hard to walk into the break room where everyone gathered and try to act natural around Craeg. He, on the other hand, had seemed totally nonplussed by her appearance or anyone else's—he'd made little eye contact with anyone, and said three words tops.

It had been about what she'd expected. And yet considering the amount of energy she needed to put in to just breathing normally around him, it had seemed unfair.

Back online, she told herself. She needed to concentrate on the training stuff. It was not only appropriate, more productive, and the reason she was in the room—it was also less likely to make her go insane.

She mostly succeeded at the goal.

Two hours later, they were allowed to get up, stretch their legs, and hit the loo. She had intended to walk down to the ladies' locker room by herself, but Novo fell into step with her.

"Mind if I ask you something?" the female said as she pushed the door open and held it for Paradise to go in first. "It's personal."

"Ah . . . sure." She picked one of the five stalls, de-pants'd it and hit the seat—and tried not to focus on the fact that she and a relative stranger were about to pee in the same place. "What is it?"

You got this, she told her bladder.

Novo naturally had no problem. The female probably had no problem with anything.

"You ever do females?"

Paradise whipped her head toward the stall wall. Her first thought? Crap, might as well do up my pants. We're going nowhere after that one.

"Did I shock you?" the female said with a laugh before she flushed.

There was the sound of a metal panel opening and then the running of water.

"Hello?" Novo prompted.

"Ah . . ." Paradise looked around as if maybe the peach metal stall walls or the white ceiling or the pale gray floor would help her out.

"So that would be a no." There was another laugh. "I'm not surprised."

For a moment, Paradise thought about trying to front

just to keep up with the coolness Novo seemed to have in spades. But similar to getting distracted in class, that was not why she was here.

"Actually, I haven't done anyone."

"Yeah, I figured that, too."

Paradise frowned. "So why did you ask?"

"I like being right."

Staring at the gray tile at her feet, Paradise thought, What the hell. "But you do? Females, that is."

"In the past. And males. I love who I love. The bits don't matter to me."

"Wow."

Novo's voice got sharp. "There's nothing wrong with that, you know."

"No, I'm not . . . I'm not criticizing or judging. I just think . . ."

"That's dirty and wrong, right."

Paradise thought about all the restrictions on her because she was an aristocrat. And then imagined what it would be like to simply be who and what she was, without excuses or compromises.

"No," she said. "I think that is really amazing."

And what do you know, on that note, she got her own job done. After she flushed, she opened the panel and was surprised, given the silence, that the female was still by the sinks.

Her face was wary, like she wanted to assess Paradise's affect.

Paradise met those intense teal eyes without hesitation as she went over and washed her hands in warm water with soap that smelled like lemon.

"In fact, I envy you," she found herself murmuring as she checked her reflection in the mirror.

No makeup and fluorescent lights were not a good combo when you hadn't slept for almost forty-eight hours— and had gone through organized torture.

"Why are you any different?" the female asked.

"I'm sorry?"

"If you like girls."

"Oh, no." She thought of her response to Craeg. And then enjoyed a couple of mental snapshots of his hand pumping under that sheet. "Yeah, no. I'm into males."

Novo shrugged and straightened. "So it still stands. Why are you any different?"

Paradise stared at her reflection, and thought about her bloodline. Her father. "Long, boring story."

"Long stories that people don't want to talk about are never the boring ones."

At the change in tone, Paradise shifted her eyes over. Novo was looking toward the door out of the bathroom, her strong body strung tight, her hands squeezing the edge of the sink so hard her knuckles were white.

"What happened to you?" Paradise whispered.

Novo shook herself back into focus. "Nothing that matters anymore. We're heading to the weight room, right?"

"Did they say that?"

"Yeah."

Paradise must have been watching Craeg walk out of the classroom. "I'm losing my mind."

"You're okay. Splash your face with some cold water. It'll bring you back—works for me all the time."

Paradise watched the female leave . . . and then she cranked on the faucet that was marked with a C.

Might as well give it a go.

Maybe it would cool off her libido, too.

Chapter Twenty-four

Sitting at the desk in Tohr's office, Butch stood the long, thin metal key up on the end that had the red tassel . . . and let the thing fall to the blotter. As gravity made it tap out, the sound was a solid *thunk*. With a curse, he picked it up, stood it on its other end . . . and let it fall. And again. And again—

"Are you ready?"

He looked up at Tohr, who'd leaned in through the glass door. "Hey, yeah, sure. Who're you sending in first?"

"Axwelle. Figured you might as well start the eval with the one most likely to be considered a sociopath."

"Perfect." He swiveled to the computer, tapped in a few commands and got the hidden video camera rolling. "Pull him out of the workout."

"Roger that."

As the glass door eased shut, Butch watched his fingers work the tasseled key some more. He hadn't wanted to say it to his Marissa, but to him and V, it was pretty clear what the thing was. The problem? When nada had come up on the Internet search, V had hit his connections in the vampire underground . . . but nothing had surfaced with any of the sex clubs or groups.

A key to get you in so you could get it on. So to speak.

Ordinarily, Butch would have wondered if people weren't hiding something or lying, but V was a legit member of the wonderful world of kink—plus the brother wasn't above using a little muscle to get information if he had to.

Yet another reason the two of them were tight.

So what else was it. Where else could he—

At the sound of a knock on the glass, he glanced up and motioned with his hand. "Hey, man. C'mon in, sit down."

As Axwelle entered, the guy made a move with his hands like he was used to cramming them in the pockets of his jeans, but then had nowhere to go with the impulse in his training uni. "Can I stand?"

"Nope." Butch nodded to the chair on the opposite side of the desk. "There. And that is not a suggestion, that's a requirement."

They had to make sure the trainee's face was in full view of the lens up in the corner behind him.

Axwelle—or Axe, as he called himself—crossed his arms over his chest and planted it in the seat. "What's this about?"

"Just want to talk to you for a little bit. Get to know you better." Butch frowned and sat forward. Then he dangled the key by its red tassel. "You recognize this?"

"No."

"Then why did your eyes just go to it?"

"Because it's in your hand and you're not holding anything else. There's nothing on the desk, either."

Butch held the tassel between his thumb and forefinger and let the thing swing from side to side. "That's the only reason, huh."

"Do I look like I worry about keys?"

"How do you know it's a key?"

Eyes that were nearly as yellow as Phury's locked on him and stayed put. "What else could it be?"

"You tell me."

"I thought this was supposed to be a get-to-know-ya. What the fuck does some whatever-it-is have to do with my ass?"

Butch studied the kid's face, looking for tells. Huh.

You know, without the half-job tattoos and piercings, the guy might have been handsome. And he might well be a good poker player, considering all the mask-in-place he was rolling.

Axe put his puss just inches from the key. "I'm still staring at it. Is this working for you?"

Butch took his own sweet time before changing subjects. The thing with liars? Silence and stillness were often the best challenge to their fronts, and he looked for tics, blinks, and twitches.

Eventually, he smiled. "You ever see someone die?"

Not on the list of questions Mary had given him to help her ascertain a trainee's psychological state. But he was good with winging shit.

"What are you suggesting?"

The thought of his Marissa crying over that dead female made him more aggressive than a bull, but he drew back on that throttle.

"Just asking." He looked at the key to give the male some "personal space." "It is one way to get to know you better, isn't it? An icebreaker, they call them, when two people go on a blind date and have to make conversation."

"You want to know if I've ever killed anybody."

"Not the question, was it. I asked, have you ever seen death happen?"

When there was no answer for a period of time, Butch glanced up. Axe wasn't looking at the key anymore. The guy was focused on the middle distance in front of his nose.

Gotcha, Butch thought.

Gentling his voice deliberately, he murmured, "Who was it, Axwelle."

"Don't call me that."

"Why, it's your name."

"I don't answer to it."

"Why."

An angry glare went point-blank on Butch like a gun muzzle. "Because I fucking don't, okay?"

"Fine, back to the Grim Reaper. Tell me the story."

"Fuck you."

Under any other circumstances, Butch would have lunged across the desk and grabbed the cocksucker's neck for that kind of attitude, but there was too much purpose behind this.

"Hmmmmm," was all he said.

Axe slammed himself back in the chair and did the re-cross thing with his arms. As his shoulders bunched up, it was hard not to approve of the heft of all that muscle. Strength without brains and a copious lack of psychotic, however, were going to do none of them any good.

"Can I go now?" Axe demanded.

"No, son, I don't think you can. And before you get all huffy on my ass, I'm going to point out to you that this wonderful little bonding time we're sharing is the first of at least three sessions."

"Are you a shrink?"

"Fuck, no, are you kidding me?" He laughed. "I take pride in my own little stretch of madness, as a matter of fact."

After all, he was seriously religious, putting his faith and the course of his life willingly in the hands of a belief system that was not concretely verifiable. And that was nuts, right?

Then again, the fact that his religion enriched his mortal coil and centered him and brought him meaning even after he had been "turned" into another species was enough proof for him.

With a shrug, he said, "The only way to get out of this office is to tell me what happened. As soon as you do, you're free to go back to the weight room and power-lift until either your knees give out on you or you begin to vomit. So much to look forward to, right?"

If Craeg had thought that sitting behind Paradise in class was bad? That was nothing compared to watching her do pull-ups.

Across the mats, and to the accompaniment of the clanking of free weights, Paradise was lifting her body in perfect form up to the chin bar and then releasing . . . and up . . . and releasing. Her knees were cocked parallel to the floor, her ass was . . . painfully tight (for him, not for her, clearly), and her torso was in control from pelvis to shoulder.

Every time she hit the low point, her breasts punched up against the loose shirt they all wore—

"Fuck," he groused as he lay back down on the bench and gripped the bar above his head.

Popping the four hundred and fifty pounds off its support, he took the weight down to his pecs and shoved it back up like the thing had insulted his dead mother.

"You want a spotter?" Novo asked.

When all he could do was grunt, she assumed the position behind his head, keeping her hands just under the now-bent bar.

"Three . . ." she counted. "Two more. One . . . good. You got it."

As she helped guide the load back into its holding position, he flopped his forearms onto his chest and caught his breath.

Novo put her face in his line of vision. "I think you need to take a break."

"Fuck that."

"No, I mean it."

"I got at least four more sets in me."

"Your endurance ain't what I'm worried about." At that, her eyes went down to his hips. "Not that I don't appreciate the view. Just not sure what the virginal object of your affections is gonna think."

Craeg lifted his head. And then sat up quick.

Novo laughed. "Yeah, why don't you take care of that and come back?"

"Damn it," he hissed, jumping to his feet.

Marching across for the door, he glanced at the Brother Vishous. "I gotta go to the bathroom."

Vishous smiled darkly. "Yeah, you do."

Punching his way out into the corridor, he wondered if everyone had noticed he had a hard-on. The only good news? Paradise seemed oblivious—which meant she was either incredibly good at hiding her reactions, which he doubted, or she was as clueless about his little problem as he hoped.

In which case he felt like an extra-huge douche bag.

He hit the door to the men's locker room so hard it flew open, striking the wall and forcing him to catch the thing before it smacked him in the face on the rebound.

"Not it, this is *not* it."

Pacing around with his hands on his hips, he realized he should never have taken her vein. That blood exchange had created some kind of connection between them such that he was aware of every move she made anywhere at any moment—and the way that shit registered?

Mr. Happy got all excited about the possibility of shaking hands with her.

Which was never. Fucking. Going. To. Happen.

More pacing. More cursing.

Still hard.

"Fuck me!" he belted out.

Yes, please, his cock replied with a kick.

For a moment, all sorts of fantasies played through his head: Slamming the thing in a heavy book. Dropping a cement block on it. Car doors, hammers, logs.

This couldn't be happening to him. The hardest part of training to become a soldier under the Brotherhood so he could avenge his family . . . could not possibly be some blond female. He just refused to believe this.

Not possible—

With another kick under his uniform, his erection seemed to be laughing at him.

Glaring down at his hips, he barked, "Shut up, idiot."

Chapter Twenty-five

Butch watched every move the kid made. From the series of fine muscle contractions under Axe's left eye to the chin itch he was rocking to the crack-of-the-neck finale.

"Tell me, and I'll let you go," he repeated.

Man, this was so much easier to do than when he'd been working for the CPD. Miranda rights? Yeah, whatever. Involuntary restraint? Blah, blah, blah. Coercion?

Well, actually he'd done some coercion even back then.

In fact, he thought back to that kid Billy Riddle who had attacked Beth before she had fallen into the vampire world and taken Butch with her. Man, he'd really enjoyed grinding that little bitch's nose into the linoleum in the emergency room. Hmm . . . that hadn't been coercion, technically—because he hadn't been after information. It had been flat-out payback for the bastard having jumped a perfectly innocent woman in an alley so he could try to rape her with his friend.

Yeah, because you could really get through to an animal like that with arm's-length handling.

Fucker.

Refocusing on Axe, Butch murmured, "I'm waiting."

Axe shrugged. "Kick me out if you want, do other shit to me if you want . . . but I don't owe you that. You don't get a piece of my soul—you haven't earned it."

Sound logic, Butch thought—and exactly what he himself would have said if he'd been sitting in that chair.

Butch leaned in. "Sooner or later, before your final acceptance, you're going to have to tell me."

"Why the fuck do you care?"

"I don't."

Well, didn't that get him a pair of bug eyes. "Then what the fuck are you asking me for?"

Butch planted his elbows on the desk and fanned out his hands, all Duh. "I need to know how you're going to handle it when you see it again. That's why. And one assessment of future behavior is past behavior. What you guys experience here in training is nothing compared to what the outside world is like. You gotta be prepared for situations when there is no time to think, when all you've got to go on to save your life or the lives of the people who are fighting with you are your instincts and your will to survive—and I guarantee you that when you get to those moments, the last thing you want is to have a lockup. The more you're exposed to trauma, the more hardened you become to it and the safer you are. And that is a really suck-ass fucking equation, but it is the goddamn truth."

Axe's eyes drifted down to his own hands.

"Go back to the gym," Butch ordered. "Think about shit. Just know you don't have forever. We're not wasting—"

"I lied."

"Excuse me."

The hard-ass, Gothed-out, degenerate-looking male inhaled slowly. "I haven't seen any. I don't know . . . what it looks like. I don't know what it feels like."

The change in affect, from hostile mask to profound sadness, was startling, but that was the way it always happened. When someone broke, when they decided to give up the goods, they became a different version of themselves, proving that self-protection and revelation were two mutually exclusive propositions.

"So why are you here?" Butch whispered. "Tell me . . . why did you come to us?"

"I don't know."

"Yeah, you do."

Butch surreptitiously reached over and made sure his phone was on silent and that the ringer on the office line was off. And when Tohr reappeared on the far side of the glass door, Butch put his palm out—and the Brother backed off.

"Why are you here, Axe?"

The minutes slowed to a crawl and the quiet noises of the office seemed to dim even further out of respect for the space they were in.

"My dad was a nobody," came the hoarse voice. "He didn't do anything with his life. He was a carpenter for the species, you know ... worked with his hands. Ma didn't want anything to do with him or me—she left before my transition. She didn't give a fuck about us. My dad, though, he stayed, and without him, I woulda been out on the streets as a pretrans, and we both know how long I would have lasted." That dark-haired, half-and-half head shook slowly from left to right. "I wasn't ... good, you know? I never have been. He didn't leave because there was no one else, I guess."

Butch made no move, no sound. If he interrupted, he was liable to remind the male that he was talking, instead of reliving his previous life internally.

It was pretty clear where this story was going.

"I like X. I like coke. I like ... some other hard-core shit. Two years ago, I went on a bender. Gone for like a week. One night, my dad tried to reach me by phone. Left me these messages—I was so fucking high that I got annoyed with him." That low voice trailed off. "I got ... annoyed."

When Axe stalled out, the haunted cast to his face was a heartbreaker.

"What did you do, son?" Butch said softly, because he couldn't help himself.

Axe cleared his throat a couple of times. Rubbed underneath his nose like the tears he was holding back were irritating the thing.

"I erased the messages." There were a couple of

coughs. "I erased . . . all the messages without listening to them."

"And then what."

"They'd killed him. The *lessers*. He was working in one of the aristocrats' houses that got hit in the raids. He was . . . dying at the time he left me the voice mails." Axe shook his head. "I went back and looked at the call log when I found what had happened and did the math."

Butch closed his eyes for a second. "I'm sorry, son."

"I didn't know about it all right away . . . I guess a son of one of the workers went there and discovered everyone? That guy, whoever he was, he took care . . . of everything. When I finally got back home—you know, three days later—there was this note that had been put on the door. Someone had called the house phone and left messages, and when there was no one returning them, they put it all . . . in a note."

"Brutal. Fucking brutal."

"I kept the note." Axe sniffed hard and shook his head. "I have the note they left. The remains are still on the estate—I think the house is in human hands now?"

"Do you want to get them back?"

"I don't know. No. No, I don't think so. Just one more way to be a bad son, huh."

"Where's your mom?"

"Heard she moved up in the world, married some rich guy, living the life. I don't know—I don't care." As the male looked up abruptly, Axe's face resumed its earlier composure, shutting the emotion down in the same way you might lock out an intruder. "So, no, I haven't seen death up close. That's one cherry I haven't popped. Can I go now?"

Butch felt like he should say something profound. But what Axe really wanted, more than some pep talk, was the exit. "Yeah. You can."

That chair made a squeaking noise against the concrete as it was shoved back hard, and then Axe steamed for the door. Before he opened it, he stopped. Looked back over his shoulder.

222   J. R. WARD

"What is it like?"

"Death?" When he got a nod, Butch did an inhale of his own. "You sure you want to know that kind of shit?"

"You said we needed exposure."

Touché, he wanted to say. Instead, Butch pictured the male going back to the modest house he lived alone in and getting really fucking drunk and slitting his wrists. Or OD'ing. Or jumping out a window.

Not a foregone conclusion, given the amount of pain lurking under the half-tats and the metal.

"I want you to move in here." Butch rubbed his large gold cross through his shirt. "Craeg's going to stay with us, you need to as well."

"What, worried I'ma go hang myself in the bathroom?"

"Yeah, precisely." When Butch just stared across the desk, those dark brows of the guy rose once again. "You'll stay here, Axe. It's safer, you're protected, and you can concentrate on what you need to do."

There was going to be a fight about this, of course. Asshats like this guy always had a—

"Okay, but I'm going to need a night or two every once in a while to . . . you know."

Interesting, Butch thought. So the poor SOB was aware, on some level, of the shit going on in his brain— and was spooked.

"You need to get laid, huh?" Butch drawled.

"Yeah."

"Don't blame you—and you can make arrangements with the *doggen* to drive you in and out. That won't be a problem."

"So . . . what is it like?"

Butch fell quiet and found himself pulling a little middle-vision-field of his own as images—gruesome, horrible images—played across his mind. For a moment, he wondered whether he should go there with the kid, but then he recognized that the truth was something that needed to be spoken even if it was terrible. Maybe especially if it was terrible.

And it had to be told to anyone who wanted to fight in this war.

If Axe couldn't handle his demons, then the last thing that was good for anybody was to give him a dagger and a gun and send him out into Caldwell's alleys.

Butch shrugged. "I used to be a homicide detective with the human police—don't ask—so I saw a lot of it. To answer the question, it depends on how old it is and how it happened. The new stuff . . . especially if it was violent . . . can be messy. Body parts really don't like to be cut, stabbed or hacked into sections, and they express their anger by leaking all over the fuck. Jesus, we're, like, seventy percent water or something? And you learn that's so fucking true when you go to a fresh scene. Pools of it. Drips of it. Speckles of it. Then you got the stained clothes, rugs, bedsheets, walls, flooring—or if it's outside, the ground cover, the concrete, the asphalt. And then there's the smell. Blood, sweat, urine, other shit. That juicy bouquet will get in your sinuses and stay there for hours afterward." He shook his head again. "The older cases . . . the smell is worse than the mess. Water deaths, with the bloating, are just ugly—and if that gas that's built up gets out? The stench will knock you on your ass. And I don't know, I wasn't too crazy for the burn deaths either. I mean, you'd think we'd realize we're not different than any other mammal—cooked meat is cooked meat, period. But I've never seen a grown man puke up his coffee and donuts over a medium rare T-bone." Butch refocused on the male. "You want to know what I always hated the most?"

"Yeah."

He motioned over his head. "The hair. The hair . . . God, the fucking hair, especially if it was a woman. Matted with blood, dirt, little rocks . . . tangled and twisted . . . lying on gray skin. When I can't sleep at night, that's what I see. I see the hair." His hands automatically began to rub themselves. "You always wore these gloves, you know . . . so you didn't get fingerprints on anything, didn't leave any of yourself behind. Early days they used to be latex—later, they were nitrile. And sometimes, when I'd handle a body, the hair would get on the gloves . . . and it was like it wanted to get into me? Like . . . you could catch death by murder somehow." He shook his head. "Those gloves were so fucking thin. And they didn't work."

Axe frowned. "Why did you have to wear them then?"

"No, no, they worked with fingerprints, you know. But I left something of myself behind in all those dead bodies. Every one of them . . . has a piece of me."

Starting with my sister, he thought. And to be accurate, she had taken the largest hunk out of him.

There was a long stretch of silence.

"You were in the human world?" Axe asked. "I mean . . . it sounds like you were—"

"Yeah, a while ago. Now . . . I'm something else." Butch cleared his throat. "G'head, get outta here. You need your workout. You, me, and Craeg will go get all your shit—and maybe it'll help me if you're in the car with that hardheaded sonofabitch. I think I'm going to have to fight to keep him from jumping out and pulling a runner."

"Yeah. Okay. Sure."

"I'm sorry about your dad. And he wasn't a nobody. Taking care of you made him count."

Axe turned away and paused again, like he was bracing himself. Then he pushed his way out into the corridor and was gone.

As the glass door quietly eased shut, Butch stared straight ahead. He hadn't intended to reveal that much to the male—he never spoke about that shit to anyone.

Putting his head in his hands, he took some deep breaths . . . and prayed to God that none of the other interviews went like that one.

Chapter Twenty-six

Paradise finally let her feet drop to the mat, but she kept her grip on the chin-up bar. Her lungs were on fire, her shoulders and biceps were screaming, and there was a line of sweat working its way from the back strap of her sports bra down her spine. The cool thing was, though, she had learned that this woozy feeling was going to pass fast, and then she would be on to the next set of reps.

Glancing over at Peyton, she found him on the treadmill, and she was impressed. He was running like a bat out of hell, big body in perfect form, his head up, eyes unfocused but alert. She'd never pegged him for an athlete—then again, all he'd done was bong lifts before.

The question was, where was—

"Hey."

As Novo came up to her, Paradise smiled. "Good job with those sit-ups. You did, like, five hundred."

"Actually it was five hundred eighty-two. Listen, Craeg just left. He looked upset. Thought you might want to go help him with his problem."

Paradise wheeled for the door, but stopped. "I don't . . . I mean, it's not like I know him."

"Do any of us? And I'm pretty damn sure you're the one he wants to talk to."

"Why's that?"

"Just a hunch."

"Ah . . . okay, thanks."

Heading for the exit, she glanced at the Brother Tohrment. "May I please be excused to go to the ladies' room?"

"You got it, Paradise."

Slipping out into the corridor, she looked left and right, expecting to find Craeg pacing or sitting on the floor. Nope. Everything was empty.

Her body cooled efficiently as she went farther down to the males' locker room. Breathing in, she caught his scent, knew he was inside—and, sensing no hint of anyone else, she went to the metal door and knocked.

"Craeg?"

When there was no answer, she pulled the door open a little and saw nothing but a concrete wall. Heading in, she went around until she was in the large open area with all the lockers. Wow. Ten times the size of the females' one, but without the couches and the nice place to sit down to do your hair and makeup. Assuming you needed to.

Man, she was so jumpy, she was talking gibberish to herself.

New level.

"Craeg?" she said more loudly.

There was the sound of running water—a sink, not a shower—and she cleared her throat. "Craeg!"

"What the fuck!"

And then there was more cursing until he marched out of a different section of the facility. Water was dripping from his face and his hands, and his T-shirt was damp around the neck.

"What are you doing in here?" he demanded, passing a palm over his wet hair, shoving the stuff back.

God, his eyes were amazing, so deeply set and such a pale blue. And his shoulders were so big. And his chest was— "Novo said you need help."

"Novo said what?"

"She told me you—"

"No, no." He whipped a hand through the air like he

was erasing his question. "Why would she—" Craeg stopped. Then muttered something like, "I'm going to kick her ass."

"Why?" Paradise frowned. "Are you okay? Do you need to feed some more—"

"No." He jabbed a finger in her face. "And never again with you. Ever."

Paradise recoiled. "I *beg* your pardon."

"You heard me." Shaking his head and pacing around in a tight circle, he focused on the tile floor. "Now will you get the hell out of here—"

"I have as much right as you do to—"

He glared at her. "You're in the males' locker room. So unless you sprouted a boom stick overnight, in fact, you do *not* have as much right as I do."

She opened her mouth. Closed it.

And she was about to leave when he made the turn and came back toward her.

That was when she saw exactly what his "problem" was.

Instantly, her body responded—and as he tripped to a halt and looked at her, it was very, very clear that he had caught her arousal.

A curious defeat, one that seemed totally counter to his personality, suffused his face and dropped his shoulders.

They stared at each other for the longest time.

"You don't have to say it," she whispered. "I know you don't want this. I know the timing is bad. I know ... that the last thing either of us needs right now is a complication. But I spent all day thinking about you, and what's the worst that can happen? Our bodies want ... what they want."

This time, when he pushed his hair back, his hand was shaking.

On her side, the trembling was in her legs, her arms, her torso. The full stem to stern bifta, as they said.

Craeg came at her slowly, as if he were giving her time

to change her mind, back away, leave. Not going to happen. She stayed exactly where she was, tilting her head up so she could meet him in the eye.

"If I kiss you," he growled, "there's no going back. I might not fuck you right here, right now, but I'll have you on your back the instant I get the goddamn chance."

She had the sense he was talking crudely to get her to reconsider, and for a split second, she did—but not because he'd used the f-word. That just turned her on even more. No, her *glymera*-trained conscience sat up and hollered, all those morals and expectations and rules rushing into the forefront of her brain and dulling the lust. If she lost her virginity to anyone it would be a problem—giving it to a commoner? She'd be stained for life. Unmateable. A source of shame upon her father, her bloodline, her class.

On the other hand, aside from somebody like Peyton, she was pretty sure that no "proper" male would want her after she had been through the training center's program, anyway. Even if she didn't fight in the war, this kind of learning did not fit into the parlor-games sort of education females were supposed to have.

The solution, she supposed, was to never get hitched.

As the thought hit her, an intoxicating relief went through her entire body, the buoyancy so powerful, she had the urge to jump—and that was when she heard Novo's voice in her head:

Why are you any different?

Locking onto Craeg's hot eyes, she marveled at how the easiest solution was in some ways the hardest. But if she never got mated, then she was free to make choices in a way she'd never dreamed.

And it was on that basis of strength that she made up her mind.

Paradise was going to back down.

Looming over the female, Craeg could feel it in his bones. In spite of her arousal, she was going to come to her senses and save them both a world of headaches. She was going to size him up, with his huge body and his raging erection, and realize that she didn't want the complications or the stress —

With an elegance of movement that terrified him, she lifted her hands and placed them on his shoulders — no, it was his pecs, because she wasn't quite tall enough. Tilting her head even further back, he was momentarily stunned by how perfectly the ugly fluorescent light from the ceiling fixtures hit her fine features and the feathers of blond hair that had escaped her tie and lines of her collarbone.

"So kiss me," she said.

In the back of his mind, he heard the sound of two Chevy trucks crashing into each other grill-to-grill.

Fuck. No backing down.

With a curse, he closed his eyes. Swayed. Realized that this was, in fact, going to happen.

Then he popped his lids back open and reached forward to touch her. Abruptly, he had a moment of awkwardness, as if he didn't know where to put his hands — her shoulders? The sides of her throat? Her face?

The sex he'd had had always been rough and quick, the kind of shit you did with human women or vampire females who didn't care who they spread for. Paradise was the opposite of all that — and that was the problem. As much as he wanted her, he wanted to do right by her.

Well, wasn't he a fucking gentlemale all of a sudden.

With shaking hands, he ended up tracing her jaw with his fingertips, and as her lips parted, he eased his head to one side and closed the distance between their mouths.

Almost.

With a mere millimeter of anticipation separating them, he whispered, "Last chance."

"I'm waiting."

So he kissed her.

The groan he let out was a combination of starvation and submission, and in the back of his mind, he became dimly aware that there was a new scent in the air, something that was part and parcel of the heat between them, but a revelation as well.

Whatever, she was soft and sweet and hesitant and strong. Everything he'd imagined her to be.

Brushing his mouth over hers, he extended his tongue and licked his way into her. And that was when the whole restraint thing went out the window—with a surge, he wrapped his arms around her and pulled her in tight to his body, letting her feel him—even at the hips, where, in spite of the two releases he'd given himself in a bathroom stall before she'd come in, he was raring to go.

Oh, God, she was so much smaller than he was, but as her breasts came up to him and her weight shifted so she was leaning against him . . .

He knew that she was the one in control.

They kissed for the longest time, and it was not nearly enough—but some inner alarm clock went off and was loud enough to cut through the roar of his need for her sex.

Pulling back, he felt a serious shot of male satisfaction as he saw that her face was flushed, and her mouth open, and her breathing rough.

He tried to think of when he could get her alone, how they could find some privacy, where it could be.

"What's your telephone number?" he asked in a guttural voice.

After she told him, she glanced around. "Do you need to write that down?"

As if. The seven numbers were tattooed on his brain.

"I'll call you." Another reason, aside from that whole pesky incinerated-by-the-sun thing, to be glad he was moving in here—he didn't have a phone of his own. "At seven a.m."

"To make arrangements to meet? I can't go out during the day. My father would kill me—and I can't sneak out. He'd know immediately."

Yeah, he could remember what it was like living with family in a small house.

Craeg kissed her mouth once. Twice. "Just answer your phone."

"I'm glad you want to talk."

"I'm not after the conversation." He let his eyes drift down over her throat to her breasts. "I'm going to teach you a couple of things."

"Like what?"

Bending at the waist, he nuzzled her throat. "You know that ache you've got right now? The one between your legs?"

"Yes . . ." she whispered.

"I'm going to show you how to take care of that by yourself. And you're going to make me come when I listen to what it sounds like." He straightened and stepped back, nodding to the exit. "Go. Before anyone finds you in here."

No reason to have her candidacy affected by this. There wasn't a no-fraternizing rule that he'd seen on the application, but come on. This was best kept under wraps.

"Go on," he repeated when she didn't move.

She just stared up at him with wide, hot eyes.

Shit, all he could think of was taking her right then and there, standing up, her legs split wide around his hips, his cock buried so far in her, he had struggle not to black out.

"*Go, Paradise.*"

Finally, she turned away. Just before she cut around the concrete partition to the door, he growled, "Answer your goddamn phone."

"I will," she said. "Right away."

Left alone, Craeg shut his lids. And wondered how in the hell he was going to make it 'til then.

Chapter Twenty-seven

Three hours later, Craeg was in the front passenger seat of a Hummer. Or nearly leaning out of it was more apt: As Butch drove him and Axe away from the training center's underground parking garage, Craeg was bent toward the windshield, trying to make sense of the strangely blurry landscape.

"We got bad weather?" Axe asked from the back.

"Nope," the Brother replied as they came up to an enormous, elaborate gate system that was like something out of *Jurassic Park*, all twenty-foot-tall concrete with huge metal bars and barricades that had to have electricity running through them.

Yeah, cuz the Brothers had already proved how they loved to play with that shocking shit.

Craeg shook his head. "You guys don't fool around with the security, do you."

"Nope."

As they progressed through the thickly wooded territory, they came up to a series of stop points that grew gradually less and less fancy and obstructive. The last one was little more than something you'd find on an abandoned farm, a rickety "old" thing that turned out to be deliberately constructed to appear that way.

So smart.

When Butch finally emerged from a clearing and took a left onto a paved road, the bizarre blurring of the landscape magically resolved itself. But it was weird, Craeg's eyes adjusted easily; his bearings did not. Were they heading west? East?

"You know where I live, of course," Axe muttered.

Butch shot a dry look into the rearview. "No, not at all."

The drive to wherever it was took about forty-five minutes, and all Craeg got out of the trip was a sense of how little he knew about Caldwell. Having spent his pre-trans life at home with his mother, he hadn't had the chance to get out all that much after his transition—because the raids had happened a mere six months later. And then following the carnage, after he had watched his mother and sister die and proceeded to learn first-hand about his father's death, he'd gone through a pe-riod of intense crazy ... then settled into a numb working schedule that had paid the bills and allowed him to find some shelter away from his parents' house.

He hadn't been back there since he'd cleaned every-thing up and buried the females of his bloodline along with the remains of his father—which he'd brought back from the aristocrats' house.

God, his father. He'd loved the guy—and to find out that a male of such worth had died because a bunch of *glymera* types had locked him and every other servant and worker on the premises out of the safe room?

And people wondered why he hated those rich bas-tards.

"You want us to wait here, Axe?" Butch asked.

Craeg shook himself and saw that they'd pulled up in front of. . . .

It was fucking Hansel and Gretel's house. That was the only comparison he could pull out of his ass. In the glow from the Hummer's headlights, the cottage was as quaint as a postcard, all whitewashed with a high peaked roof and curlicue woodwork under its eaves that was as intricate as lace.

"You," Craeg blurted. "You grew up in *that*?"

"Yeah." Axe popped his door open. "What's the fucking problem."

"Screw it, we're coming in with you," Butch announced as he killed the engine. "Mostly because I want to see all the Hummel figurines."

Craeg was going to stay in the SUV, but then figured, That's right, fuck it. What else did he have to do with his time?

Axe led them around to a side door that he unlocked with a copper key. As he went inside, the beeping of an alarm sounded, but that didn't last as he shut things off at a keypad mounted on the wall.

When the guy hit the lights, all Craeg could do was blink like a cow.

"Holy Mary, mother of . . ." Butch muttered.

"He thought she was coming back, 'kay?" Axe bitched as he tossed his keys on a spectacular slab of butcher block. "He did this for my mother."

Craeg had never seen so many red and pink roses in his life: The walls of the quaint kitchen were covered floor to ceiling with a paper dominated by the flowers and the green vine they were apparently growing on. And what do you know, the drapery over in the alcove and around the window over the kitchen sink was the exact same pattern.

"You stay here," Axe muttered. "I'll be down with my goddamn bag."

The guy's heavy footfalls sounded through the house, the thunder going up to the second floor and then drifting down from the rafters above.

"Look at this woodwork," Butch said, as he ran his hand over the carved molding around one of the doorjambs. "Incredible."

Craeg went to the carved table and sat down in a delicate chair that made him wish he hadn't eaten so much for First Meal. Looking at all the workmanship on the crown moldings and doors, on the cabinets, on even the sills of the windows, FFS, he discovered that it all formed an organic pattern that echoed the vines of the wallpaper, twisting and turning elegantly and beautifully around fixtures and entries/exits. Varnished with a clear coat, the maple or pine or whatever it was glowed as only fine wood that had been finely worked could.

"The rest of the rooms have to be like this," Butch said as he leaned out of the kitchen. "Yup. This is a masterpiece—"

Axe reappeared with a black duffel and a backpack. "On to the next—"

"Did you father do all this woodwork?" Butch asked.

"Yeah."

"He was a fuck of a lot more than a nothing."

"Can we go now?"

"Wait," Craeg cut in. "Your father was a woodworker? Mine was a floor layer."

"Oh, yeah?"

There was a pause as the pair of them locked eyes. "Did he die at Endelview?" Craeg bit out, naming the estate that had been raided that horrible night.

Axe's dark expression went straight to pitch-black, in a way that made his tattoos seem sinister. "Yeah."

"Mine, too." Craeg searched the male's face, wondering how much he knew about what had gone down there. Shit . . . it was horrible to realize that he'd handled the body of the guy's father. Someone else had done the notifications to surviving family members, though. He'd been finished at that point. "Bad night."

"Yeah." Axe cleared his throat and looked away. "So can we go?"

"No," Craeg cut in. "You two stay here while I go to my place. I'll be right back with my gear."

"You're not taking much, then," Axe drawled.

Craeg got to his feet and headed for that door again. "Don't have much."

The Brother called out just as he put a foot on the back stoop. "If you don't return here in twenty minutes, you're out of the program."

"I know," he muttered. "I know."

*   *   *

As the bus trundled to a stop, Paradise picked up her satchel and got ready to shuffle out of her row.

"So are you coming to my house?" Peyton asked as he got to his feet. "We still have two hours at least, and Anslam's coming to hang."

Ducking her head so he didn't see the flush on her face, she pretended to look for her phone even though she knew where it was, in the pocket of her parka. "I want to be home for my father."

"Annnnnd that would be dawn," he pointed out as he put his tinted glasses on. "Two hours from now."

Okay, fine, but no matter what time it was, she wasn't about to own up to the fact that all she wanted to do was watch the hands of the clock on her bedside table make their way around until the big one was on the twelve and the little guy was on the seven.

"Sorry, I have stuff to do. Call me?" Shit, she actually didn't want him to, not today. "I mean—"

"It's cool." Peyton turned to Anslam. "You ready for some bong hits?"

The other male shot a snarky smile over. "Always and forever."

As the pair of them went down the aisle, she shook her head and moved out of her seat. Guess some things were back to normal—and it was funny, with all the stress of the training, she couldn't really blame Peyton for wanting an escape that felt good. Maybe that's what she was doing with Craeg?

Talk about addictions. The way she felt around that male, when he looked at her, touched her, kissed her, was so amazing, she could see herself getting hooked on the buzz—thus the whole counting-down-the-hours thing. The trouble with all that, however, was that he wasn't something that could be bought and consumed like pot, or ice cream, or wine. He was a separate, independent entity, and it was funny, the fact that he'd chosen to be with her, even if just over the phone, was part of the high.

He was picking her. Out of anyone on the planet—

Paradise stopped in the middle of the aisle. Something had fluttered to the ground and she picked the thing up with a frown. It was a picture, an old-fashioned Polaroid type, the kind with the glossy square in the center and the white matte part that was small around three sides and big at the bottom so you could hold it and write on it.

The image was so blurry it was indecipherable, something red and pinkish with stripes.

"Peyton, really," she muttered.

God only knew what he was doing while he was high. He'd been known to rock some crazy, psychedelic stuff and try some really weird things—which, of course, he delighted in telling her about.

With the image in her hand, she shuffled down to the exit, thanked the *doggen* driver, and then opened her mouth to call for her buddy. He'd already dematerialized with Anslam, though, so she put the photograph of his bedspread, or his carpet, or his bathrobe, or his frickin' martini in her pocket.

"Did you help Craeg with his little problem?" Novo said from the shadows.

Paradise turned as the bus headed off, stones crackling under its tires. "You lied about all that."

"Did I?" The female smiled in the cold moonlight. "I don't think I did. And I was right, wasn't I. He needed you, and only you."

With a flush, Paradise remembered Craeg's body up against hers, his arousal pressing into her belly.

Not a little problem, she thought to herself. Not at all. It was big, and thick, and—

"Well?" Novo prompted.

"That is none of your business."

"So prim, so proper. S'all good, though. Glad you kids had a good time. That's what life should be about—and I figured that you guys wouldn't get it together without some help."

Paradise had to laugh. "You do not look like the match-making type, Novo."

"I'm branching out." The female shrugged her strong shoulders under her black leather jacket. "That's why we're all here, right?"

For a split second, Paradise was tempted to invite the female over. She'd never actually had a true friend. In the aristocracy, your social position determined who you were allowed to be seen with—and God knew none of the cousins she had had to make small talk with had been of much interest to her. Plus you couldn't trust them. Females like that were competing for a limited group of highly desired males—which made them as cut-throat as a school of piranha.

It was *The Bachelor* times a hundred.

Besides, Novo kind of knew about Craeg, and that made Paradise feel less like she had anything to hide—and the female certainly seemed sexual enough to have had some experience in the seduction department. Maybe a lot of it. Opening her mouth, Paradise—

Remembered where she lived.

"I'll see you tomorrow," she mumbled.

"You're not pissed off at me, are you?"

"No, I'm not at all." As she blushed, she was glad it was dark and the tree canopy cut out most of the moon-light. "I'm kind of grateful, actually."

Novo pulled another one of those shoulder squeezes of hers. "Have a good rest of the night and day. See you tomorrow."

Paradise lifted her hand. "Bye."

When she was left alone, she let her head fall back and looked at the stars. Then she moved her satchel to her chest, wrapped her arms around it and demateri-alized herself.

Re-forming on the lawn in the exact place she had the night before, she was hoping to feel a little less foreign in familiar territory.

Annnnnd that would be a big fat Nope.

Striding up to the front door, she felt just as much distance as she had the night before. This time, though, the separation was tied to Craeg.

You know that ache you've got right now? The one between your legs? I'm going to show you how to take care of that by yourself. And you're going to make me come when I listen to what it sounds like.

Just the memory of his deep, husky voice saying those words turned her body into a blast-furnace—to the point that she wanted to take her parka off even though it was forty degrees. And yet at the same time, she looked up to all those glowing windows—and wanted to vomit. The idea that she was going to get on the phone, and probably end up naked, while a male who her father wouldn't approve of walked her through it all? In the room she'd grown up in? While her father was in the house? Females like her weren't supposed—

"Oh, fuck that," she muttered as she started walking for the door.

Life was too damned short, and Craeg was too damned hot for her to waste time feeling guilty when she was doing nothing wrong in the larger scheme of things.

Remember, she told herself. You're never getting mated. You're free.

Chapter Twenty-eight

"I lied."

As Axe spoke up, Butch looked across the rose-and-vine kitchen. The male was leaning against the countertop by the stove, his arms crossed over his chest, his head tilted down so that there were great shadows where his deeply set eyes should have been.

"About what."

It took the guy a while to answer, and Axe passed the time fiddling with the row of black hoops that went down the outside of his ear. "The key. In the office."

Andjustlikethat, Butch went on full alert—not that he showed it. "Oh, yeah? How so?"

Axe rubbed under his nose, and Butch banked that tell for future reference.

"Where did you get it?" the guy asked.

"A friend gave it to me." Like he was going to come out with the dead female stuff before he needed to play that card? "A good friend."

"You're not supposed to share them. It's against the rules."

"So if I go there, will I get in trouble?" Butch asked on a flier.

"I dunno. Depends on the night. If you're wearing a mask, you might get away with it. I've never brought anybody, but the policy is plus-one as long as the guests adhere to the rules. Also, you accept responsibility if they don't. That's how you get kicked out."

"How long have you been a part of it?"

"Since before the raids. That's where I had my bender when . . . you know, the shit with my father went down. The humans there, they never knew—still don't know—what I am. So many different kinds of freak there—they just figure I'm a vampire poser."

"When was the last time you went?"

"Three or four nights ago. I didn't know how things were going to go with the training program. Figured it might be my last time for a while."

Which was about the time the girl had been found on Safe Place's lawn.

"What are you into?" Butch rolled his eyes. "And before you think I'm coming on to a student, I'm perfectly happily mated to a female I'm fully aware is too good for me—this is just to make conversation because we got nothing better to do until what's-his-face gets back."

Axe's affect loosened up, his body, too. "I like to make them submit."

"Men or women?"

"Both."

"You and V would get along just fine then. Although he's a one-female guy now, too." Butch stretched his arms over his head until his spine cracked. "When are you going again?"

"When's our next night off?"

"Will you take me and show me around? So I don't embarrass the shit out of my buddy who gave the key to me?"

"You just told me you were happily mated."

Butch shot the guy a don't-be-stoopid. "I like to watch, asshole. It's not cheating if you don't get your hands, your tongue, or your dick involved."

Axe nodded like he respected that logic. "Yeah, I'll take you. But only on a masked night. If you fuck up or get a case of the pussies, I don't want it traced back to me."

Butch thought back to a certain night with Vishous, that night when there had been certain revelations made after Butch had ... done some things that had needed doing to his best friend.

"I can handle myself," he said dryly. "Don't worry."

The sounds of heavy feet on the shallow steps to the side door announced Craeg's re-arrival.

"That was fast," Butch muttered as the male came in with only one ratty duffel.

"Told you," Craeg replied. "I don't have much."

Marissa came home early because she had a headache. And no, not one of Trez's migraines, just a dull thumper behind her eyes that made it difficult to concentrate, hard to read documents on paper, and impossible to focus on a computer screen.

Mounting the stone steps to the mansion's grand entrance, she figured out what was wrong: She'd skipped First Meal and had worked through the snack that was served every night at midnight at Safe Place.

"Dummy," she said as she entered the vestibule and looked into the security camera.

When the lock was sprung, she walked into the grand foyer and smiled at Fritz. "I'm awfully sorry to trouble you, but may I please have something to eat?"

The ancient *doggen* clasped his hands together and all but swooned, sure as if she had handed him a winning lottery ticket or the most perfect birthday present ever given to anybody.

"Oh, mistress, yes! May I get you eggs and toast? A sandwich? Soup? Something more substantial—"

She laughed a little. "Surprise me?"

"Right away! Yes, yes, right away!"

The speed with which he left and the bounce in that step suggested he had many more centuries left in him, and that was a good thing—

"Oh, heeeeey, gurl."

She turned to the billiards room. Lassiter was leaning

against the open archway, a bowl of popcorn in his hand, a giant-bag, leopard-print Snuggie covering about seventy percent of his torso, his strong, bare forearms and bare legs showing at its hems.

"Hey there . . ." She frowned as something dawned on her. "Are you wearing anything under that?"

"Of course I am." He threw a handful of popcorn into his mouth. "You wanna watch some tube with me? Right now I got a whole lot of *MacGyver* on, but I'm willing to be flexible."

Marissa opened her mouth to say no, but then figured, What the heck. She was just going to have a little snack and wait for Butch to be done at the training center. She'd texted him that she was off work early, and he'd hit her right back, telling her to sit tight; he'd be back in twenty, thirty minutes, tops.

"Sure."

"Niiiiice." The angel straightened. "What's your poison, TV-wise?"

As he turned around, she let out a squeak.

Because she was staring at his bare ass.

"What's wrong?" he asked, all concerned.

Covering her eyes, she said, "You told me you had something on!"

"A jockstrap. Duh."

At that moment, Fritz appeared next to her with a tray laden with so many covered plates that he might as well have been feeding Rhage.

"Ah . . ." Marissa rubbed her eyebrows, that headache back in full force.

"She's eating in here," Lassiter called out. "And yes, Marissa, I'll put my damn jeans on."

"Thank you, baby Jesus," she muttered as she entered the game room.

As Fritz set the tray up on the bar to the left, Lassiter pulled the Levis on and flopped down on one of the sofas that faced the enormous screen mounted over the fireplace. "FYI, if I get chafed, it's on you."

She went over and took a seat on one of the padded stools. "FYI, my mate is due in here at any moment. So you just saved yourself a whoop-assing."

Lassiter pointed the remote at the TV and called up the cable schedule. "Psssh, whatever. I can take him."

"Doubt it."

"Actually, I got nothing better to do for the rest of tonight. Think he'll want to fight? I could use the exercise."

Marissa laughed at the hopeful tone as she sat back and let Fritz pop the *cloches* off the plates and describe, with all the precision and elegance of a Nobu waiter, what was being served.

"Thank you so much," she murmured as she picked up her fork and tried the rice pilaf. "Mmmmm."

She wasn't going to eat even half of it all, but that never seemed to bother the butler. Then again, to him, the joy of serving was the very best job satisfaction he had.

"Oh, my God," Lassiter said, jerking upright. "I can't believe it."

"What? And if it's a *Beaches* marathon again, you can forget it." She rubbed the center of her chest with her free hand. "I'm *not* watching anyone die even in two dimensions."

There had been more than enough of that. Dearest Virgin Scribe, what if they couldn't find out anything about—

"It's *Melrose Place*. I love this epi—it's where Kimberly went psycho."

"Wait, wasn't she always psycho?"

"Well, yeah, but this is where she takes the wig off and you see the scar. Easily one of the most significant and influential scenes in television history."

"And to think I assumed that was, like, the human lunar landing or something."

Lassiter glanced over. "Wait, those rats without tails made it to the moon? You're kidding me. They can't even decide what time it is, clocks always flipping back and forth from season to season. And then there's their health bullshit, eat this, you'll live longer—no, strike that, it'll kill you, so you need to do this. Internet trolls. Asshat preachers and politicians. And you know, don't get me started on potholes. Why don't they fix the roads?"

Marissa threw her head back and laughed. "You don't even drive. Or care about any of those things."

The fallen angel shrugged, his gold piercings and chains gleaming like sunshine with the shift. "Just repeating what they talk about on the evening news."

Marissa shook her head with a smile. And she was about to ask him what exactly he did aside from sunning himself each noontime if there was no cloud cover, and taking up space on that couch in front of the TV—but then his eyes flicked back to her and they were dead serious. As his gaze returned to the big screen, she realized he'd picked up on her mood and was doing his best to help her out of it.

"You're okay, Lass," she said softly. "You know that?"

"I'm more than okay. I'm amaaaaaaaaaaaaaaaaaaz-ing," he sang out. "So does this mean I can put you down for a dozen of my calendars?"

With any other person in the house, she might have been tempted to laugh it off as a joke. Him, though? "No, you can't. I don't even know what they're like, but the answer is no."

"Fine, half a dozen," he tossed back. "They're only five bucks. I have to cover printing costs. Good news? There was no photographer expense—I took the pics with my selfie stick."

She lowered a forkful of chicken back to her plate. "You actually made a calendar of yourself."

"Why do you think I had my pants off."

"Lass. Really. You took twelve naked pictures of yourself—"

"Jockstrap. I was in my jockstrap, remember. I just did December's by the fire. I am so hot, it is flat-out stupid."

Marissa passed an eye around the room and shud-

dered at the number of things he'd probably put his naked ass on before settling for the hearth in front of the
banked fire. "What gave you this idea?"

He rolled his eyes. "We've only got how many nights
left in this year? I need to get 'em back from Kinko's
before December thirty-first."

From out of nowhere, she had an image of some poor
human in a FedEx Office branch getting an eyeful and a
half of the mostly naked fallen angel.

Without warning, she started to laugh so hard, tears
came to her eyes. The good kind of tears, that was.

And as she gave herself up to the angel's ridiculous-
ness, Lass just sat there on the couch, staring up at *Melrose Place*, a sly, quiet smile on his beautiful, deranged
face.

What an angel he was, she thought to herself. A total
angel.

Chapter Twenty-nine

As Butch emerged out of the hidden door under the mansion's grand staircase, his only thought was of finding his mate.

And the sound of her laughter was both an instant locator and a source of high-octane relief. She'd been so distracted as soon as she'd woken up after a day of restless sleep, the weight of what was on her mind giving her the look of someone dragging a baby grand piano around after them. But he'd promised her he would get her something on the girl, somehow, and he was beyond ready to tell her he had an in.

Striding across the mosaic depiction of an apple tree in full bloom, he entered the billiards room, and—

Lassiter lifted both his hands up from his prone position on the couch. "I put my pants back on. I was a good boy."

Butch's fangs threatened to drop and his upper lip twitched. "Excuse me? And think carefully before you explain that one. You're wicked close to the line."

Marissa took a sip from a glass of water. "It's perfectly innocent."

"I'm doing a naked calendar," the fallen angel started.

"He had a jockstrap on."

"It was all done with a selfie stick."

As the pair of them talked over each other, Butch had a sudden urge to plug both his ears, shut his eyes, and go "la-la-la-la-la." "You know, I'm good. I'm *really* good not knowing anything more."

On any of Lassiter's antics, for that matter. Bitch had a way of making the ordinary complicated and the mundane insane.

It was a gift.

Just ask the fallen angel. He'd tell ya.

"Will you excuse us for a minute," Butch said as he walked over and gave Marissa a kiss on the forehead. God, her scent smelled good in his nose, and wow, could that female make slacks and a blouse look like a goddamn ball gown. "I've got to talk to my girl."

"NFW, I'm watching *Melrose*."

"That wasn't a request, angel."

"Is there something wrong?" Marissa asked as she wiped her mouth with a damask napkin. "Did someone get hurt in training?"

He pulled out a stool and sat next to her. "Lass, you were leaving."

"The fuck I was."

Butch grimaced and hated making the offer: "You can use the couch at the Pit."

"Will you make me change the channel when you guys get back there?"

"Will you leave now if I say no?"

"Are you saying no now?"

For godsakes, Lassiter was perfectly capable of playing a round of question tennis until dawn—or one of the parties involved kicked the bucket from dehydration and exhaustion. "Yes, I'm saying no."

"Wait, does that mean I can watch *Melrose* or not? The double negative confused—"

"Jesus Christ, will you just go!"

Lassiter was muttering as he got to his feet. "How many times do I have to tell you that is *not* my name."

"I need a drink." As the fallen angel left, Butch got back on his feet and went behind the bar. Pouring himself some Lagavulin, he didn't beat around the bush, because he knew his *shellan* wouldn't want him to. "So I think I have a lead."

"You do?" She put her fork down on her plate. "What? How?"

He put two pieces of ice in a rocks glass and gave them an amber-colored bath. "That piece of metal is a key, and it gets you entrance into a private club that's for humans only."

"Oh, my God, if we can get a membership list, maybe we can find her name."

Yeah, not a country club, my love, he thought as he took a deep drink.

"How did you find this out?" she asked.

"One of the trainees belongs to it. He's taking me there ASAP—I just have to check in with the other Brothers about the next couple of nights. I think if I switch some classes around, I can free up Friday."

"So we'll go! This is amazing!" As he froze with his glass halfway back to his lips, Marissa frowned. "Why are you looking at me like that. Butch. Seriously, I am going with you."

He shook his head and followed through on the swallow. "No, I'll handle this. Don't worry, I'll let you know what I find as soon—"

"I am going with you."

As he got a good look at the set angle of her jaw, he put his Scotch down on the bar. "Marissa, this is not the kind of place you need to even drive past, much less go into. It's a sex club."

"So."

He blinked. "Honey, it's not—"

"Need I remind you what we did after the movie? Four times?"

"Marissa."

"Butch," she echoed.

To keep himself from cursing, he tossed back his drink

and poured another. "You're not up to something like that. There'll be people fucking all over the place, doing freaky shit to one another. You can't handle that."

"Or maybe it's more like you can't handle me being there."

He rolled his eyes. He couldn't help it. "You don't know what you're saying. Or what that kind of thing is like."

Marissa folded her napkin in slow, precise little squares and laid it beside her mostly full plate. "Well, we'll just find out when we go together, won't we."

"I'm not taking you there. This is not up for discussion."

"Yes, you are." She slid off the stool and picked up the tray of food. "And if I find out you went by yourself? I'm going to consider it a betrayal of the highest order of our relationship—and *that* is not up for discussion."

He tried to picture her standing next to a couple dressed in black latex getting it in the ass by a set of DD twins wearing matching purple strap-ons.

"Marissa. I'm not going to have time to handhold you," he said roughly. "My focus is going to be on fitting in, figuring out where the staff is, finding the right people to talk to. Distraction is not going to help that dead girl."

"Don't you *dare* play that card. I am fully aware of why we're going, and I'd like to point out that you're my *hellren*, not my *ghardian*. So shelve the *paterfamilias* bullshit, and pop a couple of valium before we go if you have to. But I cannot make this clearer—I'm coming with you and I'm going to help figure this all out." She leaned in. "Newsflash—just because I have a pair of ovaries doesn't mean I don't have a brain—or the right to think independently."

In the silence that followed, all he could do was shake his head back and forth. The words that were on the tip of his tongue were not going to help this—and he couldn't believe they were arguing again.

So much for the restart button they'd hit the night before.

"Or is that what you're worried about?" she challenged.

"What?"

"That I might like it."

With that little ditty dropping at his feet like a grenade, she walked off, head held high, shoulders back, a whole lot of get-over-yourself steeling her spine.

Bracing his palms against the granite countertop, he leaned into his arms and tried to keep from screaming in frustration.

At least the bottle of Lag was still three-quarters full.

He was going to need it.

Peyton exhaled a stream of smoke and let his head fall back onto his pillow. "Here."

Passing the bong over to Anslam, he closed his eyes and felt himself float about a foot over his body. The familiar sense of relief reminded him that Parry was probably right; he probably needed to not do this. But shit, after the two nights they'd just had?

He needed a little vacay.

Fuck that—he'd earned it.

"So what do you think of them all?" he asked.

The sound of Anslam exhaling just like he had was like someone laughing at the same place in a movie that you did, or enjoying the same good meal. Comradery was a nice thing.

"Boone's cool," the guy said. "Axe is a fucking freak. I mean, get over yourself, asshole with the black clothes and the spiked hair and that bullshit tattooing crap."

Peyton waited for the guy to continue. "And what about Novo."

"She is fucking *hot*."

For some reason, even though he agreed, he didn't like the idea of Anslam walking around with that opinion—or worse, popping a chub because of it.

"I don't know," Peyton muttered. "She's okay."

"Did you see her doing sit-ups? I can't believe Boone got to hold her feet. I wanted that fucking view."

"She'll break you in half." Although if this kept up, Peyton might take care of that himself. "Besides, I don't know if she does males."

"I'll turn her," Anslam said in a low voice. "I'll fucking set her right on that one—"

"What about Craeg," Peyton cut in.

"He's the guy to beat. No offense to Paradise coming in first at the end of night one, but Craeg's probably going to go the full distance."

"Yeah." At least they could both agree on that—without a coffin coming between them. "Who are you taking to the ball at her father's place?"

"Right now, no one. I like to keep my options open. Hey, before we crash, can we food up?"

Peyton opened his eyes and glanced over at the antique Cartier clock on his nightstand. "Yeah. Defo. Let me call Paradise first. I wanna make sure she got home."

"You sure you two aren't courting?"

"Nah. Friends only."

"She's a piece."

Peyton wrenched around and glared at the guy. "Watch your mouth about her."

Anslam shook his head and put his palm up. "You got some unresolved shit with her, my friend. Don't kid yourself."

Whatever.

Reaching for his phone, he called her contact out of his recent calls list and waited for her to pick up. As the connection rang, he looked around his room. His parents' mansion was a newer one, with big arching windows running down the back side that overlooked the gardens. With high ceilings and good woodwork, he'd always thought his room was airy even with all the stuffy antique crap his mother insisted on making everyone live with whether they appreciated it or not—

"Hello!"

He frowned. "You okay, Parry?"

"Oh." There was a pause. "It's you."

"Who the hell were you expecting?"

"Ah, no one. My aunt. My—her cousin. My aunt's cousin. You don't know him—her, I mean."

"Have you been smoking up?" He smiled. "Because if you have, you need to put the pipe down now and start sleeping it off."

"No, I haven't been. But you have. I can hear it in your voice."

"How?"

"Huskier than normal."

For a split second, he wondered whether she found that sexy or not. Shaking himself, he said, "I just wanted to see if you made it home. Your dad there with you by now? He must be off work."

"Yeah, we had Last Meal together. Now I'm just up here in my room."

"Anslam and I are stoned out of our minds." The guy gave a thumbs-up from the other end of the bed. "We're going to carbo-load and crash. It's going to be fabulous. Anyway, glad you're tight."

"Don't eat too much ice cream. It makes you bloat and then you complain the next day that you've lost your girlish figure."

"I have never done that."

"Really. Really?"

"Okay, fine," he muttered.

"And do I need to remind you about the cookie-dough incident."

Peyton groaned. "I could have sworn I shit my internal organs out."

"That's right. I still say you might be lactose-intolerant. Just something to consider. I love you."

He glanced at Anslam, and didn't want to say the words back in front of the guy. "Me, too. See you tomorrow—"

"Oh, hey, listen, I found your photograph."

"My what?"

"Photograph. On the bus. It fell out of your backpack or your pocket or something."

"I don't have any photographs to lose, sweet cheeks. But thanks for thinking of me—and if it involves any-thing naked and female, I'll take it off your hands free of charge. Just because I'm a straight-up Good Sam like that."

She laughed. "No. I don't know what the image is, ac-tually. I thought you dropped it, but guess not. It's an old-fashioned Polaroid."

"A Polaroid? Jesus, that's an antique."

"Well, anyway, I'll hold on to it until someone claims it. Have a good day. And you really shouldn't be smok-ing up."

"So you keep telling me. Good day, too, baby."

As he ended the call, he reached across and put his phone down by that clock. "That is one fine female."

"What was she talking about? A photograph?"

"I don't know. Some Polaroid she found on the bus." He sat up. Stood up. Tried walking. "Wow. That's some strong-ass shit. Let's go down to the kitchen the back way so no one sees us bobbing and weaving."

Chapter Thirty

As Paradise paced around her room in her bare feet, she was careful to go toe-heel, toe-heel, so that she made no noise—although considering how hard her heart was beating, she was surprised she wasn't waking people up on the other side of the river with the pounding.

Quick stop. Check the time.

Six fifty-eight. Or maybe six fifty-nine—it was hard to be precise with the old clock on her bedside, especially from across the room.

Rubbing her sweaty hands on her blue jeans, she went over and looked at her cell phone. She'd deliberately laid the thing facing up, and she stared at the black screen. She'd put the ringer on mute, but it would vibrate when Craeg called.

Any second.

Really.

Frowning, she bent down and woke the cell up, just in case she'd missed something. Which, granted, would be like someone not noticing a neon billboard in her room. Nope. No missed calls on the screen. No texts, either.

Just to be triple sure, she put her passcode in and checked the call log.

Nothing.

God, this was awful. She felt like she was standing on a parapet, looking at a long way down with nothing to catch herself on. Which was nuts—and a sign that her adrenal gland was waaaaaay over-assessing the threat to her personal safety. For godsakes, she wasn't going to lose an arm or a leg if he didn't call like he said he would. She would be perfectly fine.

And jeez, he wasn't even late yet.

Putting the phone back down, she resumed pacing.

That didn't last long. Two minutes later, she was back at the cell again.

Nothing.

Turning away, she got pissed at herself. Here she was, making this bid for independence and autonomy, and getting all GRRR about rejecting the *glymera* stuff— and yet she was worried whether some male called her for what was probably going to be a phone sesh just so he could get off.

Yeah, that really made her a feminist, right there.

Besides, she'd never had an orgasm before. What made him think that he could—

The sound of a snare drum rolling out over by the bedside had her racing back so fast she slipped on the carpet.

"Hello!" she barked as she caught herself.

There was a beat of silence. And then that deep voice, that delicious male voice, was right in her ear: "Where are you in your house."

She looked around. "My bedroom?"

"Are the lights on."

"Yes?" Funny, that ostensibly he was asking the questions and she was answering, but the reality was the reverse. She felt like she was the one making the inquiries.

"Get on your bed. Turn off the lights."

"Okay." She went over by the door and hit the switch—then she made her way back across and got up on the high mattress, kicking her shoes off and stretching out. "It's dark."

Try pitch black.

Craeg made a sound, something she couldn't identify—and the experience was amazing. With the lights off, it was as if he were right next to her.

"You kill me in class," he said in a guttural voice. "Why?"

"I can't stop staring at you. I look at the nape of your neck." That sound came again, and she realized it was halfway between a purr and a growl ... clearly, he was utterly aroused already. "I have these fantasies of going up behind you and tilting your head back. I run my hands down your throat ... under your uniform ... onto your breasts."

Paradise's eyes fluttered shut. "Oh, God ... you do?"

"All the time. Why do you think I couldn't get up out of my seat tonight."

She had an image of him frozen in the back of the classroom, no expression on his face, his big body tense. "What are you talking about?"

"I was hard. And it would have showed."

Paradise's body arched as she pictured what the front of his loose pants would have looked like, all stretched tight over that big rigid length of his.

"I need to sit down in front so I don't see you as much." As she laughed softly, he moaned. "Do that again."

"Do what?"

"That laugh. It's so fucking sexy." When she obliged, she heard rustling. "Have you ever touched yourself, Paradise?"

She had a brief image of Novo, so secure, so sexual, so confident. And she thought about lying. "No."

"I've been touching you in my head since I got back here."

More images of him flickered across the black backdrop of the darkness in the room: him fighting the Brother Butch with such honor; him pumping weights; him staring at her in the locker room.

"What are you wearing?" he breathed.

"It's like you're here with me."

"I am. What do you have on top?"

She glanced down in the dark and saw nothing. "I have a button-down blouse on."

"Don't take it off," he moaned. Or maybe that was another purr. "Put your hand inside the collar."

It seemed like the most natural thing in the world to do what he said, and the sensation of her own fingertips going over her skin made shivers rush down her body.

"Are you wearing a bra?"

"Yes."

"Can you feel one of the straps? It's warm from your skin, right?"

"Yes," she breathed.

"Loosen the top button. Do it for me. Now go inside deep—is your nipple tight against the cup?"

As she complied, she meant to answer him yes, except she was breathing too hard and her mind had gone on the fritz. But he didn't seem to mind the silence.

Craeg laughed, the deep, dark ripple thrilling her. "I want my mouth on there. I want to look up and watch you gasp when I lick at you, suck on you."

For a male who didn't say much, he sure could put a string of words together.

"I keep thinking about the clinic," she heard herself say. "Your hand under the sheets. I remember exactly what it looked like, going up and down—"

"Fuck."

"—until you—"

"Rip the shirt in half."

"What?"

"Rip the fucking thing off your body," he barked. "Put the fucking phone down and rip it in half!"

Buttons. Everywhere.

And God, that felt good, her torso arching up again as she tore the thing apart, the fastenings offering no resistance as she put her strength into the job.

Flopping back against the mattress, she scrambled to get the phone to her ear once more—and then heard him breathing harder and harder, except then he stopped.

In a tight tone, like he'd clamped his molars together, he gritted out commands for her to go under the cups of her bra and rub her nipples and feel the swells of her breasts and then get rid of the bra altogether. She didn't hesitate, and was astonished to feel her own fingertips exploring the soft skin, the tight tips, creating bolts of electricity and heat that went straight to her core. And the entire time, he was talking in that velvet voice of his, coaching her in a deliberate way in spite of the erotic charge to it all, building her up slowly, inexorably. The higher she got, the hotter, the wetter, the less she cared about the modest, lady-like crap—and the more she wanted what he was giving to her.

But she kept her wits enough to stay relatively quiet. Even though she wanted to scream his name, the idea of a *doggen* or her father trying her locked door because they'd heard something would lead to conversations she wouldn't be able to fake her way through.

"Now what," she moaned.

In the darkness of the bedroom he'd been assigned, Craeg was all in. All fucking in. The training center could have caught fire or been rocked by an earthquake and he wouldn't have cut the connection.

He had no idea what Paradise's room looked like, where her bed was, how many pillows she was up against, or what color the duvet might be. But he had a crystal-fucking-clear picture of what she'd be like, all stretched out and writhing, torn shirt hanging from her arms in two pieces, simple, modest bra undone, her breasts exposed.

Little nipples all high and tight, ready for his mouth.

"Can you feel me on you?" he demanded.

"Yes . . ." she gasped.

Good, then it was time to go down farther. Not on himself, though. He'd had to stop working his cock, because when he did, he started to orgasm and that conked his brain out: More than anything, more than getting off himself, he wanted to make this right for her.

Because this was all they'd ever have. He had no fucking intention of taking her virginity—and if he wanted to keep that resolution, then he had to make sure there was an insurmountable distance between their naked bodies: The phone shit was the only safe way to do this. She would still be able to be considered respectable afterward, because touching herself was a very different proposition than some Neanderthal like him penetrating her sex until he came hard a couple of dozen times—and robbed the male she was eventually going to mate of his due.

As long as he never got her alone for very long, he was going to be able to do right by her—and he wasn't fooling himself. Their attraction was off the chain, but after the training was done? After all this was finished, assuming they both made it through?

Separate ways. Even if they ended up working together from time to time.

Bottom line, there was no domestic future for him to offer her. Especially after he began to work on his true purpose for all this training: Revenge. On the aristocrats who had allowed his father to be killed by the enemy.

He would not rest until their blood was on his hands.

"Take your fingers and bring them down your stomach," he ordered. "What do you find?"

"The waistband of my jeans."

"Undo the button."

"Yes . . ."

There was a rustling, and then she was back talking to him. "And now?"

"The zipper."

Another rustling. During which he imagined he was the one undoing things, spreading the fly wide, taking his mouth and pressing a kiss to the lace of her panties. Or in her case, probably the cotton.

"Take the jeans off. Leave the panties on."

More shifting around, the speaker in his ear fuzzing out.

Under the light sheet that covered his naked body, he

couldn't help but grip himself and give a stroke or two. But as the top of his cock started to burn like it was going to blow, he had to stop.

Grinding his back teeth, he gritted out, "Put your hand between your thighs, spread those long legs ... do it."

He'd wanted to ease into it more, but he was too greedy. And so was she: The rippling moan she let out threw him right over the edge, his cock way done waiting for his palm to get with the program.

"Rub it," he moaned as his erection kicked under the sheets, hot jets landing on his stomach as he orgasmed. "Oh, God, Paradise, stroke yourself through the cotton ..." As she cried out, he could tell, even through his own release, that she was getting close. "Under—go under, feel the wet and the heat—feel it—oh, fuck ... it's so smooth ..."

She was panting now, and then she said his name like it was being torn out of her throat.

"Imagine my mouth on you there."

That was when she came. And so did he once again as he listened to her suck air in and blow it out, a really fucking delicious pleading, begging sound coming across the connection.

Just the sound of her release gave him orgasm number three. And four.

"Keep going," he said hoarsely, "feel my tongue lapping, my lips sucking ..."

Sometime later, when it was finally over, all they did was breathe together.

For some insane reason, he found himself wanting to be next to her and hold her—or some shit. He didn't know. All he was aware of was that he had this burning drive to make sure she was all right after what had gone down.

Now, the miles that separated them seemed like a punishment of some kind.

"You okay?" he asked roughly.

"Oh ... yes ..."

As he heard the smile in her voice, he started to grin

himself—and didn't that make him glad he was alone and in the dark. He probably looked like a complete fucking idiot.

"You're beautiful," he heard himself say. "You're amazing. You're incredible."

She laughed in a burst. "You're silly."

"Hardly. I was born without a sense of humor."

"Really?"

"Yeah. I'm the most unfunny male I know, and I never get jokes."

"You know . . . come to think of it, I don't believe I've seen you smile yet."

"Don't hold your breath." He reached over to the bedside table, opened the drawer, and took out the pack of cigarettes and the Bic lighter he'd bought on the way back to the training center. "I smoke, by the way."

Only after sex, he almost explained. But he didn't want to underscore that he'd ever been with anyone but her for some reason.

Tilting his head to the side to hold the phone to his ear with his shoulder, he fumbled around to open the Marls and take out a cancer stick. The lighter made a *shhhhht* as he fired it up, and he got a close-up visual of his fist as he brought the flame closer to his face. That first inhale was enough to make him moan all over again, and he kept the cig between his teeth as he patted around in the drawer for the ashtray, which he put on his bare chest.

"It's a bad habit," he said by way of apology. "But at least vampires don't get cancer."

As soon as he'd arranged this with her, he'd started planning about how he could get a cigarette for the afterward. Not very romantic.

Not that he was interested in romance, he reminded himself.

"So why don't you smile, Craeg."

On its surface, the question/statement, whatever it was, could have been taken as a lighthearted, jokey kind of thing, but her serious tone cut that interpretation right off.

And what do you know, it was probably the loose, relaxed, post-gasm float that made him actually answer her instead of hanging up, which was what he should have done.

"How many people did you lose in the raids?" he whispered.

"Seven cousins," she intoned with sadness. "It's just my father and me left, and the two of us were very lucky."

"I lost my immediate family. My mother and sister were at home with me. My dad was at work. They found our house address on his falsified human driver's license after they killed him. That was how they got us." He took another drag. "So that's why I don't smile."

"I'm so sorry."

"Me, too." Which was something else he wouldn't have said under other circumstances. "I couldn't save them. My mother and sister, that is."

"Oh, God . . ."

He shrugged. "I lost too much blood. The *lessers* broke the door in and I came down the stairs when I heard the noise. They attacked me, thought I was dead, so they left me. To this night, I don't know why I lived. They used machetes. I stayed conscious long enough to hear my mother scream for my sister to run—and then both of them died . . . horrible deaths." When she made a choking sound, he shook his head. "TMI. Sorry."

"I'm really . . . it doesn't feel like enough, but it's all I can say. I'm *so* sorry."

"Thanks."

"How did you survive? What . . . did someone come save you?"

"I woke up in a pool of my own blood just before dawn. I was so weak . . . I barely managed to shut the front door before the sun burned me to shreds. I crawled . . . through the house, you know, and found their . . . yeah. It was bizarre, the sight of them both lay-

ing on the linoleum, red blood everywhere, skin white—
they had reached for each other, my mom had one
hand—" He had to stop and clear his throat. "My mom
was holding her hand out for my sister and my sister was
trying to get to her. Both of their sets of eyes were
open . . . I don't know. After seeing that? Something in
me woke up. That's all I can say—and that's when it
started. That's when I decided that sometime, somehow,
I was going to find a way into the war with the Lessening
Society. It's the only way I can walk the earth without
wanting to blow my own brains out." He laughed harshly.
"Well, I also decided that I hate aristocrats—although
that didn't come for two more nights after that."

"Why . . ." She hesitated. "Why do you hate the *glymera*?"

Chapter Thirty-one

As Paradise waited for something to come back to her over the phone, her heart was beating fast again, and she had to turn on the light. Wrapping her coral-colored duvet up around her bare legs and pulling her shirt closed, she tucked her knees in tight and waited.

It was a while longer before Craeg answered her. "The first thing I did when I had any strength was try to find my father where he was working at that mansion—when I got there, it was pretty much the same as my house. Blood and bodies everywhere, but there had also been a lot of looting of paintings and silver and that kind of shit. Some of the corpses had burned up because they had been in patches of sunlight. The ones deeper in the house were still intact. I found my father . . . in the room where he had been laying a new mahogany floor. And what else did I find? The fucking open door to the safe room that the family hadn't let him or any of the other servants and workers into."

"What . . . do you mean?"

"The family who lived there, the *aristocrats* who lived there, went to take shelter in a steel-clad safe room—and they wouldn't let any of the workers in. They locked them out so they got slaughtered—I saw the open door, and their footsteps through the blood of my father and his class as they went for the exit and escaped either right before the dawn came or the following evening." There was another pause. And then in a low voice, he said, "I buried everyone but my father there. Him, I took back home. I just couldn't ... leave the others like that. A *doggen* came back while I was taking care of the bodies and told me that they'd been trying to find kin, but everyone had been killed at all of the workers' houses—just like mine. There were ... literally no survivors to tend to the dead. Oh, and that classy family? They ran. I've tried to find them—and I will not rest until I do. They lived on an estate called Endelview."

He cleared his throat roughly. "I mean, how do you do that to someone else? How do you live with yourself knowing that you could have helped somebody and didn't? The staff, the servants, they had served that family for generations. And there were a lot of those commoners in that parlor. They came there, from what I was told by that *doggen*, because the construction guys knew about the passage and herded people in the direction of that room. They were pounding on the panels to be let in while the house was sacked—I know because so many of the bodies were grouped together against the wall. But nope. They weren't good enough, important enough, worthy enough."

Oh ... God.

That was the only thing going through her mind—because she knew that story, too. Peyton had shared the terrible tale with her during one of their long, all-day phone calls about a month after she and her father had left for their safe house. The first son, a middle daughter, the mother and two cousins, had claimed to come back from out of town to discover the carnage ... but maybe they had been there all along?

And they had disappeared. Likely to a new safe house far away from Caldwell.

"Anyway, I got plans for them. When I find out where they are."

Paradise closed her eyes. "Not all aristocrats are evil."

"When you had to listen to your father come home every night with stories about how they treated him like shit while he was trying to make an honest living? Tough to find any sympathy for them—and that was before they were directly responsible not only for my sire's death, but my mother's and sister's."

"I'm sorry."

"It's okay."

No, it wasn't.

And she wasn't at all surprised when he said abruptly, "I should go. We gotta sleep."

"Yes. Yes, of course." She held on to the phone hard, trying to think of something to say. "I, ah—"

"See you tomorrow."

Click.

Taking her cell away from her ear, she stared at the thing. Naturally, there was no record of the number, because the lines out of the training center, like those from the audience house, were restricted and private.

But she wouldn't have called him back even if she could have.

Placing her phone aside, she stared across her room, her pretty, fancy room with its coral and pink tones, and silk drapery with tassels and needlepoint rugs. She couldn't blame Craeg for the way he thought or what he felt. She'd be exactly the same. But the answer wasn't him stalking some guy and murdering him to *ahvenge* those deaths. Or murdering females over all that, too.

Well, at least she hoped that wasn't the answer.

There was just so much death already within the species. Surely there was another way to atone for such a wrong?

As her phone started to vibrate, she jumped and picked it up. No number. Him? Again?

Accepting the call, she whispered, "Hello?"

There was a heartbeat of silence. Just like before.

"I'm sorry," Craeg blurted. "In case you haven't noticed, I'm shit with emotions. It's not your fault all that stuff happened before."

She exhaled in relief. "I'm so glad you called back. I didn't expect you to."

"Neither did I."

"Do you think you'll be able to sleep at all?"

"Now that I've heard your voice again? Maybe. I'll give it a shot."

"Craeg . . ."

"What?"

She fiddled with the lace edge of her duvet cover as she chose her words carefully. "That night of the raids . . . I'm not saying that the male or whoever it was who locked everyone out was right. Not at all. But eye for an eye is . . . barbaric."

"That's the way it's always been in the Old Country."

"We don't live there anymore. Times have changed. Think of all the progress that's been made, blood slavery outlawed, equality beginning to happen for females and commoners alike. You don't have to forget what happened, you don't have to forgive . . . but your response doesn't have to be murder."

"It wouldn't be murder. I would be *ahvenging* my own dead."

"But if you kill someone in cold blood, what else would you call it?" She kept her voice soft and low. "I don't want to fight with you, honestly, I don't. And I would never presume to know what that would be like, having your family . . ." As her voice caught, she cleared her throat. "I can't imagine. But if you follow through on this, you'd just be a murderer, too. You'd be no different from the *lessers*."

There was a long silence. But she knew by the lack of a *click* that he hadn't hung up on her.

"You are one of the most empathetic people I've ever met," he said finally.

"Not really."

"Yes, really. You're a good person, Paradise."

"Don't put me on a pedestal. All I'll do is fall from grace."

"Doubt it." There was a pause. "Sleep well, okay? And if you wake up in the middle of the day with the feel of someone's hands on your body, it's me. At least, it'll be me in my dreams."

"You're making me blush."

"Good. And when we're back in class, I'll try not to stare at you the whole time."

"Don't try too hard."

Now, his tone got more serious. "You've got your virtue to protect."

"My virtue, my problem. Not yours."

Craeg let out a *hrrumph.* "I'm calling you at seven again tomorrow. Answer your damn phone."

Paradise had to laugh. "Has anyone ever told you you're dominant."

"No, because I never listen to what people say to me."

"So if I mention that you're pretty amazing, too, are you going to hang up on me again?"

"Probably."

"Okay, well, then good day, and you're amazing—" Abruptly she sat up higher and pushed the phone against her ear. "Wait a minute, did I just hear a little laugh there?"

"No. Not at all."

"Liar." She smiled so big, her cheeks hurt. "You laughed. Right then and there."

"It was *not* a laugh."

"Oh, because a chuckle is so much more manly? Fine, you *chuckled*, Craeg. I caught you."

"You got to stop." Now he really let out something that sounded like . . .

"You just giggled."

"No!"

"Yes, you did." As she continued to needle him, she

figured it was the conversational equivalent of tickling him in the ribs. "You just giiiiiigggggled—"

"I got to go! Bye!"

"You're ammmmmmmmmmmmaaaaaaaazing—"

Click.

This time when she put her cell phone back down, she felt as light and frothy as the bubbles in a champagne flute.

And a little drunk, too.

Chapter Thirty-two

As night fell, Marissa cracked the bedroom door and put her head out into the hall. There were no sounds from the Pit's front room, so she padded down in her silk nightgown, her bare feet getting cold fast on the hardwood. Rounding the corner to look at the couch, she expected to find her mate asleep with his head at the kitchen end and his feet closer to her. He always slept like that, so he could see the TV better around the Foosball table.

The black leather sofa was vacant. More to the point, the Red Sox throw blanket she'd gotten him for his human Christmas holiday the year before was still folded across the back.

So he hadn't even tried to sleep at home.

The blanket was the clue. She loved her *hellren* with all her heart, but the male was constitutionally incapable of pulling that thing over his legs and putting it back when he was done. It was a running joke between them, along the lines of his not returning bottle openers to their proper place in the kitchen and never, ever starting the dishwasher.

Exhaling, she closed her eyes and leaned against the jamb.

"He didn't come back here last night."

At the sound of V's low voice, she glanced over at his bank of computers. The Brother had tilted his head

around the various screens, his super-intelligent, diamond eyes staring at her without blinking—or judgment.
And there was no reason to hide her heartbreak from
the guy. For one, he was Butch's brother for all intents
and purposes; and two, Vishous knew her so well, he'd
see through any I'm-fine lie she tried to float.

"We got into a big fight last night."

V took a drag off his hand-rolled. "About what?"

Padding over to the couch, she sat down and arranged
her nightie over her knees, smoothing, smoothing. "A sex
club."

The coughing fit would have been absolutely hysterical to watch if she'd been in a better mood—there was
something incredibly satisfying that for once she was
able to shock the unshockable Brother. Unfortunately, it
was because she was such a lame straight arrow.

"I beg your pardon?" His eyebrows were up so high,
they distorted the tattoos at his temple. "Sex club?"

The explanation was quick and to the point, and when
she was done, V's sardonic normal had returned to his
expression.

"Yeah. He'd told me he was going. Asked me to come
with him."

She couldn't hide her wince. She trusted Butch never
to cheat on her—for godsakes, as a fully bonded male, he
never noticed females on any level; they might as well be
toasters on legs for all the sexual response he had to
them. But there was something intimidating about getting V involved, maybe because it made her feel . . . ex-
cluded, even though that was crazy.

And then also inadequate because her mate needed
Vishous there, but didn't want her.

Plus it was true, V's lifestyle had always shocked her
a little—not because she thought he was a degenerate,
but because it was so sexually extreme . . . and diverse.

"You know he loves you," V muttered. "Come on."

"I know."

"And I won't get weird with him or anything."

"I don't mean to offend you."

"You didn't."

"Yes, I did." When the Brother fell silent, she knew she was right. "I just ... sometimes I don't want to be protected, if that makes sense. I mean, this issue with that female, who died in front of me—it's mine. Does that make sense? It's my ... responsibility. And I'm grateful for his help, I want his help—but getting pushed aside because I'm a 'good girl' and I can't handle certain things makes me feel like he thinks I'm weak or frivolous."

"Look, I can't get in the middle of this."

"I know. I'm sorry."

As she went to stand up, he cut in: "But he cherishes you. You're like ... you're like that Virgin Mary, that female he prays to. To him, you're the most perfect female who has ever or will ever walk the earth. Taking you to a place like that would be like him watching porn in church. He thinks of you as pure and virtuous and good, and he wants—brace yourself, I'm about to use the P-word—to protect that in a world that is cruel and filthy and disgusting."

She shook her head and thought about Butch and the whole blow-job thing. "I just don't want it to be so black-and-white. I don't want to be in a box even if he's put me there because he loves certain parts of me."

V's chair let out a creak as he sat back and exhaled a steady stream of smoke. Funny, she had hated the smell of it when she'd first moved in here. Now? It was like incense, and it meant safety and home—and she didn't even notice it most of the time.

Heck, V's presence, as chilly and intellectual as he could be sometimes, meant comfort to her now, too.

"I don't have an easy answer for that one." His brows tightened. "I mean, ya boy's kind of a right-and-wrong, black-and-white kind of guy. It's a hardwiring thing. But there're good sides of it, too. He'd never disrespect you. Never treat you badly. Never not focus on you."

"Oh, I know all that. But with where he's at now, he's getting in the way of something that is not only very important to me, but something that is within my right to do. And when you love someone that isn't cool, even if your motivations are good hearted and loving."

There was a long stretch of silence.

"Lemme talk to him."

"I'd appreciate that." She cursed quietly. "We've been having some problems this last little bit. It's breaking my heart."

"Relationships are like that. Even the best ones."

"I guess so."

"Look, he doesn't want to be with anyone but you." The Brother put his palm out. "Yeah, I know you know that, but I gotta say it again. And for better or worse, your grace and elegance and, yes, good-girlness is part of what attracts him to you. I mean, for instance, he had a shot with Xhex, but that was just sex—and all it was ever going to be. You're his type, not her."

Marissa jerked upright sure as if a bucket of ice water had just been poured over her head. *"He had sex with her?"*

Down in the training center's office, Butch sat behind Tohr's desk and stared at the shooting patterns of colorful lines that gyrated their way around the computer screen.

What he kept chewing on, what he had been chewing on all through the day, was what the hell was wrong with him. After Marissa had left him in the dust in the billiards room, he'd proceeded to get drunk, like, saturated drunk—but it hadn't done the job. Yeah, sure, his body had gotten sloppy as fuck, to the point that making it back to the Pit to crash had become an absolute impossibility.

Hell, dragging himself over to one of the sofas by the pool tables so he could pass out on the vertical had been enough of a challenge.

His brain had remained tragically clear, however.

And the worst part? For some reason, the last image he'd had of his sister—of her looking at him through the back window of that car as she'd gone off to her rape and murder—kept popping up, like his mind was a slot machine that spit out mismatched losers over and over again.

Ah, screw the "for some reason." It was Marissa's dead girl, of course. And he guessed, if he were to go sit down with Mary and get all shrinked out, that the Brotherhood's favorite therapist would tell him that the past was being kicked off by the present and he was rocking some PTSD—

The door into the supply closet was thrown wide. And he had enough alcohol in him to not jerk around and squeak like a pussy.

"V?" he said as his bestie stumbled in.

Okay, talk about your PTSD: Vishous was as disheveled as Butch had ever seen the brother, breathing hard, icy eyes wide as saucers, black hair all this way and that—and he was panting like he'd run the tunnel, not walked it.

"What?" Butch demanded. "Is Doc Jane okay? Is the Pit? Christ, what happened?"

V just marched around a little and then threw himself into Tohr's green, ugly-ass, beloved chair on the far side of the desk. Propping his head on his gloved fist, he muttered, "One of my old dreams just came true."

As Butch's panic deflated, he rolled his eyes. "And what was that."

"I just fucked you in the ass."

Blink. Blink. And then Butch started laughing. "Yeah, yeah, good joke. Okay, what did Lass do now?"

"No, I'm serious. I just screwed you. Badly. I'm really fucking sorry."

Leaning onto his forearms, Butch exhaled a curse. "No offense, there is nothing you could do that's this bad."

"I told Marissa that you fucked Xhex."

Butch's jaw unhinged, and he felt his mouth pop open. "How . . . why . . . what . . ."

V threw his hands up. "I thought she knew, true! I didn't know you hadn't told her! What the fuck, didn't you guys do that whole 'who'd you sleep with before me' shit? What the fuck!"

If Butch hadn't gone straight back into panic mode, he would have had to laugh at the guy again. V was the ultimate in unflappable, the kind of composed bastard who would sit on a gasoline can in the middle of a house fire just to take a load off.

Guess they'd figured out the criteria for his adrenal gland finally waking up. Good to know.

Bad news for Butch, though.

Putting his head in his hands, he rubbed his face. "What did she say?"

"Not much. She went down to your room, got dressed, and left for work, calm as could be. Which was what really made me shit in my pants, true?"

Butch wanted to say that it would be fine, it was going to be okay. But with the way he and his mate kept missing each other lately . . .

"How did the subject come up?" he asked.

V put both palms forward. "Look, she started talking about you guys."

"The club thing?"

"Yeah. She feels like you've got her typecast in the virgin/whore duality and you're smothering her. And listen, not that you have any interest in taking advice from me, but you gotta cut that shit out. Just because she sees a couple of humans banging in a public place doesn't mean she's going to change in any way. What do you think is going to happen? She's suddenly going to turn into the likes of me? First of all, she'd need a sex change, and second, she'd have to get a fuck of a lot more uglier — and more stupid, too, evidently."

In the silence that followed, half of Butch's brain went on overload with the Xhex thing; the other half came to a sudden realization.

Marissa was right. He felt more uncomfortable with her being in a place like that than she did.

Damn it.

"Anyway," V muttered, "you two need to talk now. And I'm sorry."

"It's okay."

"I thought I was helping. I just wanted to point out to her that she's your type. She's your girl. You don't need anything more or less from her."

"That is true." He patted around for his cell phone. "She was going to work, yeah?"

"Yeah. That's what she said when she left."

"I'll call her." As V punched up out of the chair, Butch offered his palm. "We're good, my man. It's my own damn fault. I should have told her, I guess. It's just anything that was before her doesn't matter, you know?"

V slapped palms. "I feel like fucking shit about this. If you want a *rythe*, let me know."

"Nah, but you may have to pick up my dry cleaning for a month."

"Doesn't Fritz do that already?"

"It's a human joke."

"Ah, which is why it wasn't funny." V walked over to the glass door. "When do you want that night off again so you can go to that club?"

"Might as well be tomorrow. What the hell."

"Okay. I'm taking the class to spar in the gym. Then Z is going to talk about poisoning people—you sure I don't need to get a food taster?"

"You're good. But if Z needs someone to practice on, let's get Lassiter to be the guinea pig."

"Done. So fucking done."

As Vishous walked off and the door shut silently, Butch called his mate and prayed she picked up. When things just went to voice mail, he cursed and hoped that it was because she was in a meeting and not because she was so pissed off she'd blocked him.

She wouldn't do that. Surely, she wouldn't.

Then again . . .

"Shit."

Chapter Thirty-three

Talk about adding a layer of excitement to every single second.

As Paradise went through a sparring session in the gym, and then a truly eye-opening class on how to kill things with lotions and potions, she felt like she had the most amazing secret on the planet. With every punch and kick thrown, with each note taken, question asked, and answer given to her, she had to fight to keep a smile off her face.

And part of that was that she knew Craeg was exactly the same.

From time to time, she'd catch him looking over at her with hooded eyes that suggested whatever he was thinking of, it wasn't the lesson at hand.

Instead, he was obviously back in the dark, on the phone. With her.

And gee, it was no surprise that her body wanted more of him again—so badly, in fact, that she squirmed and cracked her back and had to readjust stances and sitting positions pretty much constantly.

Nobody else seemed to know, however—although maybe that was self-delusion. And if it wasn't? Screw it. Before she'd left her house to dematerialize to the bus, she'd reread the application forms and the disclosures— namely all the stuff she hadn't shown her father because she hadn't wanted to spook him—and there was no mention of a policy prohibiting relationships.

Or romantic attachments.

Or ... whatever it was they were doing.

So they were legal as far as the regs went. They were also both of age, and yeah, sure, the idea of Peyton and Anslam finding out presented a potential complication with the *glymera*, but 1) she had so much dirt on Peyton that she could blackmail him into silence if she had to, and 2) Anslam was your typical, self-involved son of privilege who wasn't going to notice a pink elephant in the room unless it in some way benefited him.

When the final leg of the evening arrived, she walked into the weight room with Craeg ahead of her, and she allowed herself a rare ogle, measuring the breadth of his shoulders, and his towering height, and the way he walked with such leashed power.

And yup, that spectacular ass of his.

Wow.

But then it was all business as the Brother Butch gave them their marching orders, assigning people to various machines and free weights.

"Paradise, you're running tonight," he said, pointing over to the treadmills. "One hour. Break at twenty and forty for water. No incline during warm-up."

Heading across the mats, she hopped up on the nearest machine, put the stop key in, and programmed the computer for sixty minutes at a stiff clip. As the band started to whiz along, she jumped on and fell into a rhythm that was rougher than usual—then again, her thighs were tired from her having crouched in the defensive position earlier in the evening. That got better soon, though, the platform bouncing and whining to the beat of her Brooks Glycerin 12s, her breathing becoming deeper and deeper.

Craeg ended up at the squat station.

Talk about a show of shows.

The amount of weight he could handle was so great, Butch and Tohr ended up spotting him, one on each side, just in case he lost control of what had to be six hundred pounds. Positioning himself under the supported bar, he put both hands up with the wrists out, puffed some air, and grunted as he freed the load and accepted it with his body. Instantly, his face turned red and his neck muscles and veins popped as he backed up two feet to assume a stable stance.

Up . . .

. . . down.

Up . . .

. . . down.

In spite of the way he trembled on the surface of his skin, his large muscles and iron torso were rock-solid as he hefted the bar over and over again. Sweat began to run down his face, not that he appeared to notice, and there was no way she wasn't trying to imagine what his massive thigh muscles looked like under the uniform's supposedly loose pants: Those things went tight as a second skin as he dropped down because of how big his muscles got. In fact, he looked as if he were going to split them wide—

It happened so fast.

One minute, she was running with her stride, keeping up with the speed. The next, her right foot landed half on the band, half on the side rail.

She went down too quickly to catch herself, or at least catch herself with an arm or a hand. Instead, she hit the console hard, bounced, and nearly sanded her face off on the belt because the stop key she had so carefully put in the machine was not attached to her clothing.

So the treadmill just kept running.

For a second, she was too stunned to move—but then a shot of burning pain was enough to get her flipping over from wherever she'd landed. God, the nauseating stink of toasting flesh made her nose crinkle.

That was when she saw the shitkickers.

Right next to her face.

Abruptly, there were all kinds of people talking above her, and she tried to track what they were saying, but something was in her eyes. And her head hurt. Why did her head hurt?

"... Doc Jane, right away."

"... stretcher?"

"Fast. Hurry!"

Flopping around with her hand, she tried to get the sweat out of her eyes so she could see better.

Not sweat. Blood: When she looked at the palm she'd passed over her face, it was smudged with bright red blood.

Oh, crap. She'd hurt herself fairly badly.

And all because she'd been being a chick.

Damn it.

When Paradise went down across the weight room, Craeg nearly threw the barbell off to the side to run over to her. But you didn't do that with six hundred and eighty pounds—not unless you wanted to hurt yourself, or hurt somebody else.

With as much control as he could spare, he moved forward one step and relied on the Brothers' help getting the load back on the supports. Then all three of them hightailed it over. Craeg went for the stop key, yanking it out—because she was way too close to that goddamn band, her crumpled body half on, half off the fucking piece of shit.

"Paradise?" he said.

As Butch knelt down beside her, Craeg nearly yanked the guy out of the way, but that was ridiculous. For one, the Brother was a teacher. For another, there was no bigger announcement that Paradise and he were up to something than if he went all territorial over her in an emergency fucking situation.

"Paradise?" Craeg repeated. "Paradise ..."

She sat up when she heard him say her name, and

then she turned to look to him—oh, God. There was blood. So much ... fucking hell, he was going to pass out.

The Brothers barked commands at each other and then Tohr left to get help. Which meant there was a space next to her to fill, and Craeg's body took advantage of that before he had a conscious thought to move.

"I'm fine," she said, batting at hands and sitting up. "I just feel stupid. I don't need help."

Ripping off his shirt, he wadded it into a ball and pressed the fabric to the leaker over her eye. "Shut up," he muttered as she started to argue with him. "You're going to the clinic. You probably need stitches."

"It's only a little cut."

"What exactly do you think all this red stuff means."

"No reason to get hysterical—"

"I'm not the one arguing with ..."

They went back and forth, terse words crisscrossing and canceling one another out. It wasn't until they paused to take a breath that he realized everybody in the weight room was staring at them with a collective well-isn't-this-news.

Shit.

Whatever, he needed to make sure she consented to treatment first. Then he'd worry about all the conclusions that were being jumped to.

And yes, he was the one who picked her up and put her on the gurney.

And yes, if any other male, including her little buddy Peyton over there, or either of the Brothers, had touched her, he would have bitten the male's arm off.

Out in the corridor, she was still fighting with him, and he knew it was because she had scared herself and was burning off the fear.

"Ridiculous." But at least she was holding his shirt against her face. "I just need to rinse my face off and it'll stop."

"Yeah, 'cause a little water's really going to help that two-inch slice up there."

"This is overkill!"

"And you went to med school when?"

As they came up to the clinic door, he intended to go in there with her, but Butch stepped in front of him. "You need to go back to class."

Craeg opened his mouth to argue—and that was when he knew he'd lost his damn mind. He'd properly met the female, what, four nights ago, tops? This was inappropriate.

Even so, his head shook back and forth. "I'm not leaving."

"They're going to have to examine her," Butch countered. "All of her, if you get my drift."

Craeg cursed and took one last glance through the slowly closing door as Paradise transferred herself from the gurney to the exam table. As if sensing he was no longer with her, she glanced up in confusion, looking for him.

"I, ah . . ." Craeg cleared his throat. "I'd like to see her after she's finished."

"If that's cool with her, you got it."

Craeg nodded and commanded his feet to do an about-face and head back in the weight room's direction. It was a good half minute before they responded, and talk about sluggish—his legs took their damn sweet time getting him back where he needed to be.

And what do you know, Peyton was waiting outside the weight room for him.

Muttering under his breath, Craeg braced himself to fight the guy again.

"When did it happen?" the guy demanded.

"When did what happen."

"You and her."

The other male was staring up at him with a strange calmness that could have meant acceptance or preparation for attack. Funny, those perfect J.Crew looks and that aristocratic entitlement attitude, coupled with the whole fancy background, made the guy a much better eHarmony candidate for a female.

And yet Paradise, for some reason, had chosen Craeg. She had to be nuts.

"There's nothing going on between us," Craeg said.

"Don't fucking bullshit me, okay? You've bonded with her."

"The fuck I have."

Peyton's blue stare made a trip around the world. Then he frowned. "Wait, you're serious."

"What the fuck are you talking about?"

"You honestly don't recognize it. You're not aware that your bonding scent's been triggered—or of the fact that you bared your fangs at all of us when we went over to help her. You are honestly fucking unaware of all that."

Craeg blinked like a cow for a little bit. Then he looked to the left of the guy and measured the distance between his own forehead and the concrete block wall. Maybe if he hit his skull hard enough, he could cause sufficient brain damage that his short-term memory would give him a break and he could forget he'd ever met that female.

Peyton started to laugh. "You know, I want to hate you, I really fucking do. She's one of the best females I've ever known. Instead, I feel bad for you."

"Why's that," Craeg snapped.

"Because you're so far gone and you're still fighting it. This is going to be fun to watch."

"So glad I can amuse you."

Peyton had the gall to clap him on the shoulder. "You'd better take care of her properly—or I will hunt you down and kill you. Slowly."

Craeg stepped back. "I don't know what you're talking about."

"Yeah, yeah, sure you don't."

Peyton was still laughing as he turned away to open the door.

Craeg caught hold of the guy. "How do you know her?"

There was a pause. "She works at the audience house."

"That's how I met her, too."

"Just so we're clear, sometimes I think I'm in love with her, too." Peyton rolled his eyes again. "God, will you stop with that?"

"With what."

"You're snarling at me."

Huh. What do you know. His fangs had dropped and his upper lip had curled back. "Sorry."

"Yeah, you're not bonded. Not at all." Peyton crossed his arms over his chest. "Anyway, before you go Cujo on my ass, I've never even kissed her. It's not there for her. Toward me, at any rate. Just as well—I'm a total fucking asshole—and she's right, I got a couple of bad habits. Anyway, remember what I said."

"And here I was, hoping we could both forget this conversation."

"Never going to happen, my man." Abruptly, Peyton's eyes narrowed and pure aggression shone out of them. "Anyone who hurts that female is an enemy of mine. And I might be an aristocrat, but I am capable of going straight-up animal to protect what's mine. Got it?"

Craeg measured the guy. "I can't promise anything."

"What's that supposed to mean."

"I have ... things ... I need to do after this, and they don't include settling down and taking a mate. Bonding or no bonding, nothing is going to change that reality. Not even her—and she knows this."

Peyton's voice dropped until it was so deep, it was barely audible. "Then you are a fool. You are a dumb motherfucking fool." Except then the guy shrugged. "But hey, that's good news. It means I might still have a chance with her. And before I have to give you a distemper shot, fuck you. You walk away, it's on you, asshole— and I promise you, I will make a play for her serious, like."

As Craeg's inner beast stood up and roared, it was probably best that the male walked back into the weight room at that point.

Yup.

They already had one trainee in the clinic. The class didn't need two.

Especially if that second one had to be brought there in pieces.

Chapter Thirty-four

Marissa talked to Butch all night long.

Even as she conducted her staff meeting, interviewed a mental health caseworker for a job, and had a little visit with Mary, in the back of her mind, she was talking to Butch.

The imaginary scenes of her going all righteous on his omissioning ass were marked with a sound track of him agreeing with her that he was a douche bag who needed twelve kinds of therapy. The fact that, over the course of the hours, he called her three times and texted her twice didn't help his cause—then again, he could have had Perry Mason pleading his case and he would still have ended up in prison for life without the possibility of ever getting laid by his *shellan* again.

She hadn't returned any of his fingers-doing-the-walking, and she told herself she was shutting him out because she wanted to choose her words carefully first. The reality was far less laudible: She felt hurt by him, rejected by him, set aside by him, and she wanted him to get a sense firsthand for how that felt.

Which was not attractive at all.

Dearest Virgin Scribe, she'd never been a spiteful person, and she hated that the very thing she treasured most in the world, her relationship with her mate, had made her go sour.

And it was that sticky wicket that got her to leave

work early, text him that she'd be waiting for him after training got out, and resolve to have the hard conversation they needed to.

When she arrived back at the mansion and got a gander at the grand foyer, all she could think of was the number of people who walked through that space on a regular basis. As privacy was required, she decided to go sit down in the training center. For one thing, having made the decision to talk, she wanted to get going with Butch as soon as possible; for another, the Pit was too claustrophobic and she wasn't sure whether V or Jane had the night off.

God knew she didn't want anyone to overhear anything.

Leaving her coat and briefcase by the hidden door under the grand staircase, she entered the proper code, 1914, and jogged down the shallow steps. After putting in the same series of numbers again, she emerged into the underground tunnel and started off in the direction of the training center. From time to time, she had to wipe sweaty palms on the seat of her dress slacks, and she fussed with her hair, which she'd left down for once.

By the time she went through the supply closet and came out into the office, her heart was pounding, her mouth was dry and her stomach rolling.

After years of having suffered from panic attacks, she prayed her nerves weren't going to take her into that stretch of hell.

Checking the slim Cartier watch Butch had given her on their first anniversary, she figured she had a while to wait. An hour, at least.

Great, now she felt trapped in the glass fishbowl.

With a glance over her shoulder, she eyed the closet door and wondered if she shouldn't just walk the tunnel a couple dozen times under the exercise-clears-the-mind theory, but that didn't appeal. Besides, sooner or later, even if Butch didn't get her text, he'd have to go to the big house for Last Meal, and this was her best bet for catching him.

Looking over at the desk, she went across and sat in the office chair. Her log-in was accepted by the computer, and then she signed into the Gmail account she'd created for RSVPs to the Twelfth Month Festival Ball.

"Wow." She leaned in toward the screen. There were countless replies waiting. "Unless you're all declines, that is."

For godsakes, there were easily a hundred unread messages, and as she started at the top, she found ... all yeses.

We accept with pleasure your kind invitation. ...

But of course, both my hellren *and I shall ...*

With great anticipation, we do humbly accept. ...

Before she got too far into it, she opened a side drawer and took out a yellow legal pad. With a blue ink pen, she created a table with *Name, Reply*, and *Number* at the top. Going between the computer list and the paper, she marked the names and replies, and she was about halfway down the former when she got to her brother's name.

Double-clicking the bolded entry, she held her breath. And then exhaled.

He was not coming. With three polite sentences, he indicated that he would need to be at the clinic, but he certainly appreciated being included.

Funny, it was both a relief and strangely deflating. She'd expected him to come, especially after that initial female had mentioned that Havers had been the one to recommend her as event chair.

Sitting back, she thought about her whole confront-the-past goal. Wrath had long ago apologized to her, and the way he had so freely and warmly embraced Butch and their mating had meant so much. She'd never really dwelled on what had happened between her and the King, but as she considered their doomed betrothal, and then everything that had come afterward, she found that she had fully forgiven him. She bore him only love—and knew that he would speak with her if she wanted or needed him to. She truly was at peace with him, however.

The *glymera*, on the other hand? She remained incensed to the point of rage about them and their standards, but it wasn't like she could line up that judgmental bunch of bullshit artists and yell at them. Living independently from all that had been a far more healthy and successful strategy.

And as for Havers? She had been planning on talking to her brother at the ball—but that would not have been a good plan, really. Talk about needing privacy—and maybe notecards. She wasn't even sure what she would say to him.

This was the problem with resolutions. You couldn't force something until you were ready for it. And her emotions were still so volatile.

Yes, she thought. Him not attending was actually going to make her life easier. And less of a spectacle for the *glymera* peanut gallery.

The answer for speaking with him was probably a little more time and maybe . . . shoot, maybe she would sit down with him and Mary—if he'd be willing? Who knew.

Butch was her main problem. And that female who had been killed, of course.

Refocusing, she finished her tallying, closed out of the account and made an estimate of the numbers. If this nearly one-hundred-percent acceptance rate kept up, they were going to have four hundred people at Abalone's. Which was twice what she'd assumed when she'd run the food and booze costs—something that, of course, as head of the event, she was expected to cover.

Guess she'd underestimated how much they wanted to see and be seen.

Sitting back, she rechecked her watch. At least she'd blown through a good thirty minutes.

Antsy, twitchy, nervous, crampy, she fussed around with the mouse, watching the little white arrow go in circles on the screen.

Man, she was still pretty angry at Butch. Even though she'd calmed down a lot, she remained hurt and—

She frowned and stopped her arrow from wandering.

At the bottom of the line-up of icons, there was a tiny picture, a little representation of what seemed like . . . the back of her *hellren*'s head?

But that couldn't be right.

Double-clicking on the image, a sign-in popped up. The username slot was already filled in with *BUTCH DHES*, and the password was blank.

There was no title anywhere, nothing to let her know what kind of file it was. And it made her sad, but given where they were at, she was suspicious of whatever it was.

Then again, when you kept certain things from your mate, the other party was likely to start questioning pretty much everything.

Putting her fingertips back to the keyboard, she entered the password he usually used: *1MARISSA1!*

Sure enough, it got her into . . .

It was a video image, frozen and ready to be played, of Butch sitting at the desk, with the camera behind his head.

Hitting the play arrow, she triggered the mechanism and watched as her mate stared at that black key with the red tassel. There was no sound, so she couldn't hear anything, but she imagined the plopping noise the thing made every time it dropped on the blotter.

A young male came in the room.

Had to be one of the trainees.

And the pair of them started talking. Clearly, this had to be an interview with regard to the program—and it was not going well, if the other male's face was anything to go by.

When Butch held up the key, it became obvious they were talking about it.

Time for sound, she thought, fumbling around with various buttons. Talk about nowhere fast. After all kinds of F-whatevers not doing the job, she discovered that the speakers themselves required a turn-on—and still she got nothing. It took her for-frickin'-ever before she discovered that someone had unplugged the speakers from the tower for some reason.

"... what is it like?" the male asked.

Straightening, she focused on Butch's head, and he took a moment to answer the question. "Depends on how old it is and how it happened. The new stuff ... especially if it was violent ... can be messy."

"What are you talking about?" she said out loud.

"Body parts really don't like to be cut, stabbed or hacked into sections, and they express their anger by leaking all over the fuck. Jesus, we're, like, seventy percent water or something? And you learn that's so fucking true when you go to a fresh scene. Pools of it. Drips of it. Speckles of it. Then you got the stained clothes, rugs, bedsheets, walls, flooring—or if it's outside, the ground cover, the concrete, the asphalt. And then there's the smell ..."

Dear ... God, she thought as a wave of sadness overtook her.

Butch continued. "The older cases ... the smell is worse than the mess. Water deaths, with the bloating, are just ugly-looking—and if that gas that's built up gets out? The stench will knock you on your ass. And I wasn't too crazy for the burn deaths, either." There was another pause. "You want to know what I always hated the most?" He motioned over his head. "The hair. The hair ... God, the fucking hair, especially if it was a woman. Matted with blood, dirt, little rocks ... tangled and twisted ... laying on gray skin. When I can't sleep at night, that's what I see. I see the hair." He began to rub his hands together. "You always wore these gloves, you know ... so you didn't get fingerprints on anything, didn't leave any of yourself behind. Early days they used to be latex—later they were nitrile. And sometimes, when I'd handle a body, the hair would get on the gloves ... and it was like it wanted to get into me? Like ... you could catch death by murder somehow." Butch shook his head. "Those gloves were so fucking thin. And they didn't work."

The trainee frowned. "Why did you have to wear them then?"

"No, no, they worked with fingerprints, you know. But I left something of myself behind in those dead bodies. Every one of them . . . has a piece of me in them."

Marissa turned off the sound. Stopped the video.

Put her head in her hands.

"You'll be good as new in the morning."

As Doc Jane handed over a mirror, Paradise braced herself for her reflection—but actually, it wasn't that bad. "How many stitches is that?"

"Twelve. But you'll heal with no scar whatsoever."

Reaching up, she touched just under the line of tiny black knots that was next to her eyebrow. "I bled so much, you would have sworn I needed a hundred."

Doc Jane put a little white bandage over her handiwork and then the snapping sound of examination gloves being taken off echoed in the tiled room. "That area has a high degree of vascularization. You might want to feed if it's been a while—it's not an emergency at all, but you did lose some blood and you guys are working awfully hard in there."

Or, in her case, losing her concentration and making an ass out of herself.

"You can wait for the bus to take you back, or if you don't want to hang around, I can have one of the *doggen* take you out to a secure place to dematerialize from."

Dropping the mirror, Paradise tried to imagine what her father would say if he saw her face. "Can I stay here for the day? I can't . . . I don't want to go home looking like this."

V's mate smiled, her forest-green eyes kind as she pushed a hand through her cropped blond hair. "I was thinking the same thing, actually—but I'm not about to make anyone stay here unless it is medically necessary. And in your case, it's not. It's just maybe . . . a little easier on your dad."

"Is it okay if I go call him on my cell?"

"Sure. If you can't get a signal—and some people cannot—there's a landline in the cafeteria you can use."

"Thank you so much," she said as she shifted her legs off the table. "I didn't feel a thing while you were putting the stitches in."

"You're doing great, Paradise. Everybody's so proud of you."

"Thanks."

She looked down as she landed on her feet and grimaced. There were specks of blood on her Brooks—which was not a big deal as long as she didn't wear the sneakers around her father.

Yup, she definitely needed to crash here, she thought as she emerged into the corridor.

It wasn't until she'd gone down the hall and pushed open the door to the break room that she realized . . .

She and Craeg were going to be in the same facility.

For the entire day.

As her body did that math and came up with a totally buck-naked answer, she figured, What the hell, if she had to get put together with a needle and thread, she might as well take advantage of someone kissing her to make it feel better.

Mmmm.

Going over to where she'd left her satchel on the floor with some of the others' bags, she picked the thing up and put it on the nearest table. Unzipping the top, she rifled through, searching for her phone. She didn't find it.

With a frown, she turned the Bally over and dumped everything out. As she waded through Kleenex packets and her wallet and random mascara tubes and her Kindle and loose money and ChapStick and other stuff, she knew she had to get better organized. Okay, where was . . .

Her phone was *not* in there.

What the hell? Had she left the thing at home? She could have sworn she'd put it in with the rest of her junk.

Tilting the open mouth of the bag toward her, she

fished around the empty belly, and then unzipped the front pocket just to see what other useless crap—

Her phone was in that flap.

Frowning, she looked around the empty room for no good reason. The problem was, she never put the damn thing in there—she was always in too much of a hurry to bother with the unzipping. Plus she had this paranoia that she'd forget to secure the pocket back up and she'd lose her cell.

Never once had she put the phone in there.

Had someone been through her stuff?

One by one, she sorted through the items on the table. Nothing was missing that she could see, although it wasn't like she kept a detailed mental list of her necessaries. And when she checked her wallet, her ID, credit cards and cash were all still in there.

Well, if anything had been taken, it wasn't worth more than two cents.

As she put her things back in, she swallowed a load of creeped-out, but what was she going to do? Go to the Brothers with an, "Oh, my phone moved to this other pocket here and ..."

Yeah. Right.

With no bars showing on her reception, she went over to the landline that was mounted on the wall by the glass-fronted refrigerator filled with Gatorade, Coke, and juices of various sorts. When she picked the receiver off the cradle, the dial tone was just like it was at the audience house, so she hit 9 for an outside line and punched in her father's number.

Fedricah answered, and in a cheerful voice, she told the butler that she was going to spend the day at the training center because she was working on something for extra credit. She also assured him that she was going to be chaperoned.

And it was true. She wasn't going to be alone—not if she had any say in things.

Craeg was going to take care of her.

"Does it hurt?"

As she hung up, she looked over to the door. Craeg was standing in the jambs, his bare chest gleaming, his pecs and abs standing out in stark relief under the ceiling lights.

Dropping her lids, she ate up the sight of his body— and thought, actually, she did have an ache all of a sudden.

"Hello?" he demanded.

"I'm crashing here for the day."

As he went stock-still and narrowed his eyes, she held up her cell phone to him. "No bars. No service. Guess we're going to have to figure out another way to hook up at seven, won't we."

Chapter Thirty-five

Out in the training center's parking garage, Butch escorted the four trainees who were leaving to the door of the bus, making sure they all got on with their shit. Then he went back inside and walked the long corridor toward the office with a slow stride. He had no idea where Marissa was, but he was hoping, when he resurfaced up at the mansion, that she had called him back, texted him, something.

He'd left his phone on the dining room table up in the mansion by mistake. But maybe that was a good thing. He'd been driving himself crazy checking the device at First Meal.

Meandering down the empty hall toward the office, he became acutely aware that he was essentially alone in the facility: V and Tohr had already headed back to the house with Doc Jane, Manny, and Ehlena to get ready for Last Meal, and likewise, all *doggen* were working up in Fritz's big kitchen. And Paradise, Craeg and Axe were eating in the break room.

Dear Lord, what if Marissa had moved out of the Pit? he thought.

Oh, fuck, what was he going to do if—

As he opened the glass door, he froze.

"Hi," his *shellan* said from behind the desk.

She was so beautiful, sitting there with her office clothes on and her blond hair down. Man, he loved those waves falling over her shoulders like something out of

Game of Thrones, and that silk blouse with its slight hint of pink brought out her skin like she was in a magazine ad for Estée Lauder.

"I got your calls. Your texts," she said as she stared across at him.

Entering the office proper, he let the door close by itself and wasn't sure whether he should sit down in a chair. Pace. Fall to his knees and start apologizing.

"I'm sorry—"

"I'm sorry—"

They both shut up. And the silence that came next was a period of each of them waiting for the other to speak.

"Look, I should have told you about Xhex," he said, biting the bullet. "I didn't because I just ... it was before you and I were together seriously. I met her one night at Rehv's club—it was just that night, and it wasn't anything on either side. I had no idea she was going to end up living with us, and by the time she was, it was just one more thing I was leaving behind, you know?"

"I know. I get it."

He waited for her to say more, but when all she did was look down at her hands, he frowned and sat in the chair opposite from her. "You sure about that."

"Yes."

Butch shook his head at the continued quiet. "I know I'm not perfect here, but if you honestly think I want her now over you, I'm going to get pretty fucking pissed off."

"No, I know you don't."

And still she said nothing further. In the vacuum, while he tried to convince himself not to jump out of his own skin, he thought of him and Xhex high-fiving each other and joking about how he owed her because she'd saved him in a fight in an alley with some slayers. "She's one of the guys, for fuck's sake."

"I know."

Bringing up a hand, he rubbed his twitching left eye. "Do you."

Jesus, what was wrong with them? Talking had always been so easy, like breathing. Now . . . all this silence.

"Just say it," he muttered. "Whatever it is, however much it will hurt me, say it—just don't leave me sitting here wondering what the fuck you're thinking. My head's going to explode."

"Why didn't you tell me about the hair?" she said in a rush.

Butch snapped his head up. "Excuse me?"

"I saw the interview. With that trainee." She pointed to the computer screen. "I watched part of it. The part where you were telling a perfect stranger something that you'd never shared with me."

"The interview—? Oh. That."

"Yes, that."

Butch resumed scrubbing his eye. "That wasn't anything important."

"Yeah, I guess I'm stuck wondering how many other things you've decided that about? I mean, what else don't I know about you? After this long together, I thought I knew everything. . . . I thought . . ." She got choked up a little, but was able to cast that aside. "What else don't I know, Butch."

As he looked across the desk into her eyes, a feeling of unease rippled down his spine. She was staring at him as if she didn't know him at all.

"Marissa—"

"Seeing that beaten girl on the couch in the living room of Safe Place completely ruined me. The whole . . . violent ugliness of it, the suffering, the up-close pain, the way she looked at me, pleaded at me with her eyes." Marissa's slender shoulders trembled. "I didn't tell you all that because I was afraid to trigger you about your sister. I didn't talk to you because I didn't want to upset you. There. I said it. It doesn't make me happy, and it really doesn't make me feel any better . . . but that's what I've been hiding from you. Oh, that, and seeing my brother again broke my heart in half, just crumbled me. It made me miss parts of my old life, and that made me feel like I was betraying you." She put her hands up. "That's what I got. So what have you been hiding."

When he went to open his mouth, she stopped him. "Before you speak, be very aware that I love you. I love you with everything I have and all that I am. But if you do not get real with me, I'm going to go back to the Pit, pack a bag, and move to Safe Place for a while." She held his stare with unwavering eyes. "You and I are not going to survive long term, regardless of love or bonding, if you keep airbrushing things. If I keep airbrushing things. It's not a good strategy for us—and if this makes you feel like you're on the spot? As if I'm giving you an ultimatum? I don't care. If anything gets in the way of our relationship, *anything*, I will mow that shit down—even if it is you."

Butch realized he'd stopped breathing only because his lungs began to burn—and inflating them with a ragged inhale did little to improve that sense of suffocation.

Marissa shook her head gravely. "This is not about whether or not you were ever with Xhex. It's about the fact that you didn't think I could handle you telling me. Isn't it. You didn't want to hurt my feelings, and that's noble, but don't couch what happened between the two of you in terms of being 'unimportant.' That's a copout." She shook her head sadly. "The whole sex-club thing is the same. So is your issue about blow jobs—which you also refuse to discuss with me. The bottom line is, you have a very flattering, but very limiting opinion of me. You want to caretake me, but you're putting me in a prison—and no offense, I grew up in the *glymera* being told all the things I couldn't do because of who and what I was. I'm not going to put up with that anymore."

God . . . he felt like he'd been shot. And not because anything in particular was hurting. It was more that sense of encroaching cold as your blood leaked out all over the place that he was dealing with. Same sense of dizziness and disassociation from reality, too.

"So what's it going to be, Butch?" she said softly. "What are you going to do."

As Marissa fell silent, she honestly had no idea where her *hellren* was, what he was thinking about, whether he'd even heard a word she'd said. And it was weird: Her heart wasn't even hammering, and her palms were not sweaty—which, considering the crossroads they'd gotten to, was a surprise.

Then again, she'd said her bit as calmly and kindly as she could. Now it really was up to him; their future was in his hands alone in so many ways.

When he shifted in the chair, she braced herself for him to walk out, but all he did was plug his elbows into his knees and rub that shadow of a beard on his jaw. His other hand took the giant gold cross he wore out of his black shirt.

Okay, wait, now her hands were getting a little sweaty.

"I, ah ..." He cleared his throat. "That's a lot to take in."

"I'm sorry."

"Don't be."

"All right."

For some reason, the soft hum of the computer became very loud, as if her ears were trying so hard to pick up sound from her mate that they'd amplified everything else.

He cleared his throat again. "I didn't know I was so bad at this."

"Bad at what?"

"Our relationship."

"I'm still in love with you. I still want you. You haven't failed at everything—and I'm part of the problem. It's not like I've been so chatty-Cathy, either."

"Not so sure about that. The me failing part of it, that is."

Now she sat forward, too, and extended an arm across the desk even though she couldn't quite reach him—and wasn't there a metaphor in that. "Butch, don't ... please don't beat yourself up about it. That's not going to help

either one of us. Talk to me. You've got to talk to me —
that's all I'm saying."

"You're saying a lot more than that."

She threw up her hands. "I don't have to go to the club
if it's that horrific for you. I don't have to finish you off
with a blow job if it really doesn't turn you on. All I'm
saying is, you need to tell me why, and we need to talk
things through — there has to be another kind of communication that goes on other than you going silent after
you tell me it's because I'm a 'good girl and good girls
don't do that, can't handle that.'"

Butch steepled his fingers and bumped the tips against
his lips. "I didn't tell you about the nightmare stuff because I find it so fucking disturbing when it happens that
the last thing I want is to bring it up when it's not on my
mind. I get really fucking pissed off at the shit that's still
haunting me, and I feel like . . . if I talk about it, it gives
it more power over me."

She thought about her conversation with Rhage's
shellan the night before last. "I'm pretty sure Mary
would say the opposite. That the more you talk about it,
the less power it has."

"Maybe. I wouldn't know."

Marissa found herself wanting to press, but dialed
that back. She had the impression the door had been
cracked, and the last thing she wanted to do was scare
the damn thing closed.

"As for the blow jobs . . ." A flush hit his cheeks.
"You're right. I don't want to talk to you about that because I'm ashamed of myself."

"For what?" she breathed.

"'Cause . . ."

Tell me, she thought at him as he struggled. You can
do this . . . *tell me*.

His eyes flicked up to hers. "Listen, I'm not interested
in you pulling some position paper on what I'm about to
say next, okay? How I'm supposed to get over myself.
Are we clear?"

Marissa's eyebrows popped. "Of course. I promise."

"You want me to talk, that's fine. But if you come back at me with some PC bullshit, I'm not gonna take it well."

As she had never before hit him with any "PC bullshit," she was very sure he was drawing boundaries because he felt vulnerable.

"I promise."

He nodded as if they'd struck a deal. "I was raised Catholic, okay? And that would be *real* Catholic, not casual Catholic. And I'm sorry—I got taught that only whores and sluts did that. And you . . . you're everything I could ever want in a female."

Abruptly, he dropped his eyes and couldn't seem to go on.

"Why are you ashamed?" she whispered.

He grimaced so hard his whole face nearly disappeared into his brows. "Because I . . ."

"Because you want me to finish?"

All he could manage was a nod. Then he looked up sharply. "Why is that a relief for you?"

"I'm sorry?"

"You just exhaled like you're relieved."

She started to smile at him. "I thought you were never going to let me do it—and I've always wanted to find out what it's like."

Her *hellren*'s face turned beet red. Beet. Red. "I just . . . I don't want to disrespect you. And that's what my background tells me happens when you do that in a girl's mouth—you don't like her, you don't love her, you don't respect her. And yeah, sure, I should throw all that hardwiring out, but it's not so easy."

Marissa thought about her struggles with what her upbringing had left her with. "Boy, do I get that one. I feel like I should stop being bitter and insecure about my brother and my years in the *glymera*. But it's like I learned too well that that stove burned, you know?"

"Totally." He smiled a little. Then rubbed his face. "Am I as red as I think I am."

"Yes. And it's adorable."

He laughed in a short burst—but then he got serious. And stayed that way. "There's another reason. Well, with the club thing, there's another reason ... but it's crazy thinking. I mean, really crazy."

"I'm not afraid. As long as you're talking, I am honestly not afraid of anything."

Already she could feel the connection growing between them—and it wasn't the short-lived kind you got when you just had some good orgasms, but then had to return to everything that still hadn't been fixed.

This was the concrete kind. The bedrock kind.

The I-loved-my-partner-before-but-now-it's-even-more kind.

And she knew he was getting ready to talk about his sister because his entire body went still—to the point that he didn't appear to be breathing. And then a glaze of tears appeared across his beautiful hazel eyes.

When she went to get up and go to him, he slashed his hand through the air. "Don't you dare. Don't touch me, don't come over here. If you want me to talk, you gotta give me some space right now."

Marissa slowly lowered herself back into the chair. And as her heart thundered against her ribs, she had to part her lips to keep drawing breath.

"I've always been superstitious ..." he said softly, like he was talking to himself. "You know, a superstitious thinker. I draw all kinds of connections that don't really exist. It's like what I was saying to Axe about the exam gloves. On a rational level, I understand that I'm not leaving any part of me in or on those bodies, but ... it doesn't feel like that."

As he went quiet again, she stayed right where she was.

"My sister ..." More with the throat clearing. And when he finally did speak again, his naturally gravelly voice was nothing but rocks. "My sister was a good person. There were a lot of us in the family, and not everyone was nice to me. She was, though."

Mentally, Marissa recalled what she knew about the girl: the disappearance, the rape, the murder, the body being found a week later. Butch had been the last one to see her.

"But there was another side to her," he said. "She hung out with a lot of ... goddamn, this is hard to say ... but she went out with a lot of boys, you know what I mean?"

His face was pale now, the lips compressed, those hazel eyes heavy lidded as if he were replaying bad memories.

But then he just stopped. And when he didn't say anything further, she had to fill in the blanks.

"You think she was murdered," Marissa whispered, "because she wasn't being a good girl. You think maybe if she hadn't been having sex with those boys, she wouldn't have gotten into that car and they wouldn't have done what they did to her and she wouldn't have died."

Butch closed his eyes. Nodded his head once.

"And you hate yourself for thinking that because it puts the blame on her—and that's a betrayal. That's blaming the victim—and you would never, ever do that to anyone, especially not your own sister."

Now he nodded over and over again. Then wiped away a tear.

"Can I come hug you now?" she asked in a cracked voice. "Please."

When all he did was nod, she raced to him and put her arms around him, drawing him to her until she ended up sitting on the desk and he was collapsed into her lap.

Bending down over him, smelling his hair and his aftershave, stroking those huge shoulders, she felt more in love with him than ever before—in fact, what was in her heart at the moment was so tremendous, she didn't know how her body held it all in.

"It wasn't her fault," he said roughly. "And I know that. The fact that I even had that thought once—it's so fucking ugly. It's as bad as me not saving her—I might as well have put her in the car myself. Jesus, to believe her actions were the problem?" Butch sat up. "My head gets all fucked-up over it—if I had a daughter, and God forbid"— he made a quick sign of the cross over his heart— "something happened to her, and anyone tried to blame her short skirt, or the fact that she had one drink—or seventy-five, or consented to have sex and then changed her mind in the middle? Do you have any idea what I'd do to that misogynistic asshole?"

"You'd kill him, right after you murdered the perpetrator."

"Damn fucking straight. Fuck, yeah." He made a circular motion next to his head. "But then that old tape plays, and every once in a while, it spits out that horrible fucking thought—and I feel so guilty for having it that I want to vomit. In fact, right now I'm eyeing the wastepaper basket and wondering if I can make it there in time."

As his eyes locked off to the side, she wished Mary were in the room with her. Guess this was why people went to therapists—when the dam broke like this, it was probably best to have a trained professional around.

"And by the way," he tacked on, "I'm proud of my religion. The church isn't perfect, but neither am I—and it's brought a lot of good into my life. Without my faith, even with you, I'd be a shell of what I could be."

"I understand completely, and my belief system isn't any different to me."

After a period of quiet, Marissa took both of his hands. "If I go to the sex club tomorrow night, are you going to think less of me?"

"God, no."

She nodded. "And assuming you someday get comfortable with it, if I suck you off, are you going to look down on me?"

He laughed in a short burst. "I'd probably worship you even more."

"Will you still think I'm a good girl?"

"You know ... actually, yes." He sounded relieved.

"Yeah, I mean, I've never thought about it before . . . but I'll absolutely still love you."

"So you're able to get past the old thinking in regard to me, right?"

"Yes, I am."

"Like, you have a thought, you considered it, and you put it aside, right?"

"Yeah." He exhaled. "Yeah, that's exactly what I'm doing."

"So . . . why can't you do the same with your sister. Have the old thought. Consider it against everything you know about her and the way she was, and layer onto it your core belief that the blame never goes on the victim no matter what she's wearing or anything like that . . . and I'm willing to bet you'll reject the idea that your sister contributed in any way to what was a horrific, in-excusable crime against an otherwise innocent girl. I'll bet that you resolve that on your own, and probably never dwell on that part of the pain again."

He blinked once. Twice.

"Forget the blow job," he said.

"I'm sorry, what?"

Butch stared up at her with such complete devotion, it was as if she had put the world at his feet. "I think I just fell even more in love with you. And I didn't think . . . I couldn't fathom how that would even be possible."

Sure enough, his bonding scent became a roar in the room, and his hazel eyes got so full of emotion and rev-erence that she felt a little giddy.

Taking his face in her hands, she kissed him. "This is so much better than before."

"Before what?"

"If I'm going to be on a pedestal"—she pressed her mouth to his again—"I want to be there as your perfect partner, not because you think I'm the perfect good girl."

Her *hellren* started to smile. "You got it. And you got me."

As he kissed her back, she thought about what happily-ever-afters were about, and decided that true love didn't mean effortless, and ever-after wasn't about cruise control. You started with the attraction, and then you opened your heart and your soul—but all that, which was no small thing, just got you to first base.

There were many, many other trips to take to deeper levels of greater acceptance and understanding.

That was where you found the happy. And the ever-after was the work you were always willing to put in to stay close, to learn, and to grow as people together.

"I love you," he said as he wrapped his arms around her. *"God, I love you."*

Leaning away a little, she smiled and traced her fingertips over his face. She wanted to say those sacred words back to him, but somehow they didn't go far enough.

So she said the one thing that would mean even more to him. "Oh, honey . . . go, Sox."

Throwing his head back, Butch laughed so hard the sound rattled the glass door of the office. And as she smiled back at him, she thought, Yup, *I love you* could be said in many different combinations, couldn't it.

Chapter Thirty-six

It was amazing how a television could turn anything into a proper lounge.

Not that Craeg was watching *The Big Bang Theory* reruns that were on it. Still, he was glad a *doggen* had come in and set the thing up in the corner because without the pleasant chatter in the background? Sitting in the same room with both Axe and Paradise would have done his nut in completely.

He needed something, anything to keep his mind off of her.

Naturally, as he stared at the fan of cards in his hand, he had no idea what he was looking at. Across the table, however, Axe hadn't had that problem—which was why, after how many rounds of gin rummy, he owed the bastard fifty bucks.

"Well, I guess I'll head to bed," Paradise said from over on the couch.

Right. It was amazing how, when a certain female spoke a certain combination of words, it was a guaranteed fucking hard-on.

So yes, he was subtly rearranging himself under the table—before the circulation into his femoral artery was cut off completely by his erection.

Meanwhile, Paradise uncoiled herself from her tucked-in position and Craeg did a fantastic job of not watching her. At least not *directly* watching her: His peripheral vision tracked every step she took across the tiled floor to the door, and particularly noted the way she bent across one of the three round tables to grab her satchel.

"Day," Axe muttered as he shifted cards around.

Craeg grunted.

When the door eased shut, he wondered exactly how long he had to wait before he could leave—

"You can go now," Axe said with a smirk. "I'm good with solitaire—and there's some porn I'm going to watch. Which is another, more fun version of solitaire."

"I'm not that tired."

"Yeah, I know." The guy tossed back a laugh. "And listen, do me a favor—don't disrespect me by trying to pretend. After that show you put on in the weight room, how stupid do you think I am?"

"I'm not with her."

"Then you're an idiot."

"Not why I'm here." And yet even as he said it, he collapsed his hand of cards and put them facedown on the pile. "I owe you fifty."

"Forty-five. But you were going to lose this hand."

"Probably. You want it now?"

"You're good for the cash."

As Craeg got to his feet, he looked at the piercing spacers that the male had put in the holes in his face and his ears—and abruptly, he wondered exactly how many more studs of metal the guy had in places you couldn't see. "Did those piercings hurt when you got 'em?"

"Yes, that's part of why I do it. The sex afterward is sharper."

"The tats, too?"

"Yup."

"Huh. Go fig. You know, you're smarter than I thought you would be. Better card player, too."

"Because I like ink and metal, you think that makes me dumb?"

"I've led a sheltered life, what can I say."

He was over at the door when Axe spoke up. "I thought you were an asshat."

Craeg frowned and looked over his shoulder. "Based on what?"

"You're the vampire equivalent of a redneck. I thought there was nothing remarkable about you except for your size—and frankly, that's what they make Mack trucks for."

"And now?"

"I still think you're an asshat." The Goth smiled a little. "But I don't mind asshats, as it turns out. Go figure, as you say. Besides, our fathers . . ."

As the male let that one hang, Craeg was glad the guy did. "Yeah. Anyway, good day."

"Have fun, you kids."

"That's not happening."

"So you say."

Craeg stepped out into the corridor and looked all around. Everything was quiet, the proverbial coast clear, and still he stayed where he was. Down to the left, there were five single bedroom units. His was the first. Axe's was next. And Paradise's . . .

Well, three was a charm, wasn't it.

But he didn't go down to her right away. Even though he was about as romantic as a rock, he somehow ended up in his stall shower, cleaning his body as if he were about to meet the Scribe Virgin in person. And then he shaved. And even went over to the duffel bag he'd left where he'd dropped it the night before and unpacked his clothes all over the floor.

They were clean. That was about it.

Blue jeans. With holes. T-shirts. Without holes. His Syracuse Orange baseball cap.

With a curse, he settled for a pair of the uniform's loose pants and a fresh Hanes undershirt. He kept his feet bare, and he prayed, *prayed*, that he tiptoed over to her place without getting caught.

Out the door. Another left to right to check no one was around. And then he pulled a *T2* Linda Hamilton as he bounced on the balls of his feet down the bare concrete floor, making no sound at all. When he got to Paradise's room, he knocked softly.

"Come in?" she said in a high, slightly stressed voice.

No poking his head in. Nope. His whole body shot inside and he forced the door closed behind himself.

"I'm so glad," she said with a laugh. "I was worried . . . anyway."

The only light on was the one in the loo, and she'd closed that little room off for the most part: She was sitting in the semi-dark on the bed, wearing a small white robe that was belted at her waist—and nothing else.

Whoa. Legs. Lots of . . . calves, thighs . . .

As he swayed from lust, she said, "You took a shower, too?"

He nodded. Because apparently he'd left his voice out in the hall.

"Do you want to come over here?"

He nodded again.

Next thing he knew, he was standing in front of her. And then he was kneeling. Putting his shaking hands on her legs, he dipped under the hem of the robe. Her skin was just as soft as he remembered.

Dropping his head down, he ran his lips back and forth over one of her knees.

Oh, fuck him. What he needed to do was jack back up, kiss her for a while, ease her flat . . . do her right with his hands—and then get the fucking hell out of Dodge.

That was *so* not what happened.

His palms drifted down to the sides of her thighs and then traveled up—taking the robe with them. As her flesh was exposed, he watched as she trembled and her hands tightened on the bedsheets.

"Are you scared?" he asked. Because he had to be sure.

"No," she breathed.

"Do you know what I'm going to do to you now?"

"No . . ."

He nodded, keeping his lips against her knee so that he stroked her with them. "Open your legs for me."

The shivering got worse as she obeyed, exposing a pair of perfectly modest white cotton panties that just about made him come in his pants.

And her scent drove him insane.

"I'm not going to hurt you," he said in a guttural voice.

"I know. I trust you."

Craeg moved to the inside of her knee and took his sweet time, nuzzling, drawing his tongue over her thigh, running his fangs up and down.

"Put your hands in my hair," he told her. "Guide me in. You know where you want me to be. Show me."

Her touch was tentative at first, just ruffling through his short hair. "It's so soft," she whispered.

"So are you."

His hands were now up on her hips and he squeezed the bones, liking how they felt against his palms. And then for a moment, he lost his train of thought because he was struck by a powerful urge to mount her.

That would be a no, though.

Subtly, she began to pull him in and he went at her speed, working her with his lips, getting her ready for what was coming. And then he was at those panties. Looking up, he couldn't see her properly with the robe all bunched around her waist, so he freed the tie and spread the halves. She had on a little, tight muscle shirt that was white and no bra—so her hard nipples threw shadows even in the low lighting.

Groaning, he breathed in and put his lips on her core, sucking in the cotton, getting it wetter.

Her hands ripped at his hair—gone the timid touch, now a demand, and that meant it was time for a position change. Moving fast, exploding up from the floor, he made sure that the door was locked with his mind and then he swept her legs up on the bed, parted her thighs, and went back to what he was doing, kissing her, pushing her knees higher and wider so he could do her better.

Panting. She was panting and working herself against his face, her hands pulling him in tight, her body giving itself to him with an abandon that was a shock and a serious fucking turn-on. With a growl, he shoved the muscle shirt up and thumbed her spectacular breasts—and as she arched on the mattress, he was *so* ready to get those panties out of the fucking way.

But first, a little more teasing.

Staring up at her, he could feel the memories being etched in his head, the sounds and smells, the gasps and moans, the sheer beauty of her.

Paradise.

It was so much more than she expected.

As Paradise's hands dug even harder into Craeg's hair, she was riding a wave of high-octane pleasure that took her out of her body and grounded her in her flesh at the same time. The sensation of the rubbing, the friction, the heat at her core was unlike anything she'd ever known—and she still technically had her—

Nope.

With a vicious jerking motion, he ripped one side and then the other—and her panties were no more.

And then the sensations were slick and hot, nothing separating his lips and his tongue and her sex.

Thanks to what they had done the night before, she knew what was coming, so when the orgasm hit she gave herself up to it, welcoming the pumping pleasure, jerking up against the mattress, knocking the pillows off to the floor.

When she finally came back from the soaring, shimmering heights of the release, she saw him rising up between her legs.

"Take me," she ordered him. "Do it."

Grabbing hold of her muscle shirt, she ripped it off

over her head so that she lay naked and stretched out in front of his enormous body, his incredible erection, his barely leashed power. And yet he hesitated, even though the hunger on his face made him look like a demon.

"Craeg . . ." Reaching up to her breasts, she caressed herself and arched up again, the burn already back in her sex, the desperation, the sweet suffocation returning tenfold.

All he did was sit back on his heels, put his hands on his thighs, and bow his head.

"Craeg?"

"No . . ." he groaned. "I can't."

"What . . . ?"

"I'm not going to have sex with you."

Wait, huh? she thought.

When he didn't say anything else, she propped herself up on her elbows and pulled her shirt over to cover her breasts. "Why not?"

"It's . . . not going to happen."

"What's wrong? What did I do?"

"Oh, fuck, it's . . . no, you're too good, you're . . ."

"Craeg, you gotta stop that."

Enough, she thought, reaching out to him. As she ran her hands up his arms, she felt his corded muscles, knew the struggle he was forcing himself into.

"Take this off," she said, tugging at the bottom of his shirt.

She expected him to fight with her. He didn't. His arms went lax and he let her remove the undershirt, and then . . . God, he was beautiful, his smooth, hairless skin stretched over such power—and when she went to run her hands over his flesh, he let her, his head falling back, his neck and shoulder muscles straining.

And then he shocked her.

"Take my vein," he said in a rough voice. "If I can't have you . . . take from me. . . ."

Just like with the oral sex, it happened oh, so fast, her

fangs descending, her eyes locking on his jugular with a dead-serious that she'd never felt before.

With a hiss, she lunged up and struck, sinking deep, nailing him with a greed that he submitted to completely. Hauling him to the side, she laid him out beneath her and straddled his abdomen as if he were her prey, sucking at him, his taste roaring its way down to her gut, filling her up from the inside out in a way that food and rest could not do.

She was dimly aware of him stretching his arms out and gripping the headboard, bending his torso toward her, moaning as his hips pumped and thighs jerked. He was orgasming and then so was she and everything got super-crazy, super-quick, as she moved her pelvis and felt that hard ridge right where she wanted it.

But when she tried to get to his erection, when she attempted to take his pants off, he held her hands away and kept them in an iron grip. And when she protested, when she fought him, the world spun and she was on her back again.

Blood ran down his neck and his chest from where she'd penetrated him, but he didn't care.

His hands went to the front of his hips and he sprang his arousal by ripping the fly of the loose pants in half.

Paradise's eyes rolled in her head, but she forced them to focus because she wanted to see him.

Wrapping his big hand around his thick shaft, he began to stroke himself. He didn't watch what he was doing; his eyes were on hers. And in spite of the heat between them, there was something intrinsically remote about his expression.

He wasn't going to take her, she thought.

Except her confusion and disappointment got shelved as he arched up and started to orgasm all over her sex.

He might not be willing to take her body fully.

But he was marking her for all he was worth.

Spreading her legs wide, she exposed herself completely and let him torture himself on a rack of his own doing, his releases covering her core, hitting her in hot bursts that stroked her.

She might have been a virgin ... but she knew down to her soul that this was a battle he was going to lose.

Maybe not tonight, but soon, he was going to crack and make love to her.

And she couldn't wait.

Chapter Thirty-seven

Two nights later, Butch finally got free to take his *shellan* to a sex club.

Yeah, like he'd ever thought of a date night like this one?

As he waited for her in the mansion's foyer, he paced around and felt like he was pulling a Halloween in the dumb-ass getup he had on. The black leathers were fine; the black muscle shirt was also okay. The rest of the shit was . . .

What the *fuck* was he wearing?

Pulling the long black coat out in a fan, he got a whole lot of black leather, fur, and silk. The thing was huge, and yet it barely brushed the ground because he was wearing a pair of lifts that made him taller than Wrath.

New Rocks?

He'd borrowed them from Axe, and they buckled up from the toes to just under his knees. Also weighed fifty pounds, but were surprisingly stable and comfortable.

And then there was the mask. The thing was a front plate made of thin metal and plastic, and when he strapped it on and applied proper adhesive, it covered his entire face with a gray-white-and-black skeletal horror that moved when he spoke.

Yup, it was mask night down at the Poke 'n' Play, and far be it from him not to fit in with the crowd.

He took out his phone and checked the time. Marissa

had come over from the Pit to hang out with the girls to get ready—and the two of them were going to head to the club together while Axe was driven out separately from the training center.

Clomping around the mosaic apple tree, he was amazed at how okay he'd become with taking Marissa with him on this sojourn into the dark and the seedy. After that talk he and his *shellan* had had, though, it was like something had unlocked in him, some twisted, painful muscle spasm of his internal wiring had loosened and uncoiled, allowing him to breathe more easily.

He'd hated the rough spot they'd found themselves in. He fucking loved the new vista, though.

As if on cue, he sensed his mate at the top of the grand staircase. Turning, Butch looked up and—

Enagbu jioa kdf ahtaj; fjjkd powkl.

Or something to that effect.

Gone was his beautiful princess in the designer clothes. In her place was . . . a freaky-deaky erotic sexpot wearing shrink-wrapped black latex from her mile-high stilettos all the way up and over her head. The only thing that marked her identity? The long blond ponytail that came out of a hole in the top of the full-body/facial suit, those golden waves swinging free.

And then there was her mask.

It was like an industrial gas mask, with round black disks for eyes and a nose and mouthpiece that showed no part of her skin because there was a seal around the latex that covered her face. Made of black glass and burnished gray metal, it was an ugly piece of absolute art.

As she came down at him, his cock punched out an erection so quickly, he actually had to look to make sure the fly of his leathers was still intact.

Her body was . . . absolutely, fucking insane, the light stroking down the banging curves of her breasts, throwing shadows around her tight waist, highlighting her hips and thighs.

When she was finally standing in front of him, she did

a slow little turn, and holy fucking shit, the mechanized sound of her breathing made his balls tighten. Well, that and her ass. Dear God in heaven above, her—

"Well, what do you think?"

The voice that came out was not hers; it was distilled through some kind of sound box, emerging tinny and distorted and alien.

"Ojkdla hgdio lweno io."

"What?" came that electronic voice.

"He said you are fuuuuucking ammmmmmaaaazing," came a male voice from across the way.

Butch's head whipped to the side and he glared at Lassiter, who'd come out from the billiards room and was lounging against the archway. Pegging the moron with his forefinger like the thing was a gun, he snapped, "Get your miserable ass back into that fucking room before I cut your eyes out and strangle you with your own tongue."

The fallen angel put his palms up and wheeled away. "Right. Leaving. Here I am, walking back and saying absolutely nothing about her."

The retreat would have been more convincing if the bastard didn't let a huge wolf whistle rip as soon as he was out of range.

"I'm going to fucking kill him, I swear it."

"Please don't."

Refocusing, Butch just shook his head. "Oh, my God, you look . . . hey, I'm back to speaking English. Bonus."

Bringing her in close, he pressed his body against hers and felt up and down the smooth, slightly sticky suit. With a groan, he bent to the side and moved his hands down to those latexed hips and onto that ass, grabbing her cheeks, squeezing, going farther in between from behind.

"I'm not gonna make it through tonight," he groaned. "Fuck, I can barely walk."

Her sexy little laugh, distorted through that speaker, made him sway in his New Rocks.

Holy. *Shit.*

                    *   *   *

"Have you made friends in your class?"

As her father put out the inquiry, Paradise sat back in the club chair in his study. Tucking her socked feet under her, she wondered exactly how to answer him—and prayed as he rifled through the papers on his desk that he didn't look up and see her blush.

Yup, how to answer that one, she thought.

She and Craeg had spent the last two mornings talking on the phone, speaking for hours as well as . . . doing other things. So yes, they were friends of a sort—and she had plans to see him in person again, both tonight *and* tomorrow during the day.

This was what her little impromptu meeting with her father was about.

If she didn't get some skin-to-skin contact again soon, she was going to lose her mind. Phone sex was great unless you'd had the real thing.

Or almost had it.

"Paradise? Are you all right?"

She shook herself and made a show of getting out of the chair and going to the cheerful, crackling fire. The cold front that had come in the day before had gotten into the walls of the Tudor, and there were chills lurking everywhere in the house—something that would be a constant until spring's warm weather came in May.

So she had the perfect excuse to turn away from him as she picked up the poker and rearranged the logs.

"Oh, yes, I've met some lovely people and I'm enjoying the classes very much." As well as the sneak peeks of Craeg. "It's amazing the things I didn't know."

"For example?"

Well, if she purred into the phone and told Craeg everything she wasn't wearing, it was a guarantee that he'd—

As orange sparks fell into the smoldering ashes, she stopped that line of thought right quick. "Hand-to-hand combat is a science, Father. I'd never watched MMA fighting before, or learned anything about the different styles of engagement. They're teaching us various disciplines, and each one has its own strengths and weaknesses. I spar with Peyton and this other male, Craeg, a lot."

Placing the poker back in the brass stand, she pivoted around and returned to the chair. "I am very, very good at it—"

She stopped talking as she realized her father had frozen in the process of moving one sheet of paper into a pile, the bill or account statement or whatever it was hanging in the air along with his arm.

The expression on his face was akin to someone having told him his house was about to be bulldozed by humans.

"Father . . ." she said. "I'm really happy. I'm really . . . I'm learning about myself, who I am, what I want, what I can do."

He glanced at the document as if wondering what it was doing in front of him, hovering in the air. Then he seemed to snap himself back to attention.

Clearing his throat, he asked, "And what conclusions are you coming to?"

Well, the big one was that she was probably falling in love with Craeg. But considering that was going to make her father go worse than dad-statue, she needed to keep that quiet—plus she hadn't told Craeg yet, and it seemed appropriate that he be the first to know.

Falling in love. Such a huge thing, and yet so simple, too.

And quick, yes. But she had heard when bonding happened, it could be like this.

"Well, I want to do some good for the species," she said.

"Exactly how?"

"Father, that doesn't mean fighting in the war."

"Considering you were just speaking about how good you were at . . ." He rubbed his temple. "I guess I should have expected this."

"Expected what?"

"Your changing directions. What I was unclear on was how it was going to make me feel."

"I'm not changing anything."

God, that was a lie even to her own ears: She wasn't sure what her future looked like, or who precisely she was going to be at the end of the training program—however long it lasted—but she wasn't going back to the way she had been.

Those nights of being a proper female sitting in this house, or any other, waiting for the chance to come down to some social gathering was not it. And yes, that decision not to get mated—except to Craeg—had stuck.

"I wish your *mahmen* was still with us."

"Me, too." But for another reason than the one he was thinking of, no doubt. Paradise could have used some love advice. "I miss her."

"Do you know that we were well and truly in love? We had been appropriately matched by our families, but . . . we really did fall in love. She was my everything."

God . . . damn it, she thought. His subtle advocating for Peyton didn't so much miss the mark as drive a stake through her heart—because she wasn't fooled. That statement, while true and important, was without a doubt uttered in the hopes that she look favorably upon a traditional betrothal with her friend.

She had suspected for a while that that was something her father wanted for her. He liked Peyton, approved of the male's bloodline, and knew that there was already a friendship in place. In the eyes of an aristocratic head of household, what could be better for a daughter than a setup like that.

What would he think if he ever met Craeg?

Craeg, the son of what the humans would have called a

blue-collar family. Would her father even see the strength of character, the soul beneath the lack of trappings?

"I can adjust to almost anything," her father said grimly. "I can adapt to whatever you want your life to be—up to a point. The one thing that I won't budge on is your finding the kind of love your *mahmen* and I had. That is the non-negotiable for me."

Read: a male who was from the same class she was, who could provide her with the same life she had grown up in.

"Oh, Father," she said sadly.

"I'm sorry, that's just how I am."

"I know."

As the grandfather clock out in the foyer began to chime eight times, she cast off the pall that had settled in the room and got to her feet again.

"I have to be off." She straightened the clothes she had chosen for the evening. "I'm going to go out with my classmates, and then there's a project we're working on during the day, so I'll be home tomorrow night after class? And yes, there will be chaperones."

As she stared across the perfectly appointed room at him, the ambience of old wealth and distinction that hadn't been bought, but had been curated over the hundreds of years her family had had money, truly sunk in on her.

Would Craeg even be comfortable here?

Probably not.

"Father?"

"Forgive me." He looked down at the papers on his desk. "But of course, I understand you must needs be gone. Do know you are missed, however. Also know that the Brothers do not tell me much, yet what they have shared . . . makes me very, very proud of you."

That now-familiar pain in her chest, the one that came from her lying, lit off again as she thought that actually, he would not be very proud of her at all.

She intended to lose her virginity tonight to a male he would never approve of.

The trouble was, the Brothers had given no indication of how long this training program would last or what the long-term prospects for the class sticking together were. And her need for Craeg's body was making her desperate—and very conscious that time was passing with alacrity.

She wasn't going to miss her chance. And she had the sense that the more they were together, the more Craeg's priorities were changing, too. He was becoming attached to her.

Paradise could feel it.

If it weren't for the omissions with her father, she would be on cloud nine.

"I'll see you tomorrow night after class," she said in a rough voice.

"I'll be here. Do take care of yourself."

"I will." She nodded to him. "I promise, Father."

Chapter Thirty-eight

Craeg couldn't remember the last time he'd gone out with "friends." In fact, he might never have done it before.

As he pulled on his jeans and cursed the holes, he told himself to get over it. He'd never been into "fashion"—one, he couldn't have afforded it even if he had given a shit, and two, worrying about what you put on your body had always struck him as a criminal waste of brainpower.

"You look so incredibly average."

Rolling his eyes, he turned around to Axe and—

"What the *fuck* are you wearing, asshole?"

The male looked like he'd been hit with the freak bat harder than usual, his big body wearing a shiny black skin suit that smelled like chemicals and made a strange creaking sound as he walked. Black piercings were in his ears and his face, a chain running from one lobe to his fucking nose, for crissakes.

He didn't look like a pussy, though—Craeg had to give him that. Something about the bastard radiated aggression, power, strength. Sex.

Kinky sex, that was.

Axe shrugged like he was in nothing more unusual than a *granhmen's* housecoat. "I'm going to hang out with my kind. If I don't get laid my way soon, I'm going to kill myself—hell, much more of you vanilla types and I'm going to need Cialis to get it up. You're killing my burn."

"Well, no offense, but an open flame is not what you need around that getup."

And out came the mask. It was black, of course, but like he'd expected something pink and green? And it fit over Axe's features like a glove, changing his not-bad-looking-at-all face into something downright hideous—a morphing that was no longer vampire, but another species.

Alien.

"To think I assumed you were fugly before," Craeg remarked.

"Again I say, you normals are killing me."

Annnnnnnnnnnnnnnnd that was how he and a whatever-the-hell-it-was ended up riding out of the training center together.

As the bus went along, pausing at all those gates, they were both quiet, but he was damn sure they had the same things on their minds: Axe was clearly looking to get his freak all over some Goth variety of a heart-n'-a-hole, while Craeg was trying desperately to convince himself he could keep from losing control with Paradise.

Ostensibly, this whole meet-up-with-the-class thing shouldn't have been a big deal—they were just going to a regular club, with music and booze. Nothing close to where Axe was heading, for sure.

But sex was going to be front and center, at least for him.

Shit, Paradise was killing him—and he'd identified the essential problem. Since the first night of the program, he'd set up barrier after barrier to keep her away, and each one of them had crumbled. It was like he was a mountain climber and had taken a fall—and every tethering of the rope that was there to save his life had popped, one after the other.

"You know, you look like shit, and not just because you're wearing that ridiculous getup," Axe muttered.

Craeg looked across the aisle. "I look ridiculous? Have you checked in the mirror? I didn't know that crank case oil was a fashion statement."

"Stop avoiding. What's up, my man."

As they trundled along, heading for the dematerialization spot, he found himself talking. "I can't . . . You know, it's not right."

"What isn't."

"I can't do it."

"Still waiting for a noun. I know you're a redneck, but you do have a vocabulary, if rumor serves."

Craeg just shook his head. There was no way he was going to disrespect Paradise by laying their private business out—even to a guy like Axe, who seemed, if only because he was, in his own words, a committed narcissist, likely to keep shit tight.

"I don't know," Axe said as he stretched his legs out across the seats and leaned against the bus's darkened windows. "She seems different from her kind. I don't think you have to worry."

Yeah, females were totally opposite from males, weren't they.

And in this case, he was the one being a pussy. She was not. She was ready for their next level—and he suspected he might just be hiding behind her virtue: Once again, he was protecting himself. And when he thought about how she made him feel?

Still seemed like a smart . . . if perhaps unsustainable . . . plan.

Christ, they were going to end up alone at some point tonight. It was fucking inevitable. And after two phone sex seshes with her, he was more desperate than ever, a panting, starved, crazy male with an ever-ready cock, and enough orgasms on backup to dehydrate him to the point of needing Gatorade through a vein.

He wanted to believe he could keep to his resolution, he really did.

The trouble was, nothing made him more shortsighted than his name leaving her lips on a gasp.

One syllable and nothing fancy, his was not a regal name. But all she had to do was say it and he was gone,

gone, gone. Putty in her hands. Blank of any intention other than getting inside of her and staying there.

Oh, man, he was in such trouble here.

As Paradise entered the human club, shAdoWs, she looked around and thought ... yeah, no. Loud music was thumping to the point where she heard it in her skull. Dark purple and red laser beams shot this way and that through air that was thick with human smells. And the overwhelming attention she got was not anything she was interested in.

Having no idea where Craeg, Boone, and Novo were, she walked through the gyrating crowd, and as she went along, human men watched her, assessed her, hoped to catch her eye. She supposed some of them might have been considered attractive, but it was more along the lines of her wandering through someone's room and noticing a chair with a good slipcover.

The fabric might be nice, but she'd never take it home.

Or in this case, sit on the damn thing.

The building that housed the club had been a warehouse, it looked like, and there was something incongruous about its three-story-high open space nonetheless feeling claustrophobic. Then again, there were just too many people crammed into the center. Where did you just hang out, she wondered. And how did all of them know each other? Everybody seemed to be touching ... everybody that was around them.

Working her way across the floor space, she discovered there were booths along the perimeter of all that writhing. Maybe her people were there? Jeez, did she even have the right club—

"Hey, baby, come with me."

A rough hand grabbed her waist and hauled her up against a sweaty body. Glaring at the human man, she tried to push him away, but he latched hold on her wrists, yanking her in close.

"I know you want this," he slurred, rubbing his hips against her. He smelled like old cologne, older cigarette smoke—or maybe that was weed?—and a very-not-hot kind of desperation. "Kiss me."

"You've got to be kidding."

"Come on, you want it. I know you want it."

Fuck this, she thought.

With a quick jerk, she freed her right arm and punched him in the throat with her knuckles—and as he bent over and grabbed at his neck, she had to stop herself from breaking his nose with her knee.

Leaving him to gag, she turned and—

Ran smack into Craeg's enormous chest.

"I was coming to save you," he said dryly. "But I already learned firsthand you can hold your own—so I guess I shouldn't be surprised that you don't need me."

Instantly, everything about the club changed. The air was no longer stuffy; it was filled with sexual heat. The lasers weren't blinding; they were scintillating. The music wasn't loud; it was erotic.

The humans were still annoying, but come on, even true love could only do so much.

God, he looked amazing. Tall and broad, big and strong, that Orange cap on his head just like the night they'd first met. That simple white T-shirt showing off his muscles. Those jeans . . . Jesus, those worn, soft-as-skin jeans that gave her peeks of his thighs in the places that were torn.

"Dance with me," she said as she leaned into him so he could hear her over the din.

The bill of the baseball hat kept her from seeing his eyes, but she felt them running over what she had changed into before leaving the house: her low-cut blouse and her short little skirt and her tight little jacket were all for him, and they had obviously captivated the guy. He also seemed to like her hair, that she'd left loose, and what she'd done with her makeup.

"Craeg," she repeated. "Dance with me."

"I can't," he muttered.

"Why?"

"I don't, like . . . you know, move that way."

Such a lie, she thought as she remembered the feel of him on top of her. He moved just frickin' fine.

"Do it anyway." She grabbed his hips and pulled them in close. "Dance with me."

Moving against him to the beat of the music, she felt his immediate response, his arousal popping up, rubbing against her belly because he was so much taller than her.

"People are going to know," he ground out—but his hands were already on her waist, squeezing, holding their lower bodies together. "From class."

"Who cares. Like they don't already."

Novo knew. Hell, the female was part of the reason they'd kissed for the first time. Peyton? As she'd decided before, she could deal with him. Boone? He cared only about the training; she wasn't even sure the male knew anyone's name. And Axe wasn't even coming tonight. Nor Anslam. And no member of the *glymera* would ever show up in a place like this.

Live now, she thought, losing herself in being with him, close to him, held by him.

Pulling his head down to her, she whispered in his ear, "I'm not wearing any panties."

The groan that ripped out of him was louder than even the music.

"Pardon me," he said, straightening. "I gotta go do something."

"Mmmm," she purred, imagining him in the bathroom, taking care of that arousal. "And what might that be?"

"I have to go kill all the human men in this club who are looking at you. Won't take long, they're weak and can't run fast."

Throwing her head back and laughing, she felt her heart soar, especially as those strong arms wrapped around her even more tightly.

This was going to be the best night of her life. She could feel it.

Chapter Thirty-nine

The key turned out to be nothing that you put in a lock. It was more a tangible pass that got two people through a mountain of security that stood around a nondescript door to a nondescript garage structure in a seedy part of downtown Caldwell's mostly abandoned industrial park.

Following behind Butch, but ahead of the trainee he'd brought with them, Marissa found that with her mask in place, she had a confidence she might not otherwise have felt. There was something liberating about hiding your features when you were going into an environment that you didn't know how you were going to handle. It meant you didn't have to self-monitor your expression and fake composure, for one thing. For another, you could more freely try on a persona that could take whatever was thrown at them.

Because who else was going to know the truth?

In the dense darkness of the club's interior, Butch's reassuring hand reached behind and patted around to take hers, and the instant the connection was made, she felt even more confident. Nothing was going to touch her, harm her, unsettle her. Not with him here.

The first thing she became aware of was a growing thumping sound, and she assumed it was the bass beat of some music. As they rounded a tight, architecturally random corner, she discovered it wasn't a concert-worthy set of speakers doing their duty. It was the rhythmic chopping of a grind wheel that seemed to serve no purpose other than to—

Oh. Okaaaaay.

There was a woman with her legs spread underneath it, and the machine was penetrating her with . . .

Looking away, she found a male squeezed into a Lucite box, his naked body contorted, one side open so that people could . . .

Shifting her eyes elsewhere, she saw a row of exam tables, people in latex bodysuits just like hers strapped to them one after another in contorted positions, sexual organs exposed for the consumption of lines of anonymous strangers.

Okaaaaaaaaaaaaaaaay, they were in a sex club. Yup.

And it was weird, the interior space was twelve times the size it had appeared from the outside, so it must have been created by knocking out walls of other buildings, that garage thing just the start of a lineup of facilities that had been merged. Everything was dim, everyone was in costumes and masks, and sex in all its permutations and combinations was everywhere.

It was one nonjudgmental experiment and expression of eroticism after another, the moans and groans offering a soundtrack that the techno music complemented rather than overrode.

Bizarrely, she found the whole thing curiously . . . unshocking. And not really ugly, either. The people seemed genuinely turned on—and God, they were so nice. Unlike the few times she'd been out at human gatherings and been gawked at, here, people would meet you in the eye and smile, like you were part of their . . . well, club. And when she bumped into someone, the response was relaxed and nonaggressive.

It all seemed so . . . normal?

Maybe it was the unapologetic nature of it all. Maybe it was the mask hiding her identity. Maybe it was the dead-serious purpose of her being here. Whatever the combination, she was relieved.

Deep into the club, Butch, Axe, and she formed a circle. As Butch looked to her in his skeleton mask, she patted his hand and nodded, giving him the thumbs-up sign.

After he nodded back at her, he turned to Axe. The two of them leaned in and traded some words. In the meantime, she looked around for some pattern of dress that indicated who was staff.

Had the dead female come here before she died?

A series of flashes lit off over to the left and she narrowed her eyes. Someone was taking photographs of people who were strung up on rotating wheels and incapacitated as men ejaculated on them, whipped them, drew blood.

And that was when she realized . . . the farther they went, the more hard-core things had become.

Had someone taken a game too far with that female? she wondered. And killed her by mistake?

After Butch was sure that Marissa was doing okay, he was all business—and without distraction. That erotic moment with her in the foyer of the mansion had been sexual to him. Everything here in the club? Might as well have been a lawnmower for all he cared. A bowl of oatmeal. A book on Chemistry: As he started to develop a strategy in his head, he was back on his old job, his brain stepping into a set of mental clothes that at once made him hyper-aware and utterly detached from his environment.

And now to hedge his bets: He'd been debating for the last two nights whether or not to tell Axe the real reason they were all at the club. The bene was that they might get somewhere quicker; the ball slapper was that he'd potentially tip off the murderer, either directly or indirectly.

Except he had watched that tape of them talking in the office a hundred times—and he just didn't think the male had murder in him. In a fight? Yes, absolutely. Axe was a tough son of a bitch in training, capable of crushing opponents in the hand-to-hand sparring even if they were taller than he was—and he was vicious at the gun range and with dagger training, never hesitating to pull the trigger or go for the kill.

But that was a different scenario from brutalizing some female. And for all his hard-core Goth shit, he wasn't cruel and he wasn't insane.

"So I lied," he said in Axe's ear over the din of moans and techno music.

"Oh, really," the fighter countered.

"I was just following your example."

"So honored."

"I didn't get the 'key' from a friend. It was taken off a female who was beaten to death. I'm here to find out who killed her, and I'm going to need your help."

Axe recoiled. And then narrowed his eyes. Leaning back in again, he said, "How do you know I didn't do it?"

"I don't." Butch met the guy straight in the eye. "I don't know that at all."

Focusing on the stare behind that mask, he waited to see what those pupils did. With the extra stimulation around them, and the fact that his features were covered, the guy was even more likely to show a nervous reaction.

Instead, they were rock-steady.

Which yup, supported Butch's instinct that the guy hadn't been lying about having yet to see death up close and personal.

"I didn't, by the way," the male said. "I didn't kill anyone."

Butch nodded. "I figured. You've got a good conscience—you proved that with how you felt about your pops's death. Your fashion sense, on the other hand, is tragic."

"It got your ass in here."

"True, true." Butch glanced around. "So who's in charge?"

"Wait, tell me more about the female? Maybe I've seen her? Was she one of us?"

"Yup. And I don't know much more than that. There was no ID on her, just that key. She managed to dematerialize to a safe place—that's where my Marissa found her." As Axe glanced at his mate, the guy seemed mortified that anyone, especially a female, had been exposed to such a horror. "She was through her transition, with dark hair, and dark blue eyes. That's really all I got."

"Shit."

"That just about covers it."

Not for the first time did Butch wish someone had taken a photograph of her, even if it had been after she had passed. God, he wished there had been shots of the wounds, scrapings under nails, a careful search for fibers on her and her clothes. But none of that had happened, of course. Again, the vampire race had no procedures in place to handle situations like this.

And it was funny, he'd never thought about the societal weakness before. He'd been too busy fighting on the front lines to worry about intra-race problems.

Man, some simple investigative processes would have helped them so much.

Axe shook himself like he was refocusing. "About the staff—look for the red on the costumes. They tend to stay on the periphery unless there's a violation of the consent policy or if things get too out of line, in which case they'll put a stop to whatever it is. And by out of line, I mean anything more than casual bloodshed."

"Are there any cameras?"

"Probably, but I couldn't tell you where or how to get at them."

Or how to sift through hundreds of hours of streaming images—which was what you'd end up with, given the size of this place and the number of nights that had passed.

Shit.

They had just entered needle-in-a-haystack territory. And considering what was on the line here, that was about as reassuring as a knife at his throat.

Still, he'd beaten bad odds before.

"Let's go deeper," he said as he put his arm around his *shellan*. "We need to see everything."

Chapter Forty

"They have places ... places we can go."

As Craeg spoke into Paradise's ear, he was very aware of how close to the edge he was. But the more she danced against his body, the more the sex took over his brain, kicking the shit out of common sense and rationality, getting him to go all caveman. No panties? Fuuuuuuuck. He really needed to get his hands on more of her, so yeah, it was time to disappear into the back where Novo had told him there were private bathrooms you could use. After all, it was the only way they'd find any privacy tonight. Paradise was going to have to go home at dawn, and it wasn't like she could take him back to her house—not without coming out of the closet about him, which would put her father and them in a very awkward, premature situation.

Plus it was going to be a cold day in hell before he took her to the dump he lived in.

Shit, if he didn't get a release soon, he was going to lose it.

In his pants.

"Show me the way," she moaned.

Grabbing her hand, he led her through the crowd. And as he passed by the booth where Novo was giving Boone a lap dance—and quite possibly his very first hard-on—Craeg spared a wave at the female and got one in return.

As well as a very knowing look.

The private "bathrooms" were underneath the partial second floor to the north, and as they entered a dimly lit, black-walled hallway, he discovered countless closed doors. Discreet Occupied signs were flipped in the first seven they went by. Eighth was a charm.

Holding the door open for her, he growled as she passed him by to enter the little tiled room. There was a toilet stall, a sink ... and a bench—and the squat, tight space was surprisingly clean. Then again, there was a sunken drain in the middle of the floor and a sprinkler head in the ceiling.

They probably bleached 'em after every night.

Making sure the door was locked properly, he grabbed her and pulled her against him, his greedy palms getting into her clothes, feeling the fullness of her breasts, the smoothness of her ass, the heat, the wet fucking heat of her core. He was kissing her out of control already, and she was kissing him back, and God, you'd have sworn they hadn't spent three hours just that morning getting each other off on the phone.

In person, though—in person was where it was at.

And then she was backing up, drawing him with her, taking him to the sink.

With the grace of a dancer, she put her ass on the counter ... then she drew her knees up and propped her high heels against the narrow walls of the alcove.

Giving him a stunning view of her black thigh-highs and her smooth, slick, bare sex.

"You know what I want," she said. "And for once, it's not your mouth there."

Swaying on his feet, he was really goddamn aware that the moment had arrived: His willpower was down to a stump, his sex drive was a roaring engine that wasn't letting him think properly, and fucking hell ... what he was looking at.

"Are you sure?" he mumbled. While he started undoing the front of his jeans.

"Do you want me to beg?"

"No, because I'd start coming right now."

He glanced around and didn't see any cameras. But that didn't mean the fuckers weren't somewhere hidden. "I wish there was another place we could do this."

"Like I care where we are."

With that, she undid her blouse, pulled it open, and popped the cups of her bra down so they offered her breasts high and tight to him. Her blond hair was all around her shoulders, her blue eyes were at half mast, and as she ran her tongue over her lips, the tip of his cock tingled like it was going to explode.

"Please," she moaned, arching like she was in agony.

And that was all it took.

As his erection punched out of the open fly of his jeans, he took the heavy weight in his hand and closed the distance between them. Shit, he couldn't believe this was actually happening. Not the sex part; God knew he'd done that before.

It was the sex-with-*her* part that was getting to him.

Especially as he saw his head right next to everything he wanted. Shutting his eyes briefly, he wanted to say something to make it right for her, look at her in a way that showed he recognized this was a big deal for her, do anything that would turn this experience with a redneck in a club into the reverent, worshipful event it was going to be on his side.

"Yes, I want this," she said softly. "I want this with you—only with you."

Lifting his lids, he stared into her hypnotic eyes—and something strange happened. Against the backdrop of the muffled bass beats and the hundreds of humans and the burning desperation pumping in his blood, he felt an abrupt slowdown.

Make this count, he told himself. Make this special for her.

Bringing his head to her core, he brushed his flesh up and down her sex—and she jumped, then bit down on her lip with her fangs.

Her thighs began to tremble. Her breathing quickened. Her scent got heavier, headier.

With a groan of his own, he parted her sex—but he couldn't keep that up. He was about to orgasm all over her.

Arching above her, he supported his weight on his free hand.

"I'll go slow," was the last rational thing he said.

Paradise was so ready for this, her body both fluid and tense with anticipation. And then she felt him brush against her heat and she nearly orgasmed.

There were so many reasons not to do this, so many reasonable arguments why she should wait for a better moment, a better time, a more stable place in her life and Craeg's. But if the raids had taught her one thing, it was that time was a luxury no mortal could afford to squander.

And her father's words to her before she'd left had resonated not as the warning he had meant them to be, but as the statement of a goal she needed to embrace.

She was in love with this male. Yes, she hadn't known him long, and yes, it was crazy, but no, she had never felt anything close to this connection and what else would you call the emotion? And no, she couldn't control whether Craeg would stay or if he would go tomorrow night, next week, next month, next year—but he was here with her now.

And that was more than she'd ever expected.

Abruptly, a slight pressure registered, the blunt head of him pressing in. And then he was stroking the top of her sex with his thumb, driving her insane, making her feel that fizzy, exciting, burning heat that she now knew was the precursor for the release her body was hungry for.

Reaching for him, she brought his mouth to hers and kissed him, stroked into his mouth with her tongue. She was utterly unafraid. Maybe she should have been, but she almost wanted to get this behind them so that the erotic connection could be given free expression.

Craeg's hips began to roll in and retreat, roll in and retreat, each time his erection going in a little farther.

And then he shifted her around, repositioning her pelvis.

His fingers returned to her, rubbing in a circle as his body went curiously still. She was about to protest, but then the sensations were too much and her brain took a backseat as she started to come—

At that moment, in one strong, powerful thrust, he penetrated past a barrier that broke away with no pain at all.

His whole body began to shake, and the trembling was transmitted into her from where they were joined. And then he began to move inside of her, deeper and deeper, with growing momentum. Thick, he was so thick, and the fullness was . . . incredible. And then there was the feel of his mouth stroking hers as he pumped into her.

No matter what the future held for them, nothing was ever going to change the fact that he was her first.

When she orgasmed, he did, too.

And yes, it was every bit as perfect and beautiful as she could have hoped for it to be. Even in a human club, in a public place, with hundreds of strangers on the far side of a thin door . . . it was heaven.

That was what being with the right person was like, though, wasn't it.

Chapter Forty-one

When Craeg finally stilled, Paradise slumped back against the sink, and though the faucet cut into her spine, and the mirror was hard against her head, she didn't care. She was floating, coasting . . . at least until she looked down her body and saw, at the apex of her spread thighs, that his hips were pressed in tight, a part of him buried deep inside of her.

Heaven.

Too bad he looked worried—as if he thought maybe she'd fainted because he'd hurt her or something.

She wanted to reassure him, tell him that it was amazing—but her mind was too blown to let her speak coherently, so she put everything into the smile she gave him.

"God . . ." he whispered. "You're so beautiful right now."

Forcing herself to focus, she murmured, "I'm glad we did that. When can we do it again?"

"Tomorrow night. But you're going to be stiff. It's only natural."

"I'm staying the day at the training center."

His brows popped. "You are?"

"I had plans to seduce you."

"Well, far be it from me to get in the way of a goal of yours."

As he bent down and kissed her, she felt a momentary

pang as she realized he'd done this with other females, maybe even taken them for the first time, too—which explained why he'd been so good at it. But no, those thoughts weren't welcome in this space.

This was just them. Nothing else was allowed.

"How about we do it again right now?" she said, moving her hips so that her sex stroked his.

"Paradise . . . are you sure you're okay?"

She moaned a *yeeeeeeeeeeeees* in response, and then propped her hands against the sink and used what little play she had in her body to get some momentum going between them again.

What you know, it worked.

In the blink of an eye, she was off the sink and up against Craeg's body, her legs around his hips, her arms linked over his heavy shoulders, her ankles twisted behind his ass.

With a rough grip, his hands moved her up and down on his arousal, faster and harder than the first time. To help him out, not that he wasn't doing just fine, she worked with him, doubling up on the force.

More orgasms, this time over and over again, her hair flopping in both their faces, a dark scent of spices roaring from his body, the pleasure mixing their souls in a way that felt permanent.

When they finally stopped, she collapsed onto his torso, limp as a rag, hot as an oven, dizzy as if she had run for a million miles.

And that was when her phone rang.

As the electronic chiming emanated from out of the pocket of her jacket, she brought her head up. "You've got to be kidding me."

Letting whoever it was go into voice mail, she refocused and smiled at Craeg. God, she loved it when their faces were this close, when she could see each individual lash and the bump in his nose, and the shadow of his beard that was already growing in.

"Hi," she whispered.

For once, his lips actually returned the favor—and there was an endearing shyness to him as he grinned.

Reaching up to his face, she whispered, "This is how I will always remember you."

In the back of her mind, she thought . . . holy weirdness. Why was she good-byeing him? This was just the beginning—

Her phone started ringing again.

"I'm sorry," she said, frowning. "I hope there's nothing wrong."

Twisting around so she could get into her pocket, she was acutely aware that they were still joined. And when she saw the screen, she cursed.

"Really, Peyton," she muttered as she shoved the phone back where it had been. "He must know we're back here. He loves harassing people."

"Guess he's finally shown up, huh."

"You know he's like a brother to me. You really, totally know that, right?"

"Yeah. Actually, I do."

As her cell started ringing for a third time, she gritted her teeth. "My really, totally annoying brother."

"Answer it so he'll stop." Craeg rolled his hips and made her moan. "I'm going nowhere."

Hitting the accept circle, she whipped the thing up to her ear. "Will you cut this out—"

"Parry . . . ?"

The instant she heard his voice, she frowned. In all the time she had known him, he'd never sounded like that. Lost . . . like a little boy.

"Peyton? What's wrong?"

"Something very bad has happened, Parry. There's blood . . . everywhere. . . ."

"What?" She pushed back and Craeg put her down immediately. "Peyton! Where are you?"

"I'm at my cousin's . . . my cousin . . . the one who was supposed to be gone. . . ."

Paradise locked eyes with Craeg. "Peyton, Craeg and I are on the way—but where are you?"

When he stammered out an address, she repeated it, and then thrust the phone at Craeg. "I have to clean up, you stay on the phone with him—do *not* let him hang up."

Ten minutes later, Craeg was walking into a fancy human apartment building with a dark green awning, a marble lobby, and a doorman wearing a uniform that was the same color as that overhang outside.

While he hesitated and expected to get kicked out or be asked to submit to a cavity search before he stepped off the welcome mat, Paradise walked right over to the desk.

"Hello," she said in a perfectly calm and reasonable tone. "My friend Peyton came to see Ashley Murray, and he's asked us to join them."

"I'll just call up then," the man replied, reaching for the phone. "Hello? Yes, it's the front desk. Are you— great. I'll send them up." The guard nodded to the elevators. "Go ahead."

"Thank you so much," she said smoothly, and held her hand out.

At first, Craeg couldn't figure out what she was doing that for—and then he realized he hadn't moved from where he'd stopped just inside the revolving door.

Hustling over, he ignored the guard and kept his head down—because a beautiful young female was one thing, but he was very aware that he was five times her size and more likely to be viewed with suspicion. They made it into the elevator, however, and then they were getting off on some high-up floor.

The first thing they saw down the long, beige hallway was Peyton at the far end, sitting on the carpet, cradling his phone in his palms.

The scent of blood in the air was thick to Craeg's

nose, but probably wouldn't have been noticed by a human.

Paradise rushed over and knelt beside the guy. "Peyton?"

He didn't look at her until she touched him on the shoulder—and oh, God, his face was pale as chalk and his eyes were too wide. "It's bad."

"Is she . . . in there?"

"No. But the bedroom . . . God, the bedroom."

Craeg left her with her friend and pushed the door open. Instantly, the death scent grew stronger—and became ever more intense as he walked into an open room with wall-to-wall white carpeting, a white couch, and a wall of windows that, given a lack of heavy drapes, should have precluded a vampire from residing in the space.

Cold, it was very cold. And there was a stiff breeze shooting through the place.

Glancing to the right, there was nothing of note in the open galley kitchen, no mess, everything put away, a bowl of fresh-looking fruit—no, the apples were plastic, scratch that.

A hallway led off straight ahead, and there was a single light glowing down at the end. Zeroing in on it, he proceeded across the fine-napped runner.

Turning the corner, he stopped in the doorway. Across the way, a queen-size bed was stained with so much red, it was as if paint had been splashed across its white duvet and sheets and pillows and headboard.

There was some more on the floor, marking a path that went over to . . .

The sliding glass door that led out to some kind of terrace had been left open—and as the filmy white drapes wafted in the gusts, bloody handprints on the glass and the jamb were exposed and then covered, exposed and then covered.

Pivoting back to the bed, he noted the drugs on the side tables: syringes, spoons, little nubs of tinfoil. There were no condoms. No weapons. Also nothing personal—

no photographs, mementos, clutter. This was a place to fuck and do drugs and get gone before the morning. But it was expensive.

"Oh, my God . . ."

At the sound of Paradise's voice, he looked over his shoulder. "You're not going to want to come in here."

She entered anyway, and he couldn't say he was surprised.

"Where's Peyton?" he asked.

"Right here," came a dull voice from the doorway.

As the three of them stood together, he was pretty damn sure they were thinking the same thing: nobody survived something like this. Nobody.

"I need to call my father," Paradise said roughly. "This is far beyond what we should be dealing with."

Craeg shook his head as she got out her phone. "No, we need to call the Brothers."

Peyton interjected, "That's why she's phoning her dad."

As Paradise put the cell up to her ear and paced around, Craeg frowned. "What?"

Peyton shrugged. "Her father is First Adviser to the King. It's the right thing to do."

At first, the words failed to translate, the string of nouns and verbs and other shit going in one ear and out the other. But then he replayed them a couple of times . . . and felt the oddest chill go over his entire body, from eyebrow to ankle. His heart kicked in his chest. Stopped. Resumed at a bad pace.

Craeg shifted his eyes back to Paradise and listened from a great distance as she started talking urgently. He'd never particularly focused on her accent before, because he'd always been so distracted by his attraction to her. But now, the cadence, the tone, the inflection . . . it was just like Peyton's. And not because she'd assumed the lilt like some sort of poser.

In a dull voice, he said, "She isn't just the receptionist at that house, is she."

*   *   *

When Butch's phone started going off against his side, he was prepared to let the shit go into voice mail—he was in a sex club trying to get some clues to a murder for godsake. But when the damn thing kept going off, he took it out and answered.

And was not able to hear Vishous at all over the techno music. "What? Hello?"

After the connection was cut, a text from the Brother solved the confusion. The message was short and to the point, nothing but an address in the good part of downtown, the number 18, and a time duration: *5 mins.*

It was the code they used for when they were fighting and in trouble.

"We've got to go," he said aloud. Turning to Marissa, he took her arm and spoke more loudly. "We've got to leave. Now."

"What?" She came in tight against him. "But there's more up ahead?"

When he just shook his head and met her eyes, she stopped arguing. "Yo, Axe," he called out. "We need to bounce. You good?"

The guy came over. "I thought you wanted to go through everything."

"Later. See you at the training center."

The actual departure took a fuck of a lot longer than five minutes, as the process of weeding through the various sex stations and themed rooms was like trying to find your way out of 50 Shades of garden maze. As soon as they were out into the chilly, clear air, and away from the earshot of the bouncers and the line, Butch said, "I've got slayer business—"

His phone rang again, and he answered it. "V, I'm on my way, just leaving Marissa—"

The Brother was short, to the point, and very succinct, and as the call was ended, Butch lowered the phone slowly and stared at Marissa. "I think you'd better come, too."

"What is it?"

"We might have found out who the dead female is."

Minutes later, he pulled his Lexus up to the front entry of a posh high-rise apartment building that was a mere block from the Commodore. One mental scrub job on a human and an elevator ride later, and they were marching down a hallway that smelled like death. V was waiting for them.

And the brother recoiled as soon as he saw them. "What the hell? And P.S., you both look hot as fuck."

Butch tore off his mask. "I can smell the blood from out here."

Lifting her hands to remove her own mask, Marissa recoiled. "Oh, God . . . it's her. That's her scent."

V led them through an anonymous apartment to an essentially empty bedroom that reminded him of his years with the CPD. And shit, Butch's first impulse was to put himself between his mate and all the signs of a violent murder. But no more. It killed him to have her exposed to any of this, but she was right. She had to be here.

With her spine straight and her eyes clear, she went over to the bed—and fuck him, the image of her standing with her back to him as she stared at the blood-soaked duvet and pillows was going to give him a whole new category of nightmares.

Cursing, he glanced at Paradise, who was standing next to Peyton, and then he sized up Craeg, who was farther off in the corner. Finally, he assessed the scene, taking note of everything that was and was not in the room.

"Who got here first?" he asked.

Peyton lifted his hand. "I did. My cousin Allishon used this place to . . . well, you know. She leases it under a human name. I called her cell phone a couple of times to get her to come out with us—her parents had told my parents that she'd been out of touch for, like, a couple of nights, maybe a week, but that wasn't all that unusual. When I didn't hear back, I figured I'd stop by here, because she was probably partying hard. I came in through the terrace, because that's how I usually do—and yeah."

"Was that slider unlocked?" Butch asked as he lifted the billowing drapes and inspected a bloody handprint on the handle.

"It was open. But if the sun got her, it would have left burns, right? So maybe she's . . ." He trailed off as he focused on the stained bed. "She's not okay, is she."

Marissa drew her latex hood back from her head and let it hang around her neck. Going over to the male, she took his hands. "I'm Butch's *shellan*, Marissa. I'm the executive director of a domestic violence shelter. She came to us—"

"So she's there? She's alive!"

Marissa slowly shook her head. "I'm so sorry. I called my brother, Havers, and he treated her with everything he had. She did not make it."

Peyton's eyes returned to the bed and he fell silent. Then he whispered, "This is going to kill her parents. They lost my other cousin in the raids. No children now."

"So that door was unlocked or just open?" Butch asked. "And I don't mean to be insensitive, but this is a crime scene and whoever did this to her . . . we've got to nail them to the fucking wall."

Peyton shook his head. "Yeah, no—I mean, she was a wild girl. She was a partier. But she didn't deserve . . ." He cleared his throat. "The door was absolutely open."

Butch traced the marks and stains on the carpet. "The only explanation is that she somehow used the last of her strength to get out and dematerialize to Safe Place."

"How did she know to go there?" Paradise whispered. "I mean . . . thank God."

"She must have heard about us somehow," Marissa replied. "I just wish we could have saved her."

V came into the room. "I just got a text from Tohr and Rhage. They're fighting, it's a bad skirmish. I've gotta go be backup—Butch. You've got to come with me. This is an emergency."

Butch gritted his teeth and dropped a couple of f-bombs. But then he looked at Marissa. "You okay?"

Staring right at him, she said roughly, "As long as we can find out who did this, I'll be goddamn fine."

He gave her a quick, hard hug and felt a wellspring of pride in his chest. And then he gave her a very sad series of tasks.

"I want you to get a list of people she knew, human and vampire, from him." He nodded at Peyton. "Then photograph everything with your phone. The whole fucking place. Touch nothing, disturb nothing. Lock up all the doors you can. Leave from the terrace. Then go to the parents' house. They have a right to know tonight."

"I'm on it," she said.

Yes, he thought, she was.

God, he loved her. Hated this situation . . . but love, love, loved her.

One more kiss . . . and he was heading back down to his car, trying to shift his focus from one kind of emergency to another.

Chapter Forty-two

As Marissa talked to Peyton about who his cousin had been associating with, Paradise borrowed the female's phone and went through the whole place taking photographs. With every shot she captured, she thought of what she knew about the dead girl. Technically, Allishon was her cousin, too, and though it was a more distant connection than Peyton's, the loss was still acute.

Especially because she'd seen that bed.

Good ... God. Such violence.

In about fifteen minutes, she had covered the bedroom, the bathroom, the hall, and the living room—and she was turning around to do the kitchen when she saw something down on the floor.

As the place was white all over, the flash of color by the edge of the sofa really caught her eye.

Sinking onto her haunches, she pulled out ... an old-fashioned Polaroid snapshot.

With a frown, she realized it was ... red and pink. Just like the one that she'd found on the bus.

The one she'd put in her satchel after Peyton had said it wasn't his.

"What is that?" Peyton asked. "Paradise? You gonna be sick?"

She stood up and went across to him.

"It's a picture ..." As she showed the thing to him, she wondered if maybe she were jumping to conclusions.

Maybe there was another explanation. "Ah, it's like the one I found, you know, on the bus."

"Whatever. Are you finished with the pictures? We have to go talk to Allie's parents now. I need to get this over with before I lose my fucking mind."

"Two secs." She put the photo in her jacket without thinking about it and started snapping images of the kitchen. "I'm almost done."

"She has the ashes," Peyton murmured in a voice that cracked. "Marissa has them."

Paradise lowered the phone. "Oh . . . God."

"She just left to go change and pick them up before you and I head over there. I wish I had a joint with me. I didn't think. . . ." He began opening cupboards. "Oh, thank fuck."

As he took out a bottle of vodka and slipped it into his coat, she wanted to remind him they weren't supposed to disturb anything, but come on. Like she was going to bust his balls for not following the rules on a night like tonight?

"Peyton, what else can I do?"

His eyes drifted back to hers. "It is what it is. Thank you for coming with me, though."

With a grim nod, she took one last snapshot of the empty sink and bare counters. "Here. Um, where's Craeg?"

"He's in the bedroom still."

"Peyton . . . I'm so sorry."

They met in the middle and held each other tightly. She wanted to tell him that it was going to be okay, but that was already not true.

"I love you," he said.

"I love you, too."

Stepping away from him, she went to the apartment's front door, locked things up with her mind and then proceeded with him back down to the bedroom.

Craeg was where he'd been standing for the longest time, and as she went to him, she put her hand on his arm. "You all right?"

"Yeah." He turned to Peyton, breaking the contact. "Hey, man, you need anything ... I'm here for you."

Peyton went over to the male and they exchanged a hard embrace, and then all of them were out on the terrace in the stiff wind coming off the river.

Peyton left first. And then Craeg pivoted to her.

"Long night—I'd better go back. Peyton hit the training center up for me on his phone and I need to meet the bus ASAP."

"Oh ... okay." But come on, what did she expect? There had been a tragedy. Now was not the time for a long, romantic good-bye for godsakes. "So ... anyway, I guess I'll see you tomorrow night? Will you call me this morning, though? I'm going to change, then help Peyton tell the family."

"Good thing you got hold of your father."

"Yes, he's always helpful."

"I'll bet."

"It's just so ... awful." As she blinked, she saw that bed inside. "So very, very ugly. I wonder who did it?"

"Butch will find them."

"I hope so. I truly do."

"I got to go."

"Oh ... okay." Wait, she'd already said that. "Are you all right?"

"I'm fine. Don't worry about me. You'd better go, too."

For some reason, she had the strangest urge to tell him that she missed him—but that was absurd. He was standing two feet away from her. They were going to talk in a couple of hours. She was going to see him tomorrow night.

"Good day," she said.

When he nodded, she closed her eyes ... calmed herself ... and spirited away.

For so many reasons, the awkward parting had not been how she'd seen the evening ending. Not even close.

*   *   *

Craeg didn't wait long. As soon as Paradise got ahead of him, he dematerialized himself behind her, traveling on the wind, using his blood in her veins as a tracker.

When she stopped moving through the night air, he re-formed a good hundred yards away from her on the edge of a lawn that was . . .

The house before him at the top of the rise was the size of a college dorm, the kind of massive, grand structure that would be featured on television as being on some fancy university's campus or God, maybe . . . maybe it was more like a royal residence with its peaked roofs and its diamond-pane windows and all the clipped and mani-cured everything on its lawn.

It was easily twice the size of the mansion where his and Axe's fathers had been slaughtered, for example.

And as Paradise approached the front door, it was without apology—not as a staffer or a servant would. And a moment later, she was inside without ringing a doorbell or anything. In fact, as he moved to the left, he saw through leaded glass windows a uniformed butler taking her coat and bowing in deference to her.

Her father is First Adviser to the King.

Closing the distance with long strides, he watched from the cold outside as she went up the grand staircase and disappeared into what was undoubtedly an equally sumptuous second floor. Or maybe third. Or twelfth.

Even after he could no longer see her, he stayed where he was, staring through old-fashioned panes at the oil paintings, the fancy rugs, the silk on the walls—it must be silk, right?

What the fuck did he know.

Turning away, he looked out over the rolling lawn, and the bushes, and the beds of what were no doubt specimen flowers in the warm months. He wondered what the back-yard was like. Probably had a pool. An enclosure for ex-otic fucking animals. A goddamn bird sanctuary.

She had lied.

And not in a small way.

This . . . this was a big fucking deal: He'd just taken the virginity of what certainly appeared to be one of a Founding Family's daughters.

According to the Old Laws, as a commoner?

He could be put to death for that.

As anger swelled, it was less about Paradise and what she'd kept from him, and more because he had consistently overridden himself. All those internal stops he'd put up? All those resolutions he'd had? Before he'd fucked her in the bathroom at a human fucking club, for fuck's sake? He'd blown right through each and every one of them. And to top that off, he'd lost his focus with the training. Gotten sidetracked from his purpose. Wasted days when he should have been sleeping, classes when he should have been thinking, workouts when he should have been training his body with total focus.

And all for a female who cared so little for him, who was so selfish and conceited, that she had been unwilling to share some very pertinent, relevant information about herself.

Information that she had to know would have been a game changer for him.

It was a perfect storm of manipulation, that had spun him a hundred and eighty degrees away from what he'd actually wanted: Between her being a liar and his libido being out of control, he hadn't stood a chance.

Such a fool—he was such a goddamn fool.

And fools got what they deserved.

Didn't they.

Chapter Forty-three

Sitting on the edge of her mated bed, Marissa ran a brush through her hair. She had changed out of the clothes she had gotten into after she'd stripped off her latex suit, and she was now wearing one of Butch's black cashmere robes. From time to time, she brought the lapel up to her nose and smelled his scent on the fibers.

She needed the reminder of his presence. She truly did.

Dearest Virgin Scribe, there were too many things that kept going through her mind, images, sounds, smells. And as a result of the barrage, she kept wondering ... how had Butch done that for so long? How had he investigated those crime scenes, gone to the houses of the victims' families, broken that news over and over again? How had he looked into the tragic eyes of a father and a *mahmen* and commiserated with them—all the while knowing he had to get information out of them?

Information like the last time they saw their child. Last communication. Any known disagreements with people.

She had asked the questions carefully, at times holding the mother's hand or nodding to the father. There had been no reason to write anything down—she was never going to forget anything about any of it.

And now she was back here, waiting for Butch to come home safely so she could download everything.

Out in the living room, the Pit's door to the outside opened with a creaking sound, and a blast of cold air shot down the hallway—bringing with it the stench of *lessers*.

"Butch?" She shot to her feet and rushed out. "Butch . . . ?"

The groaning and cursing were an answer in and of themselves—and then she was rounding the corner into the open room and stopping short.

V had her mate in a fireman's hold, the Brother taking that bent and battered body to the leather sofa and flopping it down.

Butch was bleeding, covered in slayer blood, and half-dead.

He was also emitting that sickly sweet odor of *lessers* consumed.

As she gasped and ran over, V ripped off his own jacket, exposing cuts and bruises—and as Marissa stroked Butch's matted hair, the Brother joined the male on the sofa, entwining his warrior's body with that of his best friend's. The glow that came next started like something off in the distance, or perhaps a lantern seen through a thick fog, but soon enough, the illumination, the sacred essence of Vishous's mother, overtook the room, bright as sunlight on a sheet of metal, warm as a banked fire, and the only savior Butch had.

V's power was a curse in the wrong context, but a miracle as it was used now—because it was going to drain the evil out of her mate, rescuing him, making him strong in a way that only Vishous could.

She had never resented the connection the two had, had never been jealous that another provided something so necessary to the one she loved. She was just grateful there was a way to keep Butch from dying. Ever since the Omega had abducted him and infected him, he'd had the ability to consume slayers, destroy them in a way that "killing" them did not: Butch's consumption of their essence was a one-way ticket out of the universe.

But it came at such a cost.

Sometime later, the light began to recede and then the two of them just lay there, both exhausted. As Butch opened his lids, his hazel eyes went immediately to her and he lifted his shaking hand.

With a gentle smile, she took his palm and put it to her face, rubbing it against her cheek. "I love you, I love you. . . ."

"Okay?" he croaked out. "You?"

"Now that you're home safe, yes. A thousand yeses."

V cracked his lids and stared up at her with lolling eyes. Even though she rarely touched the Brother—because face it, Vishous was not a warm-and-fuzzy kind of guy—she reached out and brushed his cheek.

In a rare moment of tenderness, he pressed a kiss to the inside of her palm.

And then, a short time later, it was time to get her mate in the shower. As V was wasted on the sofa, Marissa helped Butch down the hall and into their room. Or almost their room. He insisted on stopping and stripping out in the hall so he could put his filthy clothes immediately into the laundry chute that dumped into the tunnel down below.

Their private bath was simple and small and cozy, and as she always did in these situations, she made Butch sit on the toilet while she got the shower to the right temperature. When all was ready, she helped him up, pushed him under the spray and propped him against the corner.

Taking his robe from her body, she stepped in with him.

He'd been hard before she did the reveal. And the instant he saw her body, his erection got even thicker.

There would be time to share their stories after this. Now? It was about finding that wavelength between them, plugging into each other, communicating without words.

Taking the soap and a washcloth, she started with his face, wiping over those features she loved so much before moving to his throat, the pads of his pecs, the ridges of his abdominals. She washed every part of him, even his arousal, which she stroked with the washcloth.

Butch arched under her touch. He was too weak to do much else, his weight sliding down until he was sitting on the built-in marble bench. With his head lazing around, he watched her work him.

And then she put the cloth aside.

Getting on her knees, she felt the warm water washing down her back as she moved in between his thighs.

He was magnificent, collapsed back into the corner, big arms lax, warrior's body exhausted.

Yet his eyes were hot.

Wrapping her hands around his cock, she opened her mouth and went down on him, swallowing as much as she could of his length, sucking on him, working him.

In response, Butch groaned and curled his hips.

She took her sweet time, plying him, going faster and then slowing down, squeezing his balls.

And then she looked up.

He was still watching her, his fangs descended, his mouth open and panting. From time to time, he seemed to try to move. The best he could manage was a flopping of his hands, though.

"Marissa . . ." he said hoarsely.

"Yes?"

While she waited for him to answer, she traced her mouth with his head. Then she ran her tongue in a circle around him.

"Finish me," he groaned. "Oh, God . . . finish me. . . ."

The smile she gave him came from deep inside.

Then, with anticipation, she went back to work.

And did her job very, very well.

Chapter Forty-four

As night fell the following evening, Paradise was pacing around her bedroom in her bathrobe.

Craeg hadn't called. Not at seven in the morning when he usually did. Not at two in the afternoon when he maybe couldn't sleep. And not at six when he was probably up and about to eat with Axe in the cafeteria.

Something had obviously changed.

And she hoped like hell it wasn't the one-and-done thing. Some males wanted only what they hadn't had yet, and although she would be shocked to discover Craeg was that much of a douche, she couldn't think what else might explain him not calling.

Except . . . they'd been so good together. Really good. And he'd been so good to her.

As for that horrific scene at the girl's apartment? Although what had happened to Peyton's cousin was tragic, she didn't think Craeg would be so affected as to suffer some kind of mental or emotional collapse—

As her phone finally fucking rang, she raced across her room.

Only to curse when she saw it was just Peyton.

When she answered, she tried to keep her voice level. "Hey. How you doing?"

After the two of them had done that sad, sad duty with the female's parents, they'd gone their separate ways for the day, but they hadn't been out of touch. He'd texted her a number of incoherent things over the hours, which she took to mean that he'd put that bottle of vodka to good use.

"So we don't have class tonight."

"What?"

"It's canceled for some reason so Anslam and I are going to Sal's Restaurant. I'm gonna invite everyone else, too."

As she struggled with the update, a crushing disappointment left her dizzy. She'd been counting on seeing Craeg and—

Peyton didn't miss a beat, telling her to meet everyone there in an hour. Then he hung up and left her to hold her phone and stare at the dark screen.

Would Craeg even join them? she wondered.

Okay, this was bullshit. She was done waiting around like some stupid chick.

Taking a deep breath, she dialed a number from memory, one that she had learned about three nights into working at the audience house. When a *doggen* answered, she smiled professionally—as if the male could see her face, as if she wasn't doing this for purely personal reasons.

"Hi, there," she said. "This is Abalone's daughter. I'm so sorry to bother you, but would you be so kind as to transfer me down to the training center's clinic?"

"Oh, but of course, mistress!" came the cheerful reply. "Was there someone in particular you should wish to address?"

"Actually . . ." Maybe this would be easier than she'd thought. "I'm trying to reach the first of the five bedroom suites down there?"

"My pleasure, please hold while I look up the extension." There was a *beep . . . beep . . . beep.* "Here it is. If you'd like to direct-dial in the future, may I give you the number?"

"Please." Grabbing a pen, she scribbled it on the side of the Kleenex box next to her. "Thank you."

"Or you may use this number always. We're grateful to serve. Please hold."

"Thank you again."

As the *beep . . . beep . . . beep* came back over the line, her palms bloomed with a flush of heat and sweat, and she had to sit down, because her legs started to shake.

Then there was ringing.

"Hello?" Craeg said.

She swallowed hard—and then got frustrated with herself. "I was hoping you'd call."

Long silence. "Hey."

"Look, I don't have the patience for this. What the hell is wrong?"

"Don't you have more important things to do?"

"What?" she said sharply.

"You know, what with your cousin having been killed. Your family must be upset, too."

"I'm more worried about you at the moment?" Naturally, she was upset about—

Paradise's anger derailed as the words he'd spoken truly sank in. "Oh."

"Yeah, I followed you home last night," he said. "Which was maybe a shitty thing to do—but considering you've lied to me about who you are and where you came from, it's a violation of privacy that was warranted. Just curious—were you ever going to tell me?"

She put her head in her hand. "Craeg . . ."

"I didn't call you because I don't actually know who I'm talking to, do I. Well, the daughter of the First Adviser to the King—Peyton was kind enough to clue me in on that one."

"Listen, I . . ."

"You what? What were you going to say, Paradise?" His voice became even more strident. "And P.S., I am legitimately sorry about what happened to that female.

As you are very aware, I've lost family, too. You remember how that went, don't you?"

Abruptly, the horrific story of his father being locked out of safety while the aristocrats hid from the *lessers* came back with vicious clarify.

"I am not like those people from that house, Craeg. And I'm insulted that you lump me in with them just because I was born into my family. Do you think I had any choice in that?"

"Oh, you're not like them. No, no, not at all—you just felt like having sex last night, so you let a commoner pop your cherry, even if that meant that technically I can be killed for the pleasure of having had your company. Yeah, you're not like them at all. You don't lie for your own purposes or anything. Nah, not you, sweetheart."

"That is *so* unfair."

He laughed in a hard burst. "Wait, wait, I know. You were waiting to give your father the best surprise birthday present ever. 'Hey, Dad, guess what! I'm with a floor layer's son—hash tag awesome.'"

Gritting her teeth, she found her emotions bouncing between anger and sorrow, regret and indignation. "I didn't tell anyone who I was. Not just you."

"Oh, I feel so much better now. Thanks."

"I didn't want to be treated any differently! You think I like being Abalone's daughter? You think I enjoy having no choices, no freedom, no—"

"So I was just part of an 'exploration' phase of yours? Great. Well, it's over on my end. No more trying out different versions of yourself on me—you're going to need to find a new piece of equipment. You know, Boone is probably available. He looked like he was seeing God for the first time as Novo was grinding on him last night."

Paradise burst up and walked around her room. "I cannot believe you're being so closed-minded."

"Closed-m—are you fucking kidding me?" He cursed. "Okay, let's try on this hypothetical. That ball, which is going to be at your house in a week—you were obviously going to ask me as your date, right? You were just waiting to tell me about it so I could go as your—oh, shit. It's called an escort, ain't it? I'd better get these details down before you introduce me to your father, and I soak fifty bucks into renting a tux."

When she didn't say anything, he laughed again. "Guess that wasn't part of the plan, huh. Oh, in case you're wondering, Axe overheard you guys talking on the bus. He told me about it after I got back to the training center and he tried to give me a hard time about dating you. I explained to him that you and I were not, in fact, 'dating,' but that I was fairly certain that if your car needed to be washed, you'd let me have at it with a bucket and a sponge."

"You are way out of line."

"And as an aristocrat, you are certainly in a position to tell me that, aren't you."

"I'm in love with you, you asshole." At least that shut him up. "That's right. I said it—where I come from, you're not allowed to say that first because you're supposed to wait for the male to do it. Oh, and you want to know what else I can't do? I can't be in the presence of any male without a chaperone. I'm not allowed to work or have a career—I was in that receptionist job solely because my father was desperately in need of help and I was the only one he could trust. I had to fight my way into the training program—and only got permission because I lied and told my father I would never fight in the war. I am expected to needlepoint, run a house, and get pregnant— and you're bitching at me that *I'm* the problem?"

"Cry me a river, okay?" he bit out. "You have never had to worry about where your next meal is coming from, you live in a fucking museum showcase of beautiful things—and pardon me, but you don't know what it's like to have people look down on you because you lost the DNA lottery!"

"You're looking down on me!" she hollered back. "Are *you* fucking kidding me right now! You're judge and jury, you've made your mind up and to hell with me! You're no different from the *glymera*—look in the goddamn mirror, Craeg. You're just as superior-acting and judgmental as they are."

As she fell silent, she was breathing hard, and her free hand was cranked into a fist, and her heart was pounding.

"This is getting us nowhere," he muttered after a moment.

"You're absolutely right. So fuck off. Have a nice life—hope all your holier-than-thou keeps you warm during the day."

Paradise cut the connection and wheeled around, lifting her arm over her head, prepared to fire the phone at the wall.

But she stopped herself. Calmed herself. Refocused.

Wow. Losing her virginity and having her first knockdown/drag-out in a relationship. Oh, and first breakup, too.

Big twenty-four hours.

Going so well.

Just great.

It took a good hour before Paradise was even back in her own body, she was so angry. And her first cogent thought was that she was not going to spend the whole night stuck in her room.

Hell, no. She had all day to look forward to for that kind of prison.

Going over to her satchel, she waded through the thing to look for her wallet. She was going to meet the other trainees at that Italian restaurant and have a drink with them—even if she only ordered a soda. And if Craeg happened to be there? Fine. Whatever.

She might as well get used to being around him.

As her hand gripped her wallet, she was about to head out—but stopped. Pulling the thing out, she put it aside on her antique French desk. Rifling through the bag, she looked through everything—and even unzipped the front pocket and checked in there.

Frowning, she headed over to her walk-in closet and proceeded to where her coats were. The one she had worn the night before was hanging with her others, and she went into the pocket on the far side.

The Polaroid she had tucked in there at the apartment was where she had left it.

Staring at the image, she put her hand over her mouth.

Back at the satchel, she double-checked one more time. Nope, the original image, the one she'd found on the bus, was gone.

She thought back to when she'd searched the satchel at the training center and found her phone in the wrong place.

Someone had gone through her bag and taken the photograph.

Maybe because it tied them . . . to a murder.

Returning to her phone, she called Peyton. "Hey," she said when he answered.

As she fell silent, he prompted, "Hello? Paradise?"

"I think . . ."

"You're breaking up."

"No, I'm not talking."

"Hold on." There was a rustling and then his voice was distant. "No, you goddamn fool. Anslam, I'm *not* doing any acid. Jesus—yeah, gimme some X."

She closed her eyes and wondered what exactly she was doing. He was in mourning. And maybe she was just being paranoid.

"Parry?" There was another rustling and then he took a drink of something. "What's up?"

"Nothing. I'm sorry."

"You're still coming out with us?"

"Not right now," she said. "I'm going to my dad's work. I, ah, I did something stupid last night."

"What was that?"

"I took something from the apartment." She stared at

the photograph, and then had to put it facedown on her desk. Even without seeing specifics, it was too gory. "I didn't mean to. That picture I found?"

"The Polaroid? The other one?"

"Yeah, I need to give it to Butch and Marissa. I slipped it into my pocket without thinking. I figure the Brotherhood's out fighting, and I can't go back to the training center, so I'll stop by the audience house and someone can take it to them later on tonight."

"Yeah. Good plan. Then come out with us?"

"Okay—I'm just going to take a quick shower and get dressed."

"You're always beautiful. See you in a few."

Hanging up, she stared at her feet. God, what if one of the trainees was involved in that death?

With a curse, Paradise brought her phone into the bathroom with her, and as she put it down on the counter, she rolled her eyes at herself. But, yes, she was going to pick up the phone if Craeg called. Although, no, he probably wouldn't. And yes, that was definitely a good thing.

In all the ways they could have crashed and burned . . . what a mess.

And frankly, she wasn't sure she wanted to work it out with him even if that was possible.

Lust, she told herself. She had been in lust with him, not love. How did you fall in love with someone after six nights, anyway.

God, she wanted to vomit, she really did.

Twenty minutes later, she was dressed in a pair of blue jeans and a cashmere sweater. She put on her regular loafers, because although it was cold, there wasn't snow forecasted yet; then she took out the coat she'd worn the night before. Putting the photograph back in the pocket, she snagged her wallet, her cell and her—

Over on the bedside table, the house phone rang. Going over, in case her father was calling to check up on her from his work, she picked the receiver up. "Hello?"

"You have a visitor."

She frowned at the voice on the other end. "An-slam?"

"Yup, it's me," he said easily. "Peyton told me to come get you."

"He did? But I'm not going to Sal's yet. I've got to do an errand first."

"I'll go with you, then."

"No, thanks. It won't take me long—"

"Are you coming down?"

Oh, for godsakes. But she didn't want to be rude. "Yup. Hold on."

"Don't hurry on my account."

Hanging up, she double-checked her hair and then left her room. As she headed for the front stairs, she hoped she could get Anslam out the door fast. She felt like hell because of the fight with Craeg, and all that yuck was compounded because she couldn't believe she'd spaced taking that Polaroid from the scene without telling anybody.

As well as the very real possibility the investigation was going to have to focus on the trainees.

Cresting the grand staircase, she saw Anslam standing down below on the black-and-white marble floor, his Saks Fifth Avenue clothes and his Gucci cologne announcing what class he was in as much as his even, rather unremarkable features did.

There was something just so . . . pasty about him, she thought.

How he'd gotten that reputation for being aggressive with females she had no clue.

When a step creaked beneath her foot, Anslam turned to face her. "Hey, girl," he said. "You look good."

"Thanks, so do you."

When she got to the bottom and he opened his arms, she went to him and kissed him on both cheeks. "Listen, I'm sorry, but I'm really just going to—"

A strange sound let off in her father's study, and she frowned, looking toward it. It was a kind of squeak, or a—

"You were going to go do an errand?" Anslam asked. "What kind of errand?"

She refocused on him. "It's nothing important. I just . . . what is that noise?"

Turning away from him, she walked forward and glanced around the ornate jamb of the library's archway—

"Oh, my God!"

Her father's butler, Fedricah, and her maid, Vuchie, were tied up in front of the desk, their mouths gagged, their feet bound.

"What in the world happened—"

Anslam grabbed her from behind and spun her around, tripping her up and slamming her face-first into the floor. As the shock and pain momentarily stunned her, he flopped her onto her back. Putting his face in hers, he looked mildly annoyed.

"Where's the photograph. What the fuck did you do with my photograph?"

While she tried to recover her bearings and pin-wheeled her arms and legs, he roughly went through her pockets.

"Ah, good girl." He put the Polaroid inside his suede jacket. "Goddamn it, Paradise—why the fuck did you have to find that? I don't want to have to do this to a female like you. It's not part of the plan."

Swallowing, she tasted blood and realized that her lip was split. "You don't . . . need to do this. . . ."

With a quick surge, he hopped up on his feet and disappeared for a moment—and when he came back, he had a Louis Vuitton briefcase with him. "Yeah, I do have to do this. Because you were going to try to take that Polaroid to your father—that's what you told Peyton. And you're such a good little girl, so conscientious, that you're not going to let it go and you're going to start thinking about the connection—and sooner or later, you're going to sneak into the cafeteria and you're going to go through my shit because you'd realize that someone in the training center must have dropped that photo on the bus and also taken it out of your bag. Nice satchel, by the way. Love Bally. Good stuff."

As he kept talking, Anslam took out a syringe. "See, because I'm attached to my work, I need to keep some part of it with me always, and pictures are the next best thing, don't you agree? Just fantastic for spiking the memory. Anyway, that's when you'd put two and two together—when you found more just like it in my bag. Then I'd be fucked—and I assure you, I am never the bottom in relationships."

As he tested that the clear fluid was live in the thin needle, her brain threatened to recede on her, the pain, the shock, the confusion, twisting and tying up her neuropathways, making any significant thought patterns impossible.

Except then she remembered what she'd been trained to do in sparring class: You got focused, you stayed focused. Got focused, stay focused.

This was not a training exercise, though—in fact, this was precisely what those lessons were supposed to prepare her for.

Not a class. No one to rescue her.

But herself.

All at once her mind went super-sharp: She was as good as dead if he injected her with whatever that was, and she was going to have only one chance at an escape.

Making a show of being helpless, she surreptitiously looked around for a weapon, something, anything she could use—

"Think of this as a compliment," he said as he looked down at her. "I'm really sure you'd eventually figure out it was me, because you're pretty fucking smart, for a girl—"

With a powerful lunge, she reared up and head-butted him right in the face. It was her only move—and she nailed him dead to rights: Anslam howled with pain and anger and fell back on his ass, clutching his nose. And she was on him, pouncing on his chest, ripping the syringe out of his hand. Depressing the plunger so the drug emptied into thin air, she tossed it aside.

With no time to spare.

Anslam roared and punched her shoulders, popping her up off him. And his next move was to clock her so hard in the jaw with his fist, she literally heard bells ringing and her vision flickered. But she couldn't afford to check out as he jumped onto her. Fighting through the pain and disorientation, she reached between the two of them and went for his 'nads, grabbing them and twisting her grip until he screamed and wrenched to the side.

Up on her feet, she went to kick him, but he caught her ankle and flipped her off her feet.

They began to roll, and in the back of her mind, she heard Butch saying that all hand-to-hand combat ended up on the ground; it was only a matter of time.

Torquing herself around, she prevented him from doing an arm bar on her, but she also failed to get him into a headlock with her thighs. A weapon, she needed—the briefcase. If she could somehow get them over there . . .

He was stronger than she was. She was faster than he was. Their bodies flopped on the hard floor, arms and legs straining, fists getting worked into torsos, more blood getting drawn on faces.

And then it happened. He somehow managed to pin her by the throat with both hands—and then he drove the back of her head into the marble floor once, twice. . . .

Fuck you! she mouthed, because she had no air.

Reaching up to his eyes, she thumbed into their sockets—

He disappeared.

Anslam just up . . . and disappeared.

For a split second, she braced herself, ready for some pummeling to hit her. But then she heard a horrible scream.

Looking up, she saw Anslam . . . levitating off the floor, his face twisted into a horrific expression of terror, blood pouring out of his mouth in a gush, feet kicking uselessly as his legs twitched.

Then he was cast aside like trash.

And Craeg was revealed like the warrior he was, his feet planted, his fangs bared . . . a bloody sword in his hand.

Dimly, Paradise realized the weapon was the ceremonial blade that her father was supposed to wear as First Adviser on special occasions, the one that his own father had owned first . . . the one that was kept on the wall directly beside the front door, as tradition required it to be hung.

Craeg came to her and crouched down. "You need medical attention. Where's your phone—where's a phone?"

"I'm okay, I'm . . . all right."

Wait, she was crying. Or was that blood? She didn't know . . .

The sound of struggle brought his head around. "Be right back."

With quick strides, he raced into the study with the sword, and moments later, Vuchie was by her side, and the butler was on the phone at the desk.

It was right about then that she realized she was seeing double.

"I think I'm going to pass out," she said to Craeg.

"Doc Jane is coming."

"Don't leave me," she told him. "I want to yell at you some more."

He got down on his knees. "Because I interrupted your fight? I apologize. I think you were going to win, by the way—but I'm not a gambling male. Sorry."

She opened her mouth to say something else . . . but it was lights-out.

Her last thought?

That as something warm enveloped her palm, she was pretty sure he had taken her hand.

Chapter Forty-five

When Craeg had materialized on Paradise's lawn, he hadn't been sure whether he'd come to fight with her or make up with her.

He honestly hadn't known. Could have gone either way.

After she had handed him his own ass over the phone, he had stormed around the training center until he'd decided, Fuck it, he was going to see her in person. He'd called for a *doggen*, gotten into the bus, and then as soon as they'd made it out to the main road, he'd told the guy he wasn't waiting for the drop-off point.

They'd negotiated to a clearing five miles away from the compound.

Then off he'd gone, to the lawn of Paradise's family's mansion.

Where he'd found the front door cracked open.

The second he'd walked in, he'd seen Paradise under Anslam, with her thumbs digging out his eyes.

And that was how he'd ended up sitting here in this . . . amazing library . . . with proverbial blood on his hands.

Looking around, he shook his head at the grand oil painting over the fireplace. The male who was depicted was staring straight out at the viewer, and Craeg could only imagine what the good ol' boy would have had to say if he'd actually been able to see a scrub-ass commoner sitting on his silk sofa. Or his son's silk sofa. Or grandson's. Whatever.

"Fuck," he muttered as he rubbed his face.

Yeah, actually, he had come over to fight with her, not make up with her. He'd come to prove his point: that she and her people were an evil in the species, and she was deluded if she thought he was going to buy any of her bullshit—

"Just stop," he groaned.

Reopening his eyes, he stared at the rug that his boots were planted on. Out in the foyer there were voices. Butch had come. V. And the butler and the maid were talking.

Paradise had been taken upstairs, and Doc Jane was—

A male appeared in the doorway of the library.

He was tall and slender, dressed in an impeccable suit that even Craeg could tell was handmade by a master. With his bright white shirt and his bloodred tie and his smart little handkerchief in his breast pocket, he was the epitome of an aristocrat.

And yup, he even had the gold signet ring on his finger.

And yes, those were Paradise's eyes staring across the still room.

Craeg took his Orange cap off as he stood up. He had an absurd impulse to retuck his shirt, or brush off his jeans . . . or something. Shit.

The male strode forward with a formidable expression on his face.

Bracing himself, Craeg cleared his throat. "Sir, I'm—"

The bear hug that hit him was so strong he felt his bones get crushed, and the guy didn't back off, he just kept holding on.

While Craeg stood there like a statue.

Over Paradise's father's shoulder, Butch stuck his head into the room. Making bug eyes, the Brother motioned for Craeg to get with the program.

Behind the male's back, Craeg put his palms up, all "what do I do?"

Butch started to madly make hugging motions.

Wincing, Craeg gingerly put his arms around the gentlemale. Patted those shoulders.

"I owe you my life," her father said in a rough voice. "On this night you have given me life anew by saving hers."

Finally, her father stepped back and he whipped that handkerchief out and wiped his red eyes. "Tell me, how may I repay you? What may I do for you? How may I e'er be of service unto you and yours."

Craeg blinked like a planker. His brain literally flatlined. And then he blurted, "My name is Craeg."

Like the guy had asked him or something.

"Craeg, I am Abalone." The male bowed. "At your service."

Before Craeg could respond to that, Peyton rounded the corner and marched over to him. "My man."

Annnnnnnnd it was time for hug number two.

As Peyton gave him a squeeze that nearly broke his ribs again, Craeg was a little more with the program on the whole return thing.

"You did my job for me," the guy said roughly.

"What are you taking about?"

"Butch told me Anslam was the one who killed my cousin."

Craeg recoiled—which was a good thing because he needed a little personal space. Ever since the danger had dissipated when he killed a goddamn classmate, he'd felt like he'd stepped into a parallel universe.

The thing was, as he'd run Anslam through like the fucker had been nothing but an animal, he'd been reacting in defense of Paradise. The reason the male had been attacking her hadn't been overly relevant at the time— and had remained unquestioned in the trippy aftermath.

Peyton told the story quickly, and Craeg followed most of it. At least, he thought he did.

Anslam and the Polaroids. Anslam and his reputation

for being aggressive with females. Paradise putting it all togther.

Abruptly, Peyton turned to Paradise's father and the two embraced.

"So how about this guy," Peyton said as the pair of them separated. "He's some kind of hero, huh."

Okay, right, it was entirely uncomfortable to have Paradise's father look at him with something close to hero worship. Yeah, wow—could he leave now? Maybe he could leave . . . he wanted to go see Paradise, but—

"He's in love with Parry, too, by the way," Peyton announced. "And she is with him."

Annnnnd that was how the whole thing between her and him got seriously, totally, fucking outted.

Chapter Forty-six

"No, I'm fine."

Paradise winced as she said the words. Then again, Doc Jane was shining a flashlight directly into her eyeballs.

"You've got a concussion," the doctor announced as she took a seat on the bed. "Do you feel sick to your stomach?"

Well, gee, yes—but whether that was because of the fact that she'd been nearly killed by a classmate or totally saved by a male she'd told to fuck off a half an hour ago . . .

"What was the question?" she asked. "Wait, yes, I'm a little nauseous, and I have a bit of a thumper."

Doc Jane smiled. "You're going to be fine. Just take it easy. And before you ask, yes, you can go to class tomorrow night, but no sparring and go easy on the workout."

"Oh. Okay." God, she couldn't imagine being back at the training center. "Thank you."

"You're welcome. I'm not going to give you anything other than the Motrin you just took."

"Oh . . . okay. Thank you."

"And you need to talk to Mary," Doc Jane said as she got back to her feet. "And no, an I'm-fine ain't going to cut it. You can expect some PTSD from this. Your body is going to heal faster than your mind will."

"Who's Mary?"

"You know, Rhage's *shellan*. She's a therapist."

"Oh."

Maybe she should follow that one up with another T-Y?

"I'm here if you need me," the doctor said before she left.

And then Paradise was alone.

It was funny, even though she was safe and in her bedroom, and there were Brothers downstairs . . . the house didn't feel quite so secured anymore. And maybe that was the point about the Mary conversation.

God . . . Anslam, a killer? Maybe even a serial killer?

He'd never shown any signs of instability. He'd seemed like a relatively normal, if slightly unpleasant person, just like her or anyone else from their class, their race.

To think she'd sat by him in training, sparred with him, talked and laughed with him—and all the while he'd been . . . brutalizing females?

It was the stuff of nightmares—before she even got to the part where he tried to murder her.

Glancing at the clock, she became even more stressed. There was only an hour before dawn came, and she didn't know where Craeg was. Had he left yet?

She needed to see him.

With a groan, she stretched across for the house phone—

"You want me to help you with that?"

Jerking back, she looked up to find the male himself standing in her doorway. He jabbed his thumb over his shoulder.

"Doc Jane told me it was okay to come in. I've got to go, and I wanted to see for myself that you were still alive."

Paradise closed her eyes and had to turn her face away. Tears came fast and furious, but she didn't want to show them.

There was a soft click as he shut the door, and for a second, she thought he'd left her. But then she took a deep breath and caught his scent.

"I met your dad," he said roughly.

Shaking herself back into focus, she forced herself to look over at him. He hadn't come any farther into the room, and that seemed apt. His face was remote, his body tense, his affect that of somebody who had already left the house even though he was arguably standing in front of her.

"You did?" she said quietly.

"Nice guy."

"He is."

Long silence. And then she decided, Fuck it, and went for a Kleenex. Blowing her nose, she snapped another free and blotted her eyes.

"Sorry, I'm kind of emotional."

"Why wouldn't you be. You nearly got killed."

Wadding up the tissues, she pitched them into the wastepaper basket by her bed and took a deep breath. "I'm sorry I said all that stuff to you. That I yelled at you."

"Don't worry about it."

"Okay." Man, for some reason that blasé response, like none of it had particularly mattered, hurt worse than her concussion. "All right."

"Look, Paradise, you and I . . ."

"Are what?" She glanced at him. "Or is it more like *aren't*. As in aren't meant to be? Is this the part where you go through all the reasons we can't be together again, including, if not especially, because of my background? Because if it is, I'm pretty sure we covered that on the phone."

When he didn't say anything, just stared at the floor as if he were counting the stitches in her needlepoint rug, she imagined he was practicing the final good-bye in his head. And that would be a good-bye to their relationship, not a never-see-you-again. Because she was not dropping out of the fucking program; that was for sure: In just these initial nights—which felt like twelve thousand years, thank you very much—she'd already invested waaaaaay too much for quitting.

"You'd better go," she said with defeat. "Just—"

"Why me?"

She frowned. "I'm sorry?"

As he looked over at her, his eyes were dead serious. "I guess, I don't understand . . . why me? You could have anyone in the species. I mean, whole bloodlines would give their arms and legs to have a son with you. You are literally the most valuable thing on the planet—and that's before they get to know how strong you are, how smart you are . . . how resilient you are. How courageous . . . and smart. Have I mentioned smart." He looked back down at the rug. "And beautiful. And then there's that voice of yours." He made a circle next to his head. "It makes me crazy, your voice. Every day, after we'd hang up the phone, I would sleep with the fucking thing on my chest. Like maybe part of your voice, part of you was still in it."

Okay, now she was tearing up for a completely different reason.

Craeg motioned around the room. "Even if you'd forgive me for being a total asshole . . . I can't give you anything like this. My parents' cottage has, like, two bedrooms and a galley kitchen. There's Formica on the counters and linoleum on the floors, and really ugly carpeting in it. The wood is fake, it's not antique. The oldest piece of furniture I own is from the seventies—and it's horrible-looking. I can't . . . I can't buy you jewelry, or cars—"

"Stop."

At the sound of her voice, he fell silent.

"I don't think like that," she whispered. "And neither should you."

"What if that changes."

And that was when she realized he'd never really shown her the vulnerability in him before. And wait, was he talking about them still being together?

"It won't," she vowed. "I don't care about any of that stuff and that is not going to change."

"How do you know?" he said softly. "Because ... I'm in love with you. And if you decide tomorrow, a week from now ... a year from now ... that this is just a fling, or that you need to be with someone who's classier than I am, I'm not going to survive that. That is one thing that will bring me to my knees and keep me there. So just let me go, okay? Put me out of my misery ... let me go."

Paradise wiped her eyes and had to smile.

"Did you just tell me you loved me?" When he didn't answer, she prompted, "I think you did."

"I'm serious, Paradise."

Suddenly, nothing in her head or her body hurt, and the fear that had been like a toxic poison in her veins was gone.

"So am I," she whispered.

"Then yes, yes I did just tell you I love you. And I'm sorry I lost it about you and your family. And I'm also an asshole for lumping you in with the people who killed my father. I don't know ... all I have to do is think back to that first night, when you didn't want to leave me on the trail? You were like that with everyone, not just me. You ... you would have locked yourself out of a safe room if it meant one more person could have fit in."

He released a shuddering breath, and wiped his face with his broad palm, like he was struggling with his own emotions.

"Craeg, all I can say is this." She waited until he looked up at her again. "I beat everyone that first night, didn't I. I was the last one standing, right?"

He nodded. "Yeah. You were amazing."

"Well, I would do that all over again right now if it meant I could prove the unprovable to you—and that is that my heart knows what it wants. It's as simple and uncomplicated as that. You can try, if you like, to layer on all kinds of reasons why I'll think differently sometime in the future, but my feelings are never going to change. I knew you were the one the first night I met you, when you walked into the audience house. I spent weeks wondering if you'd be back with your application. The night of initiation? I waited and prayed to see you come in. And when you did, all I could think of was, 'Thank God he's here.'"

She put out her hand to him. "I still think that every time I see you after I've spent some time away from you. 'Thank God . . . he's here.'"

Craeg came to her slowly, as if giving her a chance to change her mind. But then his palm was against hers. And then he was sitting on the bed next to her. And then he was leaning in and pressing a kiss to her mouth.

Except he sat back and got grave. "I'm going to *ahvenge* my father. I know you don't agree with it, but I can't change that. I'm sorry."

She closed her eyes as pain struck her in the chest. "Please . . . no. And I'm not saying that to protect some distant cousin of mine. There's been too much death already. I'm trying to protect another living thing."

"A coward who killed my father."

"Maybe there's another way of getting justice." She squeezed his hand. "Just . . . let's work on that. Maybe there's another way. Promise? For me. Do this for me."

It was a long, long while before he answered. But when he finally did, it seemed like a vow. "All right. I hate it . . . but all right."

Sitting up, she wrapped her arms around him and felt him hold her in return. "I love you."

"Oh, God, Paradise . . . I love you, too."

They stayed that way for the longest time, embracing each other, saying small things, touching, feeling, kissing.

And then there was a knock on the door.

Yeah, boy, Craeg moved so fast off her bed, he practically slammed into the wall that was farthest away.

She laughed a little. "Yes?"

"It's Butch," came the deep voice. "I'm leaving now. Craeg, you gotta come with me."

"Okay," Craeg said, heading for the door.

"When will I see you?" Paradise asked. "Tomorrow night's class is canceled also?"

He put his hand on the knob and looked over at her with hooded eyes. "Answer your phone at seven a.m. and we'll discuss it."

With that and a very hot wink, he slipped out and shut the panels quietly.

As Paradise let herself fall back against her pillows, she was grinning so hard her cheeks hurt.

Chapter Forty-seven

One week later . . .

"Wait, so where does the cumberbatch go?"

As Craeg stood in front of a full-length mirror in the Pit, he was in a panic until Butch stepped in behind him. Naturally, the Brother smiled at him like he was an idiot. Which he was.

"It's cummerbund." Butch took the banding and put it around Craeg's waist. "Damn, son, you're gonna look tight."

"How much did this thing cost?"

"Fifteen thousand." There was some fussing and tugging as things were done up at the small of his back. "And the good news is that you and I are the same kind of stocky, so it fits you like a glove."

Craeg blinked a couple of times. "Fifteen thousand? Dollars?"

"No, Pop-Tarts," Vishous said from over on the bed. "And if that makes your nuts shrink, multiply it times all the shit on those hangers over there."

Craeg glanced at the racks of clothes in the otherwise neat and tidy bedroom. "Oh, my God."

"Yeah, Saks loves him." V lit up another hand-rolled. "And Neiman Marcus."

"Fuck you, V." Butch leaned to the side and picked up a black jacket with long black tails. "Guys like Craeg and me, we have to put on some window dressing for our ladies. That's how we roll."

Personally, Craeg would rather have been in his jeans. But he had to admit the starched white shirt with its fancy white knot at the throat and the bright red suspenders and the black slacks with the satin stripes down the outsides was not a bad look.

And then he put the jacket on.

Staring at his reflection, he brushed his newly cut hair back and then shook the stuff out. "I look . . ."

"Like fifteen million bucks." Butch clapped him on the shoulder. "Now get the fuck out of here so I can get dressed, too. The misanthrope over there is staying home because he's too good for this shit, but you and I are gonna have a great fucking time."

V grunted and got off the bed. "Call me if you don't, though. I'm always good for a fistfight, and I like hitting pretty boys."

"You're just bitter you don't have a tux."

Vishous paused in the doorway and looked back at Craeg. Nodding once, he said, "The a-hole is right. You look good. She's going to be proud to be on your arm. Don't let any of those fucking morons make you feel second-class—she could pick anyone in the world, and she chose you. Also, don't offer anyone your hand first. It'll give them a chance to snub you. You let them greet you, not the other way around, 'kay?"

"Thanks," Craeg said roughly.

V nodded, and went to stalk down the shallow hall, adding, "I'm going to go sucker punch Lassiter. Then probably play some pool with him."

"Have fun, honey," Butch called out. Then he refocused on Craeg in the mirror. "Let me let you down into the tunnel. Wait for me in the parking garage. I'll drive you out."

"Okay. Hey . . . thanks."

God, that sounded so fucking lame.

Butch smiled, showing off a front tooth that was a little wonky. "I mated up, too. I know what it's like to be with a female who's—"

At that moment, Marissa stepped out of the second bedroom and . . .

Craeg recoiled. The dress . . . the diamonds . . . the dress . . .

The fucking diamonds.

The female literally sparkled white from head to foot, a blinding show of beauty and elegance in her formfitting gown.

Doc Jane jumped out into the hall. "So! How'd we do? Huh? How'd we do?"

Craeg looked over his shoulder at Butch . . . who was standing there dumb as an ox, looking like he'd seen the second coming of the Scribe Virgin Herself.

"Let yourself out, kid," the Brother said in a guttural voice. "Like *now*. I'll be there in ten minutes—no, wait . . . twenty."

As Marissa smiled at Craeg and told him he was handsome, she marveled how one could be fully clothed and completely undressed at the same time.

Then again, with the way Butch was staring at her, she was very clear on what he was thinking about.

"Come on, Craeg, I'll take you into the tunnel," Doc Jane said. "And have fun, you two."

"Go, go, go, go," Butch muttered to V's mate. "Before you see way more than you're gonna want to."

As the pair left and the door into the tunnel clicked shut and relocked, Marissa did a slow turn in front of her mate. "You like?"

Butch's reply was to fall to his knees. Like, really . . . fall to his knees so hard she wasn't sure whether the cracking was because he'd broken his bones or the floorboards.

Gathering up the skirt of her Reem Acra gown, she hustled over to him. "Are you all—"

He captured her shoulders in his hands, his hazel eyes roaming over her face. "I want to kiss you, but I don't want to ruin your makeup."

"So kiss me carefully."

And he did, brushing her mouth with a gentle stroke. "You take my breath away, Marissa. You're going to take everyone's breath away."

She smoothed his hair. "We'll see about that."

"Yes, we will."

Marissa grew serious. "Havers isn't coming tonight. It kind of surprised me. He was the one who nominated me to be head of this thing."

"Maybe it's his way of putting out an olive branch. Allowing you to shine without the complication of a lot of gossip."

"Yes." She thought of her brother by the bedside of the female who had been killed. "It's almost easier to demonize him."

"You know, when it comes to Havers, if you can forgive him . . . well, I'll never forget what he did to you, but I won't kill him if I see him. How's that?"

She laughed. "Deal. And I don't know. I guess we'll have to see what the future holds."

"I know one thing that's coming," he drawled, eyes going hooded.

"And what might that be."

Her mate rose from the floor and circled her waist with his warm hands. Leaning down, he whispered, "I'm going to be the one helping you out of this dress later."

Laughing, she put her arms around his neck and arched into him. "Does that mean I get to take your pants off at the end of the night?"

"Oh, God . . ." he groaned. "*Yeeeeeeeeeeeeeeeeeeeeeeee-eeeeeeeeees . . .*"

Chapter Forty-eight

As Paradise descended the grand staircase of her home, she held up the flowing skirt of her pale blue gown. With each step she took, she thought of the night one week before, when she had come down to find Anslam there on the marble, waiting for her as if there was nothing out of sorts, nothing wrong, nothing threatening.

For a split second, her mental wires got crossed and a shimmy of adrenaline shot down her spine.

Doc Jane had been right: The concussion had healed and so had the bruises, but her brain had a new pathway, one that had been forged quickly, but permanently. The conditioned fear response wasn't going to be a prison, though. Mary was helping her make sure of that.

As she got to the last step, her father emerged from the library. "Oh . . . Paradise."

With a dip of her head and body, she curtsied to him. "Father."

"You look like your mother."

When he held out his hands, she went to him. "That is the most perfect compliment."

"Well, it is true." Guiding her in a twirl before him, he smiled. "And I have something for you."

"Oh?"

"Come."

Drawing her into the study and over to the desk, he

presented her with a flat red box with a signature golden border. "These were hers."

"Father . . ."

"No, come now. You must open it."

Paradise's hands began to tremble as she accepted the box and toggled the top open. As she gasped, he stepped in and took the antique diamond rivière from its satin bed.

"There are forty-eight diamonds, one for each of the first forty-eight years I spent with your beloved *mahmen*. On this night, I give it to you free and clear in the same manner I give to you my love and respect. I couldn't be—"

"Wait." She stopped him. Shook her head. "I can't accept that."

"Why ever not?"

As his face fell, she closed her eyes. "I have to tell you something. It's . . ."

Unable to stay still, she began to walk in a tight circle. All she could think about was that conversation they had had about love, and class, and how he wanted her to have an aristocratic match like he and her mother had had.

But unlike before she'd gone into the training program, she had a much better sense of who she was now. And even if it broke his heart, she was going to love whoever she wanted, regardless of station, class, or ranking.

"Father, I'm in love with a male. He's a commoner, and I don't care. More to the point, I don't believe that makes him any less valuable than anyone else. Craeg is—"

"Finally!" he exclaimed. "Finally!" He pulled her in and kissed her on both cheeks. "I've been waiting all week!"

"What—wait, what?"

"Peyton told me."

"What!"

"And I agree with you. Craeg is a male of worth—and I totally approve. You may have all my blessings."

Paradise frowned and shook her head. "Father ... I don't understand. Just last week you were telling me that I needed to mate an aristocrat. I know Craeg saved my life, but you can't do a one-eighty like that and expect me to believe it."

"My darling," he said with a recoil, "when did I tell you that you had to mate a member of the *glymera*?"

"We were having First Meal before I went out—and you were saying that I had to have a mating like you and *mahmen* had. Two aristocrats set up by their families."

"No, I said your *mahmen* and I found true love. That's what I want for you. The true-love part—as long as the male is good to you, I do not care where he hails from. I have long watched the travails of our class and been summarily unimpressed. Balls and parties are fine, but one must return home with the person to whom one is mated. That is far more significant than any pedigree—and I shall make no apologies to anyone if there is talk—"

Paradise launched herself at her father and squeezed the dickens out of him. "I love you so much I'm going to cry!"

Her father, her dear, wonderful, perfect father, laughed and held her in return. "Will you allow me to put this necklace on you now? And will you finally admit that Craeg is attending to you this eve?"

"Yes, yes, he's coming! Oh, he is! I can't wait for you to meet him properly and get to know him."

"Nor can I, my love ... nor can I."

Thirty minutes later, with streams of glittering guests arriving through the front entrance and proceeding down the hall to the ballroom, Paradise thought ... well, at least she *assumed* Craeg was coming.

He'd told her he was coming.

Really, he had.

Standing just inside the ballroom's upper level, at the head of the grand staircase that took guests down to the dance floor, she searched the crowd. She didn't think it was possible that she'd missed his arrival. Certainly not with the butler announcing everyone as they came in before they descended to the party below.

She'd been well aware that he'd seemed a little uncomfortable at the idea of escorting her, but he wasn't the type to back down. Especially not where she was concerned—

"Hey, beautiful."

"Peyton," she murmured as she turned to her friend.

As they embraced, she glanced behind him, hoping to see . . . nope, no Craeg.

"Wow, nice ice." Peyton leaned in and checked out her necklace. "Where's your man?"

"I don't know." She frowned. "And I thought you were bringing that female, what's her name?"

"Oh, her. Yeah. No. Her father called mine and asked what my intentions were. I'm not about to get entangled with that stuff."

"Why didn't you ask Novo then?"

"Don't know where you got that idea." He surveyed the crowd. "Well, time to find a date. Anyone in our generation here, or is it full of old farts—wait, look, I think there's a female over there with her own teeth still."

"Peyton. You should have asked Novo."

"Who?" He kissed her on the cheek. "Laters."

As he sauntered down the red-carpeted steps into the crowd, he attracted all kinds of attention, a reminder that her best friend was a very viable commodity in the *glymera*.

The poor bastard.

And there was another reason she was worried about him, for him. Ever since the night at her house with Anslam, Peyton had closed up. On the surface he was just the same, but she knew him at a level other people didn't.

Something had changed in him, and he wasn't talking about it. Then again, a friend of his had killed a relation. That was a lot of grief to process.

God, she wished he'd talk to her. To someone.

As music swelled and couples began to make it to the center of the ballroom, she fluffed her skirts out a little and realized she'd wanted to share this with Craeg—but that might be asking too much of him. Most males would find this a snooze—or worse, a curse.

Well, fine. She didn't have to go to these things. And she could wear her damn diamonds in her bathrobe and be perfectly happy. After all, what made the necklace important was that it had been her mother's and was now hers.

Yup, her father was so right. As fancy as this crowd was, with their gowns and their jewels and their airs, it was a flat experience to stand among them. Even though she belonged here by right of birth, she was totally apart, and really pretty uninterested—

"Is there a better band coming later?"

Wheeling around, she smiled like crazy—and then stopped. Put a hand to her mouth. Took a step back.

Craeg shook his head and looked down at himself in horror. "Damn it, Butch swore to me this contraption fit. He *swore* it."

"You are . . ."

Her male was flat-out 007-gorgeous in his white tie and tails and his patent-leather shoes, looking as tall and distinguished as anybody else in the room. Although it was funny . . . she liked him just as much in his jeans and his baseball cap.

Or nothing at all. Even better.

"Wait, is that . . . my father's ceremonial sword?" she blurted, blinking through sudden tears.

Craeg smoothed the gold sheath that hung off his left hip. "He was waiting for me when I got here. He insisted I wear this tonight. He said he would have it beneath no one else's dagger hand when his daughter was presented to society with a male escort for the first time."

Paradise had to clear her throat. "That is . . . an immense honor."

"I know."

"And you got your hair cut," she said. Although as soon as she spoke, she wanted to kick herself in the ass. "I mean—"

"I was pretty shaggy."

She jumped up and hugged him. "Thankyousomuchforcomingimsohappyyourehere—"

Craeg laughed in that great baritone he had started to use and he held her in that great way he did, up close to his body so she could feel his strength. "I would have been here sooner, but my ride was getting busy."

"You made it. That's all that matters—and oh, my God, you are *hot*."

"And you are . . ." He put some space between them and seemed to look at her properly for the first time. "Wow. That is some dress, and . . . are those real? Those are real. . . . that one in the middle is the size of my thumbnail."

"It was my *mahmen*'s."

"It's almost as beautiful as you are."

As they talked, she was very aware that they were being sized up and spoken about, and there would be scandal, yes, there would be.

Fuck 'em, she thought as she hooked her arm in his. "Come with me?"

"Anywhere you take me, tonight and always."

Leading her male over to the head of the stairway, she nodded at Fedricah, who immediately bowed in deference to Craeg.

"Sire. My honor to see you this eve."

And then the *doggen* turned to the crowd and in his best, most formal voice announced in the Old Language, "*Mistress Paradise, blooded daughter of Abalone, First Adviser to Wrath, son of Wrath, sire of Wrath, and the honorable Craeg, son of Brahl the Younger, bestowed of the King's Award of Valor last eve for services rendered unto the royal court.*"

A hush silenced the crowd, and then a ripple of conversation overtook even the orchestra.

Meanwhile, Craeg recoiled. "What was all that? I got what? They did who?"

Paradise patted his hand. "My father told Wrath you saved my life, and the King gave you a title. But I loved you just as much before. You were supposed to find out tomorrow evening—I think our butler got a little overexcited."

"What?"

"Technically, you're an aristocrat now."

"WHAT."

"Pay no attention." She met him right in the eye. "It doesn't change anything—well, except tacitly tell the haters to f-themselves."

Craeg blinked and then chuckled as he looked out over the assembly. "Let's do this, my Paradise. And then maybe we can find a private spot?"

She leaned in. "I already have one in mind."

"That's my female, oh, yeah."

Stepping forward with him, she didn't look at the crowd. They weren't even in the room for all she knew.

No, she was looking at her fine male.

"You know something," she said with love as they descended to the black-and-white marble dance floor.

"What?"

"I am the luckiest female on the planet. Right here, right now."

Yup, she thought as his chest puffed with pride. She knew exactly who she was ... and who she was with— and they were a helluva pair.

"I love you," he whispered as he swept her into his arms. "Dance with me."

Read on for a sneak peek at the first book
in a new contemporary romance series by
New York Times bestselling author
J. R. Ward,

THE BOURBON KINGS

Available now from Piatkus.

B

You are cordially invited to

A Derby Brunch

in celebration of the

One Hundred and Thirty-Ninth

Running of

The Charlemont Derby

Saturday, May the Fourth

Ten o'clock

Easterly

RSVP: newarkharris@gmail.com

Chapter One

Charlemont, Kentucky

Mist hung over the Ohio's sluggish waters like the breath of God, and the trees on the Charlemont shore side of River Road were so many shades of spring green, the color required a sixth sense to absorb them all. Overhead, the sky was a dim, milky blue, the kind of thing that you saw up north only in July, and at seven-thirty a.m., the temperature was already seventy-four degrees.

It was the first week of May. The most important seven days on the calendar, beating the birth of Christ, the American Independence, and New Year's Rockin' Eve.

The One Hundred Thirty-ninth running of The Charlemont Derby was on Saturday.

Which meant the entire state of Kentucky was in a thoroughbred racing frenzy.

As Lizzie King approached the turn-off for her work, she was riding an adrenaline high that had been pumping for a good three weeks, and she knew from past experience that this rush-rush mood of hers wasn't going to deflate until after Saturday's clean-up. At least she was, as always, going against the traffic heading into downtown and making good time: Her commute was forty minutes each way, but not in the NYC, Boston, or LA, densely packed, parking-lot version of rush hour—which in her current frame of mind would have caused her head to mushroom cloud. No, her trip into her job was twenty-eight minutes of Indiana farm country followed by six minutes of bridge and spaghetti junction delays, capped off with this six- to ten-minute, against-the-tide shot parallel to the river.

Sometimes she was convinced the only cars going in her direction were the rest of the staff that worked at Easterly with her.

Ah, yes, Easterly.

The Bradford Family Estate, or BFE, as its deliveries were marked, sat high up on the biggest hill in the Charlemont metro area and was comprised of a twenty-thousand-square-foot main house with three formal gardens, two pools, and a three-hundred-sixty degree view of Washington County. There were also twelve retainer's cottages on the property, as well as ten outbuildings, a fully functioning farm of over a hundred acres, a twenty-horse stable that had been converted into a business center, and a nine-hole golf course.

That was lighted.

In case you needed to work on your chip shot at one a.m.

As far as she had heard, the enormous parcel had been granted to the family back in 1778, after the first of the Bradfords had come south from Pennsylvania with the then Colonel George Rogers Clark—and brought both his ambitions and his bourbon-making traditions into the nascent commonwealth. Fast forward almost two hundred fifty years, and you had a Federal mansion the size of a small town up on that hill, and some seventy-two people working on the property full- and part-time.

All of whom followed a feudal rules and rigid caste system that was right out of Downton Abbey.

Or maybe the Dowager Countess of Grantham's routine was a little too progressive.

William the Conqueror's times were probably more apt.

So, for example — and this was solely a Lifetime movie conjecture here — if a gardener fell in love with one of the family's precious sons? Even if she were one of two head horticulturists, and had a national reputation and a master's in landscape architecture from Cornell?

That was *just* not done.

Sabrina without the happy ending, darlin'.

With a curse, Lizzie turned the radio on in hopes of getting her brain to shut up. She didn't get far. Her Toyota Yaris had the speaker system of a Barbie house: there were little circles in the doors that were supposed to pump music, but they were mostly for pretend — and today, NPR coming out of those cocktail coasters just wasn't enough —

The sound of an ambulance speeding up behind her easily overrode the haute pitter-patter of the BBC News, and she hit her brakes and eased over onto the shoulder. After the noise and flashing lights passed, she got back on track and rounded a fat curve in both the river and the road . . . and there it was, the Bradfords' great white mansion, high up in the sky, the dawning sun being forced to work around its regal, symmetrical layout.

She had grown up in Plattsburgh, New York, on an apple orchard.

What the hell had she been thinking almost two years ago when she'd let Lane Baldwine, the youngest son, into her life?

And why was she still, after all this time, wondering about the particulars?

Come on, it wasn't like she was the first woman who'd gotten good and seduced by him —

Lizzie frowned and leaned forward over the wheel.

The ambulance that had passed her was heading up the flank of the BFE hill, its red and white lights strobing along the alley of maple trees.

"Oh, God," she breathed.

She prayed it wasn't who she thought it was.

But come on, her luck couldn't be that bad.

And wasn't it sad that that was the first thing that came to her mind instead of worry over whoever was hurt/sick/passed out.

Proceeding on by the monogrammed, wrought-iron gates that were just closing, she took her right-hand turn about three hundred yards later.

As an employee, she was required to use the service entrance with her vehicles, no excuses, no exceptions.

Because God forbid a vehicle with an MSRP of under a hundred thousand dollars be seen in front of the house—

Boy, she was getting bitchy, she decided. And after Derby, she was going to have to take a vacation before people thought she was going through menopause two decades too early.

The sewing machine under the Yaris's hood revved up as she shot down the level road that went around the base of the hill. The cornfield came first, the manure already laid down and churned over in preparation for planting. And then there were the cutting gardens filled with the first of the perennials and annuals, the heads of the early peonies fat as softballs and no darker than the blush on an ingenue's cheeks. After those, there were the orchid houses and nurseries, followed by the outbuildings with the farm and groundskeeping equipment in them, and then the lineup of two- and three-bedroom, fifties-era cottages.

That were as variable and stylish as a set of sugar and flour tins on a Formica counter.

Pulling into the staff parking lot, she got out, leaving her cooler, her hat and her bag with her sunscreen behind.

Jogging over to groundskeeping's main building, she entered the gasoline- and oil-smelling cave through the open bay on the left. The office of Gary McAdams, the head groundsman, was off to the side, the cloudy glass panes still translucent enough to tell her that lights were on and someone was moving around in there.

She didn't bother to knock. Shoving open the flimsy door, she ignored the half-naked Pirelli calendar pinups. "Gary—"

The sixty-two-year-old was just hanging up the phone with his bear-paw hand, his sunburned face with its tree-bark skin as grim as she had ever seen it. As he looked across his messy desk, she knew who the ambulance was for even before he said the name.

Lizzie put her hands to her face and leaned back against the doorjamb.

She felt so sorry for the family, of course, but it was impossible not to personalize the tragedy and want to go throw up somewhere.

The one man she never wanted to see again . . . was going to come home.

She might as well get a stop watch.

New York, New York

"Come on. I know you want me."

Jonathan Tulane Baldwine looked around the hip that was propped next to his stack of poker chips. "Ante up, boys."

"I'm talking to you." A pair of partially covered, fully fake breasts appeared over the fan of cards in his hands. *"Hello."*

Time to feign interest in something, anything else, Lane thought. Too bad the one-bedroom, mid-floor, Midtown apartment was a bachelor pad done in nothing-that-wasn't-functional. And why bother staring into the faces of what was left of the six bastards they'd started playing with eight hours ago. None of them had proved worthy of anything more than keeping up with the high stakes.

Deciphering their tells, even as an avoidance strategy, wasn't worth the eye strain at seven-thirty in the morning.

"Hellllllloooo—"

"Give it up, honey, he's not interested," someone muttered.

"Everybody's interested in me."

"Not him." Jeff Stern, the host and roommate, tossed in a thousand dollars' worth of chips. "Ain't that right, Lane?"

"Are you gay? Is he gay?"

Lane moved the queen of hearts next to the king of hearts. Shifted the jack next to the queen. Wanted to push the boob job with mouth onto the floor. "Two of you haven't anted."

"I'm out, Baldwine. Too rich for my blood."

"I'm in—if someone'll lend me a grand."

Jeff looked across the green fleet table and smiled. "It's you and me again, Baldwine."

"Looking forward to takin' your money." Lane tucked his cards in tight. "It's your bet—"

The woman leaned down again. "I love your Southern accent."

Jeff's eyes narrowed behind his clear-rimmed glasses. "You gotta back off him, baby."

"I'm not stupid," she slurred. "I know exactly who you are and how much money you have. I drink your bourbon—"

Lane sat back and addressed the fool that had brought the chatty accessory. "Billy? Seriously."

"Yeah, yeah." The guy who'd wanted to go a thousand dollars into debt stood up. "The sun's coming up, anyway. Let's go."

"I want to stay—"

"Nope, you're done." Billy took the bimbo with the self-esteem inflation problem by the arm and escorted her to the door. "I'll take you home, and no, he's not who you think he is. Later, assholes."

"Yes, he is—I've seen him in magazines—"

Before the door could shut, the other guy who'd been bled dry got to his feet. "I'm out of here, too. Remind me never to play with the pair of you again."

"I'll do nothing of the sort," Jeff said as he held up a palm. "Tell the wife I said hello."

"You can tell her yourself when we see you at Shabbat."

"That again."

"Every Friday, and if you don't like it, why do you keep showing up at my house?"

"Free food. It's just that simple."

"Like you need the handouts."

And then they were alone. With over two hundred and fifty thousand dollars' worth of poker chips, two decks of cards, an ashtray full of cigar nubs, and no bimbage.

"It's your bet," Lane said.

"I think he wants to marry her," Jeff muttered as he tossed more chips into the center of the table. "Billy, that is. Here's twenty grand."

"Then he should get his head examined." Lane met his old fraternity brother's bet and then doubled it. "Pathetic. The both of them."

Jeff lowered his cards. "Lemme ask you something."

"Don't make it too hard, I'm drunk."

"Do you like them?"

"Poker chips?" In the background, a cell phone started to ring. "Yeah, I do. So if you don't mind putting some more of yours in—"

"No, women."

Lane shifted his eyes up. "Excuse me?"

His old friend put an elbow on the felt and leaned in. His tie had been lost at the start of the game, and his previously starched, bright white shirt was now as pliant and relaxed as a polo. His eyes, however, were tragically sharp and focused. "You heard me. Look, I know it's none of my business, but you show up here how long ago? Like, nearly two years. You live on my couch, you don't work—which given who your family is, I get. But there's no women, no—"

"Stop thinking, Jeff."

"I'm serious."

"So bet."

The cell phone went quiet. But his buddy didn't. "U.Va. was a lifetime ago. Lot can change."

"Apparently not if I'm still on your couch—"

"What happened to you, man."

"I died waiting for you to bet or fold."

Jeff muttered as he made a stack of reds and blues and tossed them into the center. "'Nother twenty thousand."

"That's more like it." The cell phone started to ring again. "I'll see you. And I'll raise you fifty. If you shut up."

"You sure you want to do that?"

"Get you to be quiet? Yup."

"Go aggressive in poker with an investment banker like me. Clichés are there for a reason—I'm greedy and great with math. Unlike your kind."

"My kind."

"People like you Bradfords don't know how to make money—you've been trained to spend it. Now, unlike most dilettantes, your family actually *has* an income stream—although that's what keeps you from having to learn anything. So not sure it's a value-add in the long term."

Lane thought back to why he'd finally left Charlemont for good. "I've learned plenty, trust me."

"And now you sound bitter."

"You're boring me. Am I supposed to enjoy that?"

"Why don't you ever go home for Christmas? Thanksgiving? Easter?"

Lane collapsed his cards and put them face-down on the felt. "I don't believe in Santa Claus or the Easter Bunny anymore, goddamn it, and turkey is overrated. What *is* your problem?"

Wrong question to ask. Especially after a night of poker and drinking. Especially to a guy like Stern, who was categorically incapable of being anything but perfectly honest.

"I hate that you're so alone."

"You've *got* to be kidding—"

"I'm one of your oldest friends, right? If I don't tell you like it is, who's going to? And don't get pissy with me—you picked a New York Jew, not one of the thousand other southern-fried stick-up-the-asses that went to that ridiculous college of ours to be your perpetual roommate. So fuck you."

"Are we going to play this hand out?"

Jeff's shrewd stare narrowed. "Answer me one thing."

"Yes, I am seriously reconsidering why I didn't crash with Wedge or Chenoweth right now."

"Ha. You couldn't stand either of those two longer than a day. Unless you were drunk, which actually, you have been for the last three and a half months straight. And that's another thing I have a problem with."

"Bet. Now. For the love of God."

"Why—"

As that cell phone went off a third time, Lane got to his feet and stalked across the room. Over on the bar, next to his billfold, the glowing screen was lit up—not that he bothered to look at who it was.

He answered the call only because it was either that or commit homicide.

The male Southern voice on the other end of the connection said three words: "Your momma's dyin'."

As the meaning sank into his brain, everything destabilized around him, the walls closing in, the floor rolling, the ceiling collapsing on his head. Memories didn't so much come to him as assault him, the alcohol in his system doing nothing to dull the onslaught.

No, he thought. *Not now. Not this morning.*

Although would there ever be a good time?

"Not ever" was the only acceptable timetable on this.

From a distance, he heard himself speak. "I'll be there before noon."

And then he hung up.

"Lane?" Jeff got to his feet. "Oh, shit, don't you pass

out on me. I've got to be at Eleven Wall in an hour and I need a shower."

From a vast distance, Lane watched his hand reach out and pick up his wallet. He put that and the phone in the pocket of his slacks and headed for the door.

"Lane! Where the fuck are you going?"

"Don't wait up," he said as he opened the way out.

"When're you going to be back? Hey, Lane—what the hell?"

His old, dear friend was still talking at him as Lane walked off, letting the door close in his wake. At the far end of the hall, he punched through a steel door and started jogging down the concrete stairwell. As his foot-falls echoed all around, and he made tight turn after tight turn, he dialed a familiar phone number.

When the call was answered, he said, "This is Lane Baldwine. I need a jet at Teterboro now—going to Charlemont."

There was a brief delay, and then his father's executive assistant got back on the connection. "Mr. Baldwine, there is a jet available. I have spoken directly with the pilot. Flight plans are being filed as we speak. Once you get to the airport, proceed to—"

"I know where our terminal is." He broke out into the marble lobby, nodded to the doorman, and proceeded to the revolving doors. "Thanks."

Just a quickie, he told himself as he hung up and hailed a cab. With any luck, he would be back in Manhattan and annoying Jeff by nightfall, twelve midnight at the very latest.

Ten hours. Fifteen, tops.

He had to see his momma, though. That was what Southern boys did.

FROM #1 *NEW YORK TIMES*
BESTSELLING AUTHOR

J. R. WARD

THE BLACK DAGGER
BROTHERHOOD NOVELS

Dark Lover
Lover Eternal
Lover Awakened
Lover Revealed
Lover Unbound
Lover Enshrined
Lover Avenged
Lover Mine
Lover Unleashed
Lover Reborn
Lover At Last
The King
The Shadows

jrward.com
facebook.com/jrwardbooks

Do you love fiction with a supernatural twist?

Want the chance to hear news about your favourite
authors (and the chance to win free books)?

Keri Arthur
Kristen Callihan
P.C. Cast
Christine Feehan
Jacquelyn Frank
Larissa Ione
Darynda Jones
Sherrilyn Kenyon
Jayne Ann Krentz and Jayne Castle
Lucy March
Martin Millar
Tim O'Rourke
Lindsey Piper
Christopher Rice
J.R. Ward
Laura Wright

Then visit the Piatkus website and blog
www.piatkus.co.uk | www.piatkusbooks.net

And follow us on Facebook and Twitter
www.facebook.com/piatkusfiction | www.twitter.com/piatkusbooks

piatkus